Here's what critics a.
Stacey Wiedower's books:

"I thoroughly enjoyed the story with all of its twists and turns, and I really connected with the author's writing. I can't wait to read her other novels and I highly recommend you get a copy of all of them for yourself too!"
—*Living Life with Joy,* 5 out of 5 stars!

"(30 First Dates) was so poignant and funny and true to life. It doesn't happen often that a book inspires me outside of the pages. I liked this book so much that I decided to make my own bucket list."
—*The Bad Mommy Diaries,* 5 out of 5 stars!

"I absolutely loved this book! Highly recommended!"
—*Chicklit Club*

"This is actually my first book from Stacey Wiedower but I sure hope it won't be the last! From the beginning I got caught up in the story. Overall, a super cute beach read!"
—*Chick Lit Plus*

BOOKS BY STACEY WIEDOWER

Fixer-Upper Romances:
How to Look Happy
How to Be Loved

Unlucky in Love Romances:
30 First Dates
Now A Major Motion Picture
This is 35

Other Works:
48 Hours in New York
(short story in the Killer Beach Reads collection)

HOW TO BE LOVED

a Fixer-Upper romance

Stacey Wiedower

For my Aunt Ros, who made the best bacon sandwiches.

CHAPTER ONE

Mr. Imperfect

"You're a great girl, Quinn. The problem is all *me. I'm too picky."*

It's not you. It's me. Ouch. I pin a sullen gaze on the clouds in my coffee, contemplating the full melody of Chase Ledford's swan song as I wait for my best friends, Savy Hartnett and Jules Emmerling, to join me on the patio of our favorite lunch spot. Around us, business casual folks on lunch breaks blend seamlessly with coifed and carefree ladies who lunch. Only one group stands out—a table filled with stay-at-home moms who keep checking their phones every few seconds, almost in tandem. As I watch, the dark blonde one tilts up her phone from its spot on the table, lights up the screen, and then sets it down again, not pausing in conversation. Three seconds later, the light blonde one to her right does the same thing. They break rhythm, skipping the mousy brunette, and then the other light blonde across the table does it. Observing from the outside, it looks like a tic.

What are they checking for? My espresso no longer as interesting, I watch with tilted head as I wait for my friends to show. *Do it. Do it...* Ahh, yep. There's another one. This time it's the dark blonde again. And then, yes, yes—not to be left out, we have the brunette.

More than the others, these women are fascinating to me, with their lululemon yoga pants and boldly patterned Vera Bradley bags. Are they meant to be diaper bags or purses? It's hard to tell. One's this purple and teal paisley number, another gray and yellow chevron, and another hot pink with swirly patterns overlaid on a floral print. Surely they're meant to hold kid stuff, but there are no kids with them, apart from the dark blonde who alternates peeks at her phone with glances into a stroller with an infant carrier attached, a sunshade shielding three-fourths of its interior.

Only one woman in the group is an outlier, her nude leather satchel a smaller version of my own. There's no way she has room for pacifiers and teethers and crap in there.

That'll be me. I'll be that mom.

Hold the phone. Did I really just think that? Man, Chase must have really gotten to me last night. I've turned sentimental.

Never mind, anyway. With my track record I'll never need to worry about what kind of mom I'll be.

I keep watching the table of women as if my eyes are magnets and they're the side panel of a stainless steel fridge. *Obsess much?* I think the reason they fascinate me is because they're so clearly my age, and yet I have about as much in common with them as I do with the tableful of lawyers to their left—all white males, all younger than me, all with that Ivy League look about them (or Ole Miss, which is the wannabe Ivy League in these parts—let's just call it the "Kudzu League"). These guys have the best table on the patio, the one I wanted—the one with the huge red umbrella that completely blocks the searing sun of a May afternoon in Memphis. Already I'm sweating like a wildebeest—coffee…what the hell was I thinking?—and Jules and Savy have yet to show a single ombré hair or stilettoed toe on this patio. They're respecting my crazy-busy schedule about as much as usual.

I'm still surreptitiously watching as Nude Purse Woman slings the bag over her shoulder and stands, stooping to give awkward hugs and—yes, she actually does it—air kisses to each of the others in turn. I realize she isn't one of them, after all. Clearly she's the group's Childless Friend. She'll rush back to her office in her Mini Cooper, either cursing her fate or thanking her lucky stars that she escaped the plight of her sorority sisters, who'll soon peel out of the Overton Square parking garage in their honking-huge Honda Odysseys with stick figure families adhered to the back windows, en route to the suburbs and the Mother's Day Out pickup lines.

Yep, the Childless Friend. Now that *will definitely be me.*
I'm not a hundred and ten percent sure how I feel about that.

"Can I get you an appetizer? Some more coffee?" The server's chirpy voice pierces my thoughts. Her cheerfulness is a mask for her irritation that I'm occupying valuable real estate during the lunch rush, sipping this infernal cup of much-needed caffeine while growing more irritated by the second with Savy and Jules—especially Jules, who works like three minutes from the Square.

"No, thank you. I'm sure my party will be here any minute." I smile ruefully, trying to convey my true message: *"I'm sure I'll make my inconsiderate friends tip you extra for making both of us wait."*

Her shrug answers, *"Suit yourself."*

I am absolutely dying for a plate of "the original," aka Second Line's fries smothered in andouille sausage and gooey cheese, my favorite appetizer, but I've got to resist. They'd be glued to my thighs before I even get back to the office. And that thought, unfortunately, causes me to recall the rest of Chase's and my last-ever conversation.

"I just… I've always had this…thing, this holdup. About weight." He said the last word in a quieter voice, a glimmer of fear in his eyes, as if he thought I'd pin him down and sit on him if the walls overheard. *"It's all my mom's fault. She set my standards too high. I'm on a mission for a perfect ten."*

My face gets hot just thinking about it. Perfect ten my ass. Chase is a six, tops. A seersucker-wearing, golf-playing, Hummer-driving, Yeti cooler-flaunting jerk. The real rub is that I went into the night planning to dump *him*, but he managed to get the words out first. That wasn't the only instance where he got there first, by the way. Or at all.

I wonder if he realizes women are aware that big cars don't make up for little…

"Girlfriend."

Savy is suddenly beside the table, but I'm so wrapped up in my steam sauna replay of Chase's douchiness that I didn't see her walk in. She's standing a couple feet away with her neck craned back, giving me the Manhattan once-over.

"Uh-oh."

"What's uh-oh?" I ask, cocking my head and giving her the up-down treatment, too. No, we're not wearing the same dress. Not even the same color.

"You broke up with him, didn't you?"

My mouth drops open just a little bit. What, am I wearing it like a pair of earrings? Can she see it on my collar? I snap my lips shut and gesture for her to sit, but she keeps standing there, gaping at me. By now the whole table of lawyers is watching us—or at least watching her. That usually happens when Savy's in a room. Honestly, it probably has nothing to do with our current spectacle. She's five foot five and not much over a hundred pounds, with a D-size bra cup filled by nature, not saline. Her long, dark hair tipped in smoky purple falls in salon-perfect loose ringlets to the center of her back, and her dark brown eyes give her an exotic quality that my own grayish-blue ones lack.

"Why, Quinn? Why? What happened?" She finally pulls out a chair and drops into it, exuding genuine concern and more than a little annoyance.

I can't completely blame her. Gorgeous as she is, I've broken up with more guys in the last two years than Savy's dated in the last five. Men are intimidated by her brains, beauty, and overall self-possession, but Savy can't wrap her head around that fact and therefore denies it—she has the nerve to think the problem is with her, not them. And so even though guys are constantly drawn to us because of her, I'm the one they end up talking to because they're afraid she'll reject them. I'm like the opposite of a wing-woman.

If one of these guys ever follows through with Savy, he'll worship her for life, and though he'll undoubtedly be unworthy, I'm sure she'll do the same. Whereas, when it comes to me, guys are quick to recognize my imperfections, and I'm quick to go on the defensive. Hence Chase's and my beat-me-to-the-punch breakup competition.

I raise an eyebrow, feeling hurt by her exasperation until I remember Savy doesn't know yet *how* we broke up. She'd been rooting for Chase, but considering what he said to me, it's clear my instincts about him were right from the start.

Glancing toward the doorway of the restaurant, I heave a sigh. I'd prefer to tell the story of our breakup only once, but since Jules doesn't seem to show any signs of arriving soon—not even one of her customary "I'm running late" texts, which she sends only after she's *already* late, which means she probably hasn't even left her desk—I go ahead and launch into my tale of woe. When I get to the part about the "perfect ten," Savy's mouth puckers in outrage.

"That's not even the worst part," I say. "He finishes up by telling me, all patronizing, 'You could get there one day. You really could. There's this trainer at my CrossFit studio who's hell on wheels with glutes. The girls all call him 'the ass whisperer.'"

For once, my friend is speechless. Savy's job is knowing what to say—she's a PR exec for the fund-raising arm of St. Jude, a world-renowned cancer hospital for kids. I watch the play of emotions cross her face, smirking when her fury and indignation give way to a flash of speculation.

"No, you are not calling the ass whisperer," I say wryly. "Your ass is already perfect. It doesn't need any whispering."

She starts to say something but seems to think better of it. Then she starts again. "His *mother* set his expectations too high? What does that even mean?"

I shrug. "I don't know. I never met her. I only heard about her." Chase and I hadn't yet reached the point of meeting the parental figures, even though we'd dated for nearly six months. Today would have been our six-monthiversary, in fact. "But you want to know the worst part? If he hadn't beaten me to it, I was going to dump him last night."

She looks surprised. "Why? I thought you liked him."

I snort-laugh, inhaling a sip of the icy-cold, lemon-tinged water the server has just set in front of each of us. In fifteen seconds the glasses are already beading with perspiration. After spluttering for a full minute and inspiring stares from the surrounding patrons, I can finally choke out a response. "Mommy issues."

Savy and I are in the middle of an epic giggling fit when Jules deigns to appear on the patio at last. I spot the outside hostess pointing her in our direction, but she's hard to miss because she's wearing a pink '50s-style dress with crinoline and grasping the strings of two *helium balloons*.

She rushes to our table, flashing a toothy, apologetic grin.

"Be-yatches," she says, opening her arms wide as she comes to a halt beside my chair.

I squint up at the balloons, fully expecting them to float away in her cloud of zesty enthusiasm, but their crimped ribbon strings are double-wrapped around her wrist and clutched in her manicured fingers.

I'm trying to make out what the balloons say but can't focus past the hazy glare of sunlight. As far as I know, we're not here to celebrate anything in particular. It's Thursday. It's no one's birthday. None of us just got a job, or got engaged, or got invited, as far as I know, to a retirement party or a baby shower or even a ribbon cutting. But the next thing I know, Jules is tying the things to the back of *my* chair.

"What the...?" I put one hand up to shield my eyes and squint again at the pair of balloons, trying to make out the words. The sun is just too bright, so instead I wait till she's done knotting the bow and yank down on the strings.

"Congratulations," reads one. It's off the rack.

"SIX WHOLE MONTHS," reads the other, clearly haute couture.

I glare at her back as she moves around the table and pulls out a chair, her attention caught briefly by the table full of guys. She winks at one of them, a skinny, pale-skinned, particularly nerdy-looking boy and the only one in a full suit. In Memphis. In late May.

He must be sweating through that thing, but if he wasn't before, he definitely is now.

Men cower under Jules' attention, but not for the same reasons they shy away from Savy. Jules pulverizes everyone she meets with the sheer force of her personality, which usually enters the room before she does...in the form of her laugh, which is loud, or her voice, which is surprisingly tenor and throaty for someone as bubbly and cheerleadery as Jules.

Or in this case, in the form of two colorful Mylar balloons.

"That is so uncalled for," I say as she scoots up to the sound of metal chair legs grinding against concrete. I'm fighting the urge to untie the balloons and watch them float away over the Midtown skyline, where they can embarrass me no longer. But two things stop me: one, I don't embarrass easily by principle. And two, I have this vague vision of a deflated balloon landing in some hapless meadow or marsh, defiling the natural landscape while its string tangles in the brush, ensnaring some poor woodland creature.

Instead I sulk. "Why on earth is six months cause for celebration?" I ask. "I've dated guys for longer than six months before."

Jules and Savy raise their waxed brows with the precision of synchronized swimmers.

"Whatevs," Jules says. "Name one." She pauses too briefly for me to answer. "You can't. And that's because you're a Chandler."

"I'm a what?" I ask as Savy nods in vigorous agreement.

"You're a Chandler. Bing, bing, bing!" Since her pink dress is dotted with an allover cherry print, this strikes me as hysterical, and I dissolve into more giggles.

She cuts me off. "You find something small that's wrong with every guy you ever go out with and blow it up into something huge. His nostrils are too big. Or he pronounces it 'supposably.' Or he has mascara gunk in the corners of his eyes."

That does not even make sense. I pause to process this, shaking my head as if to clear it. "That does not even make sense," I voice out loud. "I've never dated a dude who wears mascara." *Maybe I should.* My prim and proper mother would *love* that.

Jules rolls her eyes. "Didn't you ever watch *Friends*?" she says. "Chandler Bing? Too picky for his own good?"

I'm shaking my head again. "I'm more of a *How I Met Your Mother* girl. And I'm a Ted. Holding out for the real deal. I don't want to waste my time with jerks who treat me like…jerks."

But Jules isn't listening anymore; her green eyes have grown wide as grapes. Jules is classically Irish, with strawberry hair, translucent skin, and freckles that roam endearingly across her nose and cheeks, like Annie. Her hair would be a puff of corkscrew frizz like Annie's, too, if she didn't torture it into submission with expensive keratin treatments and thousand-degree flatirons. Today she's wearing it à la 1960s housewife, teased into a pouf at the crown and flipped up at the ends. To keep the look from being too literal, she's paired the dress with dirty Converse low-tops and a vintage metal G.I. Joe lunchbox that she's carrying as a purse. Honestly, I don't know how anybody gets any work done in her office. Male or female, I'd think everybody would just sit and stare at her all day.

"What happened?" she asks in a flat voice. Again without waiting for me to answer, she adds, "You didn't."

"She did," Savy pipes in. "But you have to hear the whole story."

It doesn't matter—Jules, still willfully not listening, is already out of her chair. As Savy and I watch in open-mouthed silence, she bends down to pull something out of her lunchbox/purse and stomps around to my side of the table. She tugs down one of the two balloons—I crane my neck around and see that it's the one that reads *Congratulations*—and starts scribbling over the word with a black Sharpie marker. Before I can marvel at the fact that she carries a Sharpie in her purse, I see that she's writing something in all caps above the blacked-out word.

She takes her time, the marker squeaking dryly against the balloon's surface.

Savy and I exchange a mystified look, and finally she lets go of the string. The balloon bounces back up with a series of dull, crackling *boings*.

I have to pull it down again to read it, and when I do I can feel my face turn a hotter pink than Jules' dress. My indignation mixes with the stagnant air, radiating off of me in waves.

INTERVENTION, it spells.

"Oh, no you did not just do that," I say when I regain the ability to speak. My ears are filled with pressure, and I don't know whether to laugh, cry, or spit profanities at her.

"Oh, yes I just did," Jules announces, plopping back onto her chair with a satisfied rustling of crinoline. I glance around, and the tableful of former frat boys is openly gaping at us, frozen in the act of replacing credit cards in wallets as if conducting a Mannequin Challenge.

"How exactly are you intervening on my behalf?" I hiss, my voice a stage whisper. "Are you urging me to un-break-up with the guy who just broke up with me? Or are you suggesting I should settle down and marry the jackass who dumped me for being too fat?"

"You're not fat," Jules cries out in a ringing, offended voice, and I officially feel like the patio's live entertainment. No need to pay a jazz band! Just usher the Fat Lady and her friends to your center table and watch the drama ensue. I kid you not. A couple of androgynous teenagers are stopped on the sidewalk outside the patio's wrought-iron fence, staring at us. From the corner of my eye, I can see one of them crane his/her neck to try to read the handwritten message on the balloon.

I sigh, shifting in my chair to turn my back on the rubbernecking. "Indeed, I am not," I agree with her. And I'm not.

Really, I don't think I am.

Sure, compared to Savy's waif-like perfection I'm on the heavy side of average. But I'm two dress sizes smaller than Jules, who is also NOT fat but an Adele-like goddess, and apart from Chase I've never received a single complaint 'bout that bass. My only major problem with my body—and this is so unfair of Savy—really it is—is that all the weight chooses to settle itself on my lower half. Every ounce of Savy's fat is inside her bra cups. Whereas, for me, no matter how much thunder's roaring in my thighs, my B-cup boobs receive nary a trickle of rain.

This lower-half injustice is why I count calories and follow every diet fad I find on the internet.

But I digress.

"His words, not mine," I insist. And then I launch into an abbreviated version of the story. When I get to the "ass whisperer" part, Jules' fingers are curved so her glittery gel nails look like talons, and I think all three of us can imagine them curling around the sides of Chase's pompous, skinny neck.

"I officially apologize," she says, and it's OK because I've already forgiven her.

I actually agreed with Jules and Savy, in the beginning, that Chase Ledford had promise. He's gainfully employed, for one, and not bad looking, and he made me laugh on our first date, which is my primary requirement in any sort of romantic partner.

Of course, if I'd known he was rating the size of my ass on his own personal Richter scale, I don't think I'd have found him so funny. Nope, it's not much fun to learn you're the butt of the joke…so to speak.

I'm half smiling at my own self-deprecation and don't notice that Jules has left her seat until a deafening *POP* almost launches me off my chair. It's followed by a second gunshot, and my brain is scrambling to decide what to do—run? drop to the ground?—when I slowly begin to realize that a terrorist gunman has *not* opened fire on the Second Line patio but rather that Jules has stabbed my celebratory balloons to death with her fork.

Two servers run through the back door of the restaurant out onto the patio, their heads wildly swiveling. Nobody drops anything, but Jules is abashed anyway. "Sorry, sorry, sorry," she says in a loud voice, her layered skirt swishing from side to side as she sweeps her gaze from one corner of the patio to the other, leaving no one out.

She sits with a prim flourish. Across the table Savy mimes a director's clapboard closing by raising her stacked forearms, lifting one hand, and slapping it down onto the opposite elbow. "And…scene," she says, shooting Jules a wry grin.

Our waitress walks up then, not masking her disapproval this time. "Can I bring you ladies something to eat?" she asks. It's clear that she—and the rest of the waitstaff and, presumably, the clientele—would prefer us with our hands occupied and our mouths full. I wish the moms were still here to see what they're missing by running off to the preschool pick-up lanes, but they're not. I've been so engrossed since Jules' grand entrance that I didn't even notice them leave.

I go ahead and order "the original," knowing I won't eat it so much as torture myself with the agony of not eating it, but I deserve a little something for my trouble today—at least the *smell* of delicious, greasy carbs smothered in cheese.

And then Jules orders, and Savy, and we all pretend like this little lunch outing is normal. And it is. Just another normal day in the Quirky, Unquiet Life of Quinn Cunningham. That's totally what I'm titling my memoir someday.

* * *

My mouth falls open—an expression I maybe never fully appreciated until now. It's as if my shocked jaw suddenly stops receiving signals from my paralyzed brain.

"*London?* Are you freaking kidding me?"

OK, so this might not be the most professional way to talk to my boss, but my boss, Jen Dawson, happens to be unlike other bosses. One, we've worked together for eight years, starting out as coworkers at the same firm before the owner of said firm screwed us all over and Jen struck back by quitting and forming a partnership with a competitor. Two, when that happened she went to bat for me to bring me along with her. She totally didn't have to do that. And three, in the four years since these things happened, we've become good friends.

Her forehead wrinkles. "No, I'm not kidding." OK, one negative thing about Jen? She's so straightforward and so constantly preoccupied, rhetorical questions fly right over her head. "I'd love to take it on myself, but I am *so slammed* with the tech center project I can't get away long enough to do it justice." She pauses, chewing on her lip with her eyes far away. "Plus I think it's hard to work directly for family. I'm thrilled to do this for my brother, but I'm afraid Jane and I might tiptoe around each other too much, not wanting to offend or insult each other's tastes."

I purse my lips, mulling over that for a few seconds, as I can't relate. For one thing, neither of my sisters would hire me to do anything for them, and for another, we wouldn't hesitate to insult each other's tastes. As for my brother, he's so clueless that he needs a *life* designer, not an interior designer. And my mother…well. Yeah. Right. For now we'll just leave it at that.

Go figure that the same competence and likability that prompted Jen's brother and his wife to hire her is what prevents her from saying yes. Directly, at least.

"Plus, I trust you," she continues, and my heart fizzes in pleasure at the words. "You're a good listener, and you take no nonsense when it comes to seeing your vision through, and that's what Adam and Jane need. I love both of them to pieces, but they're not going to be easy clients. Jane's very timid and reserved, and Adam is going to say he doesn't give a flip about any of it, but that won't actually be true. When you present them with options, he'll be the one who's full of opinions, I can promise you that."

"At least I have you to lay out the psychoanalysis for me," I say, practically singing the words. Difficult clients? Who the heck cares? I'm going to *England.*

Jen smiles. "Where are you with the Perins project? Can things hold there for a little while?"

I'm nodding as I answer, my brain spinning over my current client roster. "Faye submitted the deposit for the case pieces yesterday. We ordered the upholstery last week, but the fabric's on backorder for the living room sofa. Sophie *has* to have that fabric, so we're at least eight weeks out from the install. I'd planned to call Sophie today to schedule an accessories consultation." I feel a twinge of guilt that my afternoon to-do list was derailed by my two-hour lunchtime nonintervention.

The thought zaps me back to reality for a moment, but I realize the fresh sting of Chase's breakup is already starting to fade. *Take that, Chase.* Maybe he doesn't want me, but my boss and my clients do. Who needs a boyfriend when your career is way more exciting than your sex life anyway?

Jen interrupts my jaunt into inappropriate mental territory. "What about the salon project?" She's cringing a bit, probably worried that she's imposing by dumping her brother's renovation project off on me. Ha! She has *no* idea how badly I need a break from routine right now. And designing a three-story townhouse in North London is a bigger and more fantastic break than I could possibly have imagined. When I woke up this morning, the best I'd hoped from my day was to ingest enough caffeine to make it through work and on to happy hour, where I could blot out my woe-is-me love life in a blur of red wine and vodka cocktails. I haven't slept well for the past two nights, ever since Chase basically told me my ass needs its own ZIP code.

Who cares about that now? Not me!

"We're not leaving for two weeks, right?" I say. "That's enough time for me to spec out the interior finishes and get the signage on order. And I can get Jordan or Menzi up to speed to handle whatever comes up while I'm gone."

The truth is, the Perins and SpaZone projects are only the tip of the iceberg for me right now—my appointment calendar is packed, and I have consultations with two new residential clients next week alone. But there is nothing, literally nothing, I would not reschedule or give up to get out of town right now. Out of the country? Oh, that's so, so much better.

CHAPTER TWO

———

The Bachelor Pad

Chase isn't really the problem. He's just a symptom of a lifetime of tiny little first-world problems…my weight, first and foremost, which is truly something that is outside my control. I don't stress eat, I don't binge-purge or harbor any sort of secret eating disorder, and I don't maintain a willful ignorance of nutrition or a gluttonous love of junk food. At most, I'm guilty of the same thing ninety-five percent of Americans are guilty of— my gym membership is more symbolic than productive. I don't love to exercise, so I don't do enough of it. But trust me when I tell you, my mother raised me up with a fastidious devotion to dieting, a penchant for incentivizing by buying all my clothing one size too small, and an omnipresent understanding that people do, in fact, judge books by their covers.

That hasn't made me skinnier, but it has placed a bit of a challenge, shall we say, on my relationship with my mother.

With this thought I glance in her direction. Priscilla Whitehurst Cunningham is in her customary spot—the hostess chair at one end of my parents' fussy, Federal Style dining room table. I nibble off a tiny bite of asparagus and chew slowly, watching Mother watch me. She's watching all of us, really—she has an Auror's omniscience, Mad-Eye Moody with a Veela's silvery blonde façade.

Moving my eyes from her critical gaze, I study the dining room's panoramic, vintage trompe l'oeil wallpaper, noticing for the first time that the area that receives direct afternoon sunlight from the arch of the Palladian window is fading, the upper half of the eighteenth-century chateau noticeably paler than the lower half, disconnecting it from the bucolic pastoral scenes that surround it. The room has an air of pretension that doesn't appeal to me in adulthood but carries a nostalgia so thick I can taste its tangy sweetness on my tongue. It calls up days when my sisters and I barricaded ourselves in our version of a fort, spreading out our doll beds underneath the double-pedestal table, sheltering ourselves in the speckled shadows of the French lace tablecloth and pretending to be princesses trapped in the palace while Robert the Dragon lumbered around us, a toddling, fire-breathing menace.

I glance around the rest of the room, wondering what other hints of fading glory have escaped my notice. There's a peeling seam near the crown molding on the section of wallpaper above the huge antique sideboard, and the colored glass Italian chandelier could use a detailed hit with a Swiffer duster, but other than that it's exactly as I remember it.

I'm in the chair that's been mine since I was six, Vivienne beside me. Across the table sits Viv's husband, Bradley, with their two children to his left. My father has the captain's chair at the other end of the table, nearest the large Palladian window. We gather in this formation every week for Sunday Supper, an ironclad Cunningham tradition.

"Eat with your mouth closed, dear," Mother says.

It takes me a moment to realize she's speaking to me, not one of the grandkids. *Really?* In my mother's presence I eat as sparingly as possible, owing to the fact that I'm not masochistic. And yet I've still managed to offend her delicate sensibilities.

"You're chewing like a horse. It's unbecoming."

"Dear." This single, plaintive word from my dad means nothing, though he tries his best. He's offered himself up as a human shield for as long as I can remember.

Mother shoots him a look as sharp as her French tips. "Manners and etiquette are extremely important," she says, sliding her gaze back to me. To my right I can sense Vivienne shaking with the effort to hold in her laughter.

"George, did you read or hear anything about that Altacom IPO today?" says my brother-in-law, interrupting the Let's All Dump On Quinn hatefest. It's not that he's interjecting on my behalf but rather that the animosity cloaking our family's female relationships is totally lost on him. He's singly focused on stocks and trades, bulls and bears.

"No," my father says, wiping his mouth with a cranberry-colored cloth napkin. He picks up his water glass and takes a long drink before adding, "Should I have?"

While Bradley launches into a long, dull description of some telecom company I've never heard of, Vivienne continues snickering beside me, probably waiting for my mother to fling her next insult or silently coming up with her own. I'd be stabby by now if I weren't so accustomed to this game. If not my manners, it's my clothing. If not my clothing, it's my single lifestyle. If not my lifestyle, it's my weight.

Really, it's always my weight. In my mother's eyes all my other deficiencies spiral in concentric circles out from this single, impossible-to-hide defect. She treats it like a character flaw, not a fluke of genetics.

The fact of the matter is my metabolism started out slow and never picked up speed. The freshman fifteen, for me, ascended to the sophomore twenty and the junior twenty-five. Thankfully it leveled off there, and thankfully my tall, athletic frame helps me carry it off.

I look like my dad's side of the family. My rounded posterior is in evidence on every one of my aunts—I have four of them, and they all hate my mother—and it's my legacy and birthright as much as my maternal grandmother's Miss America title or my father's family's deep political legacy, which is looking like it might end, or at least suffer its first pause in a century, with my generation.

Vivienne, who's three years older than me, was crowned Miss Tennessee in her second year at Vanderbilt, the same year Caroline, who's five years older than me, completed her residency in cardiothoracic surgery at New York-Presbyterian after graduating with distinction from Cornell. While these things were happening, I was earning my bachelor's in interior design at the Chicago Art Institute. My brother, still in college— sort of—is busy wasting his potential the way any good youngest child is supposed to do. He's currently living in Seattle and drumming in a garage band that missed the garage band movement by two decades.

My bevy of cousins on my dad's side have followed similar paths—some distinctive, some not, with the common denominator being a lack of political ambition. That left me to become the first female Congressional representative to carry the Cunningham family name...and surely you've deduced by now that that isn't happening.

I'm a disappointment all around. The forgotten middle child, the "oh, poor me."

Like I said, first-world problems.

I'm aware of my extreme good fortune to have a familial safety net while enjoying the resources at my disposal to do what *I* want to do, which is create. My only twinge of regret is the idea that I'm disappointing my dad. I think he saw me as his best shot at a successor. Growing up, my favorite pastime apart from doodling and filling scrapbooks with magazine cutouts of my future dream home was to curl up in a corner of the leather Chesterfield in my dad's study and listen to him discuss Important Political Matters with Important Political People. I had no idea what he was talking about, but I was fascinated by his competence, his power, his gravitas. Once he even gave me— only me, not Caroline or Vivienne or Robert—a "Take Your Daughter to Work Day," and I spent a full nine-to-five shadowing him in the state capitol's legislative chambers.

And now, look at me. Not only am I not a state senator, I'm not even a Republican.

But I am still a daddy's girl, and another of those tiny little problems mentioned above is that I haven't yet found a guy who's half the man my father is. Not Chase, certainly, but also not Steve, my high school boyfriend and the one who everybody but me insists is The One Who Got Away.

Especially my mom, and that's because Steve *is* a senator, and not at the state level, either. In fact, he's the youngest guy on the Hill and a prodigy whose legacy on the Harvard Law Review is still fresh. Priscilla Cunningham still hasn't forgiven me for breaking poor Stevie's heart at the tender age of eighteen—no matter that Steve was the one who screwed *me* over, literally by screwing half the cheerleading squad...and, according to rumor, two of them at the same time. And did I mention that I was *on* the cheerleading squad? Those stone-cold biatches were my best friends.

Remember that scene from *Varsity Blues* where Darcy tries to seduce Mox with her "whipped cream bikini?" Meanwhile, her boyfriend Lance Harbor is in the hospital after a devastating football injury, and Mox is in a Serious Relationship with Darcy's friend. That's pretty much what this felt like, minus the evil coach and the cast of supermodels. But there's that line, that explanation Darcy gives that's heartbreaking and almost makes you feel sorry for her gorgeous, conniving self. *"It was never about love. It was about me getting a better life."*

Well, one of my former cheerleading comrades is now Mrs. Steven Rushing Carpenter, with a house overlooking the river bluff in downtown Memphis, another house just outside DC in Virginia, and a third house in Watercolor, Florida. Last I heard they have three children and Callista doesn't work at anything more grueling than her own quadriceps and the fine art of spray tan.

Oh, and she *hates* me. Never mind that I'm the only member of our former squad without "Mrs." before my name and that *I'm* the one who got fat. Apparently she can't stand to be in the same room with me and therefore makes it her third occupation to ensure that I'm not invited to social functions whenever she's in town. I ran into her and Steve at Interim one night where I was on a date, and while Steve and I made that awkward small talk of people who once saw each other naked, Callista's evenly tanned skin turned a strange shade of purpley-orange, and she dug her claw-like nails into the arm of his suit— I saw the indentations—while gazing past me and saying sweetly, "It was lovely to catch up with you, darling." And then she continued with their previous conversation as if I wasn't still standing awkwardly beside their table. "Maximus then says to me, 'Velour is a bad idea with the salt air, no matter whether the color…'"

I didn't hear the rest of the sentence because I was already walking away, trailing a halfhearted wave behind me. I peeked over my shoulder to see Steve staring after me, lifting three fingers in return with an apologetic smile he probably got a verbal lashing for later.

Anyway, my mother still wears her disappointment over my breakup with Steve like a vintage coat with threadbare patches from having overstayed its welcome in her closet.

As if she overhears my thoughts, my mother barks my name…apparently not for the first time since her voice is agitated and sharp like a yippy dog's. I wonder how long she's been trying to flag me out of my daydream.

"Quincy," she says again, setting down her fork for emphasis. She's the only person on earth who calls me by my given name, which I received because of my parents' fear they'd never have a boy. It was my grandfather's name—my father's father, who died before I was born.

"Yes, Mother?" My tone is heavy on the sarcasm, but that's not unusual. If she notices she doesn't acknowledge it. This is our game.

"I said Marianne Caribald's son is back in town." She pauses as if waiting for a reaction, and when I don't provide one, adds, "Anthony."

My face is as blank as my memory bank. I press my lips together, my brow furrowing. Finally I shake my head and shrug. "And this should mean something to me…why?"

She stares at me coolly, as if I'm missing something rather than being intentionally obtuse. Or, more likely, as if she's trying to figure out whether to draw or play her hand.

"Well, I thought you might be interested in the fact that Anthony just finished his residency and bought a house on the Island. He's a pediatric oncologist. And by all accounts, single." She pauses, unable to keep the flutter of annoyance from dragging down her lashes. She has no poker face to speak of, despite the retinol injections. "At the very least you should be interested that a single man just bought a bachelor pad that he's likely to fill with nothing more than black leather couches and big screens. He's a prime prospect for your little business."

A jolt of indignation fizzes up my spine. My mother is insistent that my career is a passing fancy, a way to while away the time before a man sweeps me off my feet, impregnates me, and sets me up for a life of Junior League and leisure. She always calls it my "little business." Always. No matter that my "little business" has kept me off the parental payroll since grad school, thank you very much, and bought my car and my two-story townhouse that *almost* has a river view. I even have an investment portfolio.

"That's interesting information," I say cryptically. "Thank you." I'm bursting at the seams to tell her I won't be taking on new clients anytime soon because I'm leaving the country for an indefinite period, but I'm not ready to play *my* cards yet. I don't want to share my good news as a retort.

Mercifully my father chooses this moment to interject. He's used to his role as good cop, at least when it comes to me. "Did you see Gasol's last-second shot last night?"

"It was a game-winning buzzer beater. Of course I saw it," I say, grinning at him. "Were you there?"

My dad has club-level season tickets to the Grizzlies that I happily take off his hands whenever the chance arises. Sometimes we go together, a fact that mystifies the rest of my family, who wouldn't know a free throw from a three-point conversion.

"No, I gave up the tickets for a client," he says, grimacing.

Dad no longer serves in the state senate, but he still works full-time at the law office with his name on the letterhead. I'm pretty sure he'll never retire. He'll be one of those white-haired office patriarchs with endearing quirks that everybody smilingly obliges, even if they don't take his septuagenarian notions seriously.

"Shame," I say. "Let me know if Wallace can't go with you anytime in the next couple of weeks. I'll come."

"Think they'll make a playoff run?"

"Maybe," I say. "That's not why I want to come with you, though." I hedge, wanting to play this right but not sure how. Finally I just spit it out. "I'm leaving the country for a little while later this month, and I'd love to get in a game before I go."

I pick up my sweating iced tea goblet and take a sip, reveling in my fleeting status as the one with impressive news. The questions all come at once.

"Where are you going?" This is from Dad.

"How long will you be gone?" Vivienne, probably hoping it's indefinitely.

"How'd this come about?" This question is from my mother, in her usual biting tone.

Only my brother-in-law is silent. Since he travels internationally on a regular basis for his nebulous investment banking job, I'm sure this news is rather boring to him. He keeps rounding his plate, spearing bites of roasted pork tenderloin, then fingerling potato, then asparagus, always in the same order, never mixing items on his fork, as is his habit. He's a man of such rhythmic order that I can't help but wonder what he's like in bed. I know, I know, that's kind of sick. But I'm not *into* him. I just get a kick out of imagining what their love life looks like. First he sucks this, then he nibbles that, then he thrusts there. Then he does it again, round and round and round they go. I don't know—maybe there's excitement in the routine of it. Maybe it's a slow build.

But I digress.

"I'm going to England," I announce finally. "And I leave in two weeks." I've only really answered Dad's question, a fact I'm sure does not escape my mother's notice.

"Is it a market?" my mother asks. "Will you be buying antiques for the shop?"

Her voice is a notch higher than usual, and I can guess at why she's excited. Much as she's disinterested in *my* career, that's not the case for homes and design in general. She's obsessed with competing with her University Club friends for the newest, most obscure, and most expensive antique armoire or commode or breakfront. She's even more obsessed with Shilling Price, the high-dollar, high-and-mighty, only-works-on-million-dollar-plus projects interior designer who designed the main living spaces in our house roughly twenty years ago. Shilling is still around, still a Major Douche, and still getting charity features in *Veranda* every now and then. He has an office in Downtown Memphis and another in Palm Beach where he lives year-round. His style is frozen in time—still speckled with Louis XIV this and Edwardian that. Ormolu. Inlay. Swagged and tasseled draperies. Never mind that Pinterest and *Domino* and *Property Brothers* rendered these things obsolete at least a decade ago, unless they're used ironically or as elements in the ubiquitous "eclectic mix."

You'd think my mother might have hired me by now to update Shilling's old, tired design and bring our family's 1902 Colonial Revival manor into the twenty-first century, right? After all, I've been told my work is solid. And I have a knack for historic preservation—probably because I grew up in such a graceful old place. And my designs have even been featured in *Apartment Therapy* and *Garden & Gun*. But does any of this matter to my mother?

Um, no. The house remains a shrine to Shilling Price's glory days, and she remains a groupie to his outmoded expertise.

I contain my eye roll, barely. "No, Mother. It isn't a buying trip. I'll be working with a new client, a private homeowner in North London." I glance at Viv. "I'm not sure how long I'll be gone—however long it takes to get a handle on the scope of the project and get the furnishings and finishes specked out and on order. And then I'll be going back again for the install."

I'm making this up as I go; Jen and I didn't hammer things out to this level of detail, but this isn't my first out-of-market project. I've designed a row house in Boston, two condos on the Florida Gulf, and a North Woods cabin in Upper Michigan, so I know the general drill. A trip to view the space, consult with the client, measure, draw up initial plans, and present. Subsequent trips to find locally sourced items, oversee the work, and complete installation. Maybe one last trip for photo styling, if I'm lucky enough to get published.

This new project will be unusual in that I'll surely be working with new-to-me sources and I'll need to get to know the lay of the foreign land. I'm not sure how long that will take, but I thrill to the challenge. My heart swerves a beat or two off-track.

"How on earth did you get a client in England?" my sister asks, and her *"Who would hire* you *for this?"* undertone puts a pinprick in my bubble of excitement. I glance at Mother, and her lips are pressed together.

"The house belongs to my boss's brother and his wife," I say. "She doesn't have time to take the project on herself, so she's asked me to take the lead." I'd like to tell the truth—that Jen doesn't want to work directly with family, but I don't want to give my mother even more incentive to avoid hiring me. Even though I agree with Jen that working closely with family members is a bad idea—and I know there's no way Mother and I could agree on the simplest decision about color or materials or even style—it would still be nice to be asked. To be considered. To be allowed the dignity to consider the offer and defer to another member of my firm.

Much as I reject the idea that I'm seeking my mother's approval, it's hard to avoid reality when she wears her disdain of my work as prominently as her disappointment in my weight and appearance and general man-repelling tendencies.

"Ah, so she's dumped it off on you." Vivienne nods, as if there has to be some explanation outside my competence as a designer. I'm about to fire back, but her attention turns when my nephew flicks a spoonful of chopped-up fingerling potato into his sister's face. "Elijah Cunningham Cosgrove, you apologize to your sister right this second."

Vivienne jumps up and begins picking little shreds of potato peel out of Aisling's honey blonde curls. Four-year-old Elijah, ignoring his mother's command, resumes his previous occupation of smooshing his bite-size asparagus fronds into gooey green mash. Then he pinches up a glob with his fingers and stuffs it into his nose. "Look. I've got boogies." He pokes Aisling in the side as soon as Vivienne walks away, and she slaps at his hand and wails, "Mooommeeee."

"Oh, for heaven's sake." Vivienne rolls her eyes and walks back around the table, one hand on her just-visible baby bump, ignoring them.

At this my mother fixes Elijah with her Stare of Terror, and he straightens immediately in his chair, letting the glob of asparagus goo drop onto his plate.

"Eww. Gross," Aisling squeaks, and then she falls silent, too, noticing Mother's look. Nobody messes with that look.

I lift my napkin to my lips to hide my smile. My sisters might outshine me in every way, but at least Vivienne sucks at disciplining her kids. Unlike Caroline, who works long hours and whose only child is cared for most of the time by a Norwegian au pair, Vivienne, despite her master's degree in economics, has chosen the life of a stay-at-home mom—a slightly more well-heeled breed than the women I gawped at on the Second Line patio. In our mother's eyes this means she's living out her most noble calling as a woman. And yet, Vivienne hates the job. She masks her misery with an air of condescension and a tight-lipped expression she pulls straight out of Mother's playbook, but I can tell.

She doesn't have the knack…or The Look. Mother had to step in and take control. In this moment I've scored the career victory, and Viv is the failure.

It doesn't happen to me often. It almost makes up for what Vivienne says to me as she slips back into the seat to my right. Almost, but not quite.

"You know, you should avoid stretchy knits, Sis," she says, glancing past her shoulder to frown down at my midsection. "If we went somewhere together people might think we're both expecting."

Her sweet-as-honey tone belies her malice. *Why do I even bother with this lot?*

Just then my father clears his throat. "Congratulations on the new client, Quinny. When do you cross the pond?"

Oh yeah, that's why. I grin at my dad gratefully. "Two weeks."

"So soon?" He's the only one who appears dismayed. "Well, tell me when you have a night free to hang with your old man. I'll let Wallace know he needs to buy a ticket if he wants to see the Grizz clinch the division."

"That sounds great, Dad. I'm in."

"What part of London will you be staying in?" asks Bradley, my brother-in-law, with mild curiosity.

"The house is in North London. Islington, I think Jen said?"

He perks up, nodding. "I'm familiar with that area. Our London branch isn't too far away, in Shoreditch. I'm there at least twice a quarter. Maybe we'll cross paths."

"Maybe," I say, thinking it's doubtful. London is an awfully big city, and I imagine I'll be busy while I'm there, especially since I have to learn the ropes in an unfamiliar design market. I'm lost in a reverie of quaint High Street shops and posh furniture showrooms when Viv interrupts my daydreaming.

"Maybe he could introduce you to one of his single colleagues. Think how fun it would be to live abroad," she says in a musing sort of tone.

Wait a hot minute. Is this a hint of sisterly camaraderie? Is Vivienne actually happy for me?

Mic drop.

"You should really start working out more, though," she adds with a sneer. "I hear British men are even more particular than American men, especially when it comes to American women."

Ah, there's the Vivienne I know. She hasn't been abducted by aliens after all. I'm putting together a retort questioning how she came upon this shred of cosmopolitan knowledge—during playgroup? in her prenatal yoga class?—when our mother interjects.

"Parke told me there's a wonderful trainer at her CrossFit gym," she says, her voice earnest, as if Vivienne's just made an honest suggestion. "This is a bit vulgar, so I don't know that I should pass it on, especially in front of the children." She lifts a hand to shield her lips, glancing toward the kids' end of the table. Elijah is missing from his chair, and Aisling is humming to herself, running her fingers through the hair of a Barbie doll she must have smuggled in as contraband. "She told me the girls there all call him"—Mother's voice drops to a low hiss—"*the ass whisperer*."

* * *

Monday morning at work, the whole office is buzzing. Jen had shared the news with me and with her partner and coprincipal, Amanda Barnes, first, but now everybody knows about our upcoming trip. Menzi Ricewell, one of our two design assistants, is especially keyed up because she's going to be assigned work that's normally reserved for our registered designers. I've spent the morning sifting through all my open projects to figure out where things stand, what I can get done before I leave, what I can do from overseas, and what I need to delegate.

"OK, so, Sophie Perins," I say to Menzi, who's sitting beside me in one of the peacock blue leather rolling chairs surrounding the round worktable in the front corner of the shop. There are six tables like this in our workspace, a long, narrow room with a storefront that's attached to the showroom by a wide, open doorway at the center of the shop. In the showroom we have floor samples for sale—case pieces and upholstered items ordered at market, so our clients can "sit on the furniture" before making a decision and also so we always have pieces on hand in case we get a rush job. Most of what we do involves custom ordering, and that takes time. We also have a warehouse to store items, which lets Jen and Amanda keep the showroom relatively unfussy and uncluttered.

Both the showroom and the studio have exposed brick walls, concrete floors, and wide plate-glass windows that span the double-bay façade. Since we're in a strip center in Cooper-Young, an arty, eclectic area at the very heart of Memphis, there are no windows on the sides of the space. To eliminate the cave effect, suspended track lighting zigs and zags from the black-painted ceilings, and lamps dot every tabletop surface. Above each worktable hangs a Louis Poulsen mid-century pendant light.

I love our studio to the tips of my pinky toes.

"Sophie Perins," Menzi repeats in a serious voice. She's a recent graduate from SCAD, the art college in Savannah, Georgia, where Jen got her interior design degree. Jen works with their advising department to get a lot of our interns, which is how Menzi got her start with us two summers ago. She doesn't have her own client roster yet because she hasn't yet passed the accrediting exam. Menzi and our other assistant, Jordan Walker, help wherever they're needed on all the firm's projects, though Jordan is Menzi's senior by far, and part of me wishes I could work with Jordan instead of Menzi. But Jordan is tied up with her own work at the moment. "Her family owns the Pressed dry cleaning chain, right?"

"No, that's the Marins," I say, my lips curling into a tiny, wry smile. One thing you should know about Memphis—everybody here knows everybody, and which family you're from or which school you went to matters…to some people. It matters to *my* people, which is why I'll be damned if I let it matter to me. "Sophie Perins and her husband moved here last year from Brooklyn."

"Oh, that's right. She's the one whose husband clerked for a Supreme Court justice. Isn't he a bigwig at one of the major law firms downtown?"

"*Sophie* clerked for Justice Ginsburg," I correct her. "She worked for a large firm in Manhattan until they moved here. I can't remember what her husband does, but he's from Memphis, and that's what brought them down south. They want to start a family, which is why they bought the house."

Another thing to know about Memphis—it still has a good ol' boy society, with a bevy of gossiping men and women behind it. I'll never forget the time my first boss at my old firm, Candace Greenlee, asked a new client in her sweet-as-molasses, fake-as-silicone drawl, "Darling, what does your husband do?" The woman answered that her husband was a rheumatologist. Since it was my turn on the walk-in rotation, the woman became my client, and I worked with her for at least two weeks before realizing she wasn't a doctor's wife-slash-stay-at-home-mom, as we'd all assumed from her answer, but an obstetrician with her own private practice.

"Why didn't you tell me that?" I'd asked her.

"Because Candace never asked what *I* do," she'd answered with a smirk. "She only asked what my husband did."

Boy, did that put me in my place. It's true that we work with a lot of doctor's wife-slash-stay-at-home-moms in my profession, and it's also true that it's often the wives who make the design decisions for their households. But I learned that day never to assume anything.

"Oh, good to know," Menzi says, calling me back to our Sophie Perins discussion. She seems to shrink under my disapproving tone, so I smile and make my voice a little warmer.

"Two things to know about Sophie," I say. "She's very decisive. Once her mind is made up, don't try to change it, but figure out how to adapt to it."

Menzi nods gravely, tapping notes frantically into her iPad.

"And two, she hates, and I mean *hates*, mass-produced anything. I've been working to show her only items made domestically by sustainable producers, the more local the better. And art is a big driver for this project. We've planned the entire design around a large-scale abstract painting she and Denny brought with them from New York. They chose the house because it had the perfect wall to hang this painting."

Menzi stops the frantic tapping and glances up at me. "Is she going to be OK switching to work with me instead of you?" Little tremors shimmer underneath her words.

"No," I answer with a laugh. "But don't worry. We're at a good spot to stall things for a while. I'm only briefing you in case an emergency comes up while I'm away. And most of my other clients aren't scary at all." I giggle again. "OK, except Mrs. Steinbocker. But you'll get used to her."

She looks absolutely terrified.

"Seriously, don't worry," I add. "I don't have any major installs coming up. Stuff won't be coming in for SpaZone for at least another four or five weeks, and I'll be back before the final installation. I'll stay in contact with the subs, and I might need you to pop in once or twice to check on the work." I pause, eyeing her to gauge her level of freak-out, and she's nodding, so I go on. "Remember, I'm only a call or text away, and I'm sending the schedules for all of my projects to Jen, Amanda, and Faye."

Faye Epperson is our office manager and general Jane-of-all-trades. A petite, white-haired woman who's managed Amanda's business affairs for at least fifteen years, Faye doesn't have a design degree, but I guarantee you she could do any of our jobs as well as we do. Her South Georgia drawl is sweet as a ripe peach, but she's as shrewd as an IRS auditor and doesn't miss a detail.

"OK." Menzi's voice is meek and carries with it a whiff of disappointment. I remember what it's like to want more responsibility even when you're not sure you're ready for it. I felt that way most of the time at my last job, where I'm pretty sure my boss thought I was nothing more than a social climbing party girl. I'd been afraid of that when I interviewed for the job—my sister had helped me get the interview through a friend in the Junior League. As a result, none of the important projects came my way. My clients came mostly from our firm's sparse walk-ins and my own social circle, which wasn't lucrative since I refused to beg my mother to tout me to her friends. The firm's owner had been happy enough to let me revamp the firm's abysmal website and start a blog, which is something I now do for my current firm, DB Interiors, with blogging help from our design assistants.

I think forward to what else my clients have coming up and give Menzi my kindest smile.

"Rashid Harishman should be ready to move into the next phase of our master plan in the next two to three weeks," I tell her. "I've already done the space planning, and we have the major upholstery and case pieces picked out, but she's going to want a drapery consultation, and I'll need you to take the lead on presenting fabrics and giving her estimates. I've already let her know I'm going out of town, and she'll get with you when she's ready."

Menzi straightens in her chair and begins rapid-fire tapping at her screen again. "OK," she says nervously. "Will I need to take measurements?"

"Just to set up the estimates," I say. "Window dimensions are on the plans in her files. Before Faye places the order, have the installer go out to see the space and take final measurements for the workroom." I pause, my index finger pressed into the divot in my chin, something I catch myself doing when I'm thinking hard. "Don't forget to get hardware estimates, too. And check the dimensions of the window casings to make sure we order deep enough brackets."

Menzi is nodding and typing, and I'm still thinking. Spaces are quirky, especially residential spaces—corners that aren't square, shoddy DIY jobs, a wall that's an inch off here, an ill-placed receptacle there. Design work involves a lot of in-the-moment troubleshooting, and the ability to think on your feet comes with years of experience of dealing with the jillion little things that can and will go wrong on every project. I'm learning that it's even harder to do clairvoyant troubleshooting—to figure out what's going to go wrong while you're four thousand miles away.

Let it go, Quinn. I can't really help myself—I'm a control freak. It's part of the job. Honestly, it's a professional requisite. If you don't care about details, you don't go into interior design, plain and simple. Much as it kills me to let any of it go, it'll be interesting to see how Menzi handles my client roster while I'm out. Still, it makes me nervous that I can't get a read on her enthusiasm. *Is she excited or terrified?* I brush off the thought and push on.

"I'll need to turn the blog over to you and Jordan while I'm gone since I'm not sure what my schedule will look like or how much extra time I'll have," I add. "Can you handle that?"

Menzi nods, eyes wide.

"I have a file with ideas and a half-assed schedule of posts. I'll share the Google docs. Oh, and I might want to do a blog series about what it's like to do design work in the UK. If I have time to work something up and shoot you a post and some pics, can you figure out how to get that going? I'll talk to Jordan about this, too."

She nods again, tapping away at her iPad. Her forehead has two distinct wrinkles that weren't there before, which lets me know I've loaded her down enough.

"Jen is going with me for the first week to introduce me to her brother's family and help me get started, but then she'll be back. If anything major happens while I'm away, just keep me posted. I'll do what I can from London." At the last word, a thrill of expectation runs through my entire body. *London.*

I'm going to London.

I'm. Going. To. *London.*

CHAPTER THREE

———

Cheers!

It's Saturday night, a week and a half later, and Savy, Jules, and I are on another patio in Overton Square, this time at Robata, a ramen bar fitted into an old house that somehow didn't get the memo when the surrounding houses were demolished to make way for strip centers and commercial development. Robata's patio is in the front yard, as it were, of the little yellow house, and our black mesh table and chairs rest beneath an oversized umbrella though it's well after dark. Beyond the patio the street thrums with passers-by, both cars and pedestrians.

"I wish I could come visit you," Jules says for the eleven-hundredth time.

"You can," I say. "Just book the ticket. You can crash in my hotel room."

Jen and I had discussed having me stay in the extra room in Jane and Adam's house, but ultimately she decided it was more professional and considerably less awkward to book me into a bed-and-breakfast a block or so away. My expenses will be folded into the costs of the project, but from Jen's nonchalant attitude, I'm guessing budget is not a major problem for her brother, who I think is a vice president of a large insurance firm. I'm not sure what Jane does career-wise.

"I can't. You know I can't," Jules says miserably. "I'm right in the middle of the One Beale situation. Right now it's all paperwork, paperwork, paperwork. I swear if this project ever gets off the ground, I'll dance naked on the rooftop."

"You better make sure Herbert isn't around for that," pipes in Savy, and I snort.

The three of us call Herb Carpenter, the managing partner at Jules' firm, "Herbert" even though "Herb" is actually his full first name. It's short for "Herbert the Pervert," a nickname bestowed by Savy one night after a few too many cocktails. Herbert is in his midfifties with salt-and-pepper hair and a close-cropped beard. He's married with three grown children, but his come-ons to Jules are legendary. Last year he did the whole cliché thing of asking her to go along on a business trip—an architecture conference in Miami—and booking her in a room adjoining his. Late one night after a client dinner, he cajoled her into unlocking the door and, emboldened by the three-quarters empty bottle of wine on his nightstand, fondled her in all sorts of inappropriate ways and forced a sloppy, wet kiss on her.

She shut him down immediately, of course. She's engaged—even if it's the longest engagement *ever*, and Savy and I aren't one hundred percent sure she and Luca will ever tie the knot—and completely disgusted by Herbert. But ever since that trip, he's been texting her things that would definitely get him fired if he wasn't part owner of the company. So far she hasn't filed a complaint, but she's saving the text thread in case he ever throws her a quid-pro-quo situation. I know for a fact she has at least one picture of his…well, you know…because she showed it to Savy and me once when she was drunk.

We're all pretty sure Viagra was involved in that selfie.

"Guh-ross," Jules says, crinkling her perfect aquiline nose. Jules is a classic beauty—a pinup girl, basically—with porcelain skin beneath her freckles, apple blossom cheeks, and wide, jade eyes with thick, naturally curled lashes. Mixed with her flamboyant style and larger-than-life presence, she never fails to turn heads. "You girls will have to have my back," she says. "Bar the door to the roof deck."

"We've always got your back," Savy says.

"Thanks, Savannah Georgia," Jules says with a wink.

This is our little inside joke, but it's not actually a joke. Savy's full name is Savannah Georgia Hartnett, and her sisters are Alexandria Virginia and Charlotte Carolina. They have a brother named Memphis, though his middle name is Spencer, not Tennessee. Needless to say, Spence moved away after high school. A kid named Memphis growing up in Memphis was…well, it was a cruelty on the part of their parents. Even though he never went by it, from the first day of roll call every year, his classmates all knew his real name. The funniest part is that Savy's family isn't even Southern. All four kids were born in their parents' hometown in Northern Oregon. Savy's dad's job as a FedEx pilot moved them here when Savy was in the third grade.

"Anytime," Savy says, taking a dainty sip of her sake cocktail. Unlike Spence, she embraces her weird name. She explains the whole story to anybody who asks—which is pretty much everybody, since Savy is an uncommon name.

"What am I going to do without you girls for three whole weeks in England?" I wail. My cheeks are getting hot, and my fingertips are numb, which means I shouldn't order another glass of wine, but I'm sure I will anyway. This is my last hurrah with my girls before my trip-with-an-indefinite-ending. I'm telling people three weeks, but honestly it could be longer or shorter, depending on the scope of the project and the difficulty in sourcing products and lining up subs. I've wondered why Jane and Adam aren't working with a British designer, but I'm not looking a business-class plane ticket and weeks-long paid hotel stay in the mouth. I guess they just want some hometown familiarity in their foreign home.

"I know. It's going to be so weird," Jules says. "What if Savy finally meets the man who sweeps her off her feet and he carts her off to Vegas to get hitched? Who's going to fly cross-country with me to stop her from saying 'I do' to a virtual stranger in front of fake Elvis in a rhinestone jumpsuit?"

Her voice is one notch louder than its usual loud, so I know she's on her way to being hammered, too.

"Yeah, because *that's* likely to happen," Savy says. The sober one of us, as usual.

"It could happen," Jules says with an indelicate hiccup.

We finished our bowls of ramen and shared plates of yakitori at least an hour ago, which means we've been drinking for at least two.

"What's more likely to happen is that Quinn is going to meet some dashing man with a sexy British accent, and he's going to take her away from us forever to live in some thatch-roofed cottage in a picturesque village with a name like Chattingham or Hogswold. Or maybe a big stone castle with turrets and servants."

I choke on my wine and accidentally spit some from the sides of my mouth. "You've been watching too much *Downton Abbey*," I say to Savy, wiping my chin with my red cloth napkin.

"What if you do meet a guy there?" Jules muses, and I laugh.

"With my luck he'll lure me from the pub and say whatever it takes to get into my knickers. Then he'll dump me because my arse is too big."

"You're so bad," Savy says, playfully pushing my shoulder. After a few seconds her expression turns thoughtful. "You'd better not meet somebody," she adds, giving me a serious look. "If you fall hopelessly in love and move away from here, I don't know what I'd do. And Jules is getting married." She pauses again, still pensive. "Everything is changing. Life would be so boring without you two."

"Heavy," Jules says. She hiccups again and then pushes Savy's cocktail a few inches closer to her across the table. "C'mon, let's slam our drinks. Nobody's going anywhere. I refuse to grow up, and I refuse to let you two do it, either."

She picks up her glass. "To irresponsibility."

I lift mine, as well. "To irresponsibility," I echo, nudging Savy with my elbow. "And hot British guys." I give an exaggerated wink.

"To hot British guys," Savy repeats. "And not marrying them."

"To not getting married," Jules adds, her voice even louder and more emphatic. And then she tips back her glass and empties the remaining half of it down her throat. Savy raises an eyebrow and looks at me, and then we both look at Jules. I can tell Savy is about to ask but thinks better of it.

"To not getting married," we repeat in unison, and by the time we stand up, all three of us have to Uber home.

* * *

It's two days later, and I'm packed and looking around my townhouse, making sure I haven't left anything or forgotten to do anything major. I flip off the living room light and pull my enormous suitcase down my long front hallway. My hand is on the doorknob when I realize I *have* forgotten something, though I wouldn't have gotten far without it. My phone is charging in the kitchen. I roll my eyes at myself and run in to grab it, stuffing the charger into the front pocket of my carry-on bag.

As I rush toward the door, I click the home button out of reflexive habit and glance at the screen. And then I do a double-take.

There's a text on the screen, and even though his name doesn't show up—I deleted his sorry ass from my contacts the night we broke up—I immediately recognize the number as Chase's. I might have deleted his contact from my phone, but I still haven't deleted the words he used to break up with me from my brain. *"You could get there one day. You really could."* Every time I think those words I feel like punching something—Chase's stupid, flat stomach in particular. And so I try not to think them, like, ever.

I especially try not to think them when I'm lifting a spoon to my mouth, and even more especially when it's filled with something that tastes good that I know I should resist. *Damn him to the most hellish depths of hell.* It's one thing for a guy to dump you. It's quite another for him to zap all the pleasure out of a sliver of cheesecake or a chocolate-covered strawberry.

"You busy tonight?" That's all it says. As if we're on speaking terms and he has the right to ask such a question.

Yeah, I'm busy tonight. I'm busy flying far away from your rude, arrogant, presumptuous self and moving on with my life.

What's he asking for, anyway—a booty call? *Unbelievable.*

I ignore the text and swipe open my phone to see if Savy's tried to call. She's driving me to the airport so I don't have to leave my car in long-term parking for weeks. It's 8:28, and I need to be at the airport by nine, so I'm hoping the fact that she hasn't texted doesn't mean she hasn't left her apartment yet.

It's Savy, not Jules, so I feel certain she's on her way. I tap her name and call.

"I'm three minutes away," she says without greeting.

"Thank you, thank you, thank you." I could have taken an Uber, but there's something comforting about being dropped off at the airport by someone who loves you. It's like reassurance that somebody will miss you when you're gone.

"No problem. I have a meeting in East Memphis at ten anyway, so this gets me a little closer."

We're still chatting when her white CRV pulls up at the curb in front of my house. I haven't told her about Chase's text yet, but I show her the screen as soon as I've loaded my bags into her trunk and settled into the passenger seat.

"Who's that from?" she asks, checking her side mirror before pulling out into the light traffic of Tennessee Street.

"Believe it or not, Chase," I say, watching for her outraged reaction. To my astonishment, she barely raises an eyebrow.

"I'm not surprised," she says. "You haven't texted him back, have you?"

"No!" I pause for several seconds. "Why aren't you surprised?"

"Because the reason he broke up with you was ludicrous. And because you're amazing, and he knows it, and he's realized he's an idiot, and he wants you back." She says this in the tone you'd use to say, *"Well, duh."*

"Ha! That's rich. Honestly, you should write fiction."

"Maybe one day I will." Savy has a journalism degree, so it'd be a natural step. But I can't concentrate too hard on the idea of my best friend on the *New York Times* bestseller list because she has me confused with this nonsense about Chase wanting me back.

"You don't think I *should* text him back, do you?"

"Only if you're going to tell him to go screw himself," she answers in a blasé tone. "He doesn't deserve you. Obviously."

"He probably just left something at my place," I mumble, though if so, I have no idea what it could be. Trust me when I tell you, if I'd found anything of Chase's after our breakup, I'd have stuck pins in it or thrown darts at it or something worse. Tied it to a rock and tossed it into the Mississippi River in the path of a passing barge. "I'll delete it. He can deal."

"That's the spirit." We're on the interstate now, and Savy is distracted when an eighteen-wheeler swerves into the left lane in front of us to give clearance to a car in the shoulder up ahead.

Once we're past the truck, she changes the subject to her recently divorced aunt who keeps getting engaged to men she's just met online. Seriously, the latest fiancé makes three. In six months.

We gossip about it until Chase is forgotten.

The next thing I know, we're cruising up Airways Boulevard, and then I'm getting out of Savy's car and squeezing her tight, and finally I'm off to check my bag and make my way through security and meet Jen at our gate.

*   *   *

Did I mention that I've never been out of the country? Well, apart from two spring breaks in Cancun and a trip to the Canada side of Niagara Falls as a kid, but those were on the North American continent, so they don't really count. This lack of international travel is not something I readily admit, and when I do it's usually cause for surprise, considering I grew up in a fairly cosmopolitan family, went to college in a major city, and have spent time on both coasts. But I've never crossed the Atlantic. Or the Pacific, for that matter. I've never even been to Hawaii or the Bahamas. Basically I've spent my entire existence on the same land mass.

It's around eleven p.m. to my body, so night owl that I am, I'm still wide awake and ready for my tour of Westminster Abbey. But in London it's five in the morning, and the pink-tinged, foreign gray sky—my first ground-level glimpse at the other side of the world—is flooding the endless, elevated maze of glass corridors in Heathrow's terminal with hazy, filtered light.

I couldn't sleep at all on the plane; I was too excited. I might have dozed for fifteen minutes or so during my second viewing of *Allegiant*, but all in all, I'm screwed. Luckily Jen was also keyed up since she hasn't seen her brother's family, including her little nephew, Braxton, in almost a year. So we'll be battling a monstrous case of jet lag together.

Jen has been to England twice before, and during the flight she told me about her trips. The first time, she and I had just made the move from Greenlee Designs, our old firm, and Jen had merged her practice with her partner Amanda's to form DB Interiors. Jen had just begun dating her now-fiancé, Todd Birnham, and he went with her on the visit she'd been promising to make to Jane and Adam for years. Her second trip was last summer, and along with visiting England she and Todd drove up through Scotland and then flew from Edinburgh to the European mainland and spent about two weeks traveling through France, Belgium, and Germany before flying home from Amsterdam.

It sounded heavenly. I can't believe it's taken me this long to catch the travel bug, but I can feel its contagion pulsing through my body. Like punctuation for my thoughts, my blood races through my veins, and my heart pounds out a visible rhythm underneath my sweater. I can't wait to get out and explore.

"How are your feet?" Jen asks me.

She's dressed in cropped navy jeans, a striped shirt covered by a chic rose-colored blazer with the sleeves rolled up, and sensible nude ballet flats. Her straight dark hair is matted on one side from where she pressed it into a pillow for hours, forcing herself to close her eyes even though she didn't sleep. I, on the other hand, am wearing two-inch heels with my leggings and sweater dress ensemble—perfunctorily following my mother's example of treating a flight like an opening night at the theater. *"If the plane goes down, you'll go down looking your best."*

If the plane goes down, I'm pretty sure I won't give a damn what I look like, and I don't think "perfectly coiffed" is a required element for admittance through the pearly gates. But it's a good example of the many vast yet subtle ways my mother effed with my world view. At any rate, the shoes were OK up until the point that we realized we'd gotten off the train at the wrong terminal in Atlanta. After a leisurely lunch in a bland airport bar, we'd had to run past thirty gates or so to make our connection, despite our two-hour layover.

My blisters have blisters, and I'm noticeably limping.

I glance down at my cute, hellish kelly green pumps. "Well, they're pretty much telling me I'm a moron, and they hate my guts." I shoot her a wry smile.

"Sorry," she says, her forehead wrinkled with concern. Leave it to Jen to apologize for *my* idiocy. I think she might have been born on the wrong continent. She's reserved, self-effacing, and confident all at the same time—exactly how I imagine the British to be, at least in my vast experience gleaned from *Bridget Jones's Diary* and *The Holiday*. "Do you have another pair of shoes in your carry-on? Oh, here, I think I might have a Band-Aid in my purse."

She pulls us to a stop in the middle of the narrow corridor, and a bespectacled businessman in a charcoal suit steps on the back of my left heel as he dodges us. I howl in pain, and instead of apologizing, he gives me a derisive look and doesn't miss a step. Clearly he's *not* British, at least not in my estimation of the Brits. It's good that he didn't speak. If he'd had a sexy accent, it might have clouded my towering expectations of England's fair citizenry.

"I don't have another pair of shoes," I tell her. Of course I don't. That would require a level of logistical foresight I simply don't possess, at least on a personal level. I'm *not* that friend who has a Band-Aid in her purse. Or dental floss, or a spare stamp, or even loose change for the meter.

As I'm speaking I gently shove Jen to the right edge of the corridor. As together as she is, she also lives inside her own head most of the time, so she hasn't seemed to notice that Mr. Charcoal Suit isn't the only person giving us the side-eye. While she riffles through her enormous leather bag, I slip out of my pump, raise my foot, and gently knead the tender skin on my left heel bone. There's a spot that's raised and soft, a blister that hasn't yet burst. I lean against a metal hand rail and press the pad of my foot into the cool glass of the long wall behind me.

"Ahhh," I say out loud. Just the relief of having the shoe away from my skin is pure bliss. I can't believe my first memory of international travel will be foot-related.

"Well, damn. I don't have a Band-Aid," Jen says.

Two creative types should never travel together. Count on both of us to have a tape measure and paint deck close at hand nine-tenths of the time—for some reason our general absentmindedness doesn't extend to our work—but don't break a nail or get a headache and expect us to come up with the nail file or ibuprofen.

"It's no problem. I'm used to suffering for my art." I slip my shoe back on and watch for our opening to glide back into the stream of traffic. It isn't difficult. We're now straggling at the end of the stream of passengers who just disembarked our flight, and the corridor is notably less crowded. I wait for one family to pass, a petite woman wearing a hijab who's pushing a wide black stroller and trailed by a school-age daughter and twin toddlers who are spinning a human thread across the entire aisle. The mother is too lost in her own navigational struggles to be bothered by Jen and me.

By the time we're navigating the maze of signs through the arrivals gate to baggage claim, I've forgotten my torturous foot situation because I'm wide-eyed with wonder again. The terminal is filled with grainy, grayish-yellow light now, and it's like I'm watching the world wake up. Around us, people of all ages, races, colors, and styles of dress are scurrying around, toting bags as diverse as they are and shouting at wayward children or scooping up loved ones in tight hugs. I'm literally standing in the closing scene of *Love Actually*, a thousand stories and vignettes blooming all around me, the hopeful strains of "God Only Knows" whistling inside my head.

I know. I'm such a sap, right?

Who cares? At least I'm sappy in *England*.

* * *

An hour later we're on Jen's brother's doorstep. It's too early to check in to our hotel, so Jen gave the cab driver Adam and Jane's address, despite the ungodly earliness of the hour. She texted Jane on the way over, and sure enough, Jane texted right back. It's a school day for Braxton and a work day for Adam, so despite the fact that to me this morning feels like the dawn of a whole new life, to their family it's just a random Tuesday.

And then the door is opening, and we're hugging and hand-shaking and introducing and squealing and laughing, and it's all a blur because I haven't slept in roughly eighteen and a half hours.

"Quinn, it's so lovely to meet you," Jane says as she pulls me in for a delicate hug, her slim, tapered fingers pressing lightly against the edges of my shoulder blades, as though she's hesitant to let our bodies touch until she's sure my worthiness lives up to Jen's description. I imagine it must be odd to welcome a stranger full stop into your private lives based solely on a sister-in-law's tactful side step.

She confirms my thoughts. "Jen has said so many wonderful things about you. I can't wait to work with you. We're all very excited to get started and transform this old place into something that feels more like us, more like home."

I glance past her for the first time into the entry of the townhouse, and my breath catches in my throat. I've seen photos, but two-dimensional images rarely do a space justice. "This old place" is completely charming. Stunning even before we touch the first tile or newel post.

The entry hall is wide, or at least maintains the illusion of width thanks to a diagonal marble floor with tiles in a checkerboard of creamy white and rose-tinged beige. The walls are a harmonizing soft color that Jane refers to derisively as "magnolia."

"The whole of the UK is dipped in magnolia paint," she says with a wave of her hand, gesturing beyond the foyer to a formal living space visible through a wide opening arched by intricately detailed millwork. Between us and the living room is a steep stairway with a polished mahogany handrail and dark wood treads stripped with a soft beige carpet runner that shows only gentle signs of wear. The furnishings are similarly tasteful and bland, no one piece standing out. I can simultaneously see why they want a whole new space and why my primary job will be to capture the substance of the old space and keep it alive.

When she steps backward into the foyer, Jane folds into the walls of her home. She's dressed almost entirely in cream—

cream linen pants with a sharp crease down the front and cuffs that hang at exactly the right point above taupe peep-toe heels. A creamy white cardigan buttoned two-thirds up, the silky blouse underneath the only hint of color or pattern on her body—and even that is subtle, a tiny, allover print that's not quite floral, not quite paisley, set against a field of pale peach. Her light brown hair is impossibly straight and hangs in a thin satin curtain to her shoulder blades. Her voice is soft and melodic and her accent unusual—indistinctly American but inflected with traces of a Southern drawl and the occasional lilting British vowel. She and Adam have lived here for nine years, and as Jen said on the plane, "they aren't leaving." They're lifetime expats.

We're all in the foyer now, and Jen yawns widely while craning her neck to peek past Jane into a kitchen I can just glimpse through another, narrower hall behind the stairs. "Did we miss Adam and Braxton?"

"Just," Jane says. "They left about twenty minutes ago. Adam drops Brax at school on the way to his tube stop. Or sometimes Braxton's schoolmates show up at the back gate and they walk together. I can't get used to this growing independence. Do you know that all of his friends have phones now? All of them. Most of them newer models than mine. And he almost never wants me at school anymore. No more backbiting PTA mums, no more bake sales. It's enough to make me want to have another baby."

She shakes her head and draws a deep, shuddering breath, the largest show of emotion she's made so far.

Jen chuckles and says, "I won't tell Mom you said that. She'll have the shower planned before you even take the pregnancy test." Though she's laughing, her expression is sort of…preoccupied. Before I can ponder that too hard, she yawns again, and it's contagious.

"Oh, my. I almost forgot you two must be knackered." The expression sounds odd in Jane's American English. She turns on us with a stern look. "But you're not going to sleep. Sorry, nope," she adds when she sees Jen's skeptical expression. "It's breakfast for you two, and then we'll take a brisk walk around the neighborhood, and I'll show you Braxton's schoolyard. You can have a little nap this afternoon, and we'll all go to bed early tonight."

I'm sure I look shell-shocked, but Jen just looks resigned, as if she recognizes the futility of arguing.

"It's the only way," Jane adds.

Jen looks at me and explains, "Jane's a master at overcoming jet lag." In a dry voice directed at Jane's back, she adds, "She's an evil drill sergeant."

For all her mild, cool reserve, Jane's laugh is surprisingly warm. It tinkles like a wind chime in a back porch's springtime breeze.

"You can thank me in a day or so. Now c'mon. I'll make bacon sandwiches."

CHAPTER FOUR

———

Culture Clash

It's the following morning before I get a feel for my new project and a good look at Jane and Adam's regal yet relaxed home. It's an attached house, built at some fuzzy point in a past century and clad in understated brown brick. It's connected to a row of homes that all look alike, apart from the few whose exteriors are painted in muted shades of gray and cream. The front doors are mostly black, though dotted along the street are several doors painted in a specific, peculiar shade of aqua that makes these homes appear much friendlier and more approachable than the others. The aqua doorways smile and say "hey there" while the black and gray ones have their chins lifted, politely nodding as they look vaguely past your shoulder and ask "how do you do?"

Adam and Jane have a gray front door. That will be the first thing we have to change.

I make a mental note to ask Jane about a homeowner association, or whatever they call them here, and any design guidelines that might exist for the neighborhood. Based on our walk yesterday morning, I have a feeling these may be extensive. I still don't know exactly what Adam does for a living, but the community of London his family occupies is what the English might call "posh."

I finally met Adam around seven thirty last night, half an hour before Jen and I stumbled out the door to return to our B&B, which we'd checked into in the middle of the day, after our promised nap and during the hour in which Braxton had returned home from school. Jane apparently isn't usually at home during the workday. She works as a bookkeeper for a nearby dentist's office and had taken the day off to receive us and force our eyes to remain open.

Braxton, who's older than I expected—I knew he was eleven, but I guess I have no real idea what an eleven-year-old boy looks like—is a serious-seeming child with a rakish mop of dark wavy hair. He hadn't looked up from his iPad while we grown-ups talked in the living room. The only time I saw him animated was when his father had come home, and Braxton had streaked upstairs to his room and then hammered back down with the *kit* that had come in the *post* that day…apparently the uniform for his upcoming football (soccer) season.

I'm loving this new vernacular—the words foreign yet not foreign, different only in their usage. If I weren't so tired, I'd be writing a blog post just about the language.

This morning, everyone is back to their daily lives while Jen and I explore Adam and Jane's home without supervision. Jen is far too energetic for me, but then, she's a morning person. Me, I speak in monosyllabic grunts until the caffeine kicks in, and that's after seven hours' sleep and uninterrupted circadian rhythms.

"I'll stay out of your way as much as possible," Jen says, taking a delicate sip of her tea. It must be cold by now—Jane made it before she bolted out the door for work. Thankfully they also have a Keurig, so I'm not coffee-deprived.

"Don't," I say. "You know them well, so I want as much of your input as possible before you leave. Like, tell me the things they're too polite to tell me."

Considering Jane's reserved nature and Adam's long work hours, I have a feeling this might be a lot. I've worked with clients like Jane before. Getting information in the initial interview is like extracting a molar with pliers. It requires use of the tools in my psychological arsenal rather than my creative arsenal—I'll need to take cues from her body language, the colors in her closet, the fabrics and finishes and furnishings she rejects rather than what she accepts, because she's not likely to directly tell me what she likes, and she might accept things she *doesn't* like out of politeness.

Design school should include a battery of psychology courses along with drafting and CAD and color theory and lighting.

"Noted," Jen says, trailing her fingers over the uneven surface of the kitchen countertop, clad in cobalt tile with thick grout lines. It's the least attractive, though boldest, element of the entire house, apart from garish floral wallpaper in a couple of upstairs bedrooms. They'd had wallpaper removed from several rooms, Jane said yesterday—the only change she and Adam have made since moving in two years ago.

"My first piece of advice is to go through your questionnaire when Adam is at home," Jen continues. "He'll protest—he'll tell you that he'll like whatever you do, that everything is up to Jane, but when it comes down to it, Adam will be not only the one with veto power but also your primary source of information."

I nod. She'd said something to that effect back in Memphis.

"I love Jane to death, but along with being painfully polite, she's very shy. I feel like I don't know her all that well even though she and Adam have been married for ten years. That's probably in part because Adam's company moved them here about a year after they got married."

My eyebrows shoot up. Braxton is eleven, and they've been married ten years. So Jane does have an unconventional streak in her somewhere. This is important knowledge, so I file it away in my brain under the tab "creative challenge." I get the sense that coaxing out Jane's inner rebel will be the key to my success. It's what's going to take this house from wallflower to prom queen.

I make another mental note: wine will need to be present for the initial interview.

"Do you know how much work they're planning to do?"

"From what Adam said, they want a complete overhaul. That's why they called me. Adam said as long as they're investing this much money in a renovation, they might as well pay the extra travel costs to work with us, someone they already feel comfortable with."

"So this is going to take a while."

"This is going to take a while." Jen's eyes flash to mine, gauging my reaction. She has no worries there. If her face were a mirror, it would reflect nothing but my excitement. I feel like I'm taking a much-needed life break, despite the fact that this isn't a vacation—in fact, I have a feeling I'm about to work harder than I've worked in my entire thirty-two years.

"Come on," I say, and it's as if I'm smiling with my whole body. I'm practically quivering with impatience—or maybe it's just this second cup of Blonde Veranda Blend. "Help me measure the front room."

* * *

Two days later, Jen is gone, and I'm on my own in a gigantic foreign city. Todd, Jen's fiancé, flew in Friday morning, and the two of them got on a train this afternoon headed to York. From there, they're renting a car and driving up into the Scottish Highlands for a few days before flying out of Edinburgh.

"Don't get swallowed up by the Loch Ness Monster," I'd said to Jen as I'd squeezed her good-bye. It felt a little like getting dropped off by your parents at college—or, at least, how I imagine that must feel. My mother was too upset with me for going to art school to bother coming with me to Chicago, and Dad was in Nashville at the time for work. So I packed up my cute little Nissan and drove myself the eight hours up through Arkansas, Missouri, and Illinois, my cloak of righteous indignation slipping off somewhere around St. Louis. By Chicago, I wore nothing but a feather boa of freedom.

The three of us had left Jane and Adam's house together, Jen and Todd dipping into the lobby of the B&B to retrieve their bags, and that's where we'd said our good-byes. Todd, who'd spent his early twenties bumming around Europe working odd jobs, had only one slim backpack to Jen's enormous suitcase and bulging carry-on roller bag—and somewhere in there is a metaphor for their relationship. They're total opposites and so cute it hurts to look at them.

At any rate, I've just treated myself to a little nap and am about to head back over to Jane and Adam's house to get to work. With Jen's presence bringing a family reunion vibe, we spent more time socializing and sightseeing this week than actually working, though Jen and I did spend several hours checking out the Pimlico Road design district in Belgravia on Thursday after our obligatory hour spent gawking at the beefeaters at Buckingham Palace during a changing of the guard.

It's quite a hike from Belgravia to Islington, so I'm hoping I can find some good fabric shops and to-the-trade suppliers closer to home. London, I've come to learn, is *huge*. I mean, I knew it was big, but being here and experiencing it, I'm realizing I never knew what big meant. Maybe it's Manhattan's grid system or the neatly distinct boroughs or just my imagination, but even New York seems dwarfed in comparison to the size of this city. I can't wrap my head around its vastness. Jane mentioned I might want to check out Chelsea, but it's just as far as Pimlico, down near the Thames and the London Eye and all the major museums. At least I can mix in some sightseeing with my work.

The house is just a couple of blocks from the B&B—too short a distance for a cab but not quite close enough for anything but the most comfortable shoes. I've been a big city designer for less than a week, and already I can understand why urban dwellers wear sneakers or slip-ons and carry their stilettos in shoulder bags.

As I stroll along one leafy residential block toward the corner of the next, I tilt my head back to feel the sun on my face—yes, it's sunny in England, despite all reports to the contrary. So far it's been sunny every day of my trip, though I have a feeling it's false advertising. The interesting thing about the sun here is that, unlike at home where on a hot day it's sweltering even in the shade, in London you need to dress for a change in season just to walk a few blocks. On one side of the street, in the shadow of the row homes and sycamores, it's cool and crisp—cardigan weather—like twilight at a late autumn football game back home. On the other side of the street where the sun bathes the sidewalk in dappled patches of light, it's much warmer, but the rays feel strange on my skin—like I'm wrapped in a layer of cellophane the sunlight isn't quite strong enough to penetrate.

I shiver and then look both ways to cross the one-way street, trying to remember which direction the cars are coming from.

When I ring the bell, it's Braxton who comes to the door after a prolonged wait that makes me wonder if they're not home. Jane gave me a key to the front door, but right now I still feel like too much of a stranger to use it, at least without trying the bell first.

"Hallo," says Braxton politely, his accent British despite his parentage. Sort of like how kids raised in non-English-speaking households in America typically sound more like their friends and the TV shows they watch than their parents.

Braxton's accent slays me. There's something heart-melting about a kid speaking with a British accent—it's sophisticated on anyone's lips, but somehow on a child, its properness stands out in higher relief.

"Hi, Braxton." I smile at him, and he smiles warily back—the look a kid gives an adult when he's not sure how you fit into his world or whether he wants you there.

For the first time in my life, it hits me that I'm not actually young anymore. With his look-through-me expression, it's as if Braxton's just called me "ma'am." To him I could be thirty-five. Or forty-five. When you're eleven, old is old is old.

I realize I'm just standing there on the doorstep with a goofy, contemplative look on my face, so I recover with, "Are your parents home?"

"They're in the kitchen with Mr. Pemberton," he says, and then he swings the door wider, backs away, and bolts up the stairs. "I just got a notification," he calls down over his shoulder.

I didn't hear the ding. Gen Z is even more hermetically attached to their devices than us Millennials, if that's even possible. It's a scary prospect for the future of attention spans.

I close the door behind me and step through the front hall, all the while thinking, *Who the heck is Mr. Pemberton?* The name sounds like a gardener from an old fashioned children's book or a stooped, elderly uncle from a Jane Austen novel.

"Hello?" I call out as muffled voices come into hearing range. Braxton was wrong; no one's in the kitchen, but I follow the voices across the room and through a small utility space to the back door, which stands slightly ajar and opens into a glass-walled sunroom Jane called a "conservatory."

There I find Jane, Adam, and a tall, fair-haired man who must be Mr. Pemberton. He and Adam are both wearing business suits—Adam's gray with a pinstripe, though he's tossed his blazer over the arm of a wicker chair, and the other man's navy and fully in place, its fabric lustrous and its cut impeccable. I'm no snob, but it's clear whose clothing is more expensive. Mr. Pemberton must be a superior of Adam's, a senior executive at his firm or something like that.

"Hello?" I repeat tentatively, and three heads swivel in my direction.

"Oh, Quinn. I'm so sorry. I didn't hear you come in," Jane says, her hands fluttering. She turns back to the men. "And I apologize again. I was so caught up in your story. Can I make anyone a drink? A Scotch, Mr. Pemberton? Adam? Or should I put the kettle on? Quinn, what would you like?"

She's turned to look at me again, but I can't answer because the mysterious "Mr. Pemberton" has turned in my direction. My breath catches, and for a few seconds I'm at a loss for words—not a frequent problem of mine.

"Why don't I open a bottle of wine?" Adam answers for all of us, saving me from making a total idiot of myself, though this guy must be used to seeing women, and probably men, lose their power of speech in his presence.

He's beautiful—there's no other word for it. He has beautiful skin, beautiful cerulean eyes, a beautiful build emphasized beautifully by his beautiful suit.

Did I mention that he's beautiful?

He's looking at Adam now, which gives me a moment to drink him in while he's distracted. I could *lick this man off the floor*. It's too bad he's probably gay. Aren't all men who look like this gay?

I wouldn't know. I've never met one in person.

"Lovely," Jane says.

As Adam strides into the house, she picks up his suit jacket, shakes out the nonexistent wrinkles, and gestures over her shoulder to the seating area on the other side of the room, which overlooks a tiny, walled back garden. Earlier, the woven chairs with their squashy white cushions looked inviting and warm, but now, next to this perfect male specimen, they seem shabby and uninspired. I'll bet Mr. Pemberton's house is sleek and shiny, all sharp angles and reflective surfaces and retractable big-screen TVs. The perfect bachelor pad for the perfect bachelor. Because you know I've checked, of course. He isn't wearing a ring.

"I'm afraid I must be going," Mr. Pemberton says, and his voice is as hypnotizing as his looks—velvety and low, with that refined British lilt that's sexy on a far less attractive person.

"Already?" Jane's voice is surprised, and I notice she's taken on a bit of his accent herself. I figure that's a common expat problem, inflections trying themselves on without your permission, coming and going based on who's in the room. At least that's the case for me. I'm a voice chameleon, my Southern accent slipping off and on like a piece of jewelry, depending on who I'm talking to. By the time I leave England, I'll probably sound like Madonna—American with a side of wannabe.

"When will Elliott be coming to town?" Jane adds.

I glance from Jane to her guest and draw a sharp, involuntary breath when I realize Mr. Perfect is looking at me, not her. My eyes click to his just in time to see him shift his gaze northward. A fuzzy warmth skyrockets to my cheeks even though it shouldn't take me by surprise. I'm used to men staring at my chest—it's my only eye-catching feature. And I'm not showing much of it, so I can't imagine why this dreamboat is checking me out. He's so far out of my league we're playing different sports. I'm softball. He's quidditch.

He's not checking you out, dumbass. He's wondering why a strange woman just barged into these people's home uninvited. I smile tentatively at him, and he seems to come out of a trance.

He swivels his gaze sharply from me to Jane. "He's arriving in two wee—" he starts.

But Jane speaks at the same time. "Oh, my goodness. I'm sorry yet again. How awful of me to not introduce you two. Quinn, this is Ryland Pemberton, our next-door neighbor. Mr. Pemberton, meet Quinn Cunningham, a friend of Adam's sister from America and our new interior designer."

I'm mulling over his name, Ryland, and wondering why Jane keeps calling him "Mr. Pemberton" when he interrupts the thought.

"I didn't know you were renovating?" He says this with a frown in his voice that matches the new wrinkle in his forehead, his shoulder angled slightly away from me despite the fact we've just been introduced. It's as if he's warding me off.

Great. I've already managed to piss off the neighbor. But wait? What did I do? Now I'm the one frowning. Does he have a prejudice against Americans? Does he hate blondes? Women? Interior designers?

"Yes, we're finally giving the old place an overhaul," Jane says, smiling though she seems as bewildered as I am. She moves closer to me in a protective way, as if trying to compensate for Ryland's rudeness by drawing me into his closed circle.

And I thought the English were supposed to be the polite ones.

"Adam's sister, Jen, owns an interior design firm stateside, and we decided to hire her firm to help us renovate. Quinn has a fantastic eye and a real talent with historic buildings. She'll be staying with us for a few weeks as we get the work underway."

Ryland scoffs, glancing not at me but through me. "Historic buildings. I suppose this building might qualify, to an American." He sort of laughs, a hard chuckle, and I *think* he's tried to make a joke.

What an ass.

"And here we go," says Adam, sweeping back through the doorway with the neck of a wine bottle threaded through two fingers and a precarious arrangement of stemmed glasses clinking against one another in his right hand. He sets them all on a tea cart near the doorway.

"Oh, I can't stay," Ryland says. He doesn't spare a glance at me, still not acknowledging Jane's introduction. "Elliott should be here in just under two weeks," he repeats to Jane. "Thank you very much for your neighborly kindness."

Neighborly kindness? What exactly is going on here? And who is Elliott?

"Of course," Jane says. "Here, let me see you out." She shoots a perplexed look my way and hastens over to a doorway that opens to the outside. Ryland nods in Adam's and my direction without a word and then follows her out of the house and across a stone walkway through the back garden, where she unlatches a wood gate set into the ivy-covered stone fence. He steps through it without a wave or a look back.

Adam and I stare at one another for a couple of seconds. My mouth opens slightly, but I don't know Adam well enough yet to discuss what just happened with him, and so I close my mouth again, feeling like a tall, upright fish. I wish to the follicles of my hair that Jen was still here to dissect this situation with me.

I'm not quite houseguest, not quite servant. Part family acquaintance, part employee. And I'm treading on tenuous ground right now, still developing the relationship with my new clients. Adam could be close, personal friends with this Ryland for all I know. I don't want to insult him by saying what I'm thinking, which is some semblance of *Wow, your next-door neighbor is a real jackass.*

We remain frozen in place, and when Jane reenters the room, it's like a silent cue. I swivel to the doorway. Adam turns and busies himself opening the wine bottle with a corkscrew he pulls from the bottom shelf of the tea cart. Jane takes her time closing and latching the back door and then crosses the room and takes one of the two glasses of pinot grigio Adam proffers.

"Well, that was interesting," he says.

"I've never seen him act that way," Jane adds, taking her wine to the settee tucked along a half wall under the long row of windows and kicking off her heels before settling into the corner of it facing us. She glances at me. "I'm so sorry."

A long breath I didn't realize I was holding hisses out in a slow trickle, a hot air balloon exhaling pressure as it descends. Jane's shoes coming off are like a welcome sign with a scrolling LED message. *You are the wanted guest. Make yourself comfortable in our home. Forget about that strange interlude with our creepy, rude, but beautiful neighbor.*

I shrug, take the second glass from Adam's outstretched hand with a murmured "thank you," and cross the room to perch on the settee beside Jane. "It isn't your fault." I look at her as if I'm searching her face for clues. "I'm not even sure what happened."

The man hates me for no apparent reason, that's what happened. He was a big, fat jerk. That happened, too. I bristle as I replay his dismissive glance when Jane tried to introduce us. *Who the hell does this Ryland Pemberton think he is?* Suddenly an image of Chase flashes to mind. Why, lately, am I the muddy doormat men stop to scrape their boots on? What did I ever do to piss off the Y chromosome?

"What did happen, exactly?" Adam settles onto one of two cushioned wicker chairs placed against the opposite wall and flanking a narrow electric firebox. Mentally I'm rearranging the furniture, correcting the "push everything to the perimeter" instinct most people tend to follow and re-envisioning the sofa at a perpendicular angle, floating in the room with the chairs facing it, each piece taking advantage of the view and placed properly for conversation. Right now Jane and I are slightly too far away from Adam to talk comfortably.

I lean forward, expecting Jane to answer with some sort of explanation about Ryland's strange behavior, but she says, "Well, apparently the little boy will be here in less than two weeks, after the funeral and long enough for all the arrangements to be made, I guess. I'm not sure what he's going to do with him when he isn't in school. That big place all by himself. I wonder if he'll hire a nanny?"

"Nah," Adam says. "How old did he say the kid is? Thirteen?" He pauses, taking a sip. "He and Braxton should get along, at least. I hope he's an Arsenal fan."

"We'll need to keep a good eye on him." Jane's brow is furrowed.

My head swivels back and forth between the two of them as they talk, and Jane must finally notice the puzzlement on my face because she says, "Oh, sorry, Quinn. You don't care anything about our neighbor dramas, do you?"

Um yeah, actually, I kinda do. But for some reason I don't say this. I swallow my questions about the mysterious Ryland Pemberton along with my gulp of wine and lean forward to set my glass on the metal cocktail table. I slip my tablet out of the shoulder bag I'd dropped at my feet and settle deeper into my corner of the settee.

"We haven't talked much yet about the kitchen," I say, forcing Ryland's face from my mind. "Are you thinking you want to gut the space and do a total overhaul or more of a facelift?"

"Definitely gut it," Adam says. "Right, Jane?"

She nods, though she seems less certain.

"OK, then we'll need a plan for getting you through the kitchenless weeks. We won't touch the main floor bath while the kitchen reno is going on, so you'll have continuous access to a sink. It'll be a little awkward to wash dishes in there, but I'll make sure—"

Adam cuts me off. "We'll eat out. Don't worry. There won't be a lot of dish washing going on while the kitchen's out of commission. There's not a whole lot of it now." He gives a little laugh, and Jane shoots him a dirty look.

"Seriously," he says, winking at her. "The Crown's right around the corner. Are you really going to complain about sticky toffee pudding three nights a week?"

"My waistline will complain," she says, but there's humor in her voice, and I feel like I'm getting my first real glimpse into their relationship dynamic. Adam has Jen's warm brown eyes and casual good humor. It's impossible not to like him. And I already love Jane. She's soft-spoken and delicate in a birdlike way—the exact opposite of me. Something about that combination makes me feel protective of her, almost maternal, which is funny since she's the mom and I'm unlikely to ever be one myself.

"Well, I'll make sure there's a downstairs sink available for you regardless," I say, keeping us on track and trying to forget that Adam just told me something called "sticky toffee pudding" is available right up the street.

My stomach gurgles aggressively, and I ignore it, something I'm used to doing. I haven't eaten properly since I arrived here. My days and nights are in the right place, and I'm sleeping OK, but my body hasn't yet adapted to British mealtimes. Apparently for me international jet lag manifests as an eating disorder. Or maybe it's the fault of my B&B, which offers a menu nightly with boxes to check for the next morning's breakfast selections, running the gamut from "full English breakfast" to tea and toast. I never eat breakfast, but here I can't seem to resist, and it's throwing me off for the rest of the day.

On our second morning here, Jen had coerced me into ordering the full English breakfast—she's always trying to make me eat. I'd been curious enough to give it a try, and what came out was a greasy, glorious heart attack on a plate. Two eggs over easy, grilled mushrooms and tomatoes, two sausage links ("bangers") *and* two bacon strips ("rashers") and enough toast to feed my entire office. The toast was served standing up in this little silver rack alongside a china plate bearing rose-shaped pats of butter and tiny, individual pots of jam. I'd devoured most of it, and I swear I've barely been able to touch food since. Not because it wasn't delicious but because it was *too* delicious. I haven't eaten that much in one sitting since probably college.

Forcing my mind off food, I move to the next question on my list. Adam, Jane, and I chat and sip wine for an hour, finishing the pinot grigio and moving on to a French chardonnay before Braxton comes into the room—I'd forgotten he was even here—saying he's hungry, and Adam suggests we head to the pub for dinner.

My stomach growls again, and I stand eagerly, thinking I've hit the jackpot. Clients sweet as pudding, the project of a lifetime looming, amazing adventures in a fabulously exciting city beckoning outside these foreign walls.

I turn to the wall of windows and stretch my limbs that are cramped from sitting in one position too long, gazing up beyond the bricked-in courtyard, past the roofline of the neighboring building, to the hazy London sky, now shrouded in wispy gray-white clouds. Despite the cloud cover, the sky is still daytime-bright, the sun showing no sign of setting even though it must be after seven by now.

I love this place. I'm not at all used to its rhythms, its patterns—even its daylight patterns. But already I feel strangely at home.

"Ready?" Jane touches a hand to my arm as she starts to follow her family from the room.

I nod and glance one more time at the silvery sliver of sky, my brow furrowing.

The only dark spot on my personal sun is one Mr. Pemberton who, with his derisive tone and dismissive glance, made me feel as if Chase was right and I'll never be a perfect ten…and as if somehow that matters.

And now I know I won't order the sticky toffee pudding, though I want it more than anything—more than Bella wants Edward, more than Midas wants gold, more than a Kardashian wants attention.

Damn Ryland Pemberton. Damn that beautiful man to hell and back.

CHAPTER FIVE

———

Introductions

The following week passes in a blur. Over the weekend I spend more time with Jane, Adam, and Braxton—learning them, learning the house, learning the layout of the surrounding streets. I meet a few neighbors, struck by how similar they are and their lives are to the people I know back home. How similar we all are, when it comes down to it.

During the week, while Adam and Jane are at work and Braxton is in school, I start to learn the rhythms of the neighborhood. I dip in and out of local shops, seeking clues that will help me unlock the differences in this city's design market to the world I know. Along the way I pick up a few gifts—Moulton Brown hand soap and lotion for my mother, an ingenious metal tea strainer and collection of loose-leaf teas for Savy, and a mixed array of tea towels for Jules with ironic English-sounding slogans...*"For wiping up and bum flicking." "I just want to drink wine and pet my kitty." "I speak: 1. English. 2. Sarcasm. 3. Profanity." "Keep clam and proofread."*

At Jane's suggestion I take the tube to a Habitat store on Finchley Road and spend hours perusing territory that's at once foreign and familiar, comforting in that universal language of shopping. The store has a clean, modern vibe that sort of matches Jane—streamlined, tailored, neutral—giving me another clue to her tastes. I make a mental note to come back here when it's time to shop for accessories.

This afternoon, Thursday, after spending the morning making rough sketches of the living room and dining room floor plans, I head out in professional clothes but comfortable shoes—

I'm getting the hang of this—to revisit a shop that piqued my interest earlier in the week. It's the one true trade shop I've found in the vicinity of the neighborhood—a designer's studio with retail in the front, a mix of gifts and high-end accessories I recognize from European lines I've seen at market. Between the front and back of the shop is a telltale area crammed with spools of designer fabrics as well as built-in shelving that houses stacks of memos and fabric books, a sight so familiar and welcoming it wrapped me like a cashmere blanket.

I'd found it too late on Tuesday to really explore. The shopkeeper had been sweeping up and preparing to close. I'd learned from a brief conversation that she wasn't the owner but that the owner would be back on Thursday.

And so, here I am.

"Hallo. Welcome." The voice greets me about thirty seconds after I tinkle the threshold bell.

I look up from a round, pale wood table near the entry that's arrayed with pottery vessels. Small placards offer information on the artists, and a carved wooden sign reads, *We believe in fair trade.*

"Hi." I smile at the source of the greeting, though I feel a slight stab of disappointment. It isn't the same cashier who was here earlier in the week, but this person is young, definitely younger than me, with a retro-punk, urban-Millennial sort of vibe. She can't possibly be the owner I was hoping to meet.

"Ah, you're American." She seems delighted, her smile percolating through her bright, chirpy voice.

"Yes. Please don't hold it against me." I chuckle and take another look at her. She's petite, with dark hair cut into a long bob. It's piecey with product, sort of bed-tousled with spiky ends and streaks of deep red and violet running through. A tiny stud glitters in her left nostril, and she's wearing a long, striped skirt and off-the-shoulder black cropped shirt with a hot pink cami underneath. I get just a glimpse of untied black lace-up boots before manners compel me to look away, back at the wares on the table that suddenly seem buttoned-up and stuffy by comparison.

"I love Americans. Absolutely adore America, actually," she says. "Don't tell my mum."

I jerk my head back up with a grin. "Why? Does your mother not like Americans?"

"Oh no, she loves them too. I just don't want to give her a heart attack thinking I'm going to up and move stateside. She's convinced this is all a lark and I'm going to leave her with a crumbling mess to clear out." She gestures around herself at the shop, which is anything but a crumbling mess. It's tidy and well-merchandised, with a level of polish and professionalism that somehow both fits and doesn't fit the woman standing in front of me. Shades of understanding separate and reform in my brain as I realize this perky, eccentric ray of sunlight actually *is* the shop owner I've been waiting to meet. "Of course, I suppose they're not exactly handing out the visas like candy these days, right?" She gives me a cheery wink.

"I suppose not," I agree with a snort. I look more closely at her, storing up details so I can describe this experience to Jules and Savy in glorious detail. She has brown eyes with long lashes—so long I'm pretty sure she's wearing extensions—and freckles sprinkling the bridge of her nose. Her most noticeable feature, though, is her smile. It's broad and toothy, and her teeth are so small, white, and perfectly aligned that they look like baby teeth. Another British stereotype to toss straight into the bin.

"Hello, I'm Miranda." She steps closer and proffers a hand, shaking mine vigorously when I offer it to her. "That's how you do it, right?"

I chuckle, step back, and give an exaggerated curtsy. "How do you do? I'm Quinn. It's a pleasure to make your acquaintance." I make a terrible attempt at a British accent, and Miranda dissolves into giggles.

"Oh, God," she says, gasping out the words. "That was like a scene from *Henry VIII*. Very ye old-ee. Is that really how we seem to you?" She's practically quaking with glee.

"I don't know. I just got here."

"Where are you from?"

"Memphis, Tennessee."

She clutches her heart and sort of sinks into a half squat. "Oh, my God. 'Heartbreak Hotel.' Do you live near Graceland? I am absolutely *obsessed* with Elvis Presley."

I laugh, thinking *I should have known.* Already, in my short time here, I've heard a street musician playing "Love Me Tender" on the tube platform and seen vintage metal *Viva Las Vegas* and *Blue Hawaii* posters hanging behind the bar at the pub I went to with Adam, Jane, and Braxton.

Elvis is a factor of my town you can't get away from, no matter where in the world you are. And foreigners are particularly freakish about The King—at Graceland you hear every accent except Southern.

"Actually, I worked at Graceland the summer after I graduated from high school," I say, knowing it will impress her. This fact always impresses people who aren't from Memphis.

Her squeal is so loud it pierces my eardrums. "*Are you kidding me?* Were you a tour guide? What was the house like? Did you meet Lisa Marie?"

Though my laughter I tell her, "Totally not kidding. I wasn't a tour guide—all I really did was pass out headphones to the tourists before they boarded the bus to go up to the mansion. But I did get to put beer in Elvis's fridge once before a VH1 party. And, um, let's see…the house is like a '70s time warp, but the Jungle Room is as epic as you think it is. And no, I'm pretty sure Lisa Marie lives in LA."

"Can you take me home with you? Pack me in your suitcase? I've *always* wanted to go to Memphis. Sun Studio, Stax Records, Gibson Guitars. It's like, a legend. The birthplace of music. Or all the best music, at least."

I'm totally impressed with her knowledge of my city's music history—it far surpasses that of most people who live there. Most native Memphians have never been to Graceland and couldn't pick B.B. King out of a lineup.

"You can absolutely come home with me in my suitcase," I say, laughing. "But first, I think I might need your help." I gesture around myself at the shop. "I'm redesigning a townhouse about seven blocks from here, and I know absolutely nothing about the interior design market in London. Does your shop work with the trade at all? Like, will you do special ordering for independent designers?"

From the expression on her face, you'd think I'd just offered to pay her bills for a year.

"You're an interior designer? Oh, this is so exciting. I've never met an American designer before." She claps her hands twice, fast, and sort of hops up and down. She is totally tripping me out. We talk for probably a full half hour, during which she asks me a ton of questions about my design practice, my family, my life outside of work. She seems especially intrigued by my dad's political legacy and by my descriptions of the house I grew up in. She asks so many questions I can barely get in any edgewise.

While we've talked I've followed Miranda deeper into the shop. She's standing in front of the cashier's desk, where there's no register but a fancy, space age-looking iPad stand and a Square card swipe. On a long, narrow table behind the front counter, I spot a scattered array of tile samples and an open file folder, like she's been back there working on a job while manning the desk. A thrill of excitement shoots up my spine. My unlikely British counterpart, and I was lucky enough to walk right into her shop.

We're still standing near the back of the shop, chatting, when the door to the shop opens with a tinkling chime and another customer walks in, the first person to enter since I arrived. Miranda calls out a greeting and then turns to me.

"We have to meet outside of here, talk shop. Do you fancy getting drinks later, after I close up here? The pub 'round the corner, the Lion's Gate? That's where my friends and I meet. Say quarter of six?"

She gives me a teasing, speculative look and adds, "Oh, and you absolutely must meet Ian. He loves American girls. He'll drink you up like a pint of brown ale. I'll ring him up and tell him to come." And then she flashes a sly grin. "Although, on second thought, he'll like you *too* much, so be careful there. He's a cheeky one. Don't let him talk you into leaving with him."

She pauses and winks. "But don't worry. I'll take care of you." She reaches out and grabs my hand, pressing her thumb lightly into my palm before dropping it again. "I feel like we're best mates already."

"Me, too," I tell her genuinely. "I'd love to have a drink and meet your friends."

She's awesome—bubbly and warm and clearly a riot, nothing like I'd expected to encounter here. Not that I thought Londoners would be unfriendly, exactly, just that I believed the stereotype. I thought Brits were standoffish, reserved, a bit cool to outsiders. To a lesser extreme, like Ryland Pemberton.

Miranda doesn't fit my preconceived notions at all. OK, she might also be slightly crazy, but I love slightly crazy people. Just look at Jules.

When I step through the shop's door onto the sidewalk, the bell tinkling after me, my smile is so wide I feel as if it could crack my cheeks. I came in hoping for a bit of advice, and I'm leaving with a social life.

*   *   *

"I did astrophysics at university," Miranda says with a straight face, and my jaw goes slack.

"Seriously?"

"No, not seriously. Don't believe a word she says." This is from Eleanor, a tall, willowy girl with mousy brown hair and glasses, who reminds me of the Chipette with the same name. I really, really hope the fiancé she's mentioned twice is named Simon. He's coming, so I guess I'll find out.

"That's what my mum hoped I'd study," Miranda adds, rolling her eyes. "Right, like I was meant to be a scientist."

"Miranda's father does work with the European Centre for Disease Prevention," Eleanor says. She purses her lips and looks down her nose, clearly making fun. "He has top-secret clearance."

"So you're the black sheep in the family who went to art school?" I ask, grinning. "I've known you all of three hours, and it's like we were separated at birth."

"My American twin! Who's best friends with Lisa Marie Presley!" Miranda jostles me with her elbow and then comes off her chair. She slings an arm around my waist, holding her phone out with one hand and dragging me off my seat for a selfie.

I laugh and grab the phone from her hand. "Here, let me. Obviously we're fraternal twins. I'm the giant. You're the pixie."

I hold the phone a good foot higher, aiming down. "You were totally going to give me a double chin."

I snap the shot and take a look. Her smile lights up the screen.

The funny thing is Miranda practically *could* be my fraternal twin, a continent removed. This feels so much like Jules, Savy, and me hanging out at South of Beale that it's almost like I'm having déjà vu. Eleanor is Savy, minus the jaw-dropping beauty, and their third friend, Pamela, is…well, there's nobody like Jules. But anyway. Three girls who are obviously tight, hanging out at the pub. I feel like a fourth wheel.

Wait a minute—a fourth wheel is good, actually. Sort of necessary for most moving vehicles. Anyway.

"Actually, no. I didn't get my degree," Miranda says. "Dropped out in third year to follow Rex to Liverpool. Tragedy, that was." Her expression *is* tragic, absolutely heartbreaking. She probably could have a second career on the stage.

"I take it that didn't end well?"

"Bloody well right, it didn't. Ended fine for Marcy, I suppose."

I glance at Eleanor with a puzzled look, but it's Pamela who answers. "Marcy's the cow who Rex was shagging on the side. Now she's mother of Rex Junior number one and Rex Junior number two. Last Miranda heard Rex is in accountancy, and they have a cottage in Blackpool."

"I hope she's gained three stone and never puts out," Miranda says. She raises her pint glass. "To three stone and no sex."

"Three stone and no sex," Pamela and Eleanor repeat. Pamela slaps her open palm on the table, and we all tip back our glasses.

I am so in love with this crew. The beer, not so much. I suppose it's my fault—when she learned I'm not a beer drinker, Miranda told me to start slow and order something fruity, but I thought, you know, "when in Rome…" I ordered the same thing Miranda and Eleanor ordered, and it's dark brown and syrupy, in a hefty clear mug with a handle. And then I was jealous because Pamela's Belgian beer came out in a fancy stemmed glass.

"I will *not* drink to that."

I swivel to the voice, and suddenly there's a fifth body at the table and right behind him a sixth. The shorter of the two sidles up to Eleanor and slides an arm around her, which must make him the fiancé. The other guy looks around for a minute and then drags over a tall, leather-backed stool from another table, which he slides into the too small space next to Miranda, causing her to have to jump down from her stool and scoot over. There's some commotion for a couple of minutes as we all get resettled, and then the server swings by and says without question in her voice, "I'll be right back with a Guinness"—she points at the tall guy—"and a Young's Special"—she points at the fiancé (who in my head is named Simon). Tall Guy gives her a tiny nod, and she bobs off toward the bar.

"Who's your friend?" asks the tall one. He nudges Miranda, but it's Pamela who answers.

"This is Quinn, Miranda's new friend from America." Something about the way she says it tells me she wants to be the one with the information, as if she's used to speaking first and loudest to keep from being overlooked. "Quinn, this is Thomas Eppington," she adds with a nod at Tall Guy, "and Ethan Richards, Eleanor's sweetie."

Her voice gets all syrupy at the end, and Ethan-Not-Simon rolls his eyes. I notice when Eleanor stands to let him scoot onto half her chair that he's at least three inches shorter than she. I don't know them yet, but somehow it seems to fit their dynamic.

"From America…" repeats Thomas, whose arm, I notice, is very close to Miranda's on the tabletop before she subtly slides hers away and reaches for something in her purse. "What brings you into the midst of our fair group this evening?" His voice is deep, a bit standoffish.

Miranda straightens back up and pokes him in the bicep. "Don't be rude."

"I'm here on a research experiment," I say, picking up my beer and taking a slow sip, trying not to make a face. "I'm studying the mating habits of London Millennials."

Pamela chokes on her drink, and Miranda grins at me but not before I see her eyes widen with momentary alarm. *I knew it*. I knew there was something bubbling under the surface with the two of them.

Ethan-Not-Simon chortles. "Follow Tom and Miranda around for a week. That will give you all the research you need." He chuckles again, louder, but no one laughs with him. In fact, Miranda goes pink in the cheeks, Pamela looks down at the table, and Eleanor gives Ethan a surreptitious poke in the side. I glance at Thomas and see that his expression is unchanged, though a vein is twitching at his temple.

"Actually, she's working with me," Miranda says lightly in a deft subject change.

"She is?" This comes from Ethan.

"I am?" This from me.

"Yes, you are." Miranda's voice is firm. "I've decided officially to be your guide. Your guide to the London designers' trade. I'll show you to all the best shops and share my finely honed referrals list. In return, you merely have to do me the teensy, tinesy favor of allowing me to go with you to America as your stowaway." I grin at her as she glances at Ethan-Not-Simon. "Quinn lives in *Memphis*."

"No." His voice contains a note of reverence, something I'm not used to encountering when I tell people where I live. Not that I don't think Memphis is awesome, just that most people tend to think of it as flyover country. In America, Memphis is only a sought-after destination if you happen to live regionally or are passing through or have a deep, abiding passion for music history. Or for barbecue pork ribs.

"Have you met Lisa Marie Presley?" he asks, and both Miranda and I let out a peal of giggles. I can tell this beer has a higher alcohol content than anything I've tried at home. Plus I'm a total lightweight, a cheap date for sure. "What is it with you Brits and Lisa Marie?" I mutter, and everyone ignores me.

"Ethan runs a record shop in Hoxton," Eleanor says proudly, surprising me on two counts. I'd have expected her to be marrying a bookkeeper or barrister type…or, at the artiest, a literary executive. And based on Ethan's appearance, I'd have guessed the former.

"We have a whole section devoted to blues music. Robert Johnson, 'Crossroads,' all that jazz. Or blues," Ethan says, chuckling again, and I realize it isn't because he's made a joke, it's just something he does—he laughs as he utters any sentence. I look at him with closer scrutiny and see that I was off the mark with my book cover snap judgment. The little round glasses and fitted oxford-stripe shirt that read "accountant" to me at first don't give that impression at all. The glasses are sort of à la Daniel Radcliffe, and the untucked, unironed shirt is rumply and casual. His hairline is receding, but his remaining sand-colored hair is intentionally scruffy—and contains product. Definitely no bookkeeper. "I'd give a bet your clubs are fantastic," he says with another chortle.

"We have some good clubs," I agree. Inwardly, I'm chastising myself for not taking better advantage of my city's live music scene, with all its gritty authenticity. Sure, I go out a lot with my friends, but we hang out mostly in Downtown and Midtown bars and gastropubs, drinking wine or sipping fizzy cocktails until we feel fizzy ourselves. Ethan-Not-Simon has a point. "Come visit, and we'll go to some shows," I add spontaneously, the beer enhancing my generosity. "I can pack you in my second suitcase."

"Why him? He's a wanker, and he's taken."

The voice is unfamiliar, and my head jerks toward it. A third male has appeared in our midst, and Thomas has stood to try to make room for him, so I can't see his face. Our table is round and pub height—guess I know where that term comes from now—and meant for four people, tops. Miranda squeezes her stool in tighter next to mine, causing Thomas to shift his, wedging her in bench-style between us. New Guy doesn't find a free chair, so he just squeezes in and stands half beside, half behind Thomas. I suck in a breath when I finally get a look at him, and my stomach muscles tighten involuntarily. He might, *might* be even hotter than Ryland Pemberton.

Pamela distracts me by sitting up straighter and smiling at New Guy. No one has scooted closer to her, so she's the only person at the table now with leg room. It makes her stand out, like she's the type of person who's always lonely in the center of a crowd.

"Are you going to introduce me?" The guy directs the question to Miranda, I guess because she's sitting closest to me—

and because she's poking me in the ribs with the side of her hand and giving a significant nod in New Guy's direction. Getting me back for the "mating rituals" joke, I presume.

I know before she tells me that this must be Ian, the guy she'd mentioned in her shop. *"He'll drink you up like a pint of brown ale."* Even though she said it when we were alone, I feel as if it's flashing from my forehead. *"American girl. Come drink me up now."*

My breathing speeds up involuntarily. I take a swig from my beer to hide my reaction and nearly splutter at the bitter taste. It wasn't served cold to begin with, but now it's the temperature of tepid bathwater.

"Quinn Cunningham, meet Ian Murphy."

Miranda gives the history of how I came to be here for a third time. I listen as I'm talked about, feeling tongue-tied despite the buzz because Ian hasn't stopped staring at me. It's so intense it's like he's staring *into* me. I can barely look at him, though, in part because he's so cute and in part because Miranda sort-of, kind-of linked us with her comments conveying the opposite.

He's just the right height—taller than me, which is critical, but also a few inches above six feet, which is preferable—with dark, wavy hair and dark eyes that have a mischievous glint. Those eyes alone could be the source of his reputation. When he smiles, which he's doing now, they're squinty and crinkly at the corners. I can tell he's funny—he wears his good humor like other people might wear a T-shirt. And speaking of T-shirts, his is black with an elaborate gray design around the lowercase word "cobalist." I don't know if it's a bar, a band name, a brand, or what it is, and it drives home the fact that this man is a foreigner, with all the excitement that entails.

The shirt is loose and tight in all the right places, and that's how looking at it makes me feel.

"Quinn. That's an unusual name." My stomach tightens at its base when he says my name. I let out a breath when the bar attendant swings by to assess our drinks, and Ian asks for a Young's Bitter without looking away from me.

"It's a family name," I explain, and my voice rings back in my ears. I feel as if Miranda's led me out to the center ring like a prized cow. I hate feeling self-conscious. My theory with men is to keep the upper hand, in conversation or otherwise, but Ian has me totally off my game. I clear my throat and look between Ian and Ethan as I'm talking—Ian for obvious reasons and Ethan because he's such a nonthreatening presence. "I'm named for my grandfather, who was a career politician. My father wanted me to be the child who finally lived out the family legacy."

"A politician." Ian sounds impressed, though for what reason I can't fathom. Allied countries or not, American politics isn't a subject I want to touch with a jillion-foot pole right now.

"One more way we're alike, then," Miranda says. "We both refused our birthrights."

"A rebel *and* an American. What are you, like, a cowgirl?" Ian is leaning into the table, practically hanging over Thomas's arm and pressing Thomas into Miranda. As a result she's straining toward me, as close as she can get without actually sharing my chair.

"I've already warned her off of you, Ian, so you may as well give up before you begin."

I suck in a sharp breath, thinking *no, no, no*. He's looking at Miranda now, away from me.

"Warned her off of me? What'd *I* ever do to *you*?"

Ian's tone is jokey, but it's as if the sentence sucks the air out from around the table. Eleanor and Pamela both level quick glances at Thomas, and then at Miranda, and then down at the table. There's five seconds of silence, and then Ethan-Not-Simon says, while laughing, "So, Quinn, how'd you meet Lisa Marie Presley?"

* * *

When the doorbell rings I'm down on all fours, delicately picking at a peeling corner of the guest room wallpaper to see what's underneath. I have the first of the subs referred to me by Miranda stopping by in the morning to give me an estimate for stripping the remaining wallpaper from the upstairs rooms and repainting the house from top to bottom.

I scoot out from behind a faded green chair with sagging upholstery and stand up so fast that tiny pinpricks of light shimmer in front of my eyes. As soon as the head rush passes, I hurtle toward the stairs, snagging a paint deck off the corner of the bed on my way out of the room.

A vision in shocking violet greets me when I swing open the front door. Miranda is wearing eggplant fishnet stockings, a lilac miniskirt so bright it nearly glows, and a periwinkle sheer cardigan over a white tank top. Above her signature loose-laced combat boots extend slouched-down chartreuse socks. Her cat-eye black eyeliner and glittery turquoise eye shadow complete the ensemble. She should have a TV show where all the rooms are designed around her outfits.

"Oh, you're right," she says in lieu of hello, craning her neck to look beyond me. "It's lovely." She pushes past me into the foyer. "They're at work, you say?"

"Yes. Jane will be back before Braxton is home, around three."

"Ooh, let's just give it a good snoop, then." She hugs herself and does a full-body shimmy. "I just love houses. Love, love, love them."

"I know." I grin. "Me, too." I follow her into the front room—a parlor or receiving room in a past life, now an obligatory nod to a formal lifestyle that no longer exists. Jane and Adam and I talked about widening the entry between this room and the dining room and kitchen beyond, turning it into the type of open-plan living, kitchen, and dining space that exists on the pages of every American shelter magazine. Miranda has assured me that open-plan is all the rage in Britain, too, but I'm glad she's here getting a firsthand look. Even though I'm planning to salvage as much original detail as possible, even bringing back some historical references in the hardware and lighting, I don't want to butcher a graceful old building without at least getting some native context.

Watching Miranda explore the house is like watching a ballerina pirouette across a stage or an artist slash ink over a bright white sheet of paper. I know I've never looked as graceful at work. She's part of her art.

She stops in the middle of the living room, cocks her head as she assesses the fireplace, and then nods before walking on, all the while mumbling words I can't make out as she wanders through the rooms. That's something else we have in common—I talk to myself while I work, too.

"What's the plan in here?" she asks as I trail her into the kitchen.

"Opening it up, mostly. I've met with the contractor Adam wants to hire, and I suggested taking out this wall"—I gesture to the long wall behind me, now lined with long rows of upper and lower cabinets—"and expanding the island out to here." I take a big step back and draw an invisible line with my right arm and hand. "We're keeping the lower cabinets on this side of the room and replacing the uppers here with open shelving, probably stainless steel."

"Oh, very sleek and mod. I approve." Miranda claps her hands together, and I notice that her nails are painted the same chartreuse as her socks. How did I miss that before? They actually glow.

"Countertops?" she asks.

"Quartz," I reply. "I want to do a waterfall edge on the island, white with some big veining, like a calacatta look. And then honed and dark countertops for the perimeter." I step over to the existing island and grab a magazine out of a stack I've been thumbing through with Jane. I flip to a dog-eared page. "Something like this," I say, pointing, "but with darker cabinets. Jane likes my idea of a smoky deep blue, sort of a navy."

"I love it," Miranda pronounces. She taps her lip with one finger. "I have a rep I love with C&M Stonework, which did the Caesarstone on one of my commercial projects. She isn't on the list I gave. I'll text her contact to you."

"Thank you." The words don't feel adequate. I don't know how I got lucky enough to walk into this woman's shop. She's a lifesaver—an angel in fishnets and combat boots.

"Of course." She turns to look at me and grins. "You know the only thanks I need."

"Right. A cameo in Matt Damon's next film."

The list of demands following Miranda's transatlantic escape inside my luggage has grown from an introduction to Lisa Marie to personal experiences with a changing array of Hollywood stars. She's convinced all Americans know each other or at least that we all know somebody who knows somebody who knows everybody. Six degrees of Kevin Bacon and all that. I didn't know that was the kind of modern folklore that crossed cultural boundaries.

I give her an exaggerated wink.

"She thinks I jest," she mutters as she dances into the next room. And then, loudly: "Oh, wow, this is quite pretty."

I follow her voice into the conservatory, where she's already standing at the long row of windows, looking out into the walled garden.

"Isn't it? I'm not touching a thing back here, apart from updating the furniture."

"I think that's brilliant."

Our tour lasts another twenty minutes during which I share the plans I've created so far, and then Miranda has to rush out the door to open the shop. I have loads to do this afternoon before Jane gets home with Braxton, and I get straight to it— calling two more subs from Miranda's list and scheduling a second wallpaper and paint estimate and a consultation with an electrician. I've worked in plenty of older buildings, but "old" means something different in the UK than it does at home. I'm sure some surprises lurk behind these charming walls, and I want to be prepared when the inevitable problems arise.

* * *

It's after six when I make it to the Lion's Gate to continue my education of the stout versus the bitter. When Jane got home, we talked for a while about the kitchen plans and then lounged in the conservatory over more pinot grigio, which I've learned is Jane's drink of choice. Time got away from me, and I'm already buzzing before I even join Miranda and her friends— not quite my friends yet, though I'm starting to feel more comfortable thinking of them that way.

As I push through the heavy wooden door, the restless fluttering in my stomach has nothing to do with the wine and everything to do with my burning curiosity over whether or not Ian will be here tonight. I stopped myself from asking Miranda who was coming, but just barely. I'm not sure how serious she was with her warning to stay away from him, but she had to have guessed it'd increase my attraction to him by a thousand percent. She's a rebel. I'm a rebel. Rebels like bad boys. It's simple logic.

Anyway, the thought of Ian's crinkly smile, his laughing brown eyes, his sexy-as-hell accent…it makes me want to melt into a puddle right here in the doorway of the pub. Surely he's not all bad? I've dated plenty of players. He can't be any worse than Chase.

Chase. OMG, the thought pulls me up short.

I didn't reply to his text the morning we left, and in my long day of traveling I'd forgotten all about it until he'd texted me again that night—four times. It had oh-so-clearly been a booty call, and lucky for me it had been long-distance. If I'd been home I don't *think* I'd have succumbed to him, but being four thousand miles away is not only a great excuse but also a preventative measure.

I'd texted him back only three words. *Out of country.* Here's the whole exchange:

From him: *You busy tonight?*

From me: Crickets.

From him later that night (or early afternoon for me): *I'm so sorry, baby.*

From him again: *U home?*

And again: *Don't blame u for ignoring me.*

And yet again: *Can I come by tho? Want to see u.*

From me, at least two hours later (he was probably passed-out drunk by then): *Out of country.*

He's texted a few more times since that first day, but I've been so busy I honestly haven't given much thought to texting him back, apart from one terse text to say I'm in England for work. The latest text came during the night last night, and I haven't answered it. I can't believe he's still at it…he was never this persistent about seeing me while we were actually going out.

I dig my phone out of my bag to remind myself what last night's text said. *"When RU coming home?"*

"Unbelievable," I mutter to myself. And then, rolling my eyes, "Oh, for heaven's sake." I tap back, *"What's it to you, anyway?"* My fingers are flying furiously over the screen as I walk-text my way to the right side of the pub, where I'd caught a flash of Miranda purple as soon as I walked in. Sure enough, when I glance up she's waving at me wildly.

"Texting your boyfriend?" The voice comes from behind me, and I jump. Shivers race down my spine when I glance over my left shoulder and see Ian rushing to fall in step beside me.

"I don't have a boyfriend. Just texting a—hmm, how would you say it?—a wanker who used to be my boyfriend and won't go away."

"Want me to tell him to bugger off?" He reaches playfully for my phone, and I stretch out my arm to hold it out of his reach. His forearm brushes my shoulder, and my nerve endings vibrate like a just-plucked guitar string.

I'm giggling as we approach Miranda, Eleanor, Ethan, and Pamela. Miranda raises one sculpted brow at me, and I give her my wryest "I don't care" stare in return. She glances at Ian, smirks, and then carries on talking to Eleanor. "I didn't like the second one, though. Why would I watch the third?"

"This one's much funnier," Eleanor says. "You'd like it. You should watch. Besides, Colin Firth…" Her voice trails off, and Ethan-Not-Simon gives me a wounded look.

"Right in front of me," he says, shaking his head.

Eleanor pokes him in the side. "He's on my list," she says. "You have to grant me the men on my list. I allow you yours."

"I don't have any men on my list." There's a laugh in Ethan's voice, of course.

"No, Colin Firth is old now," Miranda says, ignoring them. "He's all wrinkly and pouchy and saggy. The only person I'd shag who's that old is Hugh Grant."

"Ooh, no," I say. "I mean, Hugh Grant is good-looking and all, but he's too sure of himself. A total dog. Trust me. I've dated enough of them to know."

"So you don't like confident men? Well, this bloke is out, then." Miranda bats a hand against Ian's shoulder and then stretches up on her tiptoes to grab him by the chin, jiggling her hand back and forth and smooshing his cheeks together as she adds, "He's pretty and proud of it."

Ian pushes her hand away from his face and steps subtly out of her reach. "I am not a dog," he says. "I can be whatever you want me to be. Rabbit, racehorse, lion, tiger. A cute baby kitten, perhaps?"

He's looking straight at me as he says this, and my wine-warmed cheeks are burning. In my Ian-induced haze, I'm confused. Is Miranda warning me off this guy or not? I get the feeling there's a history there but not like the history between her and Thomas.

"How do you all know each other?" I ask, waving my hands around to include everyone, diverting attention away from our public flirtation.

Miranda laughs. "Now that," she says, "is a question with a complicated answer." She peers around the table at each person in turn, as if deciding where to start. "Eleanor, Ian, and I go back to our primer school days."

"We bonded over a Marmite sandwich," Eleanor interjects with a giggle, gesturing between herself and Miranda.

"Marmite?" I ask. It's a word I've never heard before.

"Yes, Marmite. It's an English condiment, very popular here, like peanut butter in the States," Miranda explains. "Eleanor's mother always put it in her lunch pail. This awful boy, Collin, was making fun of her, saying her sandwiches made her breath smell like dirty socks, and so I—"

"She ripped the sandwich out of my hand, took a gigantic bite, and then before she swallowed it she planted this Collin with a big kiss. 'There,' she said. 'Now *your* breath smells like dirty socks, so you can shut up then, can't you?'" Eleanor looks at Miranda with clear admiration. "It was the best moment of my life."

"And we've been attached at the hip ever since," adds Miranda.

"Hey, I take exception to that," Ethan says. "The best moment of your life? What am I, chop suey?"

Eleanor chuckles. "I meant the best moment of my childhood. Meeting you was the best moment of my life, of course," she says, patting his hand. Meanwhile, she's shaking her head and giving a tiny nod toward Miranda, mouthing at me, *Not really.*

"I saw that," Ethan-Not-Simon says, his ever present chuckle erasing any actual indignation.

"Obviously, Ethan entered the group through Eleanor. They met at university," Miranda continues, moving on around the table. Next is Ian, who's standing on my left, between Miranda and me. "And Ian—"

"Eleanor and I met at work," interrupts Pamela, who's on the other side of Miranda. She hasn't said a word until now, and a piece of the puzzle clicks into place as she explains the third wheel vibe she puts off. She's only attached to this crew via one string, where the others are knitted together in a twisted ball of yarns and years and stories.

"Where do you two work?" I ask, looking at Pamela. Despite the fact that she interrupted the story I most want to hear—about Ian—it's sad that she feels like an outsider in her own circle of friends. But at the same time, I can already see that she does it to herself. Miranda looks down at the table, not hiding her annoyance very well.

"We don't work together anymore," she says. "I'm a personal assistant now to a designer with an atelier in Kensington."

"An interior designer?" I say, my interest piqued.

"No, a fashion designer," Pamela says, wearing her pride in the lift of her chin. "Anjelica Romero. She debuted at last year's Fashion Week in New York. Maybe you've heard of her?"

"No, I'm afraid not," I say. "I don't pay much attention to what's on the runways. I really only have time to read home magazines these days. And design blogs." I turn to Eleanor and ask, "Do you work in fashion, too?" I'm trying not to let my surprise show. She's adorable, especially once you get to know her, but stylewise, she's frumpy. She certainly doesn't share Miranda's fashion bravado. Today she's wearing an olive green cardigan over a nice but ordinary white blouse and denim skirt, her feet in sensible, low-heeled black pumps.

"No. I'm an editorial assistant with a magazine."

"A fashion magazine?" I feel as if I'm repeating myself, but the truth is I'm fascinated, and that's because I'd love to work at a magazine. If I hadn't gone into design, my second choice would have been journalism, like Savy. If I'd gone to Columbia or the University of Missouri or another top journalism school and gotten a job or even an internship at a respectable publication, it would have made my mother as happy as an ant at a picnic. Which is, of course, why I didn't do it.

"No." She gives a little laugh. "It's a trade journal. For the commercial embroidery industry."

Pamela snickers, and even Miranda cracks a smile.

"Shut up," she says. She looks at me. "It's a good job. I have a wonderful boss, and the office is quite laid-back. Not at all like the environment at *Slice*. I hated working there, actually. It was so cutthroat."

"*Slice*?" I ask. "What's that?" It sounds like the catchy name of a bakery in a hipster neighborhood. Somehow I don't see Pamela, in particular, slaving behind a pastry counter.

"It *is* a fashion magazine," Pamela said. "It's Scottish, based in Glasgow. And it isn't cutthroat—I don't know what she's talking about, really." She gives Eleanor an affectionate, if condescending, glance. "Eleanor and I both did an internship there after university. And when I moved back to London, I rang her up. We've been great friends ever since."

"Lovely story," says Ian, and the sudden sound of his voice raises goose bumps on my arms.

"Well, it is." A sultry pout rings through in Pamela's voice, and I realize with a start that she's flirting with him. I assess her a bit more closely—I hadn't paid that much attention to her, but now, as competition, she's more interesting.

She's blonde with large, blue-green eyes magnified by thick dark lashes with a cosmetics-ad curl. Her clothes are cute but not immediately noticeable—at least not beside Miranda's. I can't see her lower half because the table is between us, but on top she's wearing an aqua-colored, short-sleeved sweater with a chunky gold necklace and amethyst studs in her ears. She isn't stick thin but also isn't overweight, and she's shorter than me— sort of absolutely average in height and weight. Her shoulder-length hair is straight and nondescript, but I notice for the first time that it's impeccably highlighted, with three or four shades ranging from honey to butter to platinum weaved in so expertly that the dye job isn't immediately noticeable. Actually, she looks expensive.

"Yes, but we were talking about *me*." Ian grins in a way that disarms Pamela instantly, and she smiles with simpering acquiescence.

"By all means, steal the limelight."

He winks at her, triggering a strong surge of jealousy in the pit of my stomach. I didn't realize, until this moment, how much I want a chance with this Ian—probably all the more because Miranda warned me away. It's my pattern, and I'm self-aware enough to recognize it, with or without Jules' ridiculous "intervention" balloon.

I only want men who are bad for me. Men who other women flirt with and who flirt back even while I'm watching. Men who talk to my boobs rather than my face and who are sure to chew me up and spit me out once they've gotten in a few good licks and squeezes. Men like Chase, who's still sending desperate, pathetic texts that I'm now answering despite my better judgment.

There's a new one from him on my phone right now—I heard it buzz inside my purse before I hung it over the back of my chair. His reply to my "*What's it to you?*" text that I knew was a bad idea before I even clicked *Send*. It's too fake-angry to be anything but flirty.

At least I have the upper hand with him now. At least I'm *using* him to up the ante with Ian, who now knows there's someone back home texting me, wanting me.

I might make bad calls when it comes to men and I might have no luck as a closer, but no one can accuse me of not knowing the rules of the game.

As Ian starts talking—"I've known Miranda longer than any of this lot"—I nod absently, reaching behind me to pull out my phone and then setting it on the table in front of me.

"Mm-hmm," I murmur, clicking the home button and typing in the code to unlock the screen. I look at my phone, not at him, though every word out of his lips vibrates through my core.

"Since we were in nappies," Miranda pipes up, and Ian chuckles. At this, the sound of his laugh—warm, sincere, boyish, and rough all at once—I glance up and meet his eyes, unable to keep the smile out of mine.

"Really?" I ask. "Are your mothers friends or something?"

Ian laughs again, but this time his chuckle has a hard edge. "You might have said that," he says. "At one time."

I'm intrigued, and even though Chase's text, which I've just read, dropped a bombshell, I ignore the screen and look up into Ian's eyes. "What does that mean?"

Miranda sighs, as if she's told this story far too many times. "My mum," she says, a hard edge to her voice, "cheated on my dad with Ian's father."

"They grew up side by side," pipes in Pamela, who sounds almost gleeful with the scandal of it. "Next-door neighbors."

"How did you find out?" I ask, the first of a hundred questions that have popped into my head.

Miranda bursts out with a hard chuckle and says, "Funny you should ask that."

"Miranda caught them snogging in the kitchen," Ian explained. "Right in the middle of the afternoon, while her father was out of town."

"I was ditching school," Miranda says with a sheepish look. "And a good thing, too, or it might have got further than it did. I keyed in through the back door, right beside them, so there wasn't time for them to react, really, or pretend like it was something else going on. I was eleven, old enough to know. And my darling mum was half undressed. In fact, her blouse was on the floor, and when I opened the door it got caught underneath and bunched all up. I almost couldn't get the door properly open."

"Spare the details," Ian said, waving his hands in front of his face. "I don't want the visual."

"Why not? Miranda's mom's a MILF," chuckles Ethan-not-Simon. "Isn't that what you call it in the States?"

"In, like, 2005," I say, winking at him. "But you've gotten the point across, thanks."

I turn back to Miranda. "So what happened?"

It's Ian who answers. "Nothing. Miranda's mum asked her not to tell her father and said it hadn't happened before and wouldn't happen again. We have no idea whether or not that's true." He pauses, and then his voice takes on a sarcastic edge. "At least between the two of them."

Miranda shoots him a dirty look. "And about a year later, my dad left and moved to Sweden."

"Scandal!" I said. "This story is unbelievable."

"And yet, sadly, believable," Miranda says with a shudder. "Since I saw it with my own two eyes, unfortunately." She shudders again, and there's a long pause. "I never did tell my father, though a lot of good it did since he took off anyway. My mum and I have never discussed it since. And I never really see my father."

"Not that you were particularly close with him before since he worked all the time," Eleanor adds.

"True." Miranda has a weary look on her face that tells me there's more to the story. And then she changes her tone, quickly rearranging her expression. "I can't believe we've just told this sorry old tale again, and in the pub, to boot. It's so tawdry."

"Utterly sordid. Let's move on, shall we?" Ian's eyes are lit with a sort of tolerant amusement. At least they can joke about what happened.

"Though it might have been for the best. It prevented these two from any similar tawdry encounters," Ethan says, enjoying the story more than any of the rest—although maybe his laugh-talking just makes it seem that way.

"I don't think that's what prevented it," Miranda says in a quieter voice, looking up at Ian, who seems to be avoiding her eyes. "He's like my big brother."

He glances down at her when she says this. Miranda nudges his shoulder, causing his entire right side to brush up against me. The contact sends tingles up my spine.

"And besides, Thomas would've had his arse if he'd laid a hand on you, right?" Ethan says.

Even though there's a person in between us, and even though the presence of that person is making the nerve endings all over my body flicker in kaleidoscopic ways, I can sense Miranda's body go rigid. "I suppose so," she says briskly. She leans around Ian to look at me. "Ian and Thomas are best mates," she adds in a flat tone. "Since childhood, almost as long as Eleanor and me."

She stops, and even though I'm dying to ask about her history with Thomas, I can tell she's not dying to talk about it—not right now, at least. For several seconds the conversation is compressed by the weight of the elephant in the room. And then Ethan, chuckling, looks around and says, "Good God, how long have you two been standing here with no beer?" He cranes his neck to gaze between Miranda and Ian toward the bar. "Kelsey must not be here today. She'd never ignore our table like this." He drops back down to his five-foot-sevenish height.

Meanwhile, Ian says to me, "Would you like me to go up and order a pint for you?"

I wink at him. "I think I can handle it, thanks. What would *you* like?"

Ethan shakes his head and chuckles. "It's true what they say about American women. So damn independent."

"I like an independent woman," Ian says, and I catch Pamela's eye roll. "I'll have a Young's Bitter, please. Much obliged."

As I head toward the bar, I put an extra wiggle in my walk, sensing Ian's eyes following me away from the table. I hear Miranda mutter, "'Much obliged.' You wanker. Who are you trying to be, Mr. Darcy?"

I smile to myself and squeeze in between two barstools to lean against the long wood bar, wishing, for the moment at least, that I never had to leave this place.

* * *

Before going back to my bed and breakfast, I decide to make a quick stop at Adam and Jane's house. They hadn't been home when I hurried out to meet Miranda and her friends. *Oh, who am I kidding?* When I hurried out to meet *Ian* and Miranda and the rest of their friends—and I need to give them the estimates I've collected on the wallpaper project.

I ring the bell before inserting my key, just to give them a warning that I'm here, though I texted Jane to let her know I was coming. When I key in and poke my head around the door, I see Jane rushing through the door from the hallway that leads to the kitchen. And I hear voices—more voices than usual in their quiet household. *Braxton must have a friend over.*

I must be right because the first new voice I hear has the high-pitched and reedy tones of a young boy. I hear him saying, "Well, I like *her*," emphasizing the word "her" in a way that's *so* British. "But I'm not at all happy to be *here*."

Wow, that's a little rude. I inch my neck forward and strain to hear more of the conversation as Jane pushes the front door closed. A deeper voice rings out next, sending shock waves through my core.

"Now, Elliott, you must give it time. And do not be rude to Mr. and Mrs. Dawson, please. They are kind and very gracious to help us." *Ryland Pemberton.* I'd almost forgotten his existence.

Jane stops walking and glances back at me, and my eyes must be saucer-like from shock. "Visitors just arrived, and we weren't expecting them," she says to me in a whisper so low I almost can't catch the words. "But come on in. I don't think they'll be here lo—"

Her words are cut off by a wail from the boy. "*Why* must they help us?" he says. "I can walk to school and back *myself*. And I can be left alone. I am thirteen and a half."

The last word sounds like "hoff," and I shake my head. Kids with British accents are something I'm just not sure I'll ever get used to. I almost giggle but stop myself. Jane is still frozen in the center of the hallway, and she looks uncertain as to whether she should rejoin the others. I suddenly feel like an interloper.

"We will talk about this at home." Ryland's voice is low and restrained but contains a dark edge.

"This is not my home."

"Should I come back at a better time?" I ask in a stage whisper.

"No, no," Jane says, and she unfreezes and continues through the hallway and into the brightly lit kitchen. I follow.

"Hello, hello," Jane calls out in a chipper voice as she enters the kitchen. I try to make myself as unobtrusive as possible behind her, not easy when you're five-feet-nine-and-a-half-inches tall and a hundred and…well. Some pounds, anyway. "You remember Quinn, Mr. Pemberton?"

So much for my invisibility attempt. I flutter my fingers in an awkward halfhearted wave. My heart is drumming out a staccato rhythm, which annoys me. Normally when I'm around stuck-up, stuck-on-themselves men, I hold my own by holding my own chin higher. But something about Ryland Pemberton makes me feel like whimpering and cowering in the corner. Or grabbing fistfuls of that perfectly imperfect blond hair, pulling that chiseled jaw down to mine, and showing him exactly how much I refuse to let him intimidate me.

The second impulse is so shocking—and so contradictory to the first—that my actual reaction is to flicker my eyes to his and away just as fast. "Hello, *Mr. Pemberton*," I mutter in the direction of his chest, unable to keep the sarcasm out of my voice. What's with this weirdly formal means of address, anyway? It's the twenty-first century, and he lives in an urban row house. It's not like he's some Regency-era lord of the manor.

Or is he? Does Ryland have one of those bizarre, outmoded aristocratic titles, like "Earl of Somerset" or "Viscount of Salisbury" or, most likely, "Most Honourable Duke of Snobbington?" Does he own a five-hundred-acre estate with servants and silver tea services and family portraits lining the great hall? Maybe his house next door is his London pied-à-terre. Maybe he has a string of vacation homes in far-flung, exotic locales.

Get a grip, Quinn. I only realize I'm clenching my hands so tightly that my knuckles hurt because when I look up again, I notice that Ryland is staring at them, his brow furrowed into a quizzical *V*. But the moment passes quickly, and I realize he likely wasn't seeing my hands at all but some confounding image in his own head.

"We'll be going, then," he says, beckoning to a mop-headed wisp of a boy perched at one of the Dawsons' barstools. The boy looks up, and I almost jump when I catch a glimpse of his bright cerulean eyes. They're the exact same unusual shade of blue tinged with turquoise—Mediterranean waves kissed by sunlight—as Ryland's.

"Come now, Elliott," Ryland says, glancing from Jane to Adam. "Say good-bye to Braxton. I expect that you two will enjoy one another's company again soon enough."

"Good-bye, Braxton," Elliott parrots unconvincingly, not sparing a glance at Braxton, who's leaning against the counter near the sink and looking like he'd rather not enjoy the other boy's company anytime soon.

"Good-bye," Braxton mumbles, looking at Jane. "Can I go upstairs?" he asks his mom as Elliott scrapes back on the barstool and gets to his feet.

"Sure." Braxton bolts out of the room, and Jane shakes her head and gives Ryland an apologetic look. "Elliott will be fine," she says to him. "Braxton will show him the ropes, and he's welcome here anytime."

"Thank you." Ryland meets her eyes and says the words with feeling. It's the greatest show of emotion—or of authenticity or even humanity—I've seen from the man so far.

"Of course," Jane says.

With a nod Ryland turns and leaves through the back conservatory, guiding Elliott by the shoulder with one strong hand.

Jane and I watch the pair of them cross the matchbook back garden. Ryland unlatches the gate and holds it open for Elliott, who steps back quickly and then ducks under Ryland's arm, careful not to touch him. Ryland exits behind him, latching the gate smoothly and efficiently. If man were machine, Ryland Pemberton would be the top-of-the-line, highest-priced model.

"Well, then." Jane exhales loudly, as if she, too, has been holding her breath. She glances at the bag over my shoulder, and with a start I remember why I'm here.

"I've heard back from several contractors," I say, though I told her that by text before coming over here. "Give me just a minute."

I set the bag on the tile countertop and begin digging through it to find my iPad so I can pull up my spreadsheet of estimates. Without looking at her, I ask, "So Elliott is his son, then?"

Jane perches on the same barstool Elliott just evacuated and gestures for me to sit beside her. When I glance at her, she looks distracted. "What? No, a cousin," she says. "His mother was Ryland's first cousin, I believe. She died a few weeks ago, after a long battle with cancer."

"How terrible," I say. "I'm so sorry."

Jane shakes her head. "Me too. That little boy has such a tragic story. His father passed away when he was little—plane crash or train crash, I can't remember which. We don't actually know Mr. Pemberton well. We've met him at a couple of neighborhood meetings and events. And then he knocked at our back gate one night a few weeks ago, telling us about his cousin and asking if we'd mind introducing him to Braxton so he could show him around his new school. Apparently he doesn't have many living relatives, apart from an aunt in Surrey who's too old to take him in." Her voice perks up. "Oh, and you know what? It was Elliott's father who was Ryland's cousin, not his mother. His mother was American." She pauses, her face growing thoughtful. "I guess the family wouldn't have wanted to uproot the boy by sending him to a completely new country. It's pretty incredible that Mr. Pemberton is taking him in. It's got to be a shocking lifestyle change for a bachelor like him."

I see Jane eyeing the document I've opened on my tablet, but I'm not ready to stop talking about Ryland yet.

"What's his story?" I ask, digging into my bag again for my paint deck to buy more time.

"Whose story? Elliott's?" Her forehead is furrowed in confusion, and then suddenly, it clears. "Oh. You mean Mr. Pemberton's." The corners of her mouth twitch up as she catches my drift. "He's nice to look at, isn't he?" She pauses, growing thoughtful. "Not easy to get to know, though. I can't tell you much beyond what I've already said about Elliott." She glances down, seeming suddenly reticent. "He works all the time, and he travels a lot because we rarely see him here. He's a very good neighbor. He'd cross the street in front of traffic to get the door if you had your arms full. But I can't talk much about his life." Her voice falters a bit, as if she's carefully choosing her words. I file that away to ponder later.

She winks at me. "I do know that he's single. Maybe you can get to know him while you're here."

I chortle. "Doubtful." I grin at her. "He looks at me like I'm something stuck to the bottom of his shoe." I chew on the inside of my lip for a second while I mull that over. "Actually, that's not true. He doesn't look at me at all. But that's OK. That's not what I'm here for." I gesture to my iPad screen and wink back at her. "Besides, I'm happy to be getting *away* from men for a while anyway. I have enough problems back home." I'd almost forgotten about it, what with Ryland bringing his drama into the house, but Chase sent another text while I was at the pub.

"Man problems?" Jane shakes her head. "Never mind. If you're happy to be away from them, I don't want to make you talk about it."

"I'd be happy to, but it'd take all night, and I need to show you these estimates." I laugh, and then Jane laughs, and then we bury ourselves in color samples and estimates, and I forget all about Ryland Pemberton and Chase Ledford, and even Ian Murphy, who stirs up flutters in my stomach just from thinking his name.

I shake my head and center my thoughts on work.

And this is why I love my job—it's so black and white. Take something unfinished or outdated or ill-planned and turn it into something polished and beautiful and functional. Sure, it isn't instant gratification…sometimes the results don't come for weeks or months, or even years. But give me a design problem, and I *will* find a solution. Men, on the other hand, are a problem with *no* solution. No gratification. No results. Just a lot of short-term angst with no long-term benefits. Even Ian, whose name gives me flutters all over again when it pops back into my head, is sure to disappoint me as soon as someone prettier or more interesting or skinnier or more geographically available comes along.

I know, I know. I'm a real ray of sunshine, right?

Don't get me wrong—it isn't that I have no self-esteem, just that I have plenty of experience to speak from. And I'm nothing if not a realist. So I'll be sticking to color swatches and floor plans and tile samples, thank you very much. They never disappoint me.

Or look at me like I'm something stuck to the bottom of their shoe.

CHAPTER SIX

———

Playing Hard to Get

"You really can't be leaving already."

Miranda's voice rings out above the din of the pub, all of us several drinks in after spending the past two and a half hours laughing, joking, and doing far more drinking than eating. She's across the table from me, the table I've come to think of as *our table*, even though it's really *their table* and I'm just a temporary intruder who's about to lift back out of the group.

I've hung out with Miranda and her friends three more times in the last two weeks, which have passed so fast they feel like a blur of minutes and hours and days. And I'm leaving in the morning to get caught up on the work piling up at home.

"It's because of your help," I yell back to her. It's loud in here, well past the dinner hour, and actually starting to grow dim outside. "Without you I'd probably still be hunting down painters and flooring wholesalers and electricians. I can't believe how far I've gotten with the plans already."

"Well, shame on me. I should be dragging this out to keep you here."

"Yes, she should." Ian says it low enough that only I can hear, raising the hairs on my arm and making my bones feel soft. He's leaning down toward me with his elbow on the table. He's kept close to my side tonight, a fact that has me buzzing harder than the alcohol.

He leans even closer, so close that his breath rustles the fine hairs at my temple, sending a shiver from the base of my neck all the way down my spine. "Can I take you out to dinner when you get back, just the two of us?"

The question is such a shock it takes me a few seconds to answer, my stomach dancing somewhere in the vicinity of my throat. Finally I glance up at him and flutter my lashes without meaning to, a mating dance that crosses cultural boundaries. "Sure. I'd love that."

I force myself to meet his gaze. We've flirted each time I've seen him, and I knew Miranda was playing matchmaker by introducing us, but I never actually took her seriously. I didn't think Ian did, either. But the look in his eyes now says otherwise.

My breath catches. I fight a ridiculous urge to close the short distance between us and kiss him, right here in front of everybody.

"Right," he says, the movement of his mouth mesmerizing. "Excellent."

I continue gazing at his lips. They're smooth and full and look soft. His angular jaw is covered in a fine, shadowy layer of stubble.

I can't believe I'm flying out tomorrow morning. And I can't believe he's saved this question until tonight, when it's too late to satisfy what I'm ninety-nine percent sure is, at this moment at least, a mutual urge.

Maybe he gets off on sexual tension. I take a ragged breath and then swivel my head sharply when I hear my name.

"You've left room in your suitcase for me, right, Quinn?" is what Miranda has just said, and though I'm slow on the uptake, at least I heard the question. I take an extra second to answer, during which I catch the odd expression in her eyes— calculating, smug.

"I think there's a little space in my carry-on," I say. "You're so teeny-tiny I'm sure you'll squeeze right in."

"Oh, har-dee-har," she answers. "Tell that to these thunderous thighs."

Apparently unfounded body angst crosses cultural boundaries, too. Miranda's very *non*-thunderous thighs are today encased in hot pink leather pants. Above them is a black and white off-the-shoulder Flaming Lips T-shirt, and she's just had her hair dyed newly black and tinged with dusty violet, and it's spiking out from her head in tousled tufts. Instead of her usual combat boots, today she's wearing silver ballet slippers, giving her the overall appearance of a punked-out pixie, like Tinkerbell adapted for the new millennium.

"Is the project already finished? Are you coming back?" asks Eleanor, who joined the group late because of a meeting at work, so she didn't hear me give the whole spiel twice—first to Pamela, Ethan, and Miranda, who'd already heard it in her shop earlier this afternoon, and then again to Ian.

"Yes, I'm coming back. I'm not a hundred percent sure when but probably in about a month," I answer. "The house is nowhere near finished yet. But we're at a lull now where I'm waiting on work to be done and things to come in. Once the pieces start arriving, I'll come back and start putting them all together. In the meantime Miranda's saving my life again by letting me ship the bigger items to her storeroom." I shoot her a grateful look.

"It's nothing," she says, smiling happily. "It's exciting to play a part in a transatlantic project, even if I'm not the one crossing the ocean."

"You're crossing the ocean?"

Miranda visibly jumps, and we all turn toward the new, deep voice.

"Thomas!" I can't tell if she sounds excited, relieved, or annoyed. Miranda still hasn't told me the story of what happened between her and Thomas—but I know it's something. I was hoping to get it out of her tonight, but that seems unlikely now that he's shown up. "You scared me half to death."

"Sorry." He gives the group a rakish grin, not sorry in the least, and pulls himself up to the table—standing, not sitting, since Eleanor has taken the last chair. The pub is crawling with people tonight. He waves his hands around, indicating all of us. "So, go on. Who's crossing the ocean?"

"She is," Miranda says, pointing at me.

At the same time I say, "I am."

"Leaving us already?" Thomas sounds only politely interested, and I'm wondering if it's because he's relieved that I'm the one who's going and not Miranda. I'm guessing he must have done a real number on Miranda for her to be so closed off about their history, but it's clear to me, as the outsider, that he's madly in love with her. And that maybe she feels the same way, but I can't tell from her mixed signals.

As soon as I'm back in the country, I'm taking Miranda out alone and plying her with cocktails until she tells me the whole story. That's priority number one.

"It's a bloody shame," Ian answers before I can. His forearm, resting on the tabletop, brushes against the length of mine as he says this, and the shiver races down my spine again.

OK, priority number two.

Wait—no, no. Miranda is definitely priority number one. Friends come first. "Besties before testes," as Jules likes to say.

"It's not a shame, unfortunately, because if I don't get home soon and follow up on all the projects I've let slide while I've been here, I'm going to lose all my clients." I grimace, and Miranda purses her lips in sympathy. She and I talked about this at her shop earlier today. Menzi's emails and texts to me have been laced with growing levels of panic as the weeks have passed. She's had trouble handling Sophie Perins all along, but apparently their relationship is bubbling up to the boiling point.

Sophie's pieces have all arrived at our firm's warehouse, and she wants them installed before a dinner party she and Denny are hosting for Denny's office. Menzi is terrified—and insistent that she can't do "the whole install" at "that woman's house" by herself, which means I'll be working from the minute I step off the plane. I can forget about employing Jane's nifty jet lag recovery tricks on the return trip.

"Well, then, if you lose your clients, you can just move here permanently." Ian nudges me with his elbow, sending another shockwave through my body that concentrates at a sensitive point. I lick my lips, willing my time back home to pass quickly.

Why did he have to wait until I was leaving to make a move? Where was this overt flirtatiousness when I *wasn't* about to board a plane and fly four thousand miles away? Maybe it's not just the buildup of sexual tension he likes. Maybe Ian is like me, always wanting what he can't have primarily because he can't have it.

And let me be clear: that isn't good.

I'm torn between an urge to seduce him up to my room at the B&B and a simultaneous urge to turn down his date offer and forget I ever met him.

Ian is exactly my type. Let me be clear again: that isn't good.

"What's a man got to do to get a pint around here?" Ethan's laughing brogue pierces my bubble, and I follow his gaze to the bar. I've never seen the Lion's Gate so busy, and Kelsey, the server who usually brings everybody's drinks before they've even ordered them, doesn't seem to be here today.

"Drag his lazy arse up to the bar like the rest of the plebes, I s'pose," answers Thomas with a smart-alec smile.

I can't get a read on Thomas, can't decide whether or not I actually like him. On the one hand, if Miranda, Ian, and Eleanor have been friends with him for so long, he can't be too bad. On the other hand, I can't quite grasp whether the others are glad he's there, particularly Miranda—and sort of Ian, too. The group dynamic is less comfortable when he's around.

I glance at Miranda, again dying to ask what happened between them.

"I'll order the round," Thomas says. "Young's Special for you," he adds, pointing at Ethan. "What for the rest of you lot?"

As Pamela, Ian, and Eleanor shout their orders at him, I keep quiet, and so does Miranda, who's barely touched her glass. After checking with all of us, Thomas jets off to the bar, confusing me yet again by acting all genial and generous. I truly understand nothing, and I mean nothing, about the opposite sex. You'd think with almost two decades of trial and error, I'd have figured out a few things by now.

It takes a long time for Thomas to return with the drinks, long enough that by the time he comes back holding an impressive number of pint glasses, our table is already in need of more—I've sipped my Belgian witbier down to its last third, and Miranda tossed back most of her full pint in the time it takes me to drink three. Thomas starts to gather up our glasses and return to the bar, but then a harried-looking waiter finally turns up and takes care of us.

We hang out longer than usual. We've watched the pub shift from the after-work crowd, to families and middle-aged couples out for a Ploughman's Pie or Yorkshire Pudding or Bangers 'n' Mash before heading home to watch *Eastenders* or *Britain's Got Talent*, and then again to the late-nighters. This latter crowd ranges from Millennials looking for hookups to a loud group of women who seem to be celebrating something to two elderly men who've stationed themselves at opposite ends of the long wooden bar, competing for conversation time with the lone bartender. As I watch, one of the women, a brunette in a low-cut black maxi dress with a cropped denim jacket over it, walks up and gets instant attention from all three. One of the old men gets up from his chair, moves in next to her, and says something, and laughter rings out from both sides of the bar.

"You old flirt," I hear the woman say, pushing him on the shoulder and turning around with her drink, her cheeks and chest flushed with patches of the same deep shade of pink. No wait for a pint at this hour, especially if you're exposing cleavage.

Even though I'll regret it in the morning when I'm dragging my tired butt to Heathrow, I'm in no hurry to leave, knowing it's the last time I'll be in this place, with this crowd, in what might be weeks or might even be as long as two months. Thomas bows out after buying the round, claiming an early morning, and Eleanor and Ethan follow soon after.

Pamela is more animated than I've ever seen her, and more drunk. She giggles, draping herself over the table in a way that shoves her breasts up practically to her eyeballs and gives those of us remaining a good look at *her* cleavage, which is far more impressive than mine. She reaches out an arm and presses four manicured fingers into Ian's right arm, leaving a neat row of crescent moon imprints when she lifts it away.

"Whatever happened to that Joanna," she drawls. "I liked *her*." Her voice lilts up at the end, and I don't know if it's the inflection of her accent that causes the lilt or if that last sentence was directed somehow at me—because she looks at me as she says it. Her words are slurry with the effects of hours of nonstop drinking. She's had at least two pints to each one of mine.

"Oh, don't bring up Joanna," Miranda says. "That's a dirty word."

"Did she cheat on you or something?" I can't help asking.

Ian laughs, a low, husky sound that's gotten sexier as the night's gone on. "Not unless you count falling in love with my brother as cheating." I realize I've misjudged the laugh. His voice carries a hard edge of sarcasm.

"Whoa." In my beer-muddled state that's about the best reaction I can summon. "And I thought my sister was president of the World's Worst Siblings Club."

Ian laughs again. "If that's the case, then Michael is prime minister of the English chapter." He huffs another laugh. "So there you go. Something else we have in common, apparently." His voice loses its hard edge at the end.

I'm wondering how Pamela can hang out with this group so often and *not* know something as huge as Ian's brother stealing away his ex-girlfriend. Again I find myself examining her role in their group dynamic. She must be doing the same of me because she's glaring at me right now. She reaches out her claws again and digs them into Ian's forearm.

"That's *awful*," she says. "I'm sorry I asked. You know that Brian went out on me, as well." She lets go of Ian's arm and takes a big swig from her footed glass, almost draining it. "And we were *engaged*. That's why I moved back to London, you know."

No, I didn't know. Though she's directed this at Ian, I'm the one to follow up.

"When did you move here?" I ask.

"In April of this year," she says. "When I got me job." She hiccups, and even in my own drunkenness, I think how as the night's gone on, Pamela's accent has begun sounding less like Kate Middleton's and more like Eliza Doolittle's before the "fair" part of "My Fair Lady."

Well, that explains her existence on the periphery of the group. I'm pretty sure *I'm* less of a fifth wheel on this cart than she is, and I just got here. I'd feel sorry for her if her purple-polished nails weren't still pressing into Ian's arm. He subtly shifts out of her reach and inches closer on his barstool to me, causing a warmth to whoosh through my insides.

"What about that bloke who keeps texting *you*," he asks, gesturing with his head toward my phone, which has been blowing up all night with texts from Chase asking when I'm getting in. I never told him when I was coming home, but apparently he ran into my *mother* and actually asked. She was almost giddy to pass that intel off to me last time I talked to her, which was yesterday evening, or yesterday morning for her, when she called to ask for my flight number.

That woman wants me married off so badly it wouldn't matter to her if the groom had horns and carried a pitchfork.

"Is it serious?" he continues, and I shake off all thoughts of my mother with a shudder.

Miranda's the one who answers. "Is this Chase again? I thought you told him to bugger off."

"Only about five hundred times," I say, shooting her a wry look. "A day."

"Maybe don't answer him at all," Ian adds jealously, prompting Pamela to chime in.

"Or maybe she *wants* to string him along." She looks at me with wide, innocent eyes. "Are you playing hard to get?"

"I would have been pretty easy to get before he turned into a colossal ass," I mutter. *Correction. Before he pointed out* my *colossal ass.* I don't say this last part out loud, of course. Instead I add, "Funny how that works, the running back begging after *he's* the one who ended things." The last thing I want to do is share the story of how Chase thinks I'm not a "ten" to the man who's making my insides feel like Jell-O at the moment.

"Stupid git," Ian mutters.

"Just ignore him completely," Miranda agrees. "Now, and once you're home again, too. He doesn't deserve you."

Pamela harrumphs. All three of us look at her, and she hiccups. "Well, I'm off, then. Work tomorrow, you know." She shoots me a sour look. "Don't have too much fun without me."

"I need to go, too." I check my phone screen reluctantly. "My flight leaves in, oh, roughly nine hours from right now." I turn my head to watch Pamela stumble up to the bar to settle her bill and reach for my own bag from its hook under the heavy pedestal table.

"I've got it," Ian says to me with a wink. "And dinner? When you come back?"

I'm not looking at Miranda, who's on my other side, but I can feel the pleased-and-shocked vibe emanating from her tiny body. She leans over me to catch Ian's eye. "Get mine too, will you?" she says to him. "I'll pick yours up the next time."

As he shrugs in acquiescence, she says to me, "Share a car home?"

We all stand to leave. Pamela has already paid her tab and gives a little three-finger wave as she weaves through the dimly lit pub toward the door. The scowl on her face as Ian pulls me into a hug is impossible to miss. Even with my face buried against his shoulder, I hear the thud as Pamela throws her weight against the door and the sharp chirp of the entry bell which malfunctions at the vicious thrust and gives off an angry double ring.

I guess I've figured out where Pamela hoped to fit into this group. I've also just realized that in my short time in the UK, I've made an enemy. But it's hard to be too upset about it when my body is pressed against Ian's, his warmth transferring to me in a long, slow sizzle down my spine. His torso is firm, and I can feel the muscles ripple in his back as I press both hands into him.

"Have a safe trip," he says into my ear. And then, to my surprise, he plants a featherlight kiss at my temple. I resist the urge to reach up and touch the spot, which continues tingling as he walks away to pay the bar tab and even after I've followed Miranda out of the pub, onto the sidewalk, and into one of the several cabs that are trawling the street, waiting for people like us to emerge from the doorways of the multiple pubs and bars that populate the block.

"Ian's a good bloke," Miranda says, squeezing my hand after directing the driver to my B&B. "I knew he'd like you. You're exactly his type. I was hoping you'd feel the same."

"I thought you said to watch out for him?"

She pauses thoughtfully. "Ian's had a bad run of it," she says. "You heard tonight when Pamela asked about Joanna. I can't believe she did that—it was just to rankle you. Otherwise she'd have done better not to have brought her up." Miranda shakes her head. "Anyway, ever since Joanna pulled one over on him, he's been a bit…floundery, I think." She giggles. "I think I've just invented a word. Anyway, he's dated a lot, but he never has found anybody who's stuck for very long. I've been waiting for the right woman to come along for Ian, and I'm just going to say this. I want that right woman to be you."

Heat flashes through my body again, for a different reason this time. How is it possible to find such a good friend in such a short time in a completely foreign country and culture? I smile, but even as I have the thought, my warm, fuzzy feeling is overtaken by a cool wave of disappointment.

"But I'm leaving," I say. "And when I come back, it's short-term. We could never get serious." *And you don't know my history with men.* All the good ones come flirting and leave running, usually after chewing me up and spitting me out. My self-esteem has all the bite marks to prove it.

"Things have a way of working out." Miranda is nodding, and I try to banish the negative thoughts. "I have this strong feeling you're meant to be with him. Or at least while you're here, have a little fun, you know?"

My forehead wrinkles—those two things are far from the same, and the thought brings a new wave of angst. Getting involved with a guy who lives so far away doesn't seem like a good idea, especially when I think I might actually like him.

I mean, really like him. My skin is still tingling where he kissed me.

Miranda interrupts my thoughts. "You have to let me visit you in Memphis someday. I need to meet Priscilla myself, not just know her vicariously through you. And Taylor Swift."

I give her a wry look. "And when I come back, I want to have lunch with Adele. You can make that happen, right?"

She chuckles. "See, we're just like sisters."

At this I can't help but laugh, my tension erased. "Trust me. You're *nothing* like my sisters."

I'm still chuckling when the car slows on the street in front of my bed and breakfast, and after a tight hug from my newest BFF, I heave a sigh and walk up the steps into the lobby vestibule, wishing I didn't have to leave. But then a deep twinge of longing for my other BFFs hits my gut, and suddenly I can't wait to dissect everything that's happened in my weeks here with Jules and Savy.

My first real wave of homesickness hits just as I'm about to fly home, which feels poetic.

This trip has been pretty much perfect.

CHAPTER SEVEN

———

It's Not Me, It's You

When I key into my condo after an exhausting sixteen-hour travel ordeal that included a flight delay out of Heathrow and a subsequent missed connection in Chicago, I lug my gargantuan suitcase over the threshold and park it in my long and narrow foyer, schlepping my backpack off my back and dropping it with an unceremonious thud next to the suitcase. The plastic buckle on one of the straps leaves a black streak on the wall, but I'm too freaking exhausted to care.

A drop of sweat that's beaded on the tip of my nose falls and lands on my sneaker. Memphis in July is even more sweltering than I remembered.

I trudge down the hall and past the kitchen, tossing my keys onto the edge of the granite counter as I pass. When I round the corner into my living room, I stop dead, scream, and clutch my chest.

"Ohmigod, what the *hell* are you *doing* here? You scared me half to death!"

Chase is standing in front of my double French doors, facing me, his six-foot-three-inch frame silhouetted darkly against the late afternoon sun that's slanting through the shaded panes of glass. His arms are crossed tightly over his chest. I'm holding my phone out in front of me like a weapon, punching feverishly at the screen in an attempt to find the 9-1-1 buttons, but my hands are shaking too much for any success.

"I wanted to talk to you," he says, the Grim Reaper come alive. He starts toward me but then looks as if he thinks better of it, instead holding out his hands like he wants me to hand him my phone—not a chance of that—and craning his neck to try to see the screen. "What are you doing? Calling the cops? Stop that. I'm not here to hurt you."

"You could have fooled me—you looked like the freaking angel of death, standing there completely still like that. Or like a serial killer."

"I'm sorry, I'm sorry." He doesn't come closer, and eventually my heart rate slows to a somewhat normal pace, though I keep the numeric pad pulled up on my screen until I feel certain he's not here to kill me. "This was probably a bad idea."

"You *think*?"

Now that the initial shock is past, I'm doing everything I can to not look at him, hiding my shaking hands by straightening the already straight throw pillows on my loveseat. I don't want him to think it's his presence making me nervous rather than his horror movie-esque appearance in my home. I'm starting to feel convinced he doesn't mean me any harm, but still, I can't stop shaking. I move on to scooting the haphazard collection of remotes on the coffee table so their edges line up—have I mentioned I'm OCD?—before adding, "And give me back my damn key. Obviously." How did I overlook that detail before flying off into the English sunrise?

I finally look up at him. Even after all his douchiness, I can't help but feel attracted to the way he towers over me. I've always had a weakness for men who are tall enough that I have to look up at them. Of course, in Chase's case, his height isn't quite proportional with his girth…and you can take that any way you want to.

"I am sorry about breaking in like this, but you haven't been answering my texts."

I straighten up from the coffee table, my eyes narrowing.

"You mean all five hundred of them? Or just the ones that were totally inappropriate given our vitriolic *mutual* breakup? You know, in the dynamic of most relationships, ignoring someone is an unequivocal sign that you want them to *leave you alone*."

Have I also mentioned I use big words when I'm upset? Yes, I know, I have strange quirks. It's what happens when you go through life sticking out like Azrael in a world of Smurfs.

I eye the couch, tempted to sink onto it—I'm too exhausted to fight with him but especially to do it standing up. I want nothing more than a shower and a nap, and he's mucking up my plans.

I almost laugh when I remember how awful I must look. I mean, I've just come off a grueling exercise in aviary endurance, and I'm rumpled, makeup free, and drenched in sweat. But for once I'm happy to look bad. Considering how obsessed Chase is with appearance, maybe it'll jar his memory of why he broke up with me and encourage him to leave me alone…and to leave, period.

"Did you meet somebody over there?" His tone is both accusatory and territorial.

My God, he's infuriating. Who does he think he is to me, Prince Non-Charming come to throw the big girl a bone? Or, more likely, my last chance at avoiding spinsterdom?

I bulge my eyes and stick my chin out toward him as a burst of irritation propels me past him to the staircase. "None of your business?" I phrase it as a question. As in, *"Can you get it through your thick skull, already?"*

I start up the stairs, turn slightly, and add, "Do *not* follow me. And as much as I'd like you to be gone when I come back downstairs, I'm sure you won't be. So figure out exactly what you want from me, word it succinctly after I've showered and started to feel human again, and understand that you are highly, highly unlikely to get it." I step on the heels of my sneakers and bend down to peel them off before taking the last few steps at a faster pace.

"And my key had better be sitting on the kitchen counter when I come back down."

* * *

As soon as I'm in my room, I grab my phone, jotting off a group text to Jules and Savy to let them know about Chase—in case they never hear from me again, I want somebody to have documented proof of who was with me in the moments before my death.

I lock my bedroom door and take my time scrubbing the airplane funk off my body, adrenaline from my anger at Chase overpowering the jet lag and exhaustion, at least for the moment. Afterward I dry my hair, pull it back into a low ponytail, and change into comfy yoga pants and a pink Memphis Grizzlies T-shirt—napwear. Since I'm not dressing to impress, I don't bother with makeup, not even to cover up the deep, puffy circles etched below my eyes.

Before I leave the room to trudge downstairs, I grab my phone to see that Savy and Jules have both texted back. Savy's just says *OMG, keep me posted.*

Jules' is more colorful and reads *WTF??? Kick him in the balls, and tell him to get the (bleep) out!!!*

I'm chuckling when I turn the corner from the staircase into the living room, but the laugh dries up in my throat when I see Chase parked in the center of my white tufted sofa.

He looks uncomfortable, hunched forward with his elbows on his knees, as if he's afraid to touch my things for fear of further unleashing my wrath. It's a smart move on his part.

I sigh.

"OK, start talking. Why are you here?" I punctuate my question by plopping onto one of my two side chairs, modern wingbacks covered in a coral and white graphic print with aqua piping, the only bright spots of color in the room apart from a few accessories. The walls are white, the floors are pale bamboo, the pair of facing sofas is one shade off the walls, and even the rug is pale and neutral—a seagrass mat with an off-white border. It's my oasis from the Memphis heat.

Chase's brow furrows, as if he himself is unsure why he's here. He clears his throat and looks at me. "You said you were going to hear me out. You don't have to be so hostile about it."

"You're right, I did. That was dumb of me." I sigh again. "Talk, then. I'm listening." I curl my legs up underneath me and get comfortable, proving my willingness to hear him. Mainly I just want him to get this out of his system and go away so I can go back upstairs and sleep off my travel hangover.

He shuffles his feet and straightens his lanky torso out of its slouch. He clears his throat. "You want some water or something? You must be hungry or thirsty or…tired." His voice trails off. Obviously my threats about getting to the point didn't hit home.

"Chase. You are in my house. You're committing a felony by being here, by the way. If I want water, I'll get it. I want nothing more than to sleep right now, but you're preventing that from happening. So quit acting like the congenial live-in boyfriend and tell me what you want from me. And just so we're clear on the front end, I am not getting back together with you. I am not going to become your friend with benefits. I am not going to answer or even read your stalker-ish texts, and I'm not going to answer questions about who I might or might not have met because that's none of your business." As I've talked my face has grown hotter and hotter. If this were a cartoon, I'd be that character with a fire engine red face and steam coming out my ears. I try not to allow my anger to spill over into my tear ducts as I add, "And I'm sure as hell not going to change my body to suit your vision of perfection."

Chase's face etches into a deeper frown. He looks worn down. "That's what I wanted to talk to you about," he mumbles. "I want to apologize for that 'perfect ten' comment. It was bad of me to say that. Your body is fine the way it is."

Fine. Hmmphh. I glare at him, not gracing that load of crap with a response.

"No, really, I mean it," he says. "I miss it so much. I mean, I miss you. So much."

"You mean you haven't found anybody else to dump on since you dumped me, and you're tired of your most meaningful relationship being with your hand. And you were hoping I might be so grateful, as a big girl, for your gracious acceptance of my less-than-ideal body that I'd pull you into my bed for passionate make-up sex that I'd later realize was nothing more than a booty call. I've dealt with guys like you enough in my life, Chase. I'm not as naïve or desperate as you think I am."

His face finally twists into some form of animation, though the expression is hard to read. He looks…tortured. "No, that's not what I mean. What I'm trying to say is that…you're beautiful. You're beautiful, and your body is beautiful, and…I love you. I'm in love with you, and I miss you, and breaking up with you was the dumbest thing I've ever done."

For once, I'm speechless.

What they say about absence making the heart grow fonder really must be true. If I'd known leaving the country on an extended trip would have this effect on the male psyche, maybe I'd be married with a brood like Vivienne's by now. I give a little shudder at the thought—where did *that* come from?—and then realize Chase is staring dolefully at me.

The pressure in my head ebbs by slow degrees as I realize he does seem to mean what he's saying, or at least he thinks he does. This is…unexpected, to say the least. So I'm now…what? Supposed to find soothing words to let him down easy after the callous way he broke things off with me? I puff out my cheeks and plop my chin in my hands, letting out the air in a long, slow stream as I search for the right response.

"That's nice. It really is. I appreciate your apology, and I do accept it. But as for love…I'm not there, Chase. I might have loved you, one day. But I don't. Love you, that is. And I can't be with you again. After what you said to me, I'd never be able to feel comfortable in my own skin with you. I'd feel like you were constantly judging me, *weighing* me. And I would definitely never, ever get along with your mother."

This last line is carefully calculated on my part. For a mama's boy like him, it has to be a deal breaker.

But next thing I know, he's off the sofa and practically prostrating himself at my feet. "Please, Quinn. Please give me another chance. I've been miserable since we broke up. I've barely eaten anything or slept while you've been out of town. And the thought that you were over there, too far away for me to see you, possibly meeting somebody else…" His voice trails off with a choked sob. I'm frozen in place, torn between a feminine urge to comfort and a stronger urge to climb over the back of my chair to get away from him.

He looks up at me, eyes watery and filled with hope. He suddenly looks about ten years old, like a little boy who desperately wants someone to listen to his needs and take care of him. For the record, this quality is not attractive to me. I hope his mother will be very happy to have him living in her basement for the next twenty-five years.

"Chase." My voice is soft and strained with the exhaustion of twenty-two hours of near continuous wakefulness—I don't sleep well on planes—and I see the hope start to drain from his eyes at my tone. "We're not good together. This isn't meant to be." I gesture between the two of us. "I don't mean to be callous, and I think you have plenty of good qualities, but I need to be clear with you right now. I don't love you and don't want to get back together with you. I don't want to be with anybody right now. I just want to focus on my job and focus on me."

This isn't entirely true, and I wonder if he can tell—I've never been a very good liar. Throughout this conversation, Ian's face has drifted in and out of my thoughts, and right now it's front and center. The only relationship I want to focus on—the only man I'm aching to get back to—is Ian. But that truly is none of Chase's business.

He searches my face for a long moment and then slumps backward, away from my chair. I wait him out, and after an agonizingly slow minute, he finally says, "I guess this is it, then?"

I nod slowly. "This is it."

"There's nothing else I can say to show you how sorry I am?"

I tighten my lips into a line, shaking my head. I stop myself from saying, *"The damage is done."* He doesn't look like he needs further admonishment for being such an idiot.

"One last kiss, just to say good-bye?" He pauses, leaning toward me as he maneuvers to stand. He's breathing a little harder, his eyes holding mine and his pupils dilated. I can see that what's on his mind now is breakup sex. Unfortunately for him, the breakup happened weeks ago, and I haven't felt the slightest bit of regret that we didn't get one final, bittersweet roll in the hay.

I shake my head again, holding my breath until he finally looks away and then stands up and starts trudging toward the door. I stand, too, and crane my neck to give a once-over to the two-tiered island breakfast bar that separates the living room and kitchen. The countertop is completely clear.

"Um, Chase?"

He quickly turns. "Yeah?" There's that hope again.

I walk toward him, holding out my hand. "My key?"

"Oh, yeah." He digs his keys out of his right hip pocket and fumbles to get my house key off the ring, dropping the key ring once in the process. When he hands me the silver key, I hold my hand several inches below his, careful not to touch him. I grip the key tightly when it drops into my hand.

"Thanks."

Just before I close my front door behind him, he looks back at me and says, "Quinn?"

"Yes?"

"I really do think you're beautiful."

I close my eyes. "Thanks, Chase. Good-bye."

Before I even make it upstairs to my room, I've received a text from Menzi asking if I'm back yet and then another one from my client Sophie Perins asking the same thing. Apparently their tolerance of one another has reached the tipping point. I sigh and brace myself for a couple of long phone conversations, doubting I'll remember any of it later. I'm so tired I might already be sleepwalking.

*   *   *

The ensuing week is a blur of living rooms and conference rooms and color samples and project schedules. Menzi seems to have matured by a decade in the weeks I've been out, though mainly in the sense that cynicism has replaced her youthful idealism.

When you're an aspiring designer—a student or an intern—the profession looks impossibly glamorous. Glossy magazine pages, big TV reveals, gratifying "before & after" photos. In reality, intcrior dcsign is ten percent glamour, ninety percent hard work. Within that ninety percent, the breakdown is more complicated. The day-to-day work of a designer involves handling difficult personalities, making hard sales pitches, organizing myriad details, managing subcontractors, and performing manual labor—the hard parts far outweigh the fun, creative parts of the job. I learned all this years ago and have come to terms with it, and the fact is, that ten percent of awesomeness makes it all worthwhile to me. There's nothing like seeing a project you've worked like a dog to complete finally come to fruition…and seeing the light in your clients' eyes.

I'm not sure Menzi's going to get to that point of enlightenment, especially since in the seven days since my flight landed in Memphis, she's done nothing but complain about her (my) projects and talk animatedly about her boyfriend's best friend's upcoming wedding…and what it means for her own future prospects.

"I think Clayton's going to propose soon. Don't you think so? I mean, with Tucker getting married, that means all the rest of his friends are married now, or at least engaged. His SAE little brother is even having a baby. Can you imagine it? His *little* brother! Don't you think it's about time? Don't you think *he* realizes that? I mean, we've been together for two *and a half* years. I just know he's been ring shopping. Don't you think so?"

She looks up at me from the shelf of fabric memos she's making a mess of—pulling out samples with abandon from the middle of the stacks that she glances at just long enough to complain about ("Ohmigosh, this one's hideous, don't you think?") and then tossing them onto the worktable for our design librarian, Brandt, to have to reshelve later.

She pauses expectantly, and I give a noncommittal nod. Satisfied, she continues rummaging, ostensibly searching for the subtle stripe I've set her on for the Mendelssohns' guest room draperies, another client of mine who's in the midst of a whole-house renovation. I drew up the interior plans a few months ago, long before my trip, and stayed in contact with the architect and contractor while I was in England. In the meantime I strung along Betsie, the homeowner, until I got back because Menzi seemed to have her hands full enough with Sophie Perins, and every designer at our firm is slammed this summer. Now that I'm back, I'm extra-double-super slammed but can't keep putting Betsie off, and as a result I've given Menzi a new slew of tasks.

She turns to me again, a thoughtful grimace carving a sideways equal sign between her immaculately waxed brows. "Do you think you'll keep working after you get married?"

OMG, shut up and work. A visual of Chase on his knees, begging me to take him back, comes unbidden to my mind. My mother would be appalled to learn that I'd turned him down. As a matter of fact, Menzi reminds me of my mother, I suddenly realize. Now I'm the one frowning. I shake off the thought, and Menzi misunderstands the gesture.

"No? You won't keep working?"

My eyes widen. "No. I mean, no, that's not what I meant. Yes, I'll keep working after I get married. I haven't worked this hard to throw it all away in five years. I want to start my own firm one day."

I'm mulling over the fact that I've never voiced this plan out loud before when Menzi breaks into my thoughts. "*Five years?* You think it will be another *five years* before you get married? Aren't you, like, thirty?"

I can't help but laugh. "You sound like my mother." *Just like my mother. In fact, you could probably be besties.* "I'm thirty-two. That's young in today's world. And I have no desire to get married anytime soon."

"Wow, that's so…progressive of you." She says it like it's a dirty word.

I chuckle again, glad it's her and not me whose entire life's ambition hinges on whether or not Clayton What's-His-Name is friendless and emasculated enough yet to buy me a ring.

* * *

Get your ass to Local, I text.

I've been home two days, and I've yet to see Jules. Savy came over the night I got back, in the two-hour interval between my nap and my conking out again for what turned out to be a restless first night back in my own bed. But I was too groggy and jet-lagged to really talk, and besides, I need both my girls at once. I've been saving the best stories for when we're all together.

Jules texts me right back. *On way.*

Well, that's something, anyway. It means she's maybe sending one last email or three before shutting down her computer, in the meantime reapplying lipstick and probably getting distracted by something on her phone. She'll be here in, oh, forty-five minutes. And it's less than a ten-minute drive. But that's Jules—God love her, and I do.

Savy takes a long pull from the skinny straw in her cocktail, which is meant for stirring, not sipping. I watch her do it and then absently try it myself. We're both drinking Midori sours, and I suck, swallow, and then pucker my lips—all the "sour" is concentrated in the bottom of the glass.

"I think Jules and Luca are having problems," she says, apropos of nothing. She takes another long pull from the straw, and I wonder how she's keeping a straight face.

"No way," I drawl, stirring up my drink before giving it another try. It's a little better this time, more melony and sweet but still too concentrated. "They're an institution. If they ever break up, it's going to seismically alter my world view."

Jules met Luca the week before she started college, at freshman orientation. I've heard the story no fewer than a dozen times, usually from Luca after a few drinks. Sober, Luca is gregarious and warm, and drunk, he's as loquacious as ten color commentators vying for air time. He's exactly Jules' height, five eleven, with curly black hair, a face that makes him look like he's smiling even when he's not, and the type of squishy round physique that's attractive on Italian chefs and other people's boyfriends. His voice resonates, and his laugh is loud. He's the only man I can possibly imagine who wouldn't disappear in Jules' wake. He's the Marshall to her Lily.

They first laid eyes on each other outside the student union. Jules was in the middle of an impassioned speech about why she wasn't doing sorority rush ("I refuse to buy a bunch of fake girlfriends") and Luca, already recruited as an Sigma Nu pledge, walked straight up and pulled one of her two braided pigtails on a dare. Jules stayed true to her word and never joined a sorority, but she attended every single Sigma Nu function for four years in a row.

They got engaged the day Luca graduated, one semester after Jules' graduation and roughly seven and a half years ago.

To this day he's the only man Jules has ever slept with. And even though they've put off setting a wedding date longer than fifty percent of marriages last to begin with, until recently none of us had ever imagined they wouldn't one day go through with it. Luca's a medical resident. Jules is working on getting her architecture license. They've been busy.

"No, seriously. I think something's off with them," Savy says, breaking in to my thoughts. "Jules hasn't said anything about it, but she's been really distracted lately, and when I bring up Luca's name she does this weird thing where she looks off to the side, like she's looking for the closest exit."

"She hasn't said a word to me," I say, shrugging and raising one eyebrow, as if that settles it.

"Well, you've been out of the country. And besides, she's being evasive and weird. There's definitely something she isn't telling us."

"OK, so what makes you think it has to do with Luca? Maybe Herbert's been texting her more self-portraits."

"Gross." Now she makes a face—the sour liqueur didn't do it, but the idea of Herbert the Pervert sexually harassing our friend does the trick. "She would've told me if that had happened. Besides, she's got enough on him already. If he keeps trying to shove his tongue down her throat, he's just begging for a lawsuit."

"Unfortunately he knows he's untouchable. No pun intended." I pause, wrinkling my nose at the visual that pops into my head. "You know how the good ol' boys club works around here, especially at a male-owned, privately run firm. They back their own kind. If Jules said 'sexual harassment,' every one of those partners would turn on her in a hot minute."

Savy's lips turn down at the corners. She knows I'm right. In the South the glass isn't on the ceiling—it forms a wall around every person who wears a bra and doesn't have a seat saved in the golf cart. And apparently that's written in the Bible, though I've yet to actually find the verse.

"I still think it's Luca," Savy says. "Do you think he might have cheated on her?"

I snort. "Luca? He works like eighty hours a week. When would he have time to cheat? And besides, what idiot would ever cheat on Jules? That sounds more like something that would happen to me."

"Well, no, because you've never stayed in a relationship long enough for the guy to cheat," Savy says.

My mouth falls open. "Cheap shot! And that's not even true. I was with Steve for over three years. And he *did* cheat on me. Multiple times."

"Oh, yeah. That was in high school though, so it doesn't really count." She frowns but doesn't apologize, leaving me to fume over her words. I know Savy would never intentionally hurt my feelings, but that doesn't make what she said any less callous. It leaves me wondering what's up with *her* rather than with Jules. Savy is usually sensitive to a fault, especially when it comes to other people. I feel like I've missed an awful lot in my weeks overseas.

"Maybe Jules is cheating on *him*," Savy adds.

I ponder that for three seconds, forgetting my spike of irritation. "Nope," I say decisively. "Not her style. And besides, there's no way she'd leave something that big unsaid, even from thousands of miles away. I mean, I told you and Jules every significant detail of what happened on my trip even though we barely had time to talk." I pause, rethinking that statement, and add, "Except for the *very* significant details of my last night there, which I've been saving up for when you and me and Jules were all together."

The little V between Savy's eyebrows disappears and her eyes light up. "You've been holding out on me? That's not fair! I've seen you two times since your trip already. Does it have something to do with Ryland Pemberton?"

"Mr. Pemberton?" I giggle that the formal name is what comes out of me—I've been around Jane too long. But I'm wondering why Savy would jump to that conclusion instead of the obvious one. "No, Ian. Why would you think that Mr. Pemberton, I mean, *Ryland*, would have anything to do with anything?"

"I just think he sounds intriguing, that's all. Like a modern-day Mr. Darcy."

"More like Mr. Rochester," I say, remembering his perma-scowl and general scary disposition. "Although looks-wise, he's more of a modern-day Mr. Jude Law," I grudgingly allow. "But no, I barely even talked to that guy."

This is true, although recalling the intense way I caught him staring at me when he thought I wasn't looking sends a thrill from the base of my spine all the way up to my neck. I suppress it and shake my head, affixing Ian's bright and adorable image in my mind in place of dark and brooding Ryland Pemberton.

"Ian's the one I've been holding out on you about, but only because this news is so huge I don't want to have to tell it twice. Oh, thank God." I scoot back a couple inches in my chair as I spot Jules making her way to our table. As she approaches I jump up to give her a hug. In a louder, mock-scolding voice I add, "It's about damn time."

The cloud of Chanel Chance that engulfs us makes me feel like I'm finally, truly home. It's Jules' signature scent, and this is just one more thing I love about her—she's the only woman my age I know who wears perfume.

"Sorry, sorry." She says this in a way that makes it clear how very non-sorry she is, but we're used to it. And actually, she's less late than I thought she'd be.

She pulls back her chair, plops down, scoots up to the table with all her usual flamboyance, and then grins at me. "You international traveler, you. Tell us everything. And give me your phone. I want to see pictures." She reaches for my pink-encased iPhone that's resting on the table beside my silverware. "Especially of this Ryland guy."

I give Savy a shocked look. "Why are you two both obsessed with Ryland Pemberton? Did I talk him up that much?"

"Yes." Leave it to Jules to cut to the chase. "And he sounds like a hot piece of British arse."

"*When* did I talk him up?" My forehead furrows as I try to remember the texts I sent Jules and Savy the night I'd first met him. I do remember initially drooling over how beautiful he was—but that was before he brushed me aside like a broken china teacup. No, more like the housemaid who'd come into the room to sweep up the china shards. I'd gotten the distinct impression when I was around Ryland Pemberton that he regarded me as nothing more than the help.

"What did I say?"

"It wasn't really what you said, more what you didn't say," Jules says, puzzling me even more. "You talked about how beautiful he was and how perfect—"

"I remember you said you'd never seen anybody as gorgeous as him in person," Savy helpfully interjects.

"And then, nothing," Jules adds with a dramatic flourish. "You gave him this giant buildup and then moved on." She shrugs. "And so of course, we then had to do our due diligence. When you didn't answer Savy's question, we figured you were keeping it secret until you got home, and we've been dying for you to get back and tell us what happened."

I am, as the British say, gobsmacked. Which question or ludicrous point to address first? I start with, "What do you mean, due diligence?"

"Well, we had to Google him, of course. See pictures of this perfect human specimen for ourselves. And you're right—he's yummy. And such an illustrious history! So what happened?"

Her eyes are wide and overly bright, and for a second I wonder if Savy might not be right and if Jules might be using this weird assumption as a distraction technique to keep the focus off of her and whatever big secret she might be hiding. I cock my head at her, unwilling to let her distract me so easily.

"What do you mean, 'Savy's question'?"

Of course I'm dying to know what she means by "illustrious history"—and, by the way, why didn't *I* think to Google Ryland Pemberton? Maybe because I was so turned off by him? Or maybe because if there was something so "illustrious" about him, I figured Jane would have told me? Anyway.

"I don't remember Savy asking any questions about Mr. Pemberton," I add.

"There she goes with that 'Mr. Pemberton' thing again. Is that some kinky game you two play?" Savy winks at Jules.

"Ohmigosh, you guys! What the hell are you going on about? Nothing happened between me and Ryland Pemberton. I barely even talked to the man." Again, my thoughts flicker to the odd, sort of intense way I'd caught him staring at me when he'd thought I wasn't looking, and a flutter catches in my throat. Savy and Jules seem to take this as confirmation.

They look at each other. "Mmm-hmm," Jules says. "We believe you." The words are dipped in sarcasm.

"It's *Ian* you should be asking me about right now. He's the yummy one! He's the one who kissed me and asked me out the night before I left. He's the one I had to force myself not to invite up to my hotel room knowing I'd be leaving the next morning. He's the one I'm dying for you to meet and dying to get back to England to see again."

Savy frowns. "You'd better not be thinking about moving there."

Jules talks over her, adding, "Ian? Is that the guy who's friends with what's-her-name? Miranda? Isn't he, like, her ex-boyfriend or something? I kinda thought he was off limits."

"No, not her ex-boyfriend. Miranda told her that Ian was a player," Savy says, as if I'm not sitting right here.

My bubble thoroughly and disappointedly burst, I pick up my phone and unlock the screen, sliding my finger to the photo app and pulling up the scroll of images. I find a group of shots I snapped in my first week there, while I was out sightseeing, before pushing it across the table to Jules.

"Here, look at the damn houses of Parliament," I sigh, sulking. "There's a picture of Miranda and Eleanor and Ethan and Ian on there somewhere, but I guess you don't care about that one." I'm being pouty, but I don't care. They can kiss it.

"Funny you'd pick those pictures to start with," Jules says with an amused smirk. "Since that's Ryland Pemberton's stomping ground."

I look up at her with a start. I'd been assuming Ryland held some nebulous banking or bond trading or corporate executive type job. He'd had that "I'm someone important and expensive" look about him. I'd imagined him driving an impossibly pretentious car—silver or black because red was too ostentatious and therefore below him. But government? I can't see him as a harried parliamentary aide or even as a governmental higher-up. It's too servile, too altruistic for someone like him. I don't say any of this to Jules and Savy, though. "What, does he sweep the steps or something?" I laugh, annoyed that they're still fixated on Ryland when all I want to talk about is Ian.

"No, you goober," Jules says. She shoots Savy a look that's part astonished, part perplexed. "Do you really not know anything about him?"

I shrug. "Nor do I care. He's kind of a jerk, y'all."

"Well, good," Savy says, though she's wearing an expression of marked disappointment. "I don't want some English billionaire to sweep you off your feet and cause you to move away from us. Even if he does help run the country."

Billionaire? Run the country? I mean, Jane is reserved and also the picture of discretion, but would she really have kept these kinds of things from me? "I think you have the wrong guy," I say slowly. "There must be another Ryland Pemberton. There's no way this man is, like, part of the royal family or something."

"Not part of the royal family," Jules says. "Just a member of the House of Lords. And chairman of the advisory committee of one of the largest multinational corporations in the UK. There are dozens of stories about him online, mainly because he's a prominent descendant of generations of British aristocracy, and yet he actually *works*. He built his company from scratch. He was engaged once, but he never married. And he's, like, Britain's biggest catch." She giggles. "At least, besides Prince Harry. Although, I guess he's taken now. So there you go." As she talks I notice she's minimized my photos and is tapping furiously at the screen of my phone. About fifteen seconds later she shoves it in front of my face. "Here, is this the Ryland Pemberton you met?"

My brain still reeling over the words "billionaire" and "House of Lords," I gasp. Nodding, I gaze mutely at the jagged checkerboard of images that fill my phone's screen. All of them of Ryland. *The* Ryland. The Ryland Pemberton I'd met on multiple occasions, with no mistake, in the back rooms of Jane and Adam's modest Islington home. The Ryland Pemberton whose gaze had penetrated to my very core before his disdain quickly followed, putting out the slightest spark of interest I might otherwise have felt.

"That's impossible," I say, my voice breathless to my own ears. "He lives in a townhouse. A nice townhouse, yes, but an upper-middle class brownstone-type townhouse in a nice but perfectly plain neighborhood in Northern London."

Of course, Jane did say he was rarely at home. And I'd had the thought myself, while studying Ryland in the dim light of Jane and Adam's kitchen, that he probably had some large country estate that made his ownership of the townhouse make more sense. It also made sense that he'd have staff who lived in this second home and kept it up for him. And, now that I'm thinking about it, it might make sense that, if he'd inherited a castoff relative, he might put the child up there, in a nondescript second (or third or fourth) home in an area near other children and good schools and trustworthy neighbors to help look after him. To keep Elliott—or himself and his situation, more likely—out of the limelight. My mind is still spinning at a hundred miles per hour, making up stuff that I can't possibly know is true or even close to true.

Jules laughs her vivacious laugh, jolting me out of these thoughts. "Yes, but he also lives in a three-hundred-sixty-room castle on an eight-thousand-acre estate that puts Downton Abbey to shame. And he's a member of the *peerage*." She says this word with a drawn-out, pretentious lilt. "I'm surprised you're calling him 'Mister.' Isn't 'Lord Pemberton' or something like that more accurate?"

I'm still in denial. Ryland Pemberton a member of the peerage? Ryland Pemberton a *lord*? Ryland Pemberton, Jane's neighbor, whom she'd spoken with at mundane neighborhood meetings and who'd walked through the back gate of her garden with casual, neighborly confidence, the proprietor of an eight-thousand-acre estate? But then again, I *had* already guessed at a few of these things without knowing more than the sparest facts about him.

Man, how I wish I'd mentioned him to Miranda and Eleanor! I'd thought about it, but it hadn't seemed right to pass on gossip I'd gleaned from working in a client's private home, especially when Jane herself was so reticent about "Mr. Pemberton." But now that I think about it, knowing what I now apparently know, it's a good thing I didn't. My pub crew would have flipped out.

I can only imagine how much more scathingly Ryland—scratch that, *Lord Pemberton*—would look at me if I'd inadvertently shared his private address in a public pub.

I pick my chin up from the table and roll my eyes at my two best friends in the whole world, who've proven themselves to be totally, lovably absurd. "I'm flattered that you two thought I was holding out on you and that I had Britain's most eligible bachelor falling at my feet. Unfortunately I'm not going to be entertaining you on the lawns of my three-hundred-room estate as the lady of the manor anytime soon."

"Three-hundred-and-*sixty*-room estate," Jules corrects with her chin aloft.

I smirk at her, and then a giggle explodes from my chest. "And here I was so excited to tell you that a cute boy asked me out. I guess that's a little anticlimactic now, huh? Like getting a fifty-dollar gift card when you thought you'd won the lottery?" I'm shaking, practically falling out of my chair I'm laughing so hard.

Savy joins in, and then Jules loses her smug façade and starts giggling, too. "I told her you would have told me already if something had happened with Ryland," Savy says, her cheeks three shades pinker from laughter. "Your face is so easy to read. I knew you were keeping something from me the other night, but you couldn't have kept something that huge a secret."

I shake my head, tears burning at the corners of my eyes. I snatch the phone back out of Jules' hands, scrolling through photos until I find the one I took of my whole group at the pub. At the time I was trying not make it obvious that my main goal was to catch Ian on camera for this specific reason—to show him off to my friends.

"Here. He might not be a member of the *peerage*"—I adopt Jules' haughty lilt for the last word—"but he's pretty freaking cute." I pass the phone across the table, the screen facing my two best friends, holding my breath while I await their judgment. Ian's not the main subject of the photo, but he shows up clear enough at the forefront of the shot, squeezed in beside

Pamela with a gap on his other side, where I'd been standing. And he does look hot in it.

"Is he that guy on the back right?" Savy asks.

Jules, almost talking over her, says, "Oh my God. Is that a vintage Styx T-shirt? That looks straight-up from the '80s. And leather pants? I *so* approve."

"Guys," I whine. "You are totally missing the point of this." I nod toward Savy, addressing her first. "No, he's the tall guy on the front right, the most prominent person in the picture. That guy in the back is Eleanor's fiancé, Sim…um, Ethan."

Next I nod toward Jules. "And yes, Miranda's style is badass. You two would love each other." I furrow my brow. "Or hate each other. It's honestly hard to say."

My arm is starting to ache, so I drop my hand and place the phone on the tabletop between them. They both bend their heads over it as they continue to study the shot. Neither says anything, and I can't take it anymore.

"Well? What do you think of Ian? Totally cute, right?" I crane my neck to get a peek of his upside-down hotness. Looking at him, even from this angle, sends a little flutter up from the center of my stomach.

"That bleach blonde sure is draping herself all over him," Jules says.

"He's good-looking," Savy adds. "He looks like just your type." Her voice is colored with an odd tint of restraint.

"What? Why do you say that like it's a bad thing?"

Savy opens her mouth and closes it again. Jules, studying the photo anew, pipes in. "He's *too* good-looking," she pronounces. "Didn't you say that Miranda called him a player? He *looks* like a player."

"Ohmigosh, y'all. He's totally nice. Very down to earth when you get to talking to him. And Miranda was kidding when she called him a player. She's a hundred percent behind us getting together. *She* was excited when I told her Ian asked me out." I narrow my eyes, accusing them with my glare.

My friends are silent for a split second, and then Savy shrugs. "If you like him, I like him," she finally says.

"If he plays you, I'll come over there and string him up by the balls myself," adds Jules, and I shake my head and roll my eyes skyward.

"I've missed you guys so much," I say in a dry tone.

"You know you have, sweetheart," Jules says. "You know that jolly old England would have been ten times more jolly with us there with you." She's pensive for a couple seconds, her mouth turning down slightly at the corners. "Hell, maybe I'll book a ticket and go with you when you go back. I could use a break from here."

Savy gives me a pointed look, Jules' comment reminding both of us of what Savy told me before Jules arrived. I decide to take a page from Jules' own playbook and be direct.

"Why? Is something going on with you and Luca?"

For a couple seconds Jules looks as if she's just swallowed a bite of something too hot. I worry for a second, wondering if that was *too* direct. "Or at work?"

Her eyes widen, and she sits straighter in her chair. "Why would you think something's wrong with me and Luca?" She says it to me, but she's looking at Savy.

I shrug. "I don't know, what you just said? I mean, it doesn't have to be Luca. Did Herbert come on to you again? Or send you another pervy text?"

"Nothing's wrong," she says, picking up her water glass and taking a dainty sip. She looks up and glances around. "Is the waiter ever going to come? What's a girl got to do to get a drink up in here?"

I exchange a glance with Savy. Clearly she's right, and something is wrong, but it's also clear that Jules isn't ready to talk about it, whatever it is.

Funny enough, I think our server overhears because she comes hustling straight over, looking all red-faced and harried. I glance around and realize this place is full as the Mississippi River past flood stage—like it's the final happy hour before the rapture, and we're the only three who aren't aware the world is coming to an end. Our discussion's been so engrossing I haven't noticed until now how very loud it is in here.

We all order something, Jules a Velvet Elvis, Savy another sour, and me a Ghost River stout. Both women look at me like I've sprouted a third eyebrow. What can I say? Maybe it's trip nostalgia, or maybe stout beer is finally growing on me. Savy adds a duck quesadilla app for the three of us to share. Probably a good idea for me, moving so suddenly to beer, not to pour it over an empty stomach.

Jules asks me to describe in detail what happened with Chase after I got back, and we spend the better part of an hour analyzing every detail of my real-life *Psycho* encounter. Thankfully I haven't heard from him since he left my condo.

As we leave the restaurant, I realize Jules barely touched the duck appetizer or the smoked gouda fritters we ordered next. Even her drink looks like she barely took three sips from the sweating glass. This isn't like Jules—she must really be bothered by whatever it is she's keeping from us. I put my arm around her as we walk toward the door, and she slides hers around my waist and squeezes me around the middle. She'll tell me eventually. In the meantime I'm so glad to be home with my girls.

CHAPTER EIGHT

———

Flirtations

I don't get another chance to see Jules or Savy for the entire next week because I'm so slammed with work.

Sophie and Denny Perins' custom Edelman leather sofa—lipstick pink, to pull out the signature color in a huge painting that's in the same room—finally shipped to our warehouse. It's the final piece of the puzzle, so I spend all day Monday and most of Tuesday overseeing the project installation.

There's only one major disaster, a mirror that was broken during install, which our firm has to eat the cost of and repair. That wouldn't be a huge deal except it was a bespoke cast resin piece made to complement a sculpture in the foyer, and it wasn't the glass that the installer broke, which would have been simple to fix—it was the resin frame itself. Repairing it will require a specialist and cost a fortune. Unfortunately I wasn't in the room when it happened. Menzi was directing the installer, and the rest of the day she was beside herself, offering to pay for the repair herself and muttering about how she's "cursed."

She definitely isn't cursed. If she were, Sophie would have walked up during the debacle and reamed Menzi out. The two of them are polarized magnetic forces, and I wish I'd known this before giving Menzi the project.

At any rate, I explained what happened to Sophie, who was totally cool about it. And the house looks spectacular, if I do say so myself. Every downstairs wall is white except one jutted wall behind the living room fireplace, which is deep charcoal—firebox, mantel, surround, and all. That room has jolts of vivid jade green and shiny brass accents, including a show-stopping constellation light fixture that's the real deal, not the IKEA knockoff. I found it at Ochre, a tiny SoHo showroom that produces some of my favorite lighting offered by anybody, anywhere.

That room, along with the rest of the house, is designed to show off my clients' art. The lipstick pink sofa went into a family room that sports a giant canvas where most people would hang a flat screen TV. Sophie and Denny own one television, and it's in the upstairs game room. I know they want kids, and I tried to convince Sophie to plan ahead when it came to fabric and color selections, but she insisted that her children would learn how to exist among nice things.

I realize I don't know much about kids, but I do have nieces and nephews I love to pieces, and I can't see Elijah or Aisling lasting in that house for fifteen minutes without breaking something. But at least I convinced Sophie to go with leather on the sofa. One way or another, one of us will eat our words. Either Sophie and Denny will have to change their lifestyle and elements of their design style (which means another fun project for me, a definite upside to Sophie being right), or I'll be a firsthand witness to the most worldly and well-behaved toddlers in the Memphis metro region.

Anyway, apart from the mirror, the Perins project is officially off my plate. That's more than I can say for the other *eighteen* projects that have heaped onto my pile, everything from paint consults to overhauls. Menzi did less designing and scheduling and more putting off and making excuses while I was away. I'm going to have to figure out a diplomatic way to tell Jen that next time I leave for Jane and Adam's house, I'll only entrust my clients to her or Amanda, not to our junior designers. Although maybe Jordan, our other design assistant, will be available next time—the last time I left, she was in the final days of cramming for the NCIDQ exam, the national qualifying test to become registered as a professional designer. There was no way she could handle any of my workload with an eight-hour test looming ahead of her. She hasn't heard yet if she passed, but she's an ace. I'm sure she nailed it.

Menzi, on the other hand, probably won't get around to taking the NCIDQ, since she seems more interested in earning her "Mrs." certificate than any professional designation. Which is fine for her—I don't mean to judge someone else's choices. She just won't have the honor of serving as my mentee much longer. I need serious help with this workload, and it's become clear that Menzi is only serious about man trapping and scaling the social ladder.

Thanks in part to her lack of legitimate assistance, I spent Tuesday through Friday crisscrossing the county and hopping from project to project. Of my eighteen current clients, eleven needed face time, and one required me to drive two and a half hours to a lake house on the Tennessee-Mississippi border. If I thought jet lag was tiring, it doesn't hold a candle to a week chock-full of sixteen-hour workdays.

And now it's my second Sunday night at home, and I can't put off seeing my family any longer. If I try, Mother might come to my condo herself—something she never does—and grab me by the top of the arm and march me, time out-style, to my spot at the dining table. Last Sunday I played the jet lag card. This week, nothing doing.

I don't want to miss tonight anyway because my sister Caroline is in town from New York. She's here for Viv's baby shower, which Mother's best friend planned for Tuesday at ten a.m. Leave it to Mother and her friends to plan an event that doesn't account for attendees who might have full-time jobs. Granted, I'm one of only three women invited who do. Me, Caroline, and Evangeline, Vivienne's grad school roommate, who works in DC as a corporate consultant and is also flying in for the event. So actually, I'm the only person who has to fit a "tea to honor Vivienne and Baby" (the invitations were printed and embossed) into my workday.

Just as I'm heading out the door, after I've shut off the kitchen light and grabbed my keys and phone from the island countertop, my phone chimes with a text. I flip my hand over so I can see the screen and almost drop my phone.

It's from Ian.

I'd put his number in my phone after he'd asked me out. I've been texting intermittently with Miranda, but I haven't heard from Ian once since I've been back, fully aware that it's a bad sign. I also haven't texted *him*, but that's on purpose. I've read

He's Just Not That Into You. Despite my lack of luck in the love arena, I know how this game works. I know better than to chase the guy around or smother him with attention or drunk text him when I'm feeling insecure. If he wants me, he'll text me. If he doesn't, I'll cry for a couple days and force myself to move on.

At least, these are the things I've been telling myself. But now that he's texted, it's all I can do to keep from kicking my shoes off and dancing a jig in my entry hall. I caught a glimpse of the text when it popped up onscreen, but I unlock my phone and open it to get the full effect: *Been thinking about you a lot. Can't stop, in fact. When will you come back?*

"Squeeeee!"

Ohmigosh, I'm pretty sure I haven't "squeeeeed" since my college days, but this is a definite squeeing occasion. My family can wait. I set my bag down in the hallway and walk back into the kitchen, flipping on the light and perching on one of my metal barstools to answer him.

It takes me four tries to come up with something that seems breezy enough…interested but not too eager.

~~*Been thinking about you too. A LOT.*~~ (Maybe the all caps is too much…)

~~*I'm counting the days till my return.*~~ (OMG. Way cheesy. Who am I, Henry James?)

~~*What exactly have you been thinking?*~~ (Too suggestive. I mean, I'm all for sexting, but we should probably establish a texting relationship first…)

I've been thinking about you too. Don't know date yet, but prob 2-3 weeks.

I hold my breath and click *Send*.

At this point I'm going to be walking into the dining room after everybody's already seated, but I don't care. I stay right where I am, barely able to breathe. Luckily he doesn't make me wait.

That's an eternity.

Well, that's sweet. I'm feeling all warm and tingly inside when my phone buzzes again.

Been thinking about where to go on first date. You a movie-and-dinner kind of girl? Or candlelight and nighttime stroll?

OK, I think I'm swooning.

I think for a split second and type back, *Yes, please.* I didn't miss that he said *first* date, by the way. I've always preferred optimists.

LOL. I like your style.

Before I can think up a witty response he buzzes in with, *LMK when you book your flight.*

Well, it's probably for the best that this conversation is short-lived. I'm only willing to push my mother so far…

Will do. I hit *Send* and then pause to consider before adding, *Good night.* I've realized it's just past midnight in the UK. Maybe that's the reason for his sudden burst of texts—he's just left the pub, and he's drunk and lonely. I shrug. I'll take it.

About thirty seconds go by before he types back, *It is now.*

I'm dying to text Miranda, but A) it's after twelve in London, and B) my mother actually might pop a blood vessel if I'm any later than I already am. I rush out of the house and call Savy from the car to dissect every word of our exchange.

* * *

"So how did your project go in England?" Caroline asks. "You were there for a long time."

I'm surprised my sister knows how long I was overseas. She's so busy all the time we rarely hear from her, though I suspect she talks to Vivienne more than she talks to me.

"It went well. I have to go back in a couple weeks, once the furniture starts to come in and the first phase of construction is wrapped up."

"I didn't realize you were going back so soon." My mother is frowning. I'm wondering why this matters to her when she adds, "That must be disappointing to your friend Chase. He seemed very anxious to know when you were coming home."

Ah, yes. I'd almost forgotten that my mother had been the person to supply Chase with my itinerary. She always asks my sisters and me for our flight information when we travel. It's one of few ways she reveals her affection, at least to me. But this time there's nothing affectionate about it. I give her a frosty look.

"Yes, he was waiting for me when I got there. I can't imagine how he knew when I was landing."

Mother arches a penciled brow. "He seemed to want to speak to you rather urgently."

"Yes, Mother, and I didn't happen to want to speak to him. And he knew it. And in some families, parents and siblings prefer to protect their loved ones from potential stalkers."

Vivienne scoffs from across the table, the first indication that she's noticed I'm even here. I glance past her to where Elijah is squirming in his chair and Aisling is watching us with wide eyes, wishing I could reach them from across the table to pull them into a big auntie bear hug—but that's not how things are done in our family. I hope, not for the first time, that Viv is warmer as a mother than she tends to be as a sister. Lord help Aisling if she takes after me and struggles to lose her baby fat.

Glancing down the two rows of my family, I ask Caroline, "Where are Teddy and Cat?" I'd thought they were all coming.

"Catherine," my mother interjects immediately. She hates it when I call my niece by the nickname I gave her the very first time I held her, thirteen and a half years ago.

Caroline glances at me and then gives our mother an even look. "No, it's all right. She prefers to go by Cat these days."

My insides do a happy dance, since Caroline is the only one of her daughters Mother won't cross. I hardly ever have company in the defensive line unless it's my dad. I don't dare celebrate in the end zone, though, instead keeping my expression neutral.

Caroline looks at me again and continues. "Catherine had a violin concerto last night, and Teddy stayed to take her." My niece is a prodigy on the violin. I've never gotten to see one of her performances in person, but Teddy records them and posts them on a private YouTube channel.

"I want to go up sometime and see one of her concerts."

"Come anytime," Caroline says. "I was just saying to Teddy that it's been ages since a single one of you has come to me rather than making me come to you."

"Well, that's not true," Mother says. "Your father and I came up last December."

"That was two Decembers ago," Caroline argues. "And you spent more time shopping on Fifth Avenue than you did with the three of us." She laughs lightly to show she isn't actually put out about it, but I wonder for the first time what kinds of grudges Caroline holds against the rest of us. She left for college when I was in middle school, so we haven't been close, proximity-wise or otherwise, since I was around Aisling's age. It's a shame that I come from such a big family and yet none of us knows that much about the others' lives. It's the opposite of Savy's big family, which is boisterous and loud and very much into hugging.

"You know I love to come visit you," Vivienne says, patting her stomach. "But I've been a little busy these past few years." She smiles beatifically.

"Bring the kids," Caroline says. "I'm sure Cat would love it." She winks at me.

"Yeah, that sounds like *loads* of fun," Viv says dryly. "But I guess I'd have little choice. Bradley is traveling so much lately I'm not sure when he'll be home long enough for me to come by myself. And even if he were home, I'd have to get a sitter. He's not used to babysitting. He wouldn't know the first thing about taking care of these little monsters." She glances affectionately at Aisling and Elijah, then scowls and drops her voice to a low growl. "Elijah Cunningham Cosgrove, get that green bean out of your nose and put your napkin in your lap."

I snort laugh, and Caroline and Dad crack up, too. Even Mother cracks a tiny smile. And then Caroline surprises the hell out of me by saying, "You know, it's not babysitting when it's your own children. I'm sure Bradley could handle it."

If I'd been the one to say it, hell would hath rained down fury on this very table. But since Caroline said it, Viv considers the idea with tight lips and then shrugs. "Maybe."

"That's ridiculous," Mother interjects, and both Caroline and I snap our heads toward her, Caroline to protest, me to glare, since being childless myself I don't have much to bring to the debate. "The children can stay here. I think it's a lovely idea for you to visit your sister."

All three of us girls are speechless. I know our mother loves her grandchildren, but to my knowledge this is the first time she's ever offered to keep them for an extended period. I've even heard Vivienne complain before that, while her friends are all able to drop the kids with Grandma for a week while they relax and rejuvenate in Bermuda or St. Barts, she's never had that luxury because Mother is always too busy with her charity events and club commitments.

Thinking about it, Viv has probably colored all my opinions about motherhood. She makes it sound like life-ending drudgery. I should probably listen a little harder to Caroline, who's a champion for work-life balance if ever there was one. "I'd love to come up, too," I say.

Vivienne looks annoyed, but Caroline seems pleased. "You should come together," she says. "I could take a couple days off work, and we'd have so much fun in the city."

"Whatever," Viv says. "It won't happen for a while anyway. I'm in the third trimester, you know." She pats her stomach again, which forms a neat and compact ball in her lap. Even pregnant, Vivienne is skinnier than me.

Dad clears his throat, and I glance over at him.

"Speaking of Bradley's traveling, Quinn, did he ever get in touch with you while you were in London?"

My brow knits together. "You know, he did," I say. "But I was so busy I didn't get a chance to see him." In fact, I never even remembered to return his call after getting his voice mail. I need to tell him to text instead of call—I rarely answer my phone unless it's Savy or Jules or Mother or unless I have to for work. "Maybe when I go back."

"I'll remind him to find a hot British colleague to bring along," Vivienne says.

I wait for it, but she doesn't add an insult. Maybe there's hope for us yet?

"I'm sure Quinn is too busy working while she's there for any dating nonsense," Dad says, and I chuckle. I'm thirty-two, and still my father is wielding the protective vibe.

"Or maybe I don't need Bradley's help," I say pointedly, thinking about Ian and our round of texts, still so fresh in my mind I haven't come down from the buzz.

"Ooh, intriguing," Caroline says.

And then Aisling lets out an earsplitting shriek and wails, "Eww, yuck. Mommy!"

We all look over, and Elijah is picking up mashed potato with his fingers and attempting to press it onto his cheeks and chin, though most of it is sliding off and landing in drippy, buttery globs on the table and his lap. "Look, I got a beard like Daddy's," he says.

As Vivienne huffs in exasperation, I bring my napkin to my lips to hold in my giggle and Caroline does the same. I could kiss my sweet little mischievous nephew right now for his impeccable timing. My love life is the last topic I want to discuss around this particular dinner table.

* * *

Caroline flies out Tuesday just a few hours after Vivienne's baby shower "tea," and I drive her to the airport since I'm shuttling myself around the city all day anyway. My most critical tasks this afternoon are to find off-the-shelf outdoor furniture for a client who's hosting her daughter's engagement party in two weeks and to style a different client's living room for a local magazine feature about an upcoming home tour. Thanks to the shower, I dragged myself to the office at six thirty this morning to get some paperwork done for SpaZone and finalize some sketches of a law office lobby. My head is spinning.

"Your work seems to be going really well," Caroline says. She sounds happy for me, which is nice but also disorienting. I'm so accustomed to the women in my family addressing me and my "little business" with scorn. "Are you always this busy?"

"Usually," I say honestly. "Certain times of the year are busier than others. Spring and summer are always busy, and in the fall we get slammed with people wanting to get projects wrapped up before the holidays. January and February are generally our catch-up months." I glance over at her. I've always been a little in awe of Caroline, who's managed to defy our family's conventions, but with such grace and perfection that no one, not even Mother, can fault her for it. Unlike me, she's done everything right—namely, bringing a husband and child into the picture within a respectable time frame…and without gaining an unseemly amount of weight. Though, to be fair to myself, my sisters were both always skinny, while I was born with the rounded, more generous proportions of my father's side of the family.

"Well, just make sure you're taking care of yourself," she adds, the doctor in her coming out. "Burning the candle at both ends can wreak havoc on your stress levels, which can lead to all kinds of health problems."

"I'm healthy as a horse," I say. "Never felt better." I realize as I say it that it's true. Maybe I'm not traipsing in faithfully to the "ass whisperer," but I watch what I eat, and I somewhat get enough sleep. I sleep well, at least, unlike Savy, who's a chronic insomniac.

"That's good," she says. It's so weird to be talking one-on-one with Caroline, who I don't usually interact with much beyond Facebook likes and birthday texts and the very occasional family gathering. "Don't let Viv and Mother get to you, either. Viv is struggling with who she is, and that's why she's so hard on you. And Mother's very jealous of your lifestyle."

"*Mother* is jealous?" I could see her saying that about Vivienne, though I would argue the truth of it. Vivienne thinks most highly of Vivienne and always will. But our mother is the most firmly rooted person I know. She knows her place in the world, never argues it, and strongly urges the rest of us to take up her yoke.

"Definitely. She grew up in a time with fewer options, at least in her social set, and I can see that she looks at you and sees freedoms she could have had and things she could have done. You know she loves homes and architecture and design as much you do."

"But she puts down my work all the time. She calls it my 'little business.' And she's constantly on my case about finding a boyfriend and getting married."

"She just wants to make sure you're financially secure and settled."

I laugh incredulously. "That's the thing, though. I am. She just refuses to accept that I could have accomplished that on my own, without her and Daddy's help or the support of a man."

I see Caroline nodding out of the corner of my eye and glance quickly at her as we careen down I-240 at sixty-five miles an hour. She's gazing at me with empathy. "I know you are. I respect what you've done and built for yourself, and deep down I know she does, too."

I huff softly. *I doubt that.*

Caroline pauses, and I glance over again to see her forehead creased and lips pursed, as if she's trying to figure out how to word whatever she wants to say next. She catches me looking and smiles.

"You know, dating sucks, and there are a lot of duds out there, but there are also a lot of nice guys, and finding one and falling in love and getting married doesn't mean turning into Vivienne and Mother. It doesn't mean conceding your independence, even. At least not if you find the right person."

I don't know Caroline's husband, Teddy, all that well, but I can tell she's speaking from experience.

"Even Mother knows this," she adds. "She's the one who has Daddy wrapped around her pinky finger, not the other way around."

I shrug. This is true, but it also brings to mind a picture of exactly what I don't want for myself. My dad is a great guy, and he'd do anything for our family. But without him Mother has nothing—nothing she's built for herself without his influence or income. Maybe a little family money, but even that isn't something she can claim on her own merit. And if she ever walked away, she couldn't do it without taking part of Dad's wealth with her.

I've always felt sorry for myself for the way my family views me. But I guess I have it partly wrong. I guess I've always felt a little sorry for Mother and for Vivienne, too. Vivienne, especially, is trapped. If she were happy with her plight, that'd be one thing. But she's miserable—it's clear. And if *she* walked away, she'd be giving up the lifestyle she's accustomed to and probably at least some of the friends who value her place in society as much as they value Viv herself. She'd be giving up partial access to her children, whom I know she loves deeply, to a man who, by her own admission, "wouldn't know the first thing about taking care" of them.

"I can see your point, to an extent," I say. "I do want to get married one day and maybe even have a baby." *Maybe.* "I just want to know, first, that I can stand on my own two feet."

As we've talked I've exited onto Airways Boulevard, and now I'm following the signs to the airport's departures gate. Caroline pauses while I navigate the lanes and then says, "I don't think anybody has any doubt about that." She laughs. "I only hope the man who lands you has a quick wit and a strong sense of self."

I pull up at the curb, put the car in park, and grin at her. "You know, you're as bad as Mother and Viv in your own way. You're just sneakier with your love advice. And you don't make fun of me for being fat."

Caroline snort laughs before opening her car door. "You're not fat," she says. We both get out of the car, and she pulls her trim suitcase out of the trunk before adding, "Viv's jealous of you there too, you know. She wishes she had a little more junk in the trunk." She winks.

I give my immaculate, brilliant, irreverent sister a crushing hug.

"I'll plan a trip," I promise. "I'll make sure to get Viv out for it, too. After the baby's here, maybe next spring."

"You'd better."

CHAPTER NINE

———

Spearmint & Sexual Frustration

Another week blows by, and then another. I'm starting to think Jane and Adam's case pieces have gone on back order and will stay there forever when, finally, Faye lets me know the last piece I have on order arrived at the address I gave her, which is Miranda's store's warehouse.

A few days later, the upholstery is scheduled for delivery—within the coming week, but I know how that goes. All I can hope is that it arrives while I'm in town, because my trip is now booked, and I'm leaving in four days. (Yay!)

In the meantime I've been working more sixteen-hour days to get my clients in good shape for me to be gone again. Menzi will still handle aspects of a few of my projects, but this time Jen herself will be my main point of contact for any major troubleshooting. I didn't rat Menzi's shortcomings out to Jen, but Jen is sharp. She can see herself that Menzi isn't shaping up to be a long-term employee.

Plus, we're all about to get more help because the firm is hiring another full-time designer. And that's because, not only is Jen and her fiancé Todd's wedding coming up in September, but Jen is twelve weeks pregnant. She and Amanda brought us all together this morning to announce the news. There's a part of me that can't believe it. Jen's as much of a workaholic as I am, if not more so. She's my mentor and my biggest role model in the profession, both in aesthetic and in business style.

I guess what I'm saying is, maybe if Jen can do it, I can do it, too. One day.

But first things first.

I'm trying to keep my mind on my work and off the fact that in less than a week, I'll be in Ian's city again. Miranda's, too, and I'm excited to see her and Eleanor and Ethan and...well, maybe not Pamela so much. But Thomas. I'm still pulling for Miranda and Thomas.

Ian and I are texting regularly now, and we have been since that day before my family dinner a couple weeks ago. I don't think I'll be waiting long for our date once my flight lands in London, because our texts have definitely been building up to something. No sexting, exactly, but a healthy amount of flirting. Whether he is or not, I know *I'm* ready to meet face-to-face.

We'll have to meet up pretty quickly anyway because I won't be in town as long this time—less than two weeks. All I'm doing this trip is making a progress check, lining up the next wave of subcontractors for the kitchen overhaul, and getting furnishings installed now that the floor and walls are finished in the front room and dining room. There'll be at least one more trip to put finishing touches on the kitchen and conservatory.

Still, that doesn't leave much time for my budding relationship with Ian, and I'm trying not to focus on that fact. Instead I think about the tiny kiss he planted at my temple the night before I left London, and my insides go all soft and buzzy and warm.

"Quinn, got a minute?"

It's Jen, and I realize I've been staring at the same fabric memo for at least the last five minutes, lost in thought. I smile at her and stand up from my worktable. "Sure. What's up?"

"I just thought I'd go over your client list with you one more time before you leave, because *I'm* leaving tomorrow for Hot Springs to install the Wiggins' vacation house. I'll probably be back before you go, but I want to be clear on what you need, at any rate."

"You're a rock star, hot mama," I say, and Jen smirks at me.

"Mama," she muses. "It's about time, right?"

I shrug. "Seems like perfect timing to me."

Jen laughs. "You're right," she says. "Your clear view of reality has always been inspiring to me."

I cock my head at her. "Don't go all weird now that your hormones are out of whack." Even if outwardly I'm keeping up appearances—Jen and I have always bantered like this—inwardly I'm shining at her compliment.

"I'll try to keep it together." She rolls her eyes at me. "Although I've got to say, pregnancy isn't for the weak. I cried at a credit card commercial a couple days ago. And I'm already craving weird things, mostly dairy. Would you believe I went through a whole carton of cottage cheese last night? I made Todd run to Fresh Market to get more. How cliché is that?"

I laugh. "I'll make sure to add that to my future husband's job description: must be willing to procure dairy products at wife's whim. Maybe I'll put it in my online dating profile."

"One day your cottage cheese courier will come," Jen says.

I snort. "How romantic."

"Actually, it kind of is." Her eyes go all misty.

"Okay, now you're being weird again. Let's talk SpaZone before I cross the pond."

She chuckles. "Send me some pics of Adam's place while you're there. And make Braxton FaceTime me. He hardly ever does it anymore."

"Because that's what I'm so good at—interacting with children."

"He's almost a teenager, and you're cooler than I am. You have sway."

"I'll do what I can." I smile at the reminder that in just a few days, I'll be back in Braxton and Adam and Jane's neck of the woods, catching up with my friends and doing fun work and hopefully picking back up where Ian's and my last text left off.

* * *

I land at Heathrow on Tuesday midmorning, and the next night I fall back into the routine of the Lion's Gate pub. The whole group is there minus Pamela, who's on holiday with her sister in Tenerif. Her absence doesn't exactly bring pain to my heart.

Thomas and Miranda are opposite one another around the table, and I sense a coolness between them that I'm pretty sure didn't exist before. I really can't get a read on them at all.

Ian, on the other hand, is keeping close to my side, and I'm barely able to concentrate on the story I'm telling because his hand is on my thigh under the table, and each time he laughs it moves a fraction of an inch higher up my leg.

"And so the installers took down the red fixture, and now it's sitting on the patio—"

"Patio?" Ethan interrupts.

"The back garden," Miranda translates. "Go on."

"And I hope it doesn't rain because the thing is *huge*, and I've got to get a painter to pick it up and spray paint it navy, which is ridiculous, really, when you consider the cost of the thing, but there's no time to order another."

"The difficulties of doing transatlantic business," Miranda says.

"But how they came to actually install this bright-as-hell, fire engine-red chandelier that doesn't look like anything else in Adam and Jane's house is beyond my comprehension. I would have thought the electrician might realize there was a mistake, but maybe he just thought I was avant-garde."

"A red chandelier could be fantastic in the right space," Miranda says, and I nod.

"Agreed."

I'm babbling, and I realize not everyone at the table probably finds this story of my ordering snafu as interesting as Miranda and I do, but I can't think straight with Ian's hand sliding the fabric of my skirt against my inner thigh. At this rate I'm not sure he and I will make it to dinner this evening, though that's the plan.

"Are you ready to go soon?" Ian's thoughts must be traveling the same direction as mine. His voice is huskier than usual.

"Sure," I say breathlessly.

Miranda and Eleanor exchange a glance.

"I'll be right back." Ian slides off his chair and walks over to the bar to pay for our drinks.

"Where are you two kids going?" Miranda asks. Her voice has a tinge of resentment in it that confuses me, but I figure it must have something to do with Thomas.

"To some curry place Ian talked about," I say. "I've never tried curry before, so this should be interesting."

"Get the chicken tikka," Eleanor says. "It's a good starter curry. More British than Indian, really. I think it was created specifically for the English to align with our duller taste buds."

I laugh. "Thanks for the advice."

Ian walks back over then, and I hop up from my chair, suddenly nervous. I almost knock my barstool over when trying to push it up to the table. "I'm so glad to be back," I say. "It's great to see all of you."

"Cheers. Same to you," Eleanor says, and the others echo her.

"See you tomorrow?" Miranda asks, and I nod, knowing she'll expect a full accounting when I meet her at the warehouse tomorrow afternoon.

"Bye." I turn toward Ian, who threads my fingers into his and pulls me toward the door.

* * *

"I don't have any experience in long-distance dating," he says an hour or so later, when we're tucked across from one another in a gold leather booth. At each table, a pottery candle holder with shapes cut into the sides forms flickery light patterns that reflect off the glossy tabletop and the walls, which are papered in maroon and gold. We've shared an appetizer I didn't recognize but that was very good, some sort of vegetable coated in a spicy, crispy batter with an array of exotic sauces.

Around us are other coupled-up tables, and the restaurant is quiet and romantic, with a low murmur of conversation. So far Ian's reputation as a player is holding true. He's brought me to the perfect place. He's saying all the perfect things. I try to keep my head and remain on guard about being played. But it's difficult when he's plying me with wine and seducing me with delicious food and looking at me like it's me he wants to lick off his spoon.

"I don't either," I say. "This isn't like a normal first date because we've been talking for weeks. Or at least typing."

"Tell me something you haven't told me yet," he says, reaching across the table to run one fingertip along the back of my hand. His knee is touching my leg under the table. I don't think we've broken contact for more than a few seconds since we left the pub. "Tell me something about your family or your home."

I laugh lightly. "Hmm. What's something you don't know?" I think for a second. "Well, you know that my father is a politician and my mother is a drama queen." I laugh. "My oldest sister, who I don't get to see much because she lives in New York, has a daughter who's a violin prodigy and a job with a title most people can't even pronounce."

"Really?" he says. His fingers have traveled from the back of my hand to my wrist, and now his hand is covering all of mine. I'm so focused on the touch of his skin that I'm not even sure what I'm saying.

"Tell me about you, though," he presses. "What made you choose to go into design?"

"That was easy. I've always known what I wanted to do," I say. "I love art, especially making it. I love studying something blank, like a page or a canvas or a wall, seeing what isn't there, and then being the one to create something out of nothing." I pause. "It's magical to me."

I've never said this to anyone and would normally think it too cheesy or sentimental to say out loud, but it fits the mood of this place and this night and especially this warm cocoon of closeness Ian is building around us.

"That's fantastic," he says. "Actually, it's sexy." My breathing speeds up as he adds, "I'd love to watch you creating art someday."

Our server materializes out of nowhere and interrupts us by placing steaming plates atop our table. A second person spirits away the empty appetizer dish and gold-rimmed side plates.

The mood relaxes as we settle into our entrees—mine's a tikka masala, as Eleanor advised, and Ian's is something called vindaloo. I sample a bite, and it's so spicy it numbs my tongue and leaves my taste buds tingling even after chasing it with water. Ian laughs at me and offers me a piece of crispy, buttery naan.

"Tell me about your work," I say, realizing he's been asking me all the questions. I know nothing about what he does. "You're in finance, right?"

"Oh, it's a little boring, but yes," he says. "I punch numbers into a keyboard all day. Your work is much more exciting."

He brushes his leg against mine again, and I forget to ask any more questions about his job.

*   *   *

When we're finally out on the street after our meal, my jet lag has unfortunately started to catch up with me, and I yawn widely.

"You must be knackered," Ian says sympathetically.

"I'm pretty tired, yes." I smile at him, waking back up when he squeezes my hand. All this buildup, and we've yet to even kiss. I definitely don't want to appear too sleepy for that to happen.

"Can I get you a taxi back to your hotel?"

"Sure," I say, disappointed.

But when the black car pulls up to the curb, Ian slides into it after me. I give the driver the address of my inn, the same bed and breakfast I stayed in last time, and we drive away. My mind is racing. Was I planning to invite him up? Is he expecting it? Why else would he be in the car with me? I'm absolutely sure I want him to come upstairs with me, and I'm just as absolutely sure I don't. My romantic history preceding this man deems it unwise. But then again, I'll only be here for two weeks, so for anything to happen, it has to happen fast. My mind is spinning. *I'm too tired to make this decision.*

I'm vulnerable. Even I can recognize it. And I feel sure, as we approach my street and the taxi slows, that Ian recognizes it and that he's planning to take advantage of it. After all, we're so close to one another in the back seat that I'm practically on his lap, and one of his arms is around me, and his hand is on the crook of my hip, and his fingers are sliding back and forth along my thigh, and my hand is on his leg, and… *Oh, God.* With his other hand he reaches up to stroke my face, one finger tracing the line of my jaw. I feel his breath on my cheek, and it's light and tingly, with a hint of spearmint from the mints that conveniently arrived at our table with the bill.

When the car comes to a stop, Ian surprises me by instructing the driver, "Can you wait a few minutes for me, please?" The man nods once, expressionless, and Ian follows me out onto the sidewalk.

So, he's made the decision for me, then. That's probably good, since I'm so tired and defenseless, but also—I have to admit—disappointing. My body is practically humming with an electric buzz.

Ian leads me to one side of the hotel's leafy entrance, obscured from the driver's view, and then grabs my hand to pull me to a stop. The inn, with its awning-covered brick stairwell, gold railings, and enormous potted plants, is quiet, with a soft glow emanating from inside that casts scattered rays along the steps and down onto the sidewalk.

His hand is on the small of my back, pressing me against him. With his other hand he reaches for my cheek again, and then, before I can overthink it, before I can even figure out what to do with my hands or decide whether to feel grateful or frustrated that he didn't give me the chance to invite him up, his lips are covering mine, and our mouths are moving in tandem and our tongues are connected, and it's perfect. It's the most perfect first kiss I've ever experienced and maybe the most perfect kiss I've experienced, period. By the time it's over, we're both panting just a little bit, enough to make the next time inevitable but not so much to be embarrassing.

"Wow," he says.

"Wow," I echo him.

"I'll text you tomorrow?"

I nod mutely, and we separate, untwining our fingers when I reach the first step. He watches from the sidewalk until I've climbed the stairs and disappeared into the building, and then I watch through the window as he makes his way back to the car.

* * *

Unfortunately, the tighter timetable of this trip means I get to stay sexually frustrated for several more days—I don't get to see Ian again at all during the week. Because of my trips back and forth to her warehouse, I do get to spend time with Miranda, and after meeting me at the storage facility to inspect Jane and Adam's case pieces, she comes with me Thursday afternoon to check out the progress I've made on the house.

Work on the kitchen is speeding along. Demolition always seems to happen faster than any other part of construction work—I suspect the contractors find tearing things out and breaking things more fun than putting them back together. At any rate, we've reached the point in the project where restaurant dining is no longer a lifestyle choice for the Dawsons but a necessity.

Jane is home this time when I bring Miranda by, and to her credit she doesn't give Miranda side-eye for her sartorial choices. Today she's dressed in head-to-toe black, with black fingernails, black ripped skinny jeans, a black off-the-shoulder top with "heaven can wait" emblazoned across the bust in silver spangles, and a gray and black houndstooth beret. On her feet, of course, are unlaced combat boots.

By contrast, conservative Jane is wearing navy trousers with creases pressed into the legs, navy pumps, and a cream-colored blouse with puffy, long buttoned sleeves and a tie at the throat. I'm the most boring one of the bunch in my gray cropped jeans and fuchsia silk blouse, which felt bold and flirty when I put it on this morning.

"Bloody hell, it looks like somebody's let loose with the wrecking ball in this room." Miranda steps over a pile of rubble that used to be part of Jane's kitchen island.

"It might actually look better than it did before, right, Quinn?" Jane smiles over at me.

"It will soon," I reply. I smile to myself, thinking the new kitchen won't be too unlike Jane's current outfit—only a bit more modern. Creamy white quartz countertops with a waterfall edge on the island and deep blue lower cabinets. Crisp steel open shelves along the upper back wall with a long window bank opposite, overlooking the conservatory and garden. Classic, antiqued brass fixtures and hardware to accessorize the space, with clean-lined, industrial-inspired pendant lights. I can't wait to see it completed, but that won't happen on this trip. I cross my fingers that everything goes smoothly with the construction crew while I'm overseas.

"Will you take pictures and send them to me throughout the renovation?" I ask.

"Of course," Jane says. "I'm glad they're underway with the demolition. I was so tired of that dark blue tile. It's nice to finally have it gone. Do you think they'll—"

She doesn't get to finish her question, though, as the front door bangs open, causing all three of us to jump, our heads swiveling toward the sound.

Voices travel up the hall, and a few seconds later two boys emerge through the doorway and into the kitchen. "What are we supposed to do for a snack with the kitchen all messed up, Mum?" Even though his accent is more British than American, it surprises me to hear Braxton use the British word.

"The pantry cupboard is still intact." Jane points Braxton and his friend back in the direction they came, where a narrow walk-in pantry is tucked behind a doorway adjacent to the front hall. With a start I realize the boy with Braxton is Elliott, the cousin of Ryland Pemberton I met on my last trip.

They must have found common ground. From what I remember, neither boy seemed thrilled to be forced into hanging out together. Now, Elliott—lanky and awkward in that adolescent, not-quite-teenaged kind of way—disappears into the pantry behind Braxton. They're talking so loud it's impossible to continue our kitchen discussion.

"There are Heroes on the shelf on the left," Jane calls out.

"Do we have any of the good biscuits?" Braxton yells back. "The chocolate ones?"

"No, I don't think so. But I just bought crisps. They're right in front."

"I found them." Braxton emerges from the doorway clutching two full-size bags of chips in one hand and a purple package with *Cadbury's* on it in the other. "We're going upstairs."

"There's bottled water in the fridge," Jane says, and Elliott gives her a puzzled look. I wonder if it's because of her American word choice. Do they not abbreviate *refrigerator* in England? It's funny how the Dawsons straddle the two cultures so routinely. I can't remember how long Jen said they've lived here—eight years? Nine?

"When did you guys move to the UK?" I ask Jane.

She's watching as the two boys make their way up the hall. Their steps echo off the bare walls, and their voices carry more loudly than usual because of the empty front room, which is still mostly stripped of furniture, its windows bare apart from old Venetian blinds that are due for replacement as soon as the custom window treatments come in from the workshop Miranda referred to me. It occurs to me that as much as she's helped me with this project, Miranda deserves a cut of my commission. I wonder how billing is handled in the UK? I make a mental note to talk with Jen about it later.

"Don't eat crisps on the bed," Jane calls out as the two boys reach the bottom of the stairs.

"OK, Mum," Braxton calls out, drawing out the words impatiently before they clomp up the steps with all the subtlety of an African stampede.

Jane turns to me and shakes her head. "I'm sorry. What did you ask?"

I laugh. "Oh. I just asked how long y'all have lived here."

"We moved in 2009," Jane says. "When Adam was transferred to the London office from Atlanta, where we lived before. That's where Braxton was born."

"Oh, are you from Atlanta?" Miranda asks. I'm wondering if she's familiar enough with American geography to even know where Atlanta is or if she's just being polite, when she adds, "I'm absolutely obsessed with *Gone with the Wind*." She feints back, lifting the back of one hand to her forehead, and declares, "As God as my witness, I'll nevah be hungry again."

She grins, and Jane and I glance at each other and then dissolve in giggles at her attempt at an American Southern accent, even funnier coming from a punked-out London pixie hipster. And then I remember that Vivian Lee, who played Scarlett in the movie, was actually British, too. She must have had some crazy good dialect training.

"No, I'm from North Carolina originally," Jane says. "Adam and I met in college, at Clemson."

"Would that be called a Southern belle, then?" This question is asked by a deep, masculine voice, not Miranda's high-pitched lilt.

All three of us pivot in tandem again, this time toward the back door, where none other than Ryland Pemberton fills the door frame with his tall, svelte form. Or, I should say, *Lord* Pemberton. After Jules' revelation I Googled him, of course. By official title he's an earl.

"Ohmigosh, don't you ever use the front door?" I blurt out. My cheeks instantly go up in flames—not for my own sake but for Jane's. I don't embarrass easily, but I fear I've embarrassed *her*. But Ryland chuckles, easing the tension in the room and, frankly, shocking the hell out of me.

"Back door guests are best," Jane says. "My mother had that in a frame in the kitchen when I was growing up. It was cross-stitched." She smiles, and I get the feeling she's attempting to smooth over my faux pas. If Ryland appreciates this, he doesn't show it. He doesn't even look at her.

"The American returns."

His accent is clipped and off-puttingly high-brow, or maybe I just feel that way now that I know his background. At any rate, I detect disdain, which doesn't win him any points with me.

"What do you have against Americans?" I ask, trying to keep my tone light. "Our current political scandals excluded." I've heard Miranda and her friends talk enough to know the British are watching the United States' actions on the world stage as if it's an ongoing reality show. And since Ryland is a member of England's political establishment, I figure this could actually be his problem with me.

His ears turn bright pink, and his posture stiffens. I've clearly said the wrong thing. "Nothing at all," he says in a tone that's even more clipped and cold, if that's possible. "Political scandals excluded."

Oh...kay. This guy is *such* an ass. I hate to disappoint Jules, but he's too much of a jerk for even *me* to consider him a conquest. I glance at Miranda to commiserate and only then realize she's gaping at him in slack-jawed shock.

I struggle to find another witty comeback, but Miranda's reaction has me at a loss for words. I'd forgotten she doesn't know about Jane and Adam's illustrious neighbor. My lack of response doesn't matter, though, because Ryland angles his body away from Miranda and me, effectively shutting us out.

"Is Elliott upstairs?" I hear him ask in a low tone, only to Jane.

"Yes, he and Braxton arrived maybe ten minutes ago." She shoots an apologetic glance my way and moves with Ryland past the pile of island rubble, closer to the doorway that leads to the front hall. "Should I call him down to go with you?"

"No, no. If he's engaged, we can leave it there," Ryland replies mysteriously. "If I might have a word about how things are getting on?" I'm refusing to look at them, but I feel Ryland's glance as tangibly as if his eyes were to reach out and touch me.

"Of course." Jane follows him up the hallway and into a room off the foyer, probably once a small parlor but now a home office. One of the two of them shuts the door, leaving Miranda and me free to gossip.

"What..." she says. "When did..." She pauses again. "Why is he..."

The presence of a semifamous politician-bachelor-gentleman seems to have stolen Miranda's capacity for speech.

"Is that really who I think it is?"

"The one and only," I respond dryly.

"What is he doing here?"

"You got me," I say. "Though he is their next-door neighbor."

"Next-door neigh... But...but that's Ryland Pemberton. He doesn't live here, does he. Because he has an estate in Suffolk, doesn't he." I recognize that she's not actually asking but simply punctuating her statements with a question, an English tendency.

"But he does work in London," I point out. "Logic would have it that he would also maintain a city residence."

"But not *here*," she says, and though I feel a twinge of indignation on Jane and Adam's behalf, I concede internally that she's right. I'd voiced the same thought to Savy and Jules. "I mean, not that it's dodgy or anything," she adds quickly. "But just, I should expect that his second home would be nearer the city center—Kensington or Knightsbridge, or at the least Notting Hill."

"Maybe he likes to go incognito," I say.

"And who is Elliott?" she adds, ignoring me. "Is he harboring a secret love child?"

I burst out laughing. "Nothing as outrageous as that, unfortunately," I say. "He's inherited a cousin. Elliott's mother died recently in a tragic accident." I don't know why I feel the need to add this further explanation—maybe to protect Jane's role in the situation.

"And how does he know your client?" she asks, as if reading my mind.

"Well, they're neighbors, aren't they." Oh, my gosh—now I'm doing the question thing, too. If I'm not careful, soon I'll be talking with an accent. "Elliott, the cousin, is about the same age as Jane's son."

"Oh." Miranda looks unsatisfied with my answer.

She starts to ask something else, but the study door opens, and Jane and Ryland step out into the hall.

"I'll let you get back to your meeting." Ryland doesn't spare Miranda or me a glance, and I wonder if he's perturbed by the fact that a stranger has caught him out or if he just assumes Miranda is with me and likewise American. I give her a once-over, thinking if he's at all savvy, he'll recognize that's not the case. She's a poster child for London chic.

No, more likely he just sees her as "the help," the same way he regards me. As in, no regard at all. *What an ass*, I think again.

But then he turns to look at me, another of those piercing glances like the one I caught him in the day we met. It's a look that, I swear, makes me feel as if he can see through to my skin—as if I'm standing naked right here in the hallway, and Jane and Miranda aren't even here. A jolt of fire shoots down my spine, leaving me tingling from head to toe.

Just as quickly, his eyes go cold. I glance down, unable to look at him in case he really *can* see through me and my thoughts are evident on my face.

"Until next time," he says in that same maddeningly aloof tone. Only this time, there's a hint of intent behind his words, and I get the feeling, somehow, that he's counting on it.

* * *

By Friday night my patience with my own busy schedule has worn thin. I want to see Ian so badly it hurts. He calls me, and together we decide to skip the pub to spend the whole evening together, which is a bummer in that I don't get to see Miranda, Eleanor, and Ethan but also appealing because Pamela is back now from her trip. I don't really care to watch her glare daggers at me every time Ian touches my arm or laughs at my jokes, although the competitive part of me might enjoy it just a little.

I get a text from Ian saying he's out front. He's driving tonight because he wants to take me to a restaurant in a different part of the city—I didn't even know he had a car. How nice it must be to live in a city where driving is optional. As much as I love my hometown, its public transportation sucks.

I check my reflection in the mirror. I spent a full half hour flat-ironing my hair before adding a few loose waves with a big-barreled curling iron—something I almost never take the time to do. I didn't want to look like I tried too hard, so to offset my fancy hair I'm wearing less makeup than usual—which actually just means I applied my makeup in a way that makes it *look* like I'm wearing less makeup than usual, a trick I learned from Vivienne in high school before she became the Wicked Witch of the Southeast.

I apply one more coat of pink-tinged lip gloss and slip on my favorite stilettos—black patent Louboutins my boss Jen gave me because they were too loose on her. She got them from her friend Amelia Wright, who's a famous author and gets free stuff from designers when she attends red carpet events for the movies based on her books. I can't *imagine* why Amelia wouldn't keep these things for herself, but I also can't complain about her generosity—they're kick-ass shoes. I didn't bring them last time, scared they might get lost with my luggage, but the thought of a night like tonight with Ian made it worth the risk.

On my way out of the room, I glance in the full-length mirror on the wardrobe by the door. Along with the shoes I'm wearing a body-hugging black wrap dress with a deep V neckline and a subtle ruffle that follows the diagonal line of the bodice, doing an excellent job of hiding my flaws while emphasizing my assets. It's my all-time favorite dress because it makes me feel sexy and confident—curvy instead of flabby. In fact, the cut is so perfect I don't even have to wear Spanx, which means my undies are sexy, too. I try not to think too hard about that, or it'll get me all flushed and nervous.

When I descend the front steps of the hotel, I hear Ian before I see him. My head swivels toward the sound of a long, low whistle. I smile, thrilled I made the effort.

"Bloody hell, you look fantastic," he says in a low, gravelly voice when I reach the edge of the sidewalk. His car is still running, and I see that he's left the door open for me—and then I remember where I'm at and realize he's left his own door open while he rushes around the car to open the passenger-side door. The steering wheel here is on the right side of the car, not the left.

A few seconds later I process the reason for his hurry—he's parked in the taxi lane. A red-jacketed valet for the restaurant next door to the hotel is glowering at him, but when *I* catch his eye, his expression shifts, and he actually winks. Sometimes it's nice to be a woman.

"Thanks," I say as I step off the sidewalk and move past Ian to slide into the car.

A moment later he's inside, and we're hurtling away from the sidewalk at breakneck speed. "Do all Englishmen drive like your tires are on fire?" I ask, fumbling to connect the seat belt. So far I've only ridden in cabs, and it's much the same as this.

"I imagine not," he says, laughing. "This is my city driving."

"Are you from the country, then?" This piques my
interest, since I'd assumed he and Miranda and Eleanor and
Thomas grew up somewhere in the vicinity of their current
neighborhood.

"Yes, actually," he says, surprising me. "I come from
Norfolk, near the Broads."

"Oh. What part of England is Norfolk in?" I ask,
ashamed of my ignorance of English geography. I'm aware that
London is in the southern part of the country and Liverpool is up
north—a factoid I know only because I love the Beatles—but
beyond that I'm clueless.

"It's in East Anglia, north of here along the eastern
coast," he says. "My family is from Rackheath, a little village
outside Norwich. Usually people can spot out a Norfolk accent
from a mile away, but I forget that you're unfamiliar with that
nuance." He gives me a quick grin before gunning the engine to
enter a roundabout. I marvel at his boldness at maneuvering in
the heavy traffic. The lane changing and signaling and signage
make no sense to me whatsoever. I feel as if we could smash into
something or someone at any second.

"Is a Norfolk accent the country bumpkin accent of
England?" I ask, resisting the urge to shut my eyes to keep from
cringing at our impending demise. "If so, we have something in
common."

Ian laughs. "Yes, I suppose you'd say I'm a country
bumpkin. Are you as well, then?"

"No, I was born and raised in Memphis, which is urban,"
I say. "But it's in the South, which is considered the bumpkin
part of the US. Where I come from, 'Southern' is unanimous with
'hick.' Even if the stereotype isn't always deserved."

He laughs again. "I suppose here there's a romanticism
to growing up in the country," he muses. "The neighborhood
pub, the thatched-roof cottage, and all that. And really, it is
beautiful in the Broads." He pauses, his voice growing a tad
darker. "Although I wouldn't paint such an ideal picture of how I
grew up."

The comment is intriguing, but I get the feeling, based
on his expression, that he doesn't intend it to invite questions. So

I change course, saving that query for later. "And Miranda and Eleanor grew up in Norfolk, too?"

Instantly his face changes, opens up. "Yes," he says. "All of us in Rackheath. We went to primary school together. We divvied up at university, but then somehow we all ended up back together again, in the same little corner of London. It was all a coincidence, really, apart from Miranda and Eleanor."

"What about Thomas?" I ask, already knowing that Eleanor met Ethan at university. I feel like Miranda told me at some point, but I can't remember how Thomas fits into the picture.

A shadow crosses Ian's face again, though it's so brief it's more like a wisp of a cloud sweeping over the sun, as if I only imagined it. "Thomas is from Rackheath, too," he says. "He was my closest mate growing up."

"Was?" I ask. "Aren't you still close?"

Ian smiles and relaxes back a bit in his seat. I notice that, although we're still in the city, the buildings are growing a bit lower and farther apart. The early evening sunlight glints off windows and creeps into every crevasse, the busy rush-hour streets no longer cast into deep shadow by tall stone apartment blocks or skyscrapers.

"Not as close as we were as kids," he says. He glances down at my feet. "I hope you don't mind walking a bit in those shoes? I'm afraid I can't park as close to the restaurant as I'd like, though I'm happy to drop you off to wait for me."

"No, walking is fine," I say. A side benefit to the luxurious sticker price of my heels is that they're actually quite comfortable. You get what you pay for, as they say. Luckily, though, these were free.

I'm musing over the way he deftly changed the subject from Thomas when my attention is diverted by the changing scene outside the windows. Ian is driving slowly up a street that runs beside what looks to be a small river. I crane my neck to try to peek at the water, easier than it would be if I were on the right side of the car. I catch a brief glimpse of pedestrians walking along a path that's below street level. Boats in an array of bright colors —red, blue, purple, orange—line both sides of a narrow canal. The dark water appears still, its surface dappled with intermittent patches of mossy green algae and otherwise reflecting the leaves of trees that line the paths like a mirror into another world. I'm intrigued—I didn't know London had so many waterways snaking through it. The Thames was all I knew, though I'm guessing this must be some sort of tributary.

"What part of the city is this?" I ask.

"We're in East London, by the Lee River." He points off to his right. "Stratford is that way."

"Stratford, as in 'upon-Avon?'" I grin, happy to recognize the name of at least one British locale. Savy will be so excited if I visit Shakespeare's birthplace. She always has her nose buried in a book.

Ian chuckles. "I hate to disappoint you, but no. Stratford-upon-Avon is northwest of London, up toward Birmingham. This is plain old Stratford."

"There's nothing plain about this place," I say, ogling the postcard-perfect waterfront. People are strolling the sidewalks by the river and also above, at street level, in less hurry here than in the business districts we just left. I can tell parking won't be easy, and though I'm itching to get out and wander this place by foot—wishing, actually, that I'd brought along a backup pair of shoes—I watch the various city scenes unfold as we drive by, Ian circling past the entrance of one full parking garage twice as he mutters under his breath that he should have gotten a taxi.

Finally, mercifully—and apparently miraculously—an empty street space appears, and Ian wrangles his car, a gently battered Volvo hatchback that's seen better days, into it. The car doesn't seem to fit congruously with his carefully groomed, urban persona, but I don't really know him well yet, and besides, it's sort of endearing. Before long we're arm in arm, strolling amongst other strollers. It's only after we've made our way down stone steps and across a quaint, arched wooden bridge to a stretch of waterfront lined with bistros, pubs, and galleries that I remember our earlier conversation, how he clammed up when I asked about Thomas.

I can't figure out how to bring it back up without my curiosity seeming conspicuous. Then again, why do I care if my curiosity seems conspicuous?

"Tell me," I start. "What's the story with…"

Ian interrupts my question by giving my arm a gentle squeeze and pointing out a college-age guy on a yellow raft—a smaller version of the kind you take white water rafting with a group—rowing up the center of the canal. Although it's a perfectly normal thing to do on a river, he seems out of place in the midst of all these well-dressed urbanites perusing galleries and dining al fresco at trendy bistros. I squint and see that he's wearing a University of Arizona T-shirt, making me wonder how on earth he found himself in his current adventure.

Then Ian points again, this time to a group of swans swimming in a straight line, their graceful white heads held regally aloft.

"You know they're protected by the Queen," he says, a statement, not a question.

"No, I didn't know. Why?"

He laughs. "Oh, I think originally it had something to do with preventing commoners from depleting the population to ensure they were plentiful for the royal family's own feasts." He chuckles then grows thoughtful. "But now, I suppose it's because they're so beautiful. They're a part of the city, aren't they A part of London."

"That's really nice," I say, thinking that we have no counterpart to that at home. Memphis is in the midst of mallard country, but instead of revering the duck, we revere *Duck Dynasty*. Being in this place where tradition's roots run centuries deep, it feels like quite the metaphor.

"Here we are, then," he says. "My favorite café in the whole of England."

I turn my gaze from the water and see that we've stopped in front of a narrow restaurant with five or six tables scattered on the cobblestone walk, all filled. A heavy, slatted wooden door with black, barrel-style hardware is propped open, and a warm buzz of conversation drifts out to the sidewalk, along with a yummy aroma that doesn't help me place the restaurant's ethnic origin—herbs and garlic and baked breads and sweet and savory spices. The music that vibrates at a slightly louder volume than the hum of voices is poppy but soft—John Legend, I think, though I can't make out any words. I feel a deep urge to explore the inside of the restaurant and then linger here for hours.

"I'll bet you take all the women here," I say jokingly, though I'm not actually joking. I bet he *does* bring all his dates to this place—it's the most perfect date spot I could imagine.

"Nope," he says, smiling down at me. "You're the first." He pauses, his brow furrowing for a brief moment. "Well, apart from Miranda," he says. "She's the one who introduced me to this spot." His tone is oddly cagey, as if he's telling me this because he doesn't want to be caught out in a lie. I store that up for later, wondering again about Miranda and Thomas and the decades of history the three of them share. But once again I can't ask because Ian steps past the threshold and gives his name to the man behind the host station just inside the door.

He leads us to a booth for two snuggled along the side wall of the restaurant. It's the second booth from the back, where a long bar divides the dining space from a hall leading to a stairway that must lead to another dining room because two servers squeeze past each other on the open wood steps as I watch.

Despite the quaint scene outside and the building's traditional half-timber architecture, the interior is modern, with off-white walls, polished wood trim, and art mounted in frameless glass and arranged in long, graphic lines along the walls. The dark wood bar is lit from underneath, and glass shelves mounted on a wall of mirror are lined with bottles of liquors and wines and liqueurs arranged by color, making them part of the design. I make a mental note of this for the next time I work with a restaurant client.

I can't focus on the space for long, though, because Ian is talking, telling a rambling, funny story about a coworker who fell asleep in a meeting that morning, in a sunlit thirty-third floor conference room, his leather executive chair pulled up to the firm's £20,000 conference table. I note that Ian's a vivid storyteller.

"He was quietly snoring. I think he even had a bit of dribble on his chin," he says, chuckling. "I didn't notice it until I heard another mate sniggering two chairs down. Someone poked him before the vice president could call him out, but I can only imagine the lecture he received afterwards by the managing director."

"What exactly is it that you do?" I ask. I've wondered this since I met him but haven't had a good opportunity to ask.

He chuckles. "Oh, you know," he says, and I think, *No, I don't.* "I push money around. My official title is corporate finance analyst and speculative client specialist or some such nonsense, but when people ask I usually just say I work in hedge funds."

"Did you always want to work in corporate finance?" To me, it seems like the type of job I can't imagine anyone actually *wanting*, but they take it anyway because they want *money*. I get it—I was raised in a family that values moneymaking above most other skills—but it isn't a quality I find particularly attractive.

"I did always want to work in banking or business," he says. "My university degree is in international finance." He smiles. "I'm not particularly gifted in any area, no musical or theatrical or artistic talents to speak of, and I'm rubbish at grammar. But I guess you could say maths is the area where I excelled. I've always been good at numbers." He pauses and rubs his chin, staring at something beyond my shoulder. "I didn't want to go into accountancy or anything stodgy like that, so I took my aim at the financial district."

Him saying "accountancy" makes me remember the story Miranda and Eleanor told the first time I hung out with them, about Miranda's ex-boyfriend who became an accountant and moved away with his new girlfriend. My eyebrow lifts at the reminder of Miranda and her past, but I don't want to interrupt his flow to ask about Miranda and Thomas now that I'm finally learning something about *him*.

"I'm not sure it was the best choice," he continues after taking a healthy swig of the house cabernet we've ordered. He reaches to pour a bit more from the carafe on the table. "In all likelihood Matthew fell asleep this morning because he's working a second or third job. From what I've heard he's leveraged to the hilt. Makes me glad I've stayed single all these years, lived within my means." At this he gives me a surprised look, as if he's just realized he's talking to a date he should be trying to impress. Little does he know, honesty impresses me more than bragging.

"Not a great time for the finance industry, I take it. I get it—designers had it rough a few years back, too, after the US real estate bubble burst." I grimace, remembering those years. Nobody wanted to spend a cent to increase their already inflated property values, and business was slow. The market has been in recovery for a few years and finally seems to be stabilizing and even strong again, though it's always tenuous. Interior design is a luxury that's usually the first thing a home or business owner cuts when purse strings tighten, which means jobs get cut, as well, which taken all together means my profession ebbs and flows with the whims of the economy. I start to tell him this but realize he still has a frozen look on his face.

"No, it's all a bit rocky right now, what with Brexit and the uncertainty of the global economy," he says in a tight voice. He draws in a short breath before visibly relaxing the set of his shoulders and smiling at me.

"What do you do when you're not working?" I ask to lighten the mood. "Since we've established you're not arty, I take it you don't frequent the West End?" I'm trying to show off my growing London knowledge and maybe deflect from my earlier geographic faux pas.

"Guilty." He smiles. "I've never set foot in a theater."

"Never at all?"

"A West End theater," he corrects with a smirk. "I've never been to the Tate Modern, either. But then, tell me who does go to the touristy parts of their own city?"

"True," I concur. "Though I'm dying to get to the touristy parts of *your* city. I haven't actually seen much other than the insides of shops and showrooms. Tell me, what's the point of an artist spending weeks in England without seeing a single piece of English or European art?"

"For you, maybe I'd go to the Tate. You might even get me on the London Eye." He gives me a teasing smile. "And I'm afraid of heights."

"I feel privileged."

"As you should."

"But I'm afraid of heights, too, so you're off the hook."

"Well, then, we're perfect for each other."

The words warm my insides for about two and a half seconds before I realize I won't be here long enough to do much of anything with Ian on this trip, what with progress on Jane and Adam's house moving along steadily.

Even if he was kidding, the idea that Ian might be perfect for me coupled with the knowledge that we don't have much time to spend together makes me panicky. I sip my wine and lick my lips, pondering this. When I look up, he's watching me with a puzzled expression.

"What are you thinking?"

"I'm thinking that we live very far apart," I say. I try to smile but can't quite force my lips to cooperate.

He gazes at me intently. When I pick up my glass again, his eyes follow my hand and then linger on my lips. "We do," he says quietly. "But you're here now."

"True." I'm suddenly having a hard time controlling my breathing. My heart picks up speed as if I've upped the intensity on a stationary bike. It's probably good that the waiter shows up at that moment with our food, which seems to be the story of our relationship.

Our relationship.

What kind of relationship can we have? What the hell was I even thinking, saying I'd go out with a man who lives thousands of miles—an entire ocean—away? Jules is right. I need help. An intervention. Because clearly I only go for men who can't possibly be serious contenders for long-term monogamy.

I shake my head, realizing how ridiculous it is to ruin tonight by overthinking it when there's a gorgeous guy sitting across from me and gazing at me like I'm as delicious as the tapas-sized plates of glazed roast lamb and seared lemon butter scallops and prosciutto-wrapped pears with blue cheese and balsamic glaze resting between us. It's not as if I'm interviewing my future husband. This is a date. A fling. A lark, as Miranda would say.

"I'm starving." Ian's voice interrupts the strange path my thoughts have taken. "Here, try this one." He scoops up a tiny, delicate portion of lamb with the bone still attached and slides it onto my plate. Although I'm sensitive to people ogling me while

I eat—a habit gleaned from years of hawkish stares from my mother at the dinner table—I carve a sliver of the meat from the bone and lift my fork to my lips.

"Oh, my God," I moan after swallowing, licking a bit of the savory-sweet glaze from my bottom lip.

"I know. It's amazing, isn't it? The food here is heavenly."

I cut another sliver from the bone, prompting him to laugh. "Just pick it up. It's a finger food."

I laugh, too, pushing my worries out of my head. After all, Ian is right. I'm here now. I might as well make the most of this night, of this time with him—and of this food. Who cares what he thinks of how I eat or how much I eat or how the delicious, buttery glaze coating every bite is going to paste itself onto my thighs?

It might actually be a *good* thing this relationship can't go anywhere—for once I don't need to worry about which excuse he'll use to dump me later, because this time I'm the one who's leaving. I pick up the little handle formed by the bone and tear the meat off with my teeth, closing my eyes as I savor the bite.

"Now that's more like it." Ian's voice is low and husky, as though he finds it sexy to watch a woman enjoy her food, rather than a turnoff. And for me, surprisingly, that's a turn-on.

"Don't make me enjoy this by myself," I say. "I'd rather share this foodgasm, if you don't mind."

He gives a throaty chuckle and obliges, scooping another medallion of lamb onto my plate before serving one to himself. For the next half hour, we sample and share and sip and talk, the innuendos growing bolder as we volley them back and forth. I can't remember the last time I had a more relaxing meal with a man, despite the fact that this one is laced with sexual tension. Usually I can't enjoy the sensuality of dining on a date because I'm too self-conscious about my body—with every bite, thinking *he thinks I'm fat* or *I must look like a cow.*

I was attracted to Ian before, but now, buzzed with wine and filled to satisfaction with this amazing meal and the way he's let me enjoy it, the feelings he's stirring in me are almost too much to bear.

For dessert we share a sampler served on a long, narrow white platter on a stand, which the server carefully erects at the center of the table. Individual ramekins contain divine samples of deliciousness—a pear crumble with honey and some sort of sweet, soft cheese, a tiny square of cheesecake drizzled with a raspberry sauce, a mini parfait glass filled to the brim with chocolate mousse and topped with house-whipped cream, and finally a perfect, gorgeous three-bite crème brûlée.

I take tiny bites and let him finish the sweets, not wanting to take my indulgence too far—and a little worried, honestly, about the increasing snugness of my dress, especially with the thought that this night seems headed in a direction where it might come off. But I don't hesitate to use the miniature spoon to crack the caramelized sugar glaze that tops the custardy dessert.

"Mmm, I love that sound."

"You all do." Ian laughs, and I give him a hurt look.

"You've shared a lot of crème brûlées, then?" I lick a tiny bite of custard off my spoon.

He watches my mouth greedily, licking his own lips. "I feel like I've never properly shared anything with anybody until now."

A thrill races down my spine, and we talk less as we finish eating, take the last sips of our drinks, and pay the bill, though the fuzzy feeling in my nerve endings doesn't let up. I think he's feeling the same way, and even though the canal is even more charming in the deepening twilight, the lights from the restaurants and shops shimmering in jagged lines across the water's slowly moving surface, I barely see it. He takes my right arm in his left and wraps the fingers of his right hand over mine as we walk. We fit together perfectly, I notice, his height at just the right point so that he's a few inches taller than me even in my three-inch heels. In my sexiest dress at the perfect level of buzz from our dinner wines, I don't even feel ungainly next to him. He's muscular and broad and strong, and I'm fit and sexy and able to hold my own.

That lift of confidence, even more than the hum of electricity between us, is what makes this night perfect. It's what's making *him* feel perfect in this moment, like there's no one I'd rather be with more in the entire world.

Who cares what tomorrow brings, or the next day or next week or next month? Tonight is all that matters right now. All that matters ever. At least, that's the way it feels.

* * *

I realize, after making our way back up to the street and getting into his car, that the fact we aren't sharing a taxi gives him more leeway in choosing where we ultimately end up. It's a brilliant move on his part—no driver hovering nearby with the engine running while we share a good-night kiss, no moment of awkwardness in the car beforehand while I contemplate inviting him up...what it would mean, how it would look to the sweet innkeeper who I'm now on a first-name basis with, whether we're moving too fast, whether we should be moving at all, considering I'll be going home in a week and there's absolutely no chance this has a future.

There's little deliberating at all, in fact. As if that should be a surprise—with the way my entire body is humming right now, with the way his fingers are practically searing a brand into the top of my hand where they rest together near the gear shift, if we don't go someplace we can be alone together, I might spontaneously combust.

"I was thinking of taking you to a wine bar close to my apartment," he says, lightly squeezing my hand, which pulses under his touch.

"Just thinking about it? Or doing it?" I say since he's driving in a definitive direction.

"Where do you want to go?" he asks, not looking at me. The question is loaded with all sorts of innuendo that's suddenly more serious than our banter during dinner.

"A wine bar sounds fine with me." I can hear the doubt in my own voice, which is barely louder than the muted techno-pop coming through the car's speakers.

"Or, if you want, I have wine at my apartment." This time he glances over at me, and I can hear that his breathing is sort of shallow and quick, matching mine.

"That sounds nice, too."

He swallows. "My apartment it is, then."

I swear his fingers grow even hotter over mine, or maybe it's just my internal thermometer that's changed. It's reached a new setting I don't believe I've ever experienced before, not with Steve, certainly not with Chase.

I watch the changing scenery blur by and crawl by at intervals, depending on the traffic and the lights. The drive feels interminable, considering we're doing very little talking but his left hand is creeping from my hand, to my wrist, to tracing featherlight trails up my arm, to moving eventually to rest high up on my leg. In so many ways this doesn't even seem safe. I'm relieved when he finally slows the car in the middle of a block and turns into a parking garage, or a *car park*, as the sign reads.

"What part of town is this?" I ask after he comes around and opens my car door. He clasps my hand and leads me toward an elevator near his parking space.

"Battersea," he says, and I glance up at him, confused.

"Battersea," I repeat. "Isn't this south? You're not very near Islington or Miranda's shop, are you?"

"No, not really." He gives a little laugh.

"But you're a regular at the Lion's Gate?"

"I used to be," he says. "I had a flat farther north, near Hampstead, but I hated the commute. I wanted to be closer to work. I've only lived here since February." He squeezes my hand again. "I became a 'regular,' as you call it, again say, oh, around last month. When Miranda texted to tell me she'd made a new friend she felt certain I'd like to meet."

This admission makes my bones feel all soft and spongy. I'm tingling all over again, as if we're already drinking the wine he promised and my buzz is back in full swing.

We don't say much more as I walk with him out onto the street and through the front entrance of a stone apartment building. At least I assume it's an apartment building. The entrance is nondescript, just a bland, numbered door set into the stone and tucked between two shuttered commercial bays, a chemist's and a flower shop. I'm mulling over the fact that he has a car—I've heard that parking in the city for residents is ludicrously expensive, kind of like parking in New York. Since

Memphis is an easy town for driving and parking, I can't relate to this, but it does seem that he's doing well for himself, with a flat in central London, a car, and reserved parking. It's hard to believe he's still single.

When we step inside his apartment, I gaze around to get my bearings, knowing you can learn a lot—everything, really—about a person by taking in their space.

All the walls within my view are white, and the flat is relatively sparse, with the typical black leather bachelor-issue sofa and monstrous flat-screen visible in the living room at the other end of the short entry hall. The kitchen, off to my right, looks as if it rarely gets touched, no dishes on the counter, no appliances jumbling up the countertop apart from a fancy-looking single-cup coffee dispenser—not a Keurig but some sort of European counterpart.

"Do you have a roommate?" I ask, my voice reverberating through the still space even though it's only a decibel above a whisper.

"I did," he says. "Conveniently, he got sacked a few weeks back and moved back home to Yorkshire just last week. I'm in between flatmates now." He smiles with half of his mouth, something I've always found sexy, but right now it almost drives me over the edge, even if he did just casually refer to the unfortunate luck of his former roommate.

"I…feel bad for him?" I say.

"Yeh, don't," he says. "He was skimming money from clients of the firm and got caught." His face clouds with an uneasy look that disappears in another moment. I guess he doesn't want to talk badly about his friend, so I don't ask any more questions.

I step away from him, walking past the kitchen and into the hall, continuing my perusal of the flat. There's not much hanging on the walls, but I pause in front of a framed black-and-white photograph above the diminutive metal hall table where Ian tossed his keys. It's a photo of a country church with a mottled stone façade that looks as if it's a thousand years old. Tall grasses wave in fields beyond the structure, and a low stone fence extends from the side of the church and disappears at the edge of the photograph.

"That's the chapel where my grandparents were married," he says, coming up behind me and placing a hand on my right shoulder. Again, the spot where he touches me sears, even through the fabric of my dress. "It's in Ormesby, another village outside Norwich, near the sea."

"Wow." I shake my head. "How old is the building?"

He chuckles at my tone of wonder. Clearly he has no idea how very little complement there is in my country to the eons of history in this place. "Oh, I don't know. Eight hundred years, maybe? Nine hundred?"

I shake my head again, letting that sink in. "Are you close with your grandparents?"

At this he frowns slightly, making me wish I hadn't asked the question. "My nan died two years past," he says. "My grandfather about ten years before that. But yes, I was close to both of them growing up. In fact my mum and siblings and I spent summers there when I was young. Michael and I and rode our bicycles to Yarmouth just about every other day, to the shore."

"It sounds idyllic," I say.

He squeezes my shoulder again and says, "It does, doesn't it? Everything sounds idyllic when you're talking about someone else's childhood." He gives a hard chuckle and steps around me into the kitchen. He pops his head around the corner. "Red or white?"

"Oh, white, please."

White wine is universally more attractive as a date option, since it doesn't stain your teeth and turn your lips purple. But even though my answer is automatic, his question throws me off a bit—I was so engrossed in the stories of his childhood that I almost forgot the way his presence is making me practically hyperventilate.

As I hear a cabinet door open and close and glasses clink together, I venture deeper into the apartment. In the living room I set my bag down on a metal and leather chair just inside the door—a reproduction Wassily armchair, so somewhere in his minimal decorating sense, he has good taste—and visually snoop a little more. There's a tan shag carpet over pale wood flooring and another armchair adjacent to the sofa, this one off-white and stiff looking. The coffee table is metal and glass, nondescript. In this room there's nothing on the walls, but a narrow table lining a side wall holds a couple of framed pictures. I step to get a closer look. In one Ian has his arm slung around a beautiful, blonde, fifty-something woman—his mother, I presume. In another two kids sit with their backs to a thick tree trunk, one of those staged shots by a professional photographer that's meant to look random and candid. The girl, around seven or eight, is caught midlaugh, and the boy, a couple years younger, is squinting at something near his shoe.

"Is this your niece and nephew?" I ask as I hear his footsteps come up the hall. He hands me a glass.

"Yes," he says, pointing to them in turn. "That's Samantha, and he's Charles."

"Are they your brother's kids? Or, you mentioned you have other siblings?" A memory has been swimming at the depths of my consciousness since he brought up his siblings, and as I ask this question it finally bobs up and breaks the surface. At the Lion's Gate on my last trip, Miranda and Ian and Pamela talked about Ian's brother, Michael—about how Ian's ex-girlfriend had fallen in love with him. My tongue freezes in my mouth.

"I'm not sure you could say I have any brother," he says with a tight smile. I can tell he's trying to keep his tone light. "But these two belong to my sister, Charlotte. They live in Taverham, also near Norwich. Living here, I don't get to see them near as often as I should."

As he answers he moves over to the coffee table and picks up a remote control. He sits, waving a hand to offer me a seat beside him. I perch with my wine glass, leaving a few inches of space between us that seconds earlier might have crackled with an electric current but now seem to be filled up with the ghosts of his past.

I take a series of long, slow sips while he surfs a Sky TV channel guide that offers an inordinate number of stations with BBC in the name. He breezes through the list and stops on a music channel playing a soft modern rock song I've never heard before.

"It's habit," he says, gesturing to the screen. "I'll admit to having that masculine proclivity to not being able to sit in a room without something playing on a screen and some sort of noise."

I laugh, slightly too loud in my opinion, and so I reach up and cover my mouth with two fingers. He seems to get a kick out of this.

He sets his glass on the end table beside him and then turns back to me. "Are you nervous?" he whispers. The boldness of his question is startling, but I straighten my back a little, determined not to let him show me up.

"Should I be?" My voice is not a whisper. I back up a couple of inches, teasing him. "Do you have some sort of dark secret you're hiding? Some unusual feature that's usually covered up? A third nipple, maybe?" I giggle again, softer this time, but something about the word turns the atmosphere, which has been vacillating between charged and loopy and serious, on its edge.

"Are you saying you want to find out?" His eyes hold mine for a long second before he closes the distance between us and covers my mouth with his, his fingers grappling for my glass and reaching to place it on the coffee table in front of us, not breaking contact with my lips.

This kiss is serious, promising much more than that first sweet, slow kiss a week ago outside the taxi. Almost as soon as his tongue is exploring my mouth, his hands are exploring my body, roaming from my back down the sides of my dress, tracing along my stomach and moving quickly to my breast, which peaks beneath his fingers.

"Ohhh," he murmurs. Both of his hands slip to my back, and he's searching with his fingers, finding the zipper near the line of my shoulder blades and tugging it down. My fingers, not knowing how to keep up, glide in slow-motion to the buttons of his shirt, and I start undoing them, beginning in the middle, moving up and then down, making no logical sense.

Nothing about this makes sense. And if anything, that makes me want him more.

Now he's sliding the silky fabric of my dress down my torso, and I'm helping him by wriggling one arm out of a cap sleeve then the other. I'm beyond relieved to be wearing a pretty bra, lacy and royal blue, not the utilitarian, skin-colored thing I usually wear under dresses to avoid any bulges or lines.

It's all so fast…his fingers are folding down the lacy cup of my bra, his mouth is kissing a trail along my shoulder, making its way down.

"I don't usually do this so fast," I pant, feeling urgent that he understands this. It is, after all, the truth. I've never had a one-night stand. I can count the number of boyfriends I've slept with on one hand.

"I don't either," he says, and then he pauses in his work to look very seriously into my eyes. His hand, meanwhile, doesn't budge a centimeter from its new home in the crook where my hip meets my thigh. My body is pulsing to the feel of him, and my hands, finished with the buttons of his shirt, trace a path along his smooth, muscular chest that's exposed and firm under my fingertips.

"I mean that. I haven't brought a woman home since…well, I don't even want to talk about bringing other women home." His lips find mine again as I manage to feel a moment's appreciation for the fact that he's called me a woman, not a girl. Everything about him, I feel equal to, which is a sensation I've never felt with another guy. Another man.

I peel the shirt the rest of the way off his shoulders, and as he arches upward to reach behind himself and pull it the rest of the way off, the evidence of how much he wants me is clear.

My brain is muddled, but I'm still thinking about the truth of my statement, that I don't usually do this so fast. I've been hurt enough emotionally. I don't need negative sexual experiences doing further damage to my self-esteem. It took four months for me to trust Chase enough to sleep with him, and look how that turned out.

But the urgency of our situation, of my leaving in a few days, is winning out to prudency, and besides that, Ian's fingers are bunching up the fabric of my dress on my thigh, leaving me little time to think this through.

And then my fingers are traveling of their own accord to explore places south of the exposed skin of his chest, his stomach. And then the bits of fabric that remain between us are no longer between us but on the sofa, the chair, scattered on the floor.

And then, next thing I know, I'm meeting his bedroom without being properly introduced.

CHAPTER TEN

————

Long-Distance Relationships

I wake up the next morning with sunlight streaming in a window that's oriented in an unfamiliar direction. One arm is flung above my head, so numb that when I try to move it, for a couple of seconds, it doesn't want to cooperate.

This isn't one of those hungover, *what-did-I-do-last-night?* moments. I remember every second of my night with Ian, which extended very nearly into this morning. I turn my head to peek at his sleeping form, wanting to feel the warmth of him against my skin again, but the other side of the bed is empty.

For a moment I'm panicked, thinking he's run out on me and is never going to call again. It calls to mind, of all people, my mother, who's never issued a single piece of romantic or sexual advice to me or my sisters other than, before I left for college, giving me a clipped and painful version of the old adage about not buying the cow when you can get the milk for free. I shake my head to clear it of my mother—of all people to be thinking of right now—and realize that Ian can't run out and avoid me when I'm in bed in *his* apartment.

And then I hear the bedroom door open and grasp that his leaving the room must have been what woke me up. But when he comes in he's fully dressed, so I amend that thought by realizing he's left the apartment and already come back. I must really have been out cold.

"Good morning," he says. "I have breakfast. I don't cook, so I popped out to the baker's on the corner. I didn't know what you like, so I've brought home an assortment." He flashes a boyish grin, and I don't have the heart to tell him I'm not much of a breakfast eater.

"Thanks," I say, subtly wrapping the duvet around my upper body as I half sit up. I still haven't gotten used to this English situation of a fitted sheet and duvet, with no flat sheet to snuggle into.

"Oh, you're being shy now, hmm?" He crosses the room in a few strides and perches on the edge of the bed, reaching out to try to peel the duvet from my hands and peek beneath it. "You weren't so shy a few hours ago."

A hot flush spreads up my neck and flashes across my cheeks. "I'm at a disadvantage," I say, trying to keep from aiming my unbrushed-teeth mouth in his direction. I realize with some horror that I don't have a toothbrush—a situation I haven't faced before since I've never done this in quite this fashion. "I'm the only one who's naked."

Ian gives up on tugging the covers and grins at me again. "I can change that situation," he says, lifting up a corner of his black T-shirt, sending a flutter through my body as I catch a glimpse of his rippled stomach. "But I'd better not," he adds, "since my mum and sister are on their way upstairs."

"What?" I shoot up in bed so fast that I lose my grip on the edge of the bedding, leaving my upper half exposed. He snickers as I rush to tuck the duvet back around me.

"That was a nice reaction," he says. "Just what I was going for. Actually it isn't true, but they are coming into the city today. Charlotte's bringing her oldest for a day out on the town. A *girls' getaway*, mum called it. Shopping and manis and chocolates and whatever it is you ladies do."

I chuckle anxiously. "When will they be here?" I'm spinning over my options in my head, and they aren't pretty, seeing as they all end with me taking public transportation home and doing the walk of shame up the front steps of my bed and breakfast in last night's LBD and classy-hooker heels.

Ian shrugs. "They're on the train now, so not for at least an hour and a half." He isn't looking at me when he adds, "You're welcome to meet them if you like. Although get ready for some heavy questioning from my mum because I don't speak with her about my dating life often."

I can't tell from these statements if he wants me to meet them or not. But my own gut reaction is that we're not ready for this—no matter how well I got to know him last night, and from my recollection it was pretty well.

"I'll let you have your time with them," I say. "I know it doesn't happen very often." He'd said something to this effect last night. Feeling supremely awkward and exposed, I add, "Which direction is the shower?"

I shower quickly and wrap myself in a towel—it's fluffy and smells freshly laundered, with an unfamiliar, sweetly floral scent that's incongruous with the bachelor pad vibe and makes me smile. I brush my teeth using my finger and Ian's toothpaste, which I find by scrounging around in the cabinet hanging on the wall near the sink. When I step back into Ian's bedroom, I dress in my same blue bra and panties and snug black dress, which he kindly laid out on the bed for me while I was in the shower.

To his credit, as we nibble on pastries and drink the coffee he made in his Nespresso machine—no tea for this Englishman, apparently, though I see that he does have the requisite electric kettle—Ian offers to drive me back to the inn.

"That's OK. I can get an Uber," I say, thinking that'll be less humiliating than dragging my mismatched—fancy dress, no makeup—clearly morning-after self all the way across town on the Underground.

"Are you sure?" His forehead is wrinkled in consternation. "I would never ask you to do that under other circumstances. I'm the one who dragged you all the way here."

I smile gently. "You hardly had to drag me."

At this he gives me a tender look and steps toward me, drawing me into an embrace. He kisses my forehead then pulls back to give a sweeping look down my body and says in a low voice, "That dress is a knockout. You didn't leave me a choice, really."

Once his lips leave mine, which is a blissfully long moment later, I whisper, "I'm glad I came."

At the same time we say, "No pun intended."

Ian bursts out laughing and kisses me again. "We really are perfect together," he says when he releases my lips. "That proves it."

It seems as if he really means it, and this makes me sad rather than happy. All I can think of is the fact that I'm leaving again and won't be back for weeks, maybe even a couple of months. The most promising relationship I've found myself in since…well, possibly since ever, and it's doomed before it can even start.

* * *

"You did *what*?" screeches Savy on the phone in a voice that doesn't sound like Savy. She never screeches.

"You *slept* with him? You don't ever do that." She says it in a sort of accusatory tone. "You practically require a contract before you'll sleep with a guy."

"You make me sound like Christian Grey," I say wryly. "I wouldn't have raced to call and tell you this if I thought you'd react this way." I pause and then add in a quieter voice, "I really like him."

If I'm being honest with myself I can't come to any other conclusion, though I've been trying to convince myself otherwise all morning. I've been playing my own devil's advocate, mentally chronicling all the red flags…his past with his ex and his brother, which he clearly hasn't gotten over. His reticence about his work. The brooding look he gets when he thinks he's said too much, which he did more than once, about his brother, about his office mate, about his roommate. Plus, I'm just not used to a guy being so clearly, unabashedly into me. Maybe it's because usually when I meet men, I'm with Savy.

"Well, that's different, then," she says. "And I wasn't judging you anyway. You know that. If you like him this much, I'm sure I'd approve." I can tell she's trying to make up for her flippancy a minute earlier. Savy is constantly tuned in to other people's feelings and hates to make anyone feel bad. It's part of her people-pleasing nature.

"I think you would like Ian," I say, warmth spreading through the center of my body as my voice wraps around his name.

"So, nothing to report with the British lord, then?" The disappointment in her voice makes me laugh.

"Ryland Pemberton?" I remember our odd encounter in the hallway outside Jane's demolished kitchen, the piercing assessments of me he seems unable to hide. "Definitely not. I saw him a few days ago, and he was every bit as stuck-up and rude as he was the last time I was here." I pause, remembering his hush-hush meeting with Jane in her office. "I do wish I knew the story of him and Elliott, though."

"The boy who's living with him, the cousin?"

"Yes. Although I don't believe Ryland actually lives there. It's kind of like he owns it on paper and only uses it as his hideaway from his public life. And Jane and Adam are part of his cover." All of this is gelling in my head only as I voice it aloud. I haven't given Ryland Pemberton much thought this trip since I've been so wrapped up in Ian, but now the size and shape of the weirdness of his situation seems patent.

"Hmm, that's really weird," Savy says, knocking me off my train of thought. "And how about Miranda? How is your newest friend this trip?"

I can't tell if there's a twinge of jealousy hidden in the question, but Savy and Jules have both expressed a sort of veiled skepticism about Miranda and her whole crew, Ian included. Jules, especially, thinks it's weird that Miranda drew me into her circle so readily. Even Jen, my boss, expressed surprise that I had such an easy time finding a London designer to partner with and help guide me through the web of sources and subcontractors, with so little expectation in return.

But that's just because they don't know her, I think. Miranda is the most laid-back, open, and friendly person I think I've ever met. And usually I'm skeptical of people—my upbringing didn't exactly warm me to the motivations of other women, especially tiny, gorgeous, pixie-like women who can seemingly get what they want with a mere bat of their fluttering lashes.

"Miranda is good," I say. "I've seen her a couple times this week because of work, but I haven't met up with the rest of the crew much on this trip since I've been with Ian."

Now that I think about it, it is a teeny bit odd how easily Miranda has accepted—encouraged, even—my absence from her and from our budding friendship so I can spend time with Ian.

It's like she really meant what she said, that she wants me to be the woman who mends Ian's troubled past. Why, I'm not sure. But I'm grateful for it. My past has its troubles, too, and following Chase and his put-downs, Ian's adoration is like a dip in a cool stream after a sunburn—a healing balm that no excuse or apology from Chase could ever compare to.

My skin flashes with heat as I think about last night. I've only been away from Ian for about two hours, and I'm craving him as much as I've ever craved chocolate or cheesecake or Chinese takeout or caffeine or, in college, nicotine. Maybe this is the key to losing weight…love.

My breath catches in my throat. Did I really just think the *L* word?

I've never been in love before, not even with Steve, who I'd worshipped and followed around like a faithful puppy throughout high school, even though he'd kicked me when nobody else was looking by making fun of me or, more often, by laughing along when his friends made fun of me, rarely ever coming to my defense. Even though I'd been aware of the rumors that he'd cheated on me with multiple girls who were all prettier, thinner, and more popular than I was, I'd clung to Steve because I thought I didn't deserve him, because I thought he made me better than I was on my own, because he'd won me some semblance of approval in the eyes of people like my mother, who was happy to see her "heavy daughter" with an attractive trophy on my arm in prom pictures. But I hadn't loved him. Not really. Not even before I'd figured out that all of the above was complete and utter crap.

I'd never loved Chase, not when I gave in and slept with him, not when I let myself travel down the path of thinking maybe we had a future. I'd told myself I thought I could fall in love with him, but that's certainly not the same thing.

Do I love Ian? The question sounds bizarre in my head. For one thing, it's way too soon to be asking it. For another, lust is definitely in the way of any other feelings I might have for him.

But the emotions he's stirring in me are huge, bigger than any I've ever felt before, too big to pinpoint or name. Just the thought of it is exhilarating, like a promise I can't tell anyone but that's certain to change my life. I can't really explain it, but I have a good feeling about him. And my instincts—often negative, generally accurate—don't tend to let me down.

And then I remember that I'm leaving again soon, and my entire being is a balloon with a pinprick-size hole, the air letting out slowly but deflating just the same. This is how it feels sometimes to be me—like a drifting balloon, so much promise, so much happiness to convey and enjoy and give, if only I could keep the air inside.

I'm leaving.

And Ian can't come with me.

"Quinn?" Savy's voice sounds far away. "Quinn? You there? Can you hear me?"

"Yeah, I'm here." I have no idea if she's been saying things that I haven't heard. I feel as if a lifetime's worth of revelation has just dropped onto my shoulders, and it's too heavy to bear. I sigh. "What'd you ask? Miranda? She's good."

I pause, realizing I'd better pay attention since I've been too busy this trip to talk much to Savy or Jules and we have loads to catch up on. How funny that when I dialed, I was blissful, ecstatic to tell my best friend about my night. Now I'm anxious to get off the phone, but it isn't Savy's fault. Eventually this realization would have dropped onto me regardless, smothering last night's bliss.

"She's good," I repeat in a dull voice. "Like I said, I haven't seen as much of her this trip."

"Oh. Yeah," Savy says, sounding confused. "Did you hear any of what I said about Jules? The connection must have faded out for a minute."

"Jules? No. No, I didn't hear you." I don't elaborate, letting her think the call cut out rather than admit I wasn't paying attention.

"Have you talked to her at all?"

"Not in the last couple of days," I say. "Why, what's up?"

"Oh, my God. You really haven't talked to her at all?"

Now she has my attention.

"No. I texted her a couple times last night, but it was morning where you are, and I just figured she wasn't up yet. I haven't heard from her." I pause, waiting for Savy to respond. "Why? *What's going on?*"

I hear Savy blow out a breath. "I don't think I need to tell you anything," she says. "I'll let her talk to you when she's ready. She might just be waiting to tell you in person."

"Now you're really freaking me out. Is it her and Luca? Did he cheat on her? Did she cheat on him? Are they calling off their engagement?" When she doesn't respond, my shrill voice gets shriller. "*You can't do this to me.* If you weren't going to tell me anything, you shouldn't have brought it up."

"No, you're right, I shouldn't have," Savy concedes. "Because it's not mine to tell. I just figured she would have talked to you already. She really might be waiting to talk to you until you get home."

"Well, clearly that's not happening now," I say. "Because I'll be calling her the second we hang up." I blow out a long breath. "I love being over here, but I hate being so far away from you guys."

"I know," Savy says. "It's totally weird. Even through the phone line, I can tell you're far away. It sounds different."

And in one week, it will sound that way when I talk to Ian on the phone. If, that is, we can even last past my transcontinental flight. Last night might really have been a one-night thing, and I might have to just be OK with that.

I push Ian out of my head, for the moment at least—I know it won't last. "I'm going to let you go and call Jules," I say. "I'll probably be calling you back."

"OK," Savy says. "Do call me back if you can. Oh, and Quinn?"

"Yeah?"

"I really am happy for you about Ian. I think you did the right thing last night."

"Yeah. Thanks. I think so, too." And I really do.

At least, if last night or this week or one month or two months of long-distance communicating is all we get, I'll have one amazing night to dream about, on the opposite side of the world, for the rest of my days on earth.

* * *

Jules doesn't answer when I call, but I keep calling back, hanging up each time before the call goes to voice mail. After five tries, I finally text her and say, "Pick up, already."

I wait her out, staring at my phone screen long enough that I get bored and click open Facebook. Finally, about two minutes later, she texts back.

"Chill out, woman. I was in the damn bathroom."

I dial again, and she answers almost before it rings.

"Savy told you" is the first thing she says.

"Told me *what*?" I ask, exasperated. "Nobody's told me a freaking thing."

"She didn't tell you?" Jules voice is wavering, like she's on the verge of tears.

"What's going on, Jules?" I ask. "Has something happened with you and Luca? And no, Savy didn't tell me whatever it is. She just asked me if I've talked to you."

Jules heaves out a long, heavy sigh. "Oh, God."

That's all she says.

"What? Honey, what's wrong?"

"This is a complicated thing to explain, and I really hate to tell you over the phone," she says. "But you've left me no choice, being over there." She pauses for a long time, but I wait her out, not wanting to interrupt. "So…yeah. Me and Luca are over." She sniffs, and I can tell even over the international airwaves that she's trying hard to hold back her emotion.

"What happened?" Even though I guess I was expecting this, based on her recent behavior, it's still a shock.

She lets out a strangled laugh, not a ha-ha laugh, more a cry of disbelief. "Well, I guess I should start at the beginning," she says.

"Yes, please do." I'm a little disgruntled that she's obviously been keeping things from Savy and me for some time, but I'm sure she's had her reasons.

"It all started a couple of months ago. Before you left for England the first time," she says, and my jaw drops. She's been keeping a secret from us for *two months*? "Well, way before that, probably, but that's when I found out."

"Found out? So he *has* been cheating on you?" I can't imagine it. Luca adores Jules. He's always been so good to her, doting and loving and admiring and respectful. I just can't see it at all.

"No, no, it's not like that," she says. "I mean, maybe he has cheated on me. I guess maybe…yes, well, emotionally he's been cheating on me, for sure, but I don't think there's been any physical act."

"This isn't making a lot of sense, hon," I say gently. "Tell me what you found out and how."

"I was getting ready for work one morning. This was a few weeks ago," she starts, speaking so slowly it's painful. "And I realized Luca had left his phone at home. He'd left sometime in the night or in the early morning hours. You know his shifts are so crazy."

She pauses for me to acknowledge her with an "mm-hmm."

"So, I was standing there trying to figure out how to get it to him, because obviously I couldn't text him to tell him I had it. And I knew he'd need it for work or at least want it throughout the day, so I was figuring I'd stop by the hospital on my way into the office, even though I was already going to be hella late and—"

"Jules," I interrupt her. "You're killing me here."

"Sorry, sorry." She sniffs again. "So, while I'm standing there holding the phone, a text comes in."

"And it's from a girl?" She can probably hear the shock in my voice. What a horrible, cliché way to find out your fiancé is cheating on you. I feel so bad for her I'm trembling.

"No." At this she pauses for a long time. "It was from a *guy*. Somebody named Jake. His name was programmed in, so it showed up onscreen."

There's a long moment of crackling silence as this sinks in. And then I say, "And so…and so Luca is…gay?"

She takes a sharp inhalation of breath. "It was pretty clear from the text."

"What did it…what did the text say?"

She takes another deep breath. Her voice is wobbly when she answers. "It said, 'Great talk last night, man. I'll be waiting for you in the same place. We can take this as slow as you need to, especially considering you haven't told Jules yet.'" She breaks down, a sob in her voice as she adds, "'I miss you.'"

"That's what the text said?" I ask to clarify. "It said, 'I miss you?'"

"Yes," she whispers.

"Wow." My voice is shaky, too.

"Yeah."

"What...what happened? I mean, what happened next?"

She sniffs again. "Well, nothing. I mean, not for a while. I was just in so much shock. I left his phone on the bathroom counter and pretended I hadn't seen it. I...I didn't know how to just come out and ask him, and obviously I knew it had to be tearing him up, too."

I can hear her softly crying, and my heart is reaching out to her, trying to fold her into a hug over a phone line and four thousand miles away. I reach up to swipe the tears from my cheeks.

"That day in Local," she continues, "when you got back. Well, first of all, I'm sorry I wasn't around much after your trip. I didn't know how to talk to you or Savy about it. I mean, I know I should have told you first thing, but I was...I don't know. Embarrassed? Like, humiliated? I mean, I know this has nothing to do with me, and this is just who he is, but it was like everything I knew about myself was suddenly different, and a lie, and I just needed time to process it, you know? And..." Her voice trails off.

"Honey," I say in as soft a voice as I can manage. "There's no need to apologize to me or to Savy. It's understandable that you needed time. I'm just sorry I wasn't there to help you through this. Because yeah, it isn't your fault. One hundred percent nothing to do with you."

I pause, and for several seconds neither of us speaks. Finally I ask, "So, I take it he knows you know now?"

"Yeah," she says. "He still...he still didn't tell me. I kept waiting. I think he just—you know he's a good guy..."

"I know he is," I agree.

"And so I think he just didn't want to break my heart. Like, he just couldn't do it. And days kept going by, and weeks, and I kept resisting the urge to break into his phone and see what else he and Jake were texting about, see if things had progressed beyond talking…"

I'm stock still as she pauses, barely even breathing, not wanting to interrupt.

"And so finally I just asked him about it," she says.

"Wow," I breathe. "How? What did you say?"

"I waited up for him last Wednesday night after his shift. I got home around six, and he'd texted to say not to wait up, that he'd be home after midnight. But I did wait up. And…" She pauses again. "And I'm not proud of this, but I texted Ryan, one of his buddies from med school, another resident, and asked if he knew what time Luca's shift ended, said I couldn't get hold of him."

"And…?"

"And he said he and Luca were on the same shift, and he was leaving at eight."

"And so Luca had four hours unaccounted for."

"Four hours with Jake," she says with resignation. "I knew that had to be it."

"Wow."

She continues as if she doesn't hear me. "So he finally came in around one a.m., and I was sitting up in the living room, watching like my fifth episode of *Game of Thrones*, and he keyed in all quietly, and I think it scared the hell out of him when he saw me sitting there, staring at him."

She pauses long enough for me to say, "And then what happened?"

"Well," she says. "I think he knew then. I think he knew from the look on my face that I knew. So I ask him, 'Is there anything you want to tell me?'" She chokes on a sob and continues, the words breaking up around her sobs, "And he said, 'Oh, my God, Jules. I'm so sorry.'"

Neither of us speaks for a couple of minutes, both of us crying on separate ends of the phone line. Finally she tells me more about the night, about how Luca had held her for three hours straight, how they were so exhausted the next morning that they both called in sick to work. How he was already moving out of their apartment, his stuff packed in boxes that still lined the hallway while he figured out where he was going to go. How neither of them had told their parents yet.

"Oh, honey," I say to her when the stories and our tears seem to have run their course. "I'm so, so sorry."

"I know." She blows her nose. "I knew things weren't right between us," she says. "I've known for a long time." There's another long pause. "You know we hadn't had sex in like five or six months. And before that, it was a while. A long while, probably. I don't know. I mean, since he started his residency, he's been so busy all the time, and his hours were so crazy and our schedules almost never overlapped. There always seemed to be a reason, a reason I could make it seem OK…"

She pauses. "I'm sorry I didn't talk to you about it."

"Don't be sorry," I say. "God, don't be sorry. Some things are so private you can't even tell your best friend. And sometimes saying it out loud makes it seem like it might be true."

"Yep," she says. "You nailed it. I didn't want to admit there was a problem because I didn't want there to *be* a problem. I really loved Luca, really." Her voice grows soft. "I still do."

"I know," I whisper. "I'm so sorry."

And I can't tell her anything about Ian, not tonight. My news is nothing compared to hers, and my earlier angst and even sorrow over my situation is suddenly nothing, too. Talk about gaining perspective.

Sometimes love isn't enough. And sometimes, it is. I don't know where things will go with Ian, but right now it doesn't matter. It will matter when it matters, and Ian will be there or won't be there. But one thing's for sure—Jules will be there. And suddenly I'm ready to get home.

CHAPTER ELEVEN

———

I Never Expected You

The next morning I'm a kaleidoscope of emotion. I'm devastated for Jules and Luca, and at the same time, I have to admit, bemused over Luca's situation. How could he not have known in all the years he spent with Jules that he was attracted to men? Did some part of him know all along? How long has he been lying about it, to Jules, to the rest of us, to himself?

Jules is the most feminine woman I know, not to mention the most loyal, the most kind, the most generous person I can imagine. The idea of her not being loved in every way, in all the ways she deserves, is unthinkable. But these qualities also make her the perfect person for Luca, especially now. If anybody can help Luca navigate the rough waters he's wading through, it's her.

I can't imagine how either of them picks up and starts again from this point, but I hope they both can, and soon. I love them both too much to think of them hurting like this.

The part of me that longs to be back home, in Memphis, helping Jules through this terrible time in her life is warring with the part of me that's longing for Ian. He called last night after his family left and asked if I could come over, and I turned him down. I didn't tell him about Jules—I was still processing it, and he's still new. Somehow it felt like a disloyalty to talk about her situation to an outsider, even if I'm crazy about him.

Besides, there's also a part of me that doubts what happened with Ian, what I let happen, and where I let things go—hell, where I helped take things. When I say I don't rush in, I mean I really *don't rush in*. The sex, the feelings, the…all of it, it's scaring the hell out of me. Especially now. Especially when I look at Jules and Luca, the two people I was most certain were meant for each other and would be together forever, and see how ephemeral, how fragile, our ties to each other really are.

I know Jules would talk me down from this if she were in a different place and I were admitting all of this to her. She'd tell me it was a load of crap, that my potential feelings for Ian have nothing to do with her relationship with Luca, that I'm just being my typical self, scared to commit and looking for the quickest route to the door.

Of course, she's never dealt with trust issues, really, until now. Her parents are still together and cute in that dorky, geriatric kind of way—her dad's the type of guy who flicks a dish towel at her mom's tush with a wink on his way through the kitchen. They still hold hands. And Jules has been with Luca forever, since they were practically kids. Her relationship history, both familial and romantic, is the stellar opposite of mine.

No guy has ever given me a reason to trust him before.

Friday night, I trusted Ian. I trusted that he wasn't using me and trusted that the spark between us, the chemistry, that it was *real*. What I felt for him then and what I still feel, it's deeper than a crush, more serious than a one-night stand. It's different somehow from the way I felt about Chase, or Steve, or any other guy I've ever been with. But now, in the light of day and in light of what I know about Luca, what he's been hiding, I'm not sure I can trust the way Ian feels about *me*. I mean, it's not as if he's given me a reason to trust him—if anything, he's been piling up a list of reasons for me not to trust him. And I barely know him, at any rate. Sure, Friday night was amazing. Incredible. One of the best nights of my life, if not *the* best.

But that's one night. He still has plenty of room to disappoint or betray or belittle me, given time. In my experience it's definitely coming. And this is without even considering the very really obstacle between us, that little matter of the Atlantic Ocean. In eleven days I'm flying back across it, and the breadth of it will surely dampen the spark of what's happening between us, like the first cool drizzle after a hot, steamy summer.

I don't feel like getting out of bed, but I can't waste a minute of my limited time here wallowing in my situation, or Jules', even on a Sunday. So I drag myself off the four-poster in the bedroom that's become like a second home and into the bath, where I choose to use the antique clawfoot tub rather than the modern shower unit fitted into a corner of the en suite.

I hear my phone buzz with a new text while I soak, but I don't rush to get out of the tub, taking my time to shave my legs, lather my hair, and enjoy the hot, steamy spray of the Euro-style nozzle as the rivulets of shampoo run down my neck and shoulders and back.

After I've wrapped myself in a fluffy white towel, brushed my teeth, moisturized from head to toe with the luxurious Moulton Brown products provided by the B&B, and then applied a touch of makeup—procrastinating before I head back over to Jane and Adam's house to check on any progress I've missed since Friday morning, in case there's been any—I pad into the bedroom and notice the phone screen light up with another message. I sigh, not really wanting to talk to anybody at the moment, preferring to remain in my own head.

Are you around today? It's Ian again. My eyebrows knit together, surprised at his persistence. Usually, in my experience, guys are mostly absent at the start of a relationship, either intentionally playing games to make a girl sweat or less intentionally nonchalant, not realizing the female in the situation is fretting over every minute that a call or text does or doesn't come, placing outsized meaning on every minor interaction.

I left him roughly twenty-four hours ago, and already he's texted me multiple times, even sending me a cute pic of himself with his niece outside the My London Girl store—a UK take on the American Girl phenomenon, apparently—yesterday afternoon. He called last night, and now he's texted twice already this morning.

Last night, before talking to Jules, I'd have sold my soul for this kind of attention. Now I just feel sort of numb, even a little wary.

Yes, I type back as I walk over to the wardrobe, where I've hung or folded most of the contents of my suitcase. *Planning to work a little bit. Leaving for client house in a few.* I set the phone on a ledge of the wardrobe while I flip through the padded hangers. It buzzes again as I pull from the hanger a simple shift dress in a cornflower blue that's almost the exact shade as my eyes; it's my favorite casual dress.

I walk over and lay the dress and my towel on the bed while I grab underwear. I start toward my suitcase, propped open on a luggage rack beside the wardrobe, but the pull of Ian's new text is too strong to resist. I reach over and snag my phone, swiping open the screen while I sort through my panties and bras to find the ones I always wear with this dress.

I pick them up—nude and utilitarian—and then immediately drop them again when I read the words on the screen. *Oh, oops. I'm outside your hotel. Any chance I can coerce you to change your plans?*

What?? My eyes swivel wildly toward the window, which doesn't make a lot of sense as it overlooks a rear courtyard and not the street view, so I couldn't see Ian outside if I tried. Somehow it makes the moment more panic-inducing—and funnier—that I'm standing here naked, as if he's got X-ray vision and knew exactly what he was doing by texting me now.

Thinking about Ian and being naked overtakes my senses for a couple seconds, and then I giggle and lean against the edge of the wardrobe, feeling a heady, overwhelming sense of relief from the comedy of the situation, which I needed. I've definitely been dwelling too much on the tragedy.

I'm still laughing, shaky inside, almost giddy, when I text back, *I'm listening. What do you have in mind?*

While I wait for him to text me back, I riffle frantically through my suitcase, dropping the boring nude panties and replacing them with a less boring, lacy nude pair that still won't show through my dress. I pick the push-up bra instead of the full-coverage granny version. I ask myself why I'm doing this when I've just been going over all the many reasons why things with Ian could never work out long-term, and finally I think about Jules, about the advice I know she'd give me if she knew my situation, and decide, *Long-term, long-schmerm. Why the hell not?*

Life is short. A girl—a woman—deserves to have a little fun.

*　*　*

"She really said that?"

"Yes. Vivienne is a bitch on wheels. And of course, I love her dearly." My mouth turns up at one corner, as what I've said is the absolute truth and one of the purest paradoxes of my life.

Ian and I have spent a lazy afternoon wandering the blocks around Spitalfields, dipping in and out amidst the famous market's stalls, which alternate with authentic, handmade goods by local artisans and bulk-ordered, touristy trinkets. Even better, with Ian's guidance I've gotten to know the real, hidden markets, which are thriving with life and tucked away in back-alley warehouses with rollaway doors, open only on Sundays. Along with stalls stuffed to bursting with vintage clothes that Jules would absolutely die over, there's aisle after aisle of stands proffering ethic foods, emanating with rich, aromatic, and distinctly foreign combinations of herbs and spices like turmeric, coriander, clove, cumin, curry, and any number of hot peppers. We sample several things in thin, boat-like cardboard takeaway containers dotted with grease that we blot off our hands with too-small paper napkins.

I buy gifts for my nieces and nephew, Aisling a baby doll with hand-stitched clothing and blonde ringlet curls that remind me of hers, Elijah a handmade wooden airplane with a painted red stripe and a miniature wood pilot whose arms and legs are jointed so he can stand beside his plane or be fitted into the cockpit. The maker, a stooped Irish pensioner with white hair in tufts, was selling his work himself, and Ian and I talked to him long enough to learn snippets of the life story that brought him from Cork to London in the early '70s. For Cat, I find a vintage book of violin compositions that includes Paganini's Caprice No. 24, which I know is her favorite.

I pick up a funky fitted T-shirt with the Union Jack screen printed over a backdrop of crop circles that's quirky and weird and totally Jules, along with a magenta leather clutch for Savy made by an artist whose pink hair and outrageous fashion choices could give Miranda a run for her money. We talk to her for several minutes as well—long enough for me to learn that the panel of robin's egg blue fabric stitched into the leather of Savy's purse came from a dress the artist bought in a random £5 grab bag of vintage clothes that were destined for the rubbish bin. Savy will love that story—she loves supporting struggling artists, and she loves the items she owns to have a story, period.

And now we're settled into a booth with all my packages in a noisy Brick Lane curry house, where I'm picking at my lamb rogan josh and basmati rice not because they're not delicious— I'm actually developing quite a taste for curries—but because I'm still full from our nibbling in the market stalls and because, as our day closes in on nighttime, the more jumpy and tight with anticipation my stomach is getting, and I know that, in any case, I don't want to overeat.

Plus, now we're talking about our families, and since Ian is finally starting to open up a little, I want to drag out this conversation as long as possible.

"I know what you mean," Ian says. "I suppose I still have brotherly feelings toward Michael, despite the fact that he's treated me literally like a first-class cuckold."

I try not to chuckle, considering the seriousness of the subject, but I'm pretty sure I've never heard anyone actually use the word "cuckold" in conversation before. Oh, how I love the English. I also love how Ian says "literally," which he sprinkles generously throughout his sentences. It's a three-syllable word off his tongue, not four. "Lit-ral-ly." And it usually means the opposite of whatever he's trying to convey.

"What happened?" I ask gently, looking at the table instead of him. "With Joanna and Michael, I mean."

I glance up to see his surprise that I know—or at least, that I remember—his ex-girlfriend's name from the one brief conversation at the pub.

"Oh, I don't know that you want to hear that sad story."

"Only if you want to tell it."

I catch his eye, and he shrugs. "I've nothing to hide about it, I suppose. She wasn't my one great love or anything. We met while I was spending some time back home. I was between jobs after dozens of us got the sack at the investment brokerage I previously worked for—the financial crisis in the States made its ripples here, too, you know. Anyway, I was sharing Michael's flat and working in the business office of a mortgage lending broker in Norwich whilst sending resumes to all the bigger investment offices in London." He pauses and takes a sharp breath, glancing down at the table before meeting my eyes again. "Actually I met Joanna through Michael, through the group of friends he was hanging around with at that time. We're only a year apart in age, Michael being the younger. Joanna and I struck up a conversation at the pub, and we dated for, oh, three or four months. It was only after I landed the job with my firm and broke the news to my family that I was leaving for London again that I found out about Joanna and Michael."

"What happened that made you find out?"

I can't help asking. I'm enthralled.

"Nothing too dramatic." He shrugs again—almost *too* nonchalant, which makes me wonder how much this conversation is costing him. "A mutual friend from the group sat me down and told me, thought it'd be better than me finding out accidentally, by catching them snogging in the flat when I came home or something like that." He pauses thoughtfully, nibbling off a corner of naan, chewing, and swallowing before going on. "I confronted Joanna, who admitted to the whole thing readily— it was eating her up that she was coming between brothers. I never did confront Michael, however. It wasn't eating *him* up— that was the problem. We haven't actually spoken since."

"And they're still together?" I ask, eyes wide.

"They're still together," he says with a nod.

"How long ago did this happen?"

"About eighteen months hence," he says. He rips off another, bigger, bite of naan before adding, "The wedding is in October."

"Wow."

"That about sums it up."

We both sip and chew in silence for a couple of minutes.

"And then to top it off, now my firm has rumors of another big round of redundancies. Based on my luck, I'm not holding my breath that my position is steady at all. Especially after what happened with Ewan." His mouth closes over the word in a strange way, as if he wishes he could suck it back in.

"Ewan?" My forehead wrinkles as I try to place the name. I don't think he or Miranda have ever mentioned a Ewan.

"My old flatmate," he says, rubbing his forehead, a gesture I'm coming to realize means he's agitated or talking about something uncomfortable. I lean forward automatically, eager to unlock more of his mysteries.

"He got the sack recently, like I said," Ian continues. "And the situation wasn't pretty. He was doing something shady with the figures on his accounts and apparently skimmed off a few tens of thousands of pounds that he transferred into an offshore account. But he wasn't very good at it, obviously, and he got caught before any real, substantial damage was done."

He heaves a long, wracking sigh, looking so glum I want to crawl across the table and give him a hug. But something is bothering me—something that could explain everything from his reticence to his single status, and that something scares me more than a little.

I open my mouth to ask the question on my mind, close it again, and then decide to ask anyway. What have I got to lose?

Besides him, that is. Besides everything.

"What does Ewan's situation have to do with you potentially losing your job?"

I feel insensitive for asking since Ian has already shared one hard luck story and is clearly struggling to discuss this one, but I hold my breath to wait for his answer, knowing I have to ask for my own sake and wondering if he'll be pissed or if he'll clam up again. Either way, I fully expect his reaction to be a deal-breaker—for this to be the reason I pick not to be with him, as Jules would characterize it.

My muscles are rigid, my whole body tense with anticipation.

"Nothing," he says quickly. Too quickly.

"I mean, I had nothing to do with any of it," he amends. "I didn't know it was going on until everybody else did, when our managing director sat us all down and told us what had been going on—to gauge our reactions, I think. But afterwards he asked me to stay behind, and he questioned me separately from the others. I'd never met with him one-on-one before, never done anything so good or so dreadful that I'd had to answer directly to him, so I'm sure my nervousness didn't help matters. But it was clear that, as I'd lived with Ewan, the powers that be suspected that I played a role, that I was some sort of accomplice in the situation. I'm still not one hundred percent sure they believe I wasn't involved."

At this his face twists in authentic despondency, and to my surprise, I find that I believe what he's saying, that he truly didn't know. If it isn't true, I've never met a better actor.

He glances up at me, directly into my eyes. "I met him through a company noticeboard," he says. "I needed a flatmate and answered an advert. We roomed together four months and barely even crossed each other's paths."

He studies the candle flickering on the table between us. "I'm daily afraid of being served subpoena papers," he says in a soft voice and then chuckles nervously when he looks up at me, shaking his head. "Hardly third-date material to be sharing, is it? I suppose I should also tell you I'm supporting my mum after my deadbeat drunk of a father disappeared a year ago, lit-rally vanished in the night, leaving a monsoon of creditors raining in his wake. She gets daily threats in the post, and the phone never stops ringing. This was why I had to drop everything yesterday—she so rarely gets away from it all to do something for herself."

I'm not sure what expression is frozen on my face, but seeing it, Ian chokes out a hard, somewhat acidic laugh. "I'm sure you're ready to run screaming from the restaurant by now. I'm such a catch." His eyes, when they focus on mine again, are bleak.

"My God, Ian" is all I can choke out. "I'm so sorry. For all of it." Between his stories and Jules', I feel like I've put to use my entire range of emotions in the last twenty-four hours.

"Thanks for that," he says, rubbing his forehead again. "Now, are you willing to let me see you back to your inn myself, or would you rather I call you a taxi?" He shoots me a tense, lopsided smile to show me he's kidding, but probably only halfway.

"I'm not running away," I say with intensity, leaning toward him. "You can't help your bad luck. Why does that make you not a catch?"

I'm tripping over my tongue a little, still shell-shocked by the bomb of information—too much at once, maybe, but that seems par for the course in this sped-up, urgent, deadline-driven romance we seem to be sharing.

He studies me for a long moment. "Really?" he finally asks.

"Really."

If anything, I'm more attracted to him now that he's not hidden beneath a shroud of unanswered questions. In fact, the intense bubble our conversation has formed around us is charging the atmosphere—I can actually feel it change—and bringing us closer, and there really only seems to be one direction we can take this overwhelming rush of feeling. He covers my hand with his.

"Thank you," he says, his voice thick. "Thank you for believing me. Thank you for not running away."

He pauses, shaking his head and giving me a slightly dazed look. "I never expected this."

"Never expected what?" I imagine I know what he's saying since I'm also feeling things I'm not sure how I can even convey, but I want to hear him say it.

"I never expected *you*," he says. "I mean, I *liked* you. You, you're"—he gestures toward me—"you're gorgeous, aren't you. And sophisticated and clever and lovely. But I thought we were having a bit of fun." He looks sheepish. "I mean, not that I'm not having fun…"

His voice trails off as warmth floods my body.

"I think I know what you mean."

"You do?"

"I'm leaving soon," I say, and he starts to shake his head, to protest, but I hold up a finger to stop him. "I'm only here for a short time, and this was supposed to be a fling, just something fun and someone interesting and foreign to meet and go on a date or two. An adventure. But…"

His hand grips mine a little tighter as he leans in across the tabletop. "But…" he prompts.

"But I like you," I finish lamely, unable to express it in deeper terms. "I really, really like you."

"I really like you, too." His voice is very soft, his eyes filled with a tenderness I've never seen in anyone's before. I feel like I could melt onto the tabletop, like I could melt right off the earth at this moment and leave happy.

And then a server stops beside our table to refill water glasses and whisk away forgotten plates, and the spell is broken as we pay the bill and gather my packages and make our way out of the restaurant and onto the teeming, noisy sidewalk.

The whole way back to his flat—where we head without even a need to discuss it—despite towing my bulky shopping bags and navigating the tunnels and platforms of three tube stops and walking the half block from the Underground to Ian's building, it's as if I'm floating, my feet not once meeting the ground. Our conversation has been lighter, not just in topic, which is a given, but light as in airless, a shared giddiness that's clearly mutual, like a weight's been lifted and we've reached a new, unspoken understanding.

It's happened very quickly, far more quickly than I would ever deem prudent, but it feels as if we've turned an invisible corner into a Real Relationship.

And later, when he slides my dress over my head and my hands and lips roam to find their now-familiar favorite places on his body, I feel whole and healthy and unfettered and beautiful and loved.

CHAPTER TWELVE

———

Blasts from the Past

A week and two days later, I'm on the job, standing in the midst of Jane and Adam's kitchen, wearing a hard hat since the contractor is now removing the 1970s-added dropped ceiling to open up the space and free the electrical team to install the recessed lighting I've specified.

I wish the subs were further along on their individual jobs so that, A) I could see some of the installation getting underway before I have to leave again, and B) obviously, so the project comes together quicker and I can fly back over here to Ian again sooner. But I know how renovation works—here's a hint: it isn't fast—and it seems to move even slower in this country than it does at home. I'd hoped to at least be past the demolition phase before getting on another plane, but no such luck.

It's the middle of the day, and Adam is at work, Braxton at school, and Jane at some sort of women's luncheon. I'm consulting my plans and trying to work out what date I'll need the painters to return for the kitchen walls and ceiling. My mind is halfway on the paint schedule and halfway on Ian, lingering particularly on certain details of last night that haven't left my mind entirely all day.

Since his flat isn't nearby and since I have so much work to do in the short time I'm here, Ian has set up camp in my hotel suite and caught an extra-early tube ride to work each morning during the week, rather than me staying at his place. Spending nights apart is not an option we've even discussed—apart from work, we haven't left each other's side since he turned up at my

B&B a week ago Sunday. Flying away from him, which I'm doing the day after tomorrow, will be physically painful. I can't even think about it, or I'll be too upset to get anything done.

"Mind your head," the contractor calls down from his perch in the rafters, in a similar intonation to the "mind the gap" recording that repeats on London's train platforms. Seconds after he says it, a crumbling hunk of plaster covered with bits of old insulation crashes to the floor several feet to my right, adding to the mess in the room, which by now shows almost no resemblance to Jane and Adam's former kitchen—or to any kitchen, for that matter. Only the capped pipes emerging from the floor and walls in places give a hint to the intention of the space.

"Bloody hell, it's like a war zone in here."

My whole body swivels to the sound of the unexpected voice.

Ryland Pemberton is picking his way over the rubble, trying to avoid the worst of the dusty mess with his expensive-looking shoes. I sweep a glance up his body, my eyes narrowing.

"Where the hell do you *come* from?" I ask. "It's like you crystallize out of nowhere. Don't you ever just ring the doorbell?"

He gives me a tight-lipped smile. "I prefer to keep a low profile," he says, confirming mine and Savy's and Jules' suspicions.

"And why is that, exactly?" I'm not sure where my brashness is coming from, speaking to an important public figure like this—maybe because Jane isn't here. Maybe because any stab of attraction I might have felt around this man in the beginning has disappeared, a casualty of my feelings for Ian and of Ryland's own unpleasantness.

As I assumed he would, Ryland ignores my question. "Is Jane at home?" he asks in a new tone, clipped and professional.

"No, she isn't, actually. It's just me and this lot." I gesture up toward the ceiling and then out toward the conservatory, where another couple of tradesmen are carefully dismantling part of the exterior wall to make way for the new windows.

"Mmm, that's unfortunate," Ryland mutters.

"Gee. Thanks." I smile to show I'm kidding, but he doesn't smile back. What a jerk.

"That isn't how I meant it," he says, looking at me—as in, actually gazing in the direction of my eyes and acknowledging me as a human—for the first time. There's no hint of humor in his voice, merely impassive relaying of the facts. "You Americans take every statement so personally."

"You certainly like to stereotype," I shoot back, suddenly determined to get a rise out of the guy. He's like an automaton, or at the least like one of the Buckingham guards, the Beefeaters—as if it's part of his official duties to exhibit no emotion whatsoever.

And just that easily, I've won. A wave of confused and conflicting sentiment flickers across his face, handsome like a Ken doll's and every bit as plasticized.

He mutters something under his breath that sounds like, "God, you're so like her."

It's not at all what I expect, and I'm sure my surprise reads easily on my face. "What do you mean?" I ask in a perplexed voice. "I'm so like who?"

"Whom." He says it automatically, like a tic. He must be a real pleasure to spend time with on a regular basis. "And never mind, then. I'm not meant to be a bother to you."

He starts to turn away, but there is no way I'm letting him leave here without some sort of explanation for that statement.

"No, really," I say, reaching out and touching his arm before he can walk away from me. "What did you mean? Who do I remind you of? Or, if you'd prefer, *whom* do I remind you of?"

He pulls his arm away sharply, as if my touch burns into the surface of his suit jacket, searing straight through to the skin below.

His expression seems torn between not wanting to bother with a response and wishing to say whatever he has to say to extricate himself from my presence. His eyes are conflicted for a moment, and then finally he gives a tiny shake of his head, lips pursed.

He blows out a sharp, efficient exhalation.

"You look exactly like a woman I once knew," he says. "Elliott's mum, in fact." He pauses, his cerulean eyes flashing to mine for the briefest of moments. "It's absolutely uncanny."

His voice is low, almost reverent, causing my mind to spin with a tilt-a-whirl of confusion. Didn't Jane say Elliott's mum was Ryland's cousin's wife? Why would he call his cousin's wife "a woman I once knew?" Before I can collect these thoughts enough to formulate a response, Ryland adds, "She, too, was American."

My brows are knitted together, and my head is cocked slightly to one side, trying to make sense of this new, nonsensical information. When I look back up at him, another question on my lips, Ryland is gazing at me with consternation, maybe even a trace of panic. As if he knows he's said too much.

While I watch, his entire demeanor changes, becomes glossed over with that impassive, professional glaze. "Well," he says, lacing his fingers and bending them backward, cracking his knuckles in a way that hardly seems aristocratic. "I'm off, then. Will you please convey to Jane that I stopped by? I need to speak with her."

"Of course," I say.

With no further pleasantries, he spins on a polished heel and returns to the back door through which he came.

*   *   *

I know I shouldn't spread gossip about Ryland Pemberton—if not to protect the man himself then to protect Jane's mysterious role as his confidant. And I don't mean for it to come out. But late Tuesday night, after a long, dusty day at the townhouse, a long, hot shower in my hotel suite, and a longer, hotter encounter with Ian that started in the stairwell of the B&B—because we couldn't keep our lips away from each other long enough to make it to the door—I'm lying languidly in the middle of the queen-size bed, curled into Ian's side, his hand tracing a lazy pattern along the length of my left arm, and it just slips out, apropos of nothing.

"Have you ever met Ryland Pemberton?" My mind is on a conversation I'd had with Jane just before I left the townhouse, when I'd finally remembered to tell her Ryland had stopped by. She'd asked me what time he'd come, and when I approximated as best I could, a pair of parallel worry lines had appeared between her eyebrows. She'd asked me specifically what he'd said, and then she'd seemed frantic, glancing at her watch, fretting out loud over whether or not she should call him.

I left a couple minutes later, puzzling over it on my walk back to the inn. By the time Ian arrived, I'd forgotten all about it…until now.

"No," Ian says, drawling out the long *o* sound for several seconds until it has a question mark at the end of it. "I know *of* him, of course." He pauses. "Why? Do *you* know Ryland Pemberton?"

I *so* wish I could hit rewind on the last thirty seconds and un-ask the question. But at the same time, the tiny twinge of jealousy in Ian's voice is sort of adorable.

I chuckle and flip over to face him. "Yes," I answer, looking up at him. "He's a friend of my client's."

"Really?" he asks, his forehead crinkling. "And…so you've met him at your client's house, then?"

Definite jealousy. *Oops.* I need to find a way to shut this down. Which doesn't explain why I next say…

"Yes. He has a young cousin who hangs out with my clients' son. I was just…wondering how much you know about him. Like, if he's ever been married, or if he's had any high-profile relationships. I mean, I can just Google it, I guess. I just thought, you know, living here in London, you might know something about him."

While I'm talking, Ian's lips turn down into a full-on frown. "Do I need to be worried about this line of questioning?"

I giggle nervously. "No. God, no. Never mind. It was just a silly thing that popped into my head." He's still frowning, gazing at me seriously, and so I add, "He's a total prick, and that's basically why I'm curious about him. Trust me, you don't need to be worried."

His forehead clears. "He looks like a total prick," he agrees. "I've always figured him for a right wanker."

"Well, you would be right." I grin at him, loving that he's jealous, loving the lilt of his voice when he uses cute British slang. However, I need to get off this topic, and there's one surefire way I know to distract Ian very thoroughly. So I employ the method.

I don't know if Ian thinks any more about our conversation over the next couple of hours before we fall asleep wrapped in each other's arms, but I can tell you for certain it doesn't take long for me to get Ryland Pemberton off my mind.

* * *

I spend the day before I leave tying up loose ends—calling and emailing and, in the case of the electrician, personally tracking down my subs to make sure the timeline is understood by all. Of course, no one will follow it ultimately, and I'll be on the phone again, making the rounds as best I can from across the ocean to reshuffle the deck. No matter where you try to do this, the process works much the same, and it's like pushing the first domino and stepping back to watch the line fall neatly in a row. When one domino falls astray—when the tile layer doesn't get the grout down on the scheduled day, for instance—the whole train stops, and the orchestrator of the process—in this case, me—has to line them all back up again.

Once I've done everything I can to ensure that my schedule and instructions will be reasonably followed, I say my good-byes to Jane, Adam, Braxton, and Elliott, who's becoming a fixture in the Dawsons' household, and head out for the Lion's Gate. I haven't been there since my first night back in London, and as a result, I haven't seen much of Miranda or her friends on this trip, with one notable exception.

I would feel bad about that, normally. We've all had that friend who's the picture of devoted friendship—always ready to shop for shoes, or talk on the phone, or meet for brunch—until a guy enters the picture, and suddenly she's cutting you off midsentence, three minutes into your first phone conversation in two weeks, because Kevin's beeping in. But Miranda, especially, seems thrilled that I've been spending all my time with Ian. When I stopped by her shop this morning to confirm delivery times with her assistant, she didn't want the two of us to come to the pub tonight, not even with me leaving in the morning.

"It's your last night together," she said. "We'll see you again in a few weeks. Have fun with Ian." She waggled her eyebrows like a scoundrel in a vaudeville skit.

But I miss the group, especially Eleanor and Ethan-Not-Simon, and I still haven't gotten to the bottom of Miranda's mysterious past with Thomas. So I tell her we'll be there and convince Ian of the same. He doesn't seem to mind like she does, though he does warn me that I'd better be planning to sleep on the plane tomorrow because turning in early to prep for my long day of travel is not an option.

Around five thirty I'm pushing through the wood doors of the pub, scouring the place because a bunch of strangers are occupying "our" table. At first I think I'm the first one to show up, but then I hear Miranda's trilling laugh and spot her chartreuse pleather jacket all the way across the room, in the back left corner of the pub opposite their usual spot by the big front window. My stomach dips when I see that Pamela is here—at least I've managed to avoid running into *her* this trip—but I'm happy when I spot Eleanor with Ethan-Not-Simon in his usual place by her side.

I cross the room, disappointed that Ian hasn't made it yet but unsurprised. He texted only twenty minutes ago to say he was leaving the office.

When we leave here, our plan is to spend the night at his place so he can drive me to Heathrow in the morning—both because the airport is closer to his flat and because he insists—and so my bags are already packed and lined up by the door of my suite for us to swing by and pick up on our way to Battersea.

"Well, look who it is!" Ethan-Not-Simon chuckles out a greeting, holding up his hefty, handled beer mug in welcome.

"Hallo," Eleanor says, smiling warmly at me as I slide into an available chair—a low armchair rather than a high barstool because we're in the part of the pub loosely designated as the dining area. Not that you can't eat in the front or drink in the back, but there's a hazy delineation between the dimmer, buzzier bar side and the brighter, more open, kid-friendlier restaurant side. Indeed, there are about three families back here having dinner, including one that's clearly American, the boy with his Mets cap and bright blue Nikes, the dad wearing a

Syracuse sweatshirt, both kids tapping and swiping at the screens of their tablets and both parents hooked into their phones like an IV line, nobody talking to any of the others until the boy lets out a whoop at something that happens on his screen and the mother reaches out to lay a hand on his arm and shushes him almost as loudly.

"So how long are you in town this time?" Ethan asks. His laugh comes along with a wink in Miranda's direction, an inside joke I don't get.

"I'm leaving in the morning, unfortunately."

"No, you're *not*." He says it with an air of shock. "Couldn't be bothered to spare some time for your new friends while you're here, could you? Only *one* new friend is that important, is he?"

He and Miranda exchange another smirk, and I finally get that she's put him up to it. She knows I'm self-conscious about the way I've blown them all off for Ian this trip. I stick out my tongue at her.

"You're right," I say. I glance at the clock on my phone. "Speaking of which, he should be here any minute. I can't wait till he gets here so we can ditch you guys."

Eleanor chuckles along with Ethan. But Pamela, who's looked as if she's been sipping on a cup of lemon juice ever since Ethan said "one new friend," rolls her eyes.

"Don't worry. We all know where we rate," she says, smiling so we can see she's joking, but it's obvious to me that she's not. I wonder if the rest of the group has picked up on her crush on Ian. For that matter I wonder why Miranda picked *me* to introduce to Ian when another willing candidate sits here with her at the Lion's Gate on a regular basis.

Then Pamela pushes a hand through her hair and says, "I'm *sooo* wiped out today. I had to turn up at Claridge's to do an interview with Emma Watson. It was a junket for her new Universal film." It's such an obvious humble-brag that I realize I've answered my own question. She fake yawns and then eyes us all sharply to make sure we look impressed.

"Bloody hell," Miranda says. "You didn't tell me that. Why didn't you get me in as your photography assistant or something like that?" She presses out her chest and tosses her head back. "I'd look rather lovely in a press badge."

"Oh, it was very last minute," Pamela says, frowning and clearly enjoying the spotlight. "Another editor was supposed to do it, but she was stuck at home with the stomach flu."

"What was very last minute?" asks Ian, and I almost fall off my chair as I pivot to the sound of his voice.

"My interview with Emma Watson," Pamela says in a bored tone, waving a dismissive hand in the air. I now know the reason for the timing of her announcement, as she's sitting with a clear view of the door and would have seen Ian walk in.

I suppress a very strong desire to roll my eyes but force myself to indulge her instead by asking, "What was she like?" Meanwhile, Ian plops into the chair next to mine and promptly scoots it over so he can wrap my hand in his, resting his arm on the tabletop so our twined fingers are in view.

Pamela takes another hit off the lemon juice, flinching at our obvious intimacy as she answers, "Oh, very distracted, really. She was absolutely bored to be there, you could tell. But she liked a question I asked about the International Women's Awards. She was still talking when the publicist was shooing me out of the room."

I give Miranda a phony glare. "You're supposed to be introducing *me* to British celebrities, remember?"

"Ah, if I'm not mistaken, it's you who has the connections," she answers in a mischievous tone. "Where are my autographed blue suede shoes, hmm?"

Pamela interrupts our banter, clearing her throat loudly before saying, "I heard a tidbit of gossip from one of the other reporters, the entertainment columnist from *The Globe*." She waits until all eyes are on her again before leaning into the table—her upper arms squeezed tightly against her body in a way that reveals maximum cleavage—and whispers, "He said she's up the duff." She peers around the table to gauge everyone's reaction, continuing to serve as her own human Wonderbra. I can't help but sneak a glance at Ian to see if he's noticed, but he's looking over his shoulder and trying to get the attention of a server.

Hiding my smile, I say, "She's what?"

At the same time, Miranda says, "What? Nooo. Whose is it?"

Oh. Pregnant. There's still a lot of British slang that leaves me scratching my head.

"I don't know. He wouldn't say," Pamela says, looking disappointed. "But I bet it's that American bloke she's been spotted around with."

"*If* it's even true," pipes in Eleanor. "You know eighty percent of the celebrity rumors circulating in the London media are one hundred percent crap."

"She is so very private, isn't she?" adds Miranda.

Ethan-Not-Simon chuckles, his eyes twinkling. "Hey, Ian, I heard that Posh and Becks are off again. Didn't you hear that? It has to be true. Oh, and Kanye is definitely shagging one of Kim's sisters. I got that from my roommate's cousin's roommate who came into the shop last week. He has a friend who has a friend who works for the BBC."

Pamela reaches across Eleanor to swat Ethan's arm. "Stop making fun. This is *actually* potentially true information. It's a bona fide source."

"Bona fide," Ethan says solemnly, nodding at Ian and me.

Pamela goes a little red in the face. "Anyway," she says loudly, "I think it's lovely, if it's true. She'll be a good mum."

"A yummy mummy, that one. Yes, there I agree with you." Ethan-Not-Simon nods along. This time it's Eleanor who swats him.

"Oh, stop it. You're awful," she says. And then she glances at Miranda and Pamela in turn and adds, "I have some news. It might not be as exciting as Emma Watson's baby daddy, but it is actually true."

Pamela scowls at her as Miranda says, "Well, what is it, then?"

Eleanor smiles. "We've set a date. We're getting married on sixteenth December." She puts her chin in her hand and adds with a satisfied, dreamy smile, "A Christmas wedding."

"Oh, that's lovely," Miranda exclaims. "Congratulations, you two."

Even Pamela brightens at the news, though she does say, "Only four months time? That's terribly fast for making plans."

Amidst all of our enthusiastic congratulations, Miranda raises her glass for a toast. As soon as we've clinked glasses and raised a "cheers" to the news, Thomas walks up.

"What are we celebrating?" he asks.

"Mine and Ellie's impending nuptials," Ethan laughs.

"Ah, right. Well, congratulations, then." He pulls up a chair from a neighboring table and squeezes it in beside Miranda's, all of us shifting accordingly to make room. He reaches out and delivers Ethan a fist-bump.

"The gang's all here," Miranda says affectionately, sweeping a glance around the table and smiling. I notice her eyes stop just short of Thomas's and that she's shifted a bit farther left in her chair, away from him. "It's a nice send-off for this one." She nods a head in my direction.

"Oh," Thomas says. "So you're off again?"

"Yes, leaving to go home in the morning." Ian squeezes my hand, and I swallow the lump in my throat. At that moment the server appears beside our table to deliver Pamela and Ethan-Not-Simon another pint and to take Thomas's order. Most of the group orders food, but since Ian and I plan to pick up food on the way to his place—I still haven't tried English fish and chips in England, and he has a favorite takeaway spot near his flat—we stick to drinks only.

"We should get out of here," he whispers in my ear after twenty minutes or so, and I nod.

"Whenever you're ready," I whisper back, picking up my drink and taking a long sip.

But we stay another half hour, laughing and joking and listening to Eleanor and Miranda making plans for Eleanor and Ethan's wedding, each of us chiming in occasionally with ideas—mine mostly design-related, Thomas's mostly about the "stag night," and Pamela's mostly refuted by Eleanor, who wants a small, simple ceremony in the small parish church in her hometown, not a big, flashy London-esque affair.

I watch Thomas and Miranda out of the corner of my eye, and though she never relaxes her position straining away from him, he does seem to inch closer and closer to *her*. I resolve that this time I *will* remember to ask Ian about Miranda and Thomas after we leave the pub.

I'm hesitant to leave my new friends, knowing it'll be weeks before I make it back again, but eventually Ian's hand moves from my hand to my leg, where it inches up until it finally reaches a point where I jump slightly and giggle, my entire body tingling at what his touch promises. I nudge him with my shoulder and narrow my eyes to give him a playfully dirty look. And then I glance up to see Miranda watching us shrewdly.

"You two are adorable," she pronounces, and I roll my eyes, downplaying the attention.

"Oh, yes. You're just adorable," Ethan-Not-Simon echoes in a high-pitched voice, and Eleanor swats him again.

"I haven't married you *yet*," she reminds him.

"So you're together, then," Thomas says, ignoring them. "I thought so but wasn't sure. Nobody tells me these things anymore." I see Eleanor and Ethan exchange a swift, nervous glance, and it makes me burn with a new flare of curiosity.

"Yes, they're together," Miranda says. "And you probably want to be alone together, don't you?" She gives me a pointed look, putting emphasis on the word "alone." It's actually pretty embarrassing, and the tips of Ian's ears go red.

"Yes, she's very keen on seeing that these two end up together," Pamela says. She's been quieter this last half hour, since Eleanor's news and wedding planning talk stole the thunder of her celebrity encounter. I realize, seeing the lineup of empty glasses in front of her, that she's been putting back pints rapidly in the short time Ian and I have been here. As I have this thought, she gives a small hiccup.

Miranda laughs. "Don't listen to her. She's quite drunk." She seems as if she wants to downplay Pamela's announcement, but honestly, I'm not sure why. From my perspective Pamela's words are nothing but the truth. Miranda has pushed me toward Ian since our very first conversation in her shop, on the first days of my first trip.

"No, I'm not," Pamela insists, her voice getting a little louder, her cheeks ruddy and her eyes laser-bright when she focuses them on me. "She *is* keen on playing matchmaker. Seeing as how Quinn is so very rich, and Ian is in desperate need of a trust fund heiress, especially when he loses his job. Isn't that right, Miranda?" Her gaze shifts to Miranda, whose pixie-like features are frozen in a mask of dread. And then she looks at Ian. "It'll be hard to find another job in the city, won't it, if they give you the sack? People do talk…"

Her voice trails off, and I can feel Ian by my side, rigid as a petrified tree limb. His hand, still resting on my leg, has clenched into an angry fist. I can't look at him, though, because I'm frozen in shock myself.

My brain is making a thousand little connections, synapses joining as memories shift and bubble to the surface and click together in my brain. All those questions Miranda asked during our first conversation in her shop, about my family and my father's political legacy and my business, and the eager way she immediately took me under her wing. The speed with which she invited me into her tight little group, urging me to come here that night to meet her friends. Even the way she seemed to want to turn me off of Ian at first—playing hard to get on his behalf, maybe?—and then, incongruously, pushing us together.

And the way Ian, apparently, never hung out here anymore and only started coming again once Miranda convinced him he needed to meet *me*. What exactly had she said to get him to come?

My whole body starts quaking as the implications of Pamela's words begin to fully sink in. If Miranda has been plotting this from the beginning, does that mean Ian's been in on it the whole time? Is that how and why our relationship became so intense, so serious, so fast? It never has made sense to me that Ian—gorgeous, flirtatious Ian, so very much my type and so very out of my league—found me as irresistible as I found him. I know who I am, and I'm just not a supermodel. I'm not a Savy. I'm not a Jules. I'm comfortable with that. But still, Ian had made me feel beautiful. He'd made me feel loved.

Hot tears are rising up behind my eyelids, welling at the corners of my eyes. I wriggle my leg out from under Ian's hand and shift away from him in my chair.

A shocked silence hangs above the group for several more seconds, during which Pamela, who now looks slightly appalled at what she's done but doesn't seem able to stop, adds,

"And since she's in love with you, she wants to help you herself, doesn't she?" Pamela glares at Ian as she says this. "But she doesn't have the means because her business is hanging on by its fingernails. Isn't that right, Miranda?" She hiccups again and then shoves up from her chair, banging her knee on the underside of the table as she stands. "Oh, bloody hell."

I'm too livid to look at Ian, but Miranda is directly across from me, and her face, frozen in a mask of outrage, is directly in my line of sight. Beside her, Thomas's features are chiseled from stone, his jaw tightly clenched and a vein throbbing on his forehead.

Pamela hiccups again and wobbles on her stilt-like heels. "I've had enough of you lot." She glances around the table, her face twisted with disgust. Her eyes grow narrower as they rest, finally, on me. "God, I hate all of you. Except you, Ellie. I'm sorry, and congratulations, really." She doesn't look at Eleanor as she plucks her bag from the back of her chair, slings it over a shoulder, and walks in an unsteady line toward the front of the pub, stopping at the bar to slap some money on the bar top on her way to the door.

No one speaks for at least thirty seconds. I don't think anyone is even breathing. And then it seems as if their words come from all sides at once.

"None of it is true," Miranda bursts out, her eyes imploring mine. "She's crazy, that one. Absolutely loony as a bird. You can't believe anything she says. You know she's a drama queen, right? Surely you know that. She thrives on it. You do know that, right? You *don't* believe any of it, do you?" The words are fast, almost running together, her voice reedy and high-pitched. Her cheeks are flushed a scarlet so deep it's almost purple.

I couldn't answer her questions even if I tried, my brain still frozen on the words "since she's in love with you." She meant Miranda, right? Obviously she meant Miranda. *Is Miranda in love with Ian?* The question spins around my brain at a million RPMs, round and round and round.

It doesn't make sense. But then again, in some very real ways, it does. It explains a few things, at least.

"She's been very jealous of you," Eleanor adds, her tone placating, apologetic. "And she's had a very tough time letting go of her ex-fiancé. And she's always fancied Ian." At this her face flushes slightly, as if she's said too much. As if *she's* the one who's said too much.

Ethan-Not-Simon's lips are moving like a fish's, opening and closing—like he wants to weigh in and diffuse the situation with a joke, his usual M.O., but can't find a thing that's funny about it to say.

And Ian. I haven't looked at him, and can't, but I can feel him. His hand is on my leg again, not stroking it affectionately, as he was doing earlier, but rather like he's holding it down so I can't run. I push his hand away without looking at him. I don't see how I can ever look at his face again.

"I…" I start to say but can't finish. "I…" I jerk my chair backwards several inches. "I have to…I have to go."

I fumble to unhook my bag from the back of my chair and clumsily stand, tripping over a table leg as I try to extricate myself from the tangle of chairs, too many for the size of our table. I avoid looking at any of them as I scrounge around inside my bag for my wallet, opting to follow Pamela's lead by paying on my way out. When I do find my wallet and look inside it, my jumbled brain can't make sense of the foreign bills and coins. And then I think, *To hell with it*. Ian or Miranda can pick up my tab. It's the least they can do, either of them.

With Miranda's and Ian's voices trilling in my ears, Miranda's shrill and Ian's desperate, I pick my way through the tables and toward the door. My eyes are blurring with tears, but I can see enough to comprehend that the entire restaurant is fixated on our little scene.

The table of Americans all watch me as I pass, the daughter's eyes wide and her mouth agape. "Mommy, why is that lady crying?" she asks in a youthful trill.

Just before I reach the door, my fingers already stretching for the handle, a strong hand clasps my shoulder.

"Quinn." Ian's voice is cracked, broken. "You have to believe me, I didn't—"

But I can't listen. I shake off his hand, my skin searing where he's touched me, and without looking at him I yank open the door and step out onto the sidewalk. I know that he's followed me because he's still saying my name, over and over. "Quinn, let me explain. Quinn, please. Quinn, stop, please? Please, will you stop?"

Mercifully I don't have to keep listening to him and don't have to hail a taxi because one's right there. I step to the edge of the sidewalk and bend slightly to catch the eye of the driver, who nods. It all happens in a matter of seconds.

I open the car door and slide numbly into the back seat. The driver begins to pull away from the curb before I even give him an address.

I glance back once— I can't help myself—and see that Ian is still standing there, on the street where the black car was just parked, both hands stretched out toward me as if he's trying to reach for the car's bumper to drag me back. His face is anguished, and tears are streaming down both his cheeks.

I can see his lips, his gorgeous, full lips, still forming themselves around the shape of my name. *Quinn.*

CHAPTER THIRTEEN

———

Fine Art of Avoidance

My phone, beside my left elbow, buzzes with a new text. I squeeze my eyes shut, wondering if it's from him. *Again.* Maybe not. Maybe it's Savy, or Jules, or one of my clients. But it's probably from him, considering he's texted me no fewer than six dozen times since the night, now nearly two weeks ago, when I left him standing on the street and took a blurry-eyed cab ride back to my hotel.

I know he'd tried to come after me, but the innkeeper wouldn't let him up without my permission, and I'd already told her not to. As I'd spent nearly five weeks of my summer under her roof, she knew me pretty well by then. When I'd explained the situation, probably making little sense through my blubbering hysterics, she'd listened with a knowing, pitying look.

I could block his number—probably *should* block his number—but no, masochist that I am, I've read every text. There's really no need for Ian to torture me when I'm so skilled at torturing myself.

I try to ignore it. For a full thirty seconds I actually manage to keep my eyes on the massive, rectangular book of Romo wallpaper memos I'm flipping through, sitting at the table closest to the long front window of the studio. But the pull is too strong and, as we've established, I'm weak. I flip the phone over just as Jen, my boss, blows past my table in a hurry, the heels of her nude pumps click-clack-clicking on the concrete floor of the shop. Even pregnant, Jen's in her ever-present heels. My tendency to use wardrobe cues when assessing a client's style to work out the aesthetics of a space? Yeah, that comes from Jen.

She's always impeccable—stylish without pretension, modern yet timeless, a walking advertisement for her work.

She stops in her tracks, not quite to the door. "Hey, Quinn, do you know if Ed's been here yet today?"

Ed is our FedEx guy, and he's such a regular daily fixture at the studio that we're on a first-name basis. Deliveries come in here all the time, except the freight deliveries, like upholstery and big case pieces, which arrive by semi and go straight to our Broad Avenue warehouse.

I drop my phone as if it's stung me, feeling caught even though Jen has no idea what she's catching me at. "No clue." I give her a blank look. She knows nothing about anything that went on during my weeks in England apart from work, though I've almost told her about Ian a dozen times or so. She's even asked me if I met any hot guys over there, but I can't talk about him. Not yet. Just, not at all, really. I've suffered some breakups and betrayals in my time, but this one's on another level.

She shrugs. "OK. I'm waiting on a mirror from Stray Dog. It might go to the warehouse, but it's small enough that I think it'll come here. I'm running out to Crosstown to meet the countertop guy. Do you mind checking the packages for me when he comes and texting me if it's here?"

I shrug. "Sure, no problem."

The way she cocks her head and stares at me makes me self-conscious again. I suppose my voice is dull, though I hadn't really noticed—I'm not sure I'd notice if I fainted in the middle of the shop or if someone flung a tile sample and it hit me in the head—but Jen keeps staring long and hard at me.

"Are you all right?"

"I'm fine." It's an automatic answer. I've given it to Menzi and Jordan. I've given it to Amanda, my other boss, and to Faye, our office manager. I've given it to Mother and to Vivienne and to my dad. I've also given it to Savy and Jules when they've been daft enough to ask, but mostly they know I'm wallowing in a deep, murky riverbed of misery.

A river that's filled with texts. Dozens of them.

"Oh…kay." Jen's eyes cloud over with distraction again, leaving me relieved. "Well, I'll be back before the shop closes, but probably not till four or after if anybody asks."

"Got it." I try to put some life in my voice this time, but it doesn't fool her. She zeroes in on me with her gaze again.

"Take it easy, OK? You haven't been back that long, and you worked like crazy over there. I know you've got lots to do here, too, but your clients understand. You deserve a break. I don't want you killing yourself over work."

This gets a genuine smile. "You're one to talk." Jen's a legendary workaholic.

"Yeah, well, I have to take care of myself these days, don't I?" She pats her teeny-tiny baby bump and gives a small, private smile. "Not just me I'm overworking now." She glances down at her watch—she's one of the few people I know who still wears one—and adds, "On that note, I'd better run if I don't want to be up here all night. I've got to measure again and completely redraft the cabinetry plan for the refrigerator wall—there's a structural beam behind the fur-down that we didn't know about." She grimaces. "It's gonna delay things by a week, probably. If we're lucky. And they need to be in by Labor Day."

"That sucks." I purse my lips in understanding because it really does. It's amazing how one little kink can set everything back. And kinks are inevitable on every project; the only question is whether they land in the category of minor annoyance or epic, budget-busting disaster.

Talking to Jen has made me feel a little more human, so I'm bummed when she grabs the door handle, ending our conversation.

"Good luck," I tell her.

"Thanks." She smiles. "Luck would definitely come in handy today."

Isn't that the truth. Only for me, lately, luck's just not a tool in my toolkit.

* * *

"What does it say?"

Savy lunges for my phone, but I snatch it away before she can grab it.

"More of the same."

It's roughly a week later, and we're sitting in Savy's pink living room—yes, her living room is pink, and no, it's not Pepto Bismol. It's a subtle shade of champagne I helped her pick out that complements her creamy skin and looks chic behind her mish-mash of mid-century modern furniture and quirky thrift shop art. The centerpiece of the room, which I also helped her find, is a gray crushed-velvet sofa with button tufting on the back and seat cushions but modern straight arms and mid-century legs. It's delicious. Anyway, we're both sitting on it, at opposite ends, each nursing a glass of rosé prosecco that Savy bought to cheer me up—and waiting on Jules. Always, always, always waiting on Jules, bless her heart.

"What does 'More of the same' mean?" Savy says, eyeing my phone jealously. "More *I'm sorry* and *I miss you* and *Please answer my calls*?"

"No, more of, *I didn't know. I swear*, and *Pamela was lying* and *I'm sorry* and *I miss you* and *Please answer my calls*." My voice actually has a bit of life in it until I remember the one distinct text he sent this morning, the one that hurts my heart the most, the one that said, *I'm looking at the picture you liked, the church in Ormesby where my grandparents were married. I so wish I could take you there.*

Ian's melancholy, my melancholy, pierces my heart, and when I speak again I'm back to my new, dull monotone. "It's a load of crap, clearly. There's no way Ian wasn't in on it. No way." I've repeated this so many times now to Jules and Savy that it doesn't even hurt so much anymore. I think I'm on the sixth stage of the five stages of grief: numbness.

"I know you keep saying that, but don't you think there's a *chance* he could be telling the truth? If he were lying, why would he still be texting you every five minutes?"

"First of all, no, I don't think there's a chance he could be telling the truth. And why is that? Because *Miranda* isn't texting me every five minutes. If Miranda was so keen on matching us up to improve Ian's financial situation, wouldn't *she* be lying on his behalf right now, insisting he didn't know?" I've gone over this a thousand times and from a thousand different angles in my head, but it's the first time I've said it out loud.

"Hmm." Savy sits back into the sofa cushions, furrowing her brow for a long moment. "What does she have to gain from that, really?"

I look at her sharply. "Well, that's easy. If she's in love with him and eventually sees *herself* with him, doesn't it benefit her to improve his financial situation? Especially if her own business is on the rocks?"

"That only works if Ian was in on the *whole* thing," Savy says emphatically. "If he was in love with her, too, and she knew she had a reasonable chance of ending up with him, and they were plotting this together. If not, though, and really think about this." She leans toward me and waits until I roll my eyes over to look at her. "If not, then Miranda is embarrassed. She's embarrassed as hell, too embarrassed to talk to Ian *or* to you. I mean, no matter what Ian's part is in all of this, the fact remains that there's a good chance that Miranda was using you. Using both of you."

I chew on the inside corner of my lip, the same spot I've been gnawing gouges into for the past week and a half, and try to think through her logic.

"I don't think Miranda feels shame," I say finally. "You're giving her too much credit. Everything about her is brash and bold. If she really did what Pamela says she did, think about how shameless *that* was. There's nothing about her that equals restraint." I shake my head back and forth vehemently, working at the spot on the inside my mouth so hard I can taste blood. "I think she just doesn't care enough to try to reach out to me at all. Now that there's nothing she can get from me."

I've already called around and found another warehouse in London to receive my shipments. I've also had Faye call Miranda's assistant to arrange for my movers to shift Jane and Adam's things from Miranda's storage facility to my own.

None of that was cheap, but instead of passing the cost on to my clients I'm taking it out of my own commission. Jane and Adam shouldn't have to pay for my own epic mismanagement of my personal life. I also asked Faye to cut a check against my commission to compensate Miranda for her time. I want no obligation to that woman hanging over me at all and no reason to ever have to contact her again.

And the same goes for Ian.

"Maybe," Savy says thoughtfully, and I have to really concentrate to remember what point of mine she's answering. My thoughts these days are like the wispy fronds of dandelion buds. The slightest conversational shift sends them drifting on the breeze, impossible to grasp even as I watch them float away. "But she has to have some element of niceness inside her for you to have liked her so much. And for Eleanor to have stayed friends with her for so many years. That's her name, right? Eleanor?"

A spasm of regret pings my chest as I think about Eleanor and Ethan Not-Simon. How I'll never see them again. How I won't be invited to their wedding, though I probably couldn't have gone anyway. There's no way Eleanor could have been in on this. I might have been a terrible judge of character when it came to Miranda, but I'm sure that Eleanor and Ethan are as kindhearted and genuine as they appear to be. You can't fake their type of niceness.

But then my mind drifts to Thomas, and I don't know which of my impressions I can or can't trust. Thomas is an enigma—I never did get a good read on him. And his past with Miranda… What on earth happened between him and Miranda? Somehow I feel there must be a tie to me in all of this, but why I think that, I couldn't begin to pinpoint. Obviously I'm placing too much substance on my own significance in their lives, the same way I did with Ian.

I think I always knew, underneath, that Ian's interest in me wasn't real. I just don't inspire that kind of intensity in men. I never have. I'm the one who's cheated on—or, once, the one who was cheated *with*, as in the case of Brevin, a smooth-talking, handsome South African lawyer I met at a Peabody rooftop party. I didn't learn until *after* making out with him for two hours in a dark corner of the party and then, afterward, in the front seat of his BMW, that his fiancée was asleep in their apartment a few blocks away. But the point is, I'm never the fiancée.

"Quinn?"

Savy's voice cuts through my thoughts, my ongoing monologue of self-deprecation that's kept me company most of my life.

"Yeah." I sigh. "What'd you ask again?"

"Eleanor," she says, and I wince. "Eleanor is someone you trusted, right? Maybe you could talk to her to try to figure out the truth of what happened. Do you have her cell number?" She eyes my phone again, causing me to snag it off the arm of the couch and slide it under my thigh.

"I'm *not* contacting Eleanor," I say. "Her loyalty is with Miranda anyway, not me."

"Yes, but—"

I cut her off. "Savy, look. Ian is over, in the past. I just want to put this behind me."

"But—"

"But what? What he and Miranda did was awful. Unforgiveable. It was epic, even for *me*. I don't want to see or speak to him ever again." The thought of never seeing Ian again adds another puncture to my mottled heart, but I swallow the lump in my throat. "Besides, I didn't think you were even a fan of Ian's. You were pushing for me to seduce the nobleman." I manage a smirk that comes off more as a grimace. "*Mr. Pemberton.*"

Saying his name reminds me of our last interaction, that day in Jane's demolished kitchen, and I realize with a start that I never even told Savy or Jules about it. With everything else that's happened, I'd almost forgotten it even took place. "Ohmigod," I gasp.

"What?" Savy's eyes are wide as she gazes at me with concern, as if she's scared I'm losing my grip on sanity. Which, maybe I am.

I launch into the story of how Ryland seemed to melt as he stared at me, his rigid, proper posture coming undone before my eyes as he admitted my resemblance to someone else…someone he'd known, someone he must have loved. Savy's riveted to every word, and I take advantage of it—at least now we're finally off the subject of Ian.

"W-o-w," she breathes, separating each letter into its own syllable. "You really had the British guys falling all over you."

I snort. "That's one way to put it. I'm like the female version of that character in *Love Actually*, the ugly guy who goes to America and suddenly has beautiful women inviting him home with them."

"You're not ugly," Savy says, and I roll my eyes at her.

"Yeah, yeah. I know I'm not ugly. But I'm not exactly the swan, either." Uttering the word "swan" makes me think of Ian again, of our conversation as we strolled the bank of the canal on our first real date. And suddenly I'm right back where I started—the thrill of relaying the Ryland story short-lived. I see the concern return to Savy's face as my brief spark fades.

"You are *not* ugly," she repeats. "You've got to stop being so hard on yourself. I know it's tough, having all that negativity drilled into you by your mother and your awful sisters all your life—"

"Sis*ter*," I say, coming to Caroline's defense. Viv, sure, we can go with awful. Caroline's only fault is that she left home too soon to stick up for me once Vivienne became such a witch.

"Sis*ter*, fine. Anyway, they're just jealous of you. Even your mother. She's jealou…"

Her voice fades out as our phones chirp simultaneously with a new text, and I'm relieved. I've heard all this before.

"It's Jules," Savy says, eyes glued to her phone.

"It's about time," I say. "This is ridiculous, even for her." I peer over Savy's shoulder to check the time on her screen. "She's…what? Forty minutes late?"

"She wants us to come to her place," Savy says. She stretches out her arm to hold the phone closer to me so I can read the text.

It says, *Can you guys come here instead?*

"Well, that's really nice of her," I grumble. "An hour of waiting, and she tells us to come to *her*." Instantly I feel a pinprick of guilt—I'm mad at the world, yes, but I shouldn't take it out on the two people who love me the most, apart from maybe my dad.

"Something must be wrong," says Savy, jumping up. Leave it to her to put herself in Jules' shoes and come to that conclusion while I sit here thinking the worst of someone I love. And just as quickly, I know she must be right. I look up at her with alarm.

"Let's go," I say.

Our unfinished glasses of wine are left to bead with perspiration and slowly release their bubbles as I sling my heavy purse over my shoulder and lead the way to the door. Savy doesn't even bother to turn off the lights.

* * *

We go through Jules' doorway in reverse, me trailing behind Savy as I hop along trying to put my shoe back on—I accidentally stepped out of my flip-flop in my rush to get from the car to Jules' front porch.

Jules lives in a petite, green clapboard cottage on Mud Island, a neighborhood of candy-colored houses on a small strip of land just across a bridge from Downtown, on the banks of the Mississippi River. Her house doesn't have a river view since it's buried in a row of zero-lot-line neighbors, but she walks her dogs morning and night on the sidewalks that wind along the waterfront, through a tree-dotted park. I squint in the sharp sunlight and breathe in the mingled scents of the river breeze, the fresh-cut grass of a neighbor's lawn, the lilac bushes Jules planted on either side of her navy front door.

Once I've fumbled my way in and closed the door behind me, I'm immediately struck by the expression on Jules' face. It isn't misery or distress, as I'd envisioned. Rather, she looks sort of shell-shocked or in awe. I can't imagine what else Luca could have done to shock her—to shock any of us—at this point.

"Is Luca here?" I ask, looking around. The living room is haphazardly cluttered, as usual—not so much as to make her seem like a slob but more in a way that makes you feel like plopping down and putting your feet up as soon as you enter. The navy and white striped couch is squashy and scattered with pillows in multiple colors and patterns. The chipped coffee table is painted in a cheery green just a couple shades off the exterior. The hardwood floor is layered with a large sisal mat topped by a fluffy faux-sheepskin throw. One corner of it shows chew marks from one of her two fur-babies, probably Keisha, a sharp-tongued Pekingese who's currently dancing in circles around my feet. I stoop low enough to scratch behind her ears.

"No." Jules looks at me curiously, her eyes oddly bright. "Luca moved out. You know this."

Savy shoots me a dirty look, and only then do I realize my mistake in bringing him up. "Yeah. I'm sorry," I say, a lump in my throat. I shake my head to focus—I've been so caught up in my own misery that I'm off my game. But I'm clearheaded enough to recognize that Jules' right to her grief in mourning the loss of an almost thirteen-year relationship trumps mine. "I'm sorry," I repeat in a whisper.

Jules waves a hand dismissively. "It's fine." Her voice, too, is breezier than it should be, with a note of exhilaration I haven't heard from her since she confided Luca's story. "He was just here, in fact. You guys barely missed him."

"Luca? Was here?" Wow, I really am tripping over my tongue today. Probably because of the giant foot in my mouth.

But I'm legitimately confused, and I can tell from Savy's face that she is, too. Could Jules and Luca be getting back together? But…no. Right? Luca's *gay*. Somehow Savy and I are saying these things to each other with our eyes, in that way that only best friends can.

Savy grabs Jules' hand and marches her over to the sofa. Keisha darts out from under my legs and jumps onto the couch before Jules sits all the way down—she almost sits on her but at the last second scoops her onto her lap and starts absently stroking her fur. Miles, on the other hand, hasn't budged a centimeter since we came through the door. A twelve-year-old, sixty-pound bulldog, he's sprawled out in the room's only patch of waning afternoon sunlight, slanting in from the sidelights beside the front door.

"What's going on?" Savy demands.

"Weeeell…" Jules drags out the word, looking suddenly unsure of herself. And then she bursts into tears.

"Oh, honey," Savy croons, lunging across the couch to pull Jules against her shoulder, in the process eliciting a yelp from Keisha, who's literally caught in the middle. I trip over my flip-flop again in my rush to reach them. Within seconds we're in a friend-sandwich with Jules in the middle. Keisha, finished with us crazy ladies, slinks off the sofa and hides under the coffee table, where she collapses against one of its legs with a sigh.

"What's wrong? What's happened?" I ask, glancing at Savy.

Jules swipes at her eyes with an index finger. "I'm sorry. I'm sorry," she says, sniffling loudly. "It's just. I just. Oh, God, this is just all so much."

And then, to our wide-eyed amazement, she bursts out laughing.

We let her get it out for a long moment, until I can't hold it in anymore. "What's happened?" I say again. "What's so much? What did Luca say to you? What did he do?"

At this she laughs harder, or cries—it's getting hard to tell.

"What did he do," she repeats, not a question. "That's a funny way to put it." She chokes out another giggle. "A very funny way to put it."

Savy reaches over and grabs Jules' hand. "Jules." Her voice is firm. "You're killing me. I don't know how to help you right now. Do you need a hug or a Xanax? Help us out."

"I'm sorry," she says again. "I'm sorry. I'm just…I'm trying to wrap my mind around it. Here. Let me just…I'll just show you." She stands up suddenly, bumping a shin into the coffee table. Keisha springs up, backs up from the table by a couple feet, and starts barking sharply.

"Hush, baby," Jules calls over her shoulder as she rushes from the room.

Savy and I exchange a mystified glance. This is strange behavior, even for Jules. I'm sure I'm not alone in wondering if the weight of Luca's admission is sinking her to the brink of a nervous breakdown.

"What the…" Savy says, but before she can finish the sentence Jules is running back into the room, panting slightly and holding something gingerly out in front of her. I glance at it—and then do a double take and peer harder.

It looks like a…

"Is that a pregnancy test?" As I say it, Savy and I both shoot off the couch, rushing over to her. Keisha's in a frenzy at this point, still barking as she prances between and around us. Even Miles moves his head and lifts a droopy eyelid before collapsing back into his original position. Savy and I crowd right up into Jules' personal space, all three of us gazing slack-jawed at the stick. It shows two very bright, very distinct pink lines.

"What the hell?" I bellow.

"Holy crap," Savy exclaims.

"How did this happen?" we say in unison, and then we glance at each other and Jules bursts out laughing.

"In the usual way," she says with a snort. "Well," she amends, her voice several notes softer, "not so usual, I guess."

"Is it Luca's?" I blurt out, never one for subtlety. "How? When?"

Savy looks as if she's at a total loss for words.

Jules drags in a long, deep breath and then gazes at each of us in turn. "Well, I didn't tell you this, but…"

* * *

Thirty minutes later, Savy and I are both three intersections north of a buzz. Jules, unable to imbibe herself, has begged us to drain the contents of her bar cart so she doesn't, as she put it, "have to stare at it longingly for the next nine months."

Over the course of getting us drunk, she's managed to get the story out. And no, grief didn't lure our chaste friend into a one-night stand, though she had a tough time convincing Savy otherwise at first.

It turns out that on the night Luca made his confession, roughly six and a half weeks ago, the two of them spent the wee-nighttime hours cuddled up and spooning together on their bed. Their emotions were raw and hot, and the atmosphere was charged with sweetness and nostalgia and love, even if their love had morphed into something platonic over time. And at some point in between their laughter and their tears and their reminiscing and their stroking and their comforting kisses, they'd had sex. Good-bye sex. One-last-time sex. First-sex-they'd-had-in-months sex.

Telling us this part, Jules actually blushed. Because, as she said, "It was good." She was looking down as she said it, unable to look us in the eye. "It was really, really good. I'll be honest with you, it was probably the best sex we'd had since before Luca even started med school."

And then *Savy* blushed, because she—and it's to my credit, and admittedly shock, that it was her who said this and not me—asked, "And he could..." She paused. "You know...get it up?"

Jules seemed to struggle with her answer. Meanwhile, I could tell Savy was mortified and fighting to keep from bursting out with a string of apologies, but I held my hand up behind Jules' head where she couldn't see. Not because I was so eager to learn the details but because Jules seemed like she really needed to share them.

"Yes," she finally said. "He didn't have any trouble with that." She paused, closing her eyes. "He told me it isn't that he's not attracted to me anymore. He said it isn't me, that it isn't like that, that my body doesn't turn him off. It's just that, male bodies turn him on, and he didn't want me to have to...to have to live with that. With knowing that." She sniffled hard, clearly working to hold herself together. "And he couldn't..." This time, the tears leaked through and streaked down both her cheeks, so quickly and copiously it was hard to tell her cheeks had just been dry. "And he couldn't hold back that part of himself anymore, either. After trying to deny it for so long, he wanted to act on it. He wanted to...and he didn't want to cheat on me, to let me down in that way."

The three of us cried together after that, long and hard.

There's one part of the story she still hasn't told us, though, and I'm not so drunk yet that it's escaped my notice.

"Wait," I blurt out, holding my hand up, even though nobody's leaving and nobody's said anything for at least thirty seconds. That's the tequila talking. The good stuff. The Don Julio Jules picked up in Cancun during a work conference.

Jules and Savy both look at me. "But, what are you going to do?" I ask.

"What am I going to do?" Jules cocks her head at me, staring at me as if I've lost my mind. "What do you think I'm going to do? I'm going to have a baby."

"So you're going to...you're going to keep it?" I know Jules, as a Catholic, has strong opinions about abortion and probably wouldn't consider that path in any normal situation, but this situation is...wow.

She's silent for a long moment during which Savy hiccups softly and presses her fingers to her mouth. She's a lightweight, always has been.

"Yes, I'm going to keep it," Jules says in a quiet voice, as if she's voicing the thought to herself as much as she is to us. "I know it won't be easy, that single parenting is anything but easy, but…I mean, I know that I just found out about this, and it *is* a shock, but…I want this baby. And Luca does, too. He was ecstatic when I showed him the test."

She glances up at us. Both Savy and I are riveted, hanging on to every word. I know that I, at least, am completely in awe of my friend.

She continues. "Now that Luca is…well, this might be the only path he has to becoming a parent, at least a natural parent. And I know he'll be there for the baby, and for me, and I *want* to raise a baby with him. I've always wanted to see him become a father. He'll be a great dad."

She's quiet again, but neither Savy nor I dare interrupt. I'm not sure either of us is even breathing.

"He's my…he's my best friend. I mean, apart from you guys, and I love him, and I always will. I know we can do this."

It's quiet as a church on Saturday night as we each process Jules' words. And then all at once we let it out. It's hard to tell who lunges first, but suddenly we're crying and hugging and laughing and talking over each other.

"*We* know you can do this," I say, tears running down my cheeks. "I think it's wonderful. Jules, you're going to be a great mom."

Jules' eyes grow as wide as the comic book vixens she resembles, and she gazes at me, assessing me for a long moment. "You really think so?"

I nod vehemently. "I really do. There's no question." Savy is nodding along with me. And then we're all smiling and hugging and crying again.

When we finally separate, Jules plops back into the couch cushions. She stares off into the distance for a few seconds and then glances between us, her eyes still round with amazement. "I'm pregnant."

"You're pregnant," Savy repeats, sounding just as amazed.

And we all squeal, and Savy's foot raises up and bangs into the coffee table, and her cocktail goes flying off its glass coaster and right over the edge of the table, spattering lime juice and tequila and triple sec and who knows what else all over Jules' white sheepskin rug. Keisha's barking up a riot, and Savy is apologizing profusely, as Savy is prone to do, but Jules just waves a hand in dismissal.

"Eh, who cares? Soon I'm going to have to get used to spills and messes and crumbs and toys to trip over and…" Her words trail off until she finally says, eyes filled with wonder—and tears—again, "I'm having a baby."

From the squealing and the crying and the laughing, I'm scared Keisha's going to have a doggie heart attack. But she'd better learn to tolerate noise.

Jules is having a baby. My best friend is having a *baby*.

CHAPTER FOURTEEN

———

Friends & Frenemies

It's three days later, and I know I have to do something about the Ian situation.

By situation, I mean the fact that it's now been more than three weeks since I left London, and he's still texting me. The texts are getting less frequent, but now he's calling *more* frequently, flooding my voice mail inbox until it fills up and I delete the messages, one by one, without listening to them.

It's one thing to read his words on a screen. Hearing his voice might be something I don't recover from.

The tone of his texts has changed. He sounds more despondent now, less hopeful. It's funny—I mean, not ha-ha funny, but sort of ironic—that when Chase was sending me all those annoying texts on my first trip to London, Ian offered to "tell him to bugger off." Turning his words back on him seems like a special kind of cruelty, so instead I'm simply not responding.

Radio silence.

But I can't stop reading his texts.

And I have to be honest—they have me questioning myself. If Ian were plotting with Miranda to seduce me, steal my heart, and run off with my supposed trust fund, wouldn't he have stopped trying to contact me by now? Savy certainly thinks so. Jules, too.

But, I argue with them, what if that's his game? What if he's wearing me down to win me back, only to play me for a fool in the long run anyway? That's exactly the type of thing that would happen to me.

I'm standing at the vanity in my bathroom, putting on makeup in preparation for tonight's Sunday Supper with my family and thinking about all of this, about Ian's texts, when, funny enough, my phone chirps with another one.

Considering what time it is—a few minutes after six—this text probably isn't from Ian. It's after midnight in London and a work night. I don't have time to check since I'm supposed to be at my parents' house by six thirty, but thinking it might be Jules, I rush out of the room to grab my phone off the dresser anyway.

When I see that it *is* Ian's number flashing across the screen, I want to scream.

I want to hurl my phone against the wall.

I want to scream *and* hurl my phone against the wall and yell at him to just stop, stop already. I almost, *almost* want to text him back to tell him that he's driving me bloody crazy.

I flick my finger angrily across the screen to swipe it open and get to my text messages, preparing to…I'm not sure what. Block his number, finally? Tell him to go to hell? Call him, *lit-rally* call him, to tell him how pathetic it is to drunk-text your ex after midnight?

My head is exploding with the pressure of the angry replies I'm dying to unleash on him. My anger getting the better of my judgment, I stab my phone screen to open the text, sure it's more of the same. And then his words hit me like a hook punch to the gut.

I'm just going to say this. I love you. Ordinarily I'd think I'm mad for saying it, knowing it will almost certainly scare you away. But I love you, I know I do. I can't stop thinking about you. I can't bear this. Please, please talk to me.

I sink onto the edge of my bed, my anger melting away, the spaces it occupied filling up with despair. "How could you?" I whisper, too livid even to cry.

This is the lowest he could possibly go, lower than I would have given him credit for. Sure, he doesn't know the full miserable details of my romantic history. He doesn't know how long I've been waiting to hear someone say these words to me and mean them. I've heard them very, very few times in my life, even from my own family. If my mother has ever said it, I was too young to remember. My father implies it in his actions, but he's not vocal with his emotions. Steve said it when we were in high school, but that didn't count—he was only saying it to get in my pants.

And Chase, don't even get me started on Chase. If Chase thought he was in love with me, it was because he'd awoken to the very real possibility that he might be living in his mother's basement for the rest of his life. He's further proven this point by not contacting me at all, not once, since he stalked me home and I kicked him out of my apartment. I mean, I told him not to, and it's not like I *wanted* him to, but if he really had been in love with me, could I have dissuaded him so easily? I really don't think so. Love doesn't work that way.

And I should know, because I can't stop thinking about Ian either, the way he just told me he can't stop thinking about me. Only, there's one of us who's telling the truth, and it isn't him.

My tear ducts finally overtake my fury, and within seconds my entire face is wet. So much for the makeup I was in the middle of applying, and so much for being only marginally late to dinner.

I curl up into a tight ball on my comforter, grab my pillow, and wrap myself around it, giving myself over to the sobs wracking my body. I can't stop crying for what feels like a long, long time. I realize how much I've been holding it in.

How I haven't let myself grieve the loss of something that felt real.

How I've downplayed it even to Jules and Savy, to my best friends in the universe, because I couldn't admit even to myself how much he'd hurt me. I've made jokes about it with them, about Ian's texts and about our "instant chemistry" (rolling my eyes when I said this) and even—and this thought brings on a whole new body-shaking spasm of tears—about our physical chemistry, about how good the sex was. I joked with them that it was "lust at first sight." I didn't tell them how he made me feel whole, how he made me feel beautiful, how he held me and touched me and kissed me like I was something precious, how I'd never experienced anything remotely like it before, and how it all felt so *real*.

By the time I've cried it out, I look at my phone and figure my family must already be well into dinner and moving on to dessert. I force myself to stand and drag my heavy, damp body to the bathroom, where one glance in the mirror tells me I'm not leaving my condo anytime soon. My eyes are veiny and bloodred with dark circles underneath from smeared eyeliner. My cheeks are slashed with angry streaks of red and pink where I've been pushing off the hot tears repeatedly with my palms. My hair, which I'd carefully flat-ironed, is matted up on one side, and my linen sundress looks like I rescued it from the street after a line of semi trucks drove over it.

Mother, I'm sure, is furious. No one misses Sunday Supper, not when we're in town and conscious and anywhere outside the emergency room. I sigh and send a quick text, knowing she won't see it during dinner. She also has a strict no-cell-phones-at-the-table rule.

While the phone is in my hand, I allow myself to look at Ian's text one more time. As I read the words, my eyes blur back over with tears, and I quickly swipe at the screen to delete it. I hesitate there, with my finger hovering above the word *delete*, for probably a full minute, but I can't hit the button.

Instead I close out of my texts, telling myself I just want to be able to show it to Jules and Savy later so we can dissect it together, and then I step into the shower for a second time to wash off my hot, wretched misery and start the getting-ready process all over again.

I'll still go. At the least I'll go and play with Aisling and Elijah for a bit and endure Viv's stinging commentary, knowing nothing she says can come anywhere close to hurting me as much as I've already been hurt today. At least, since I missed dinner, I won't have to endure watching my mother watch me put every bite of food into my mouth.

When I step out of the shower and hear my phone chime with another text, my stomach lurches so violently I think for a second I might actually throw up. I ignore the phone for as long as I can—long enough to towel dry my hair, wrap the towel around my body, apply facial moisturizer, and rebrush my teeth to get the tear-sour taste out of my mouth. And then I can't stand it any longer, and I head for my bed to get my phone, my heart hammering with every step.

I start with surprise when I see that the text isn't from Ian, as I'd feared, but from Mother. I can't believe she's texting me before dinner is over and cleared from the table, and…honestly, I'm surprised she's texting me back at all. She usually ignores my texts, always pretending she doesn't know how to work her smartphone, though she certainly can use it to order multi-thousand-dollar case pieces from 1stdibs and One Kings Lane.

She must really be pissed is my first thought. But then I see the text and yell, "Holy crap!"

Viv's in labor.

Nobody's even *at* my parents' house because Viv's water broke, and everybody rushed out in the middle of dinner to caravan to the hospital.

I dash off a text to let Mother know I'm on my way, and then I run back to the bathroom to finish getting ready, skipping the makeup this time apart from two quick dabs of concealer to mask the dark circles under my eyes. I towel dry my hair again, toss on another sundress, and grab my purse and keys on my way out the door.

* * *

"How's it going?" Breathless, I'm asking the question before anybody even realizes I'm in the room. My dad jerks his head up from *The Commercial Appeal* sports section, and Mother looks up from her knitting.

Yes, knitting. She took it to heart several years back when Julia Roberts and several other Hollywood stars touted the therapeutic, stress-relieving benefits of clicking needles into strands of plush, designer yarn. She and her club friends found a posh little Midtown yarn and fabric shop with weekly wine nights, and thus a hobby was born. To be honest it's one of my favorite things about my mother. It makes me feel like maybe there's some sort of warm, fuzzy part of her personality I've been missing all these years. Sure, she's hidden it well from *me*, but just knowing it's there is somehow comforting.

"Where have you *been*?" Mother's voice is sharp and accusing, killing the warm fuzzies. She looks me up and down, and though she doesn't say what she's thinking, she doesn't have to. Her disapproval is etched into the tight line of her lips.

"Is she still in labor?" It's only been about twenty-five minutes since I got Mother's text, but I know from Vivienne that second and third labors tend to move quicker than the first.

"Yes," Mother says calmly. "Eight centimeters dilated. She's not ready to come out yet."

"She?" I look at Dad, puzzled. "Did Viv find out the sex already?" This confuses me because she's made a big deal about wanting to be surprised this time. It surprised *me* when she told me because I thought for sure she'd want to have one of those big, Instagrammable "reveal parties" that are all the rage in her mommy circles.

"Your mother is quite certain it's a girl," Dad says.

"She's carrying high and all over," Mother says. "If it were a boy, she'd be carrying low and out front."

"Isn't that an old wives' tale?"

"If so, it exists for a reason," Mother says. "I've never known it to be wrong."

I resist the urge to roll my eyes, hoping against all hope that my new *nephew* will emerge from the uterus having my back.

"I'm here, I'm here. Is she pushing yet?"

This time I can't stop my eyes from rolling as the grating, nasal voice of Becca Strazinsky, Viv's high school best friend, penetrates the dim peacefulness of the Baptist Memorial Women's Hospital maternity ward waiting area.

Mother drops her knitting and stands to welcome Becca into a genuine, if restrained, embrace, complete with double air kisses. Mother has always liked Becca as much as I dislike her. Which baffles me, considering there's nothing about Becca— other than her family pedigree—that's remotely refined or conservative enough for Pricilla Whitehurst Cunningham to like. Becca's voice is too loud and her clothes are too tight—case in point, tonight she's wearing a royal blue, low-cut, clingy sheath dress and leopard-print heels *in a hospital waiting room*. Plus, she was Vivienne's bad-influence friend, the one who introduced the cigarettes and acquired the pot and circulated the dog-eared copy of the *Kama Sutra*. But she belonged to the right Carnival Memphis Krewe and lived in the right ZIP code and went to the right schools, starting with Hattison girls' school, which is where she and Vivienne met in seventh grade.

Caroline and I didn't go to Hattison—we went to the co-ed St. Michael's, but Mother apparently thought Hattison was a better fit with Viv's delicate sensibilities. There's a long-standing joke in Memphis that if you want your daughter to marry a doctor, you send her to Hattison, and if you want her to *be* a doctor, you send her to St. Michael's. It worked on one of us, at any rate. And I would have been a disappointment no matter what path I'd chosen.

Becca interrupts these thoughts by turning and giving me a sweeping glance that mimics the one Mother just gave me. "Quinn, look at you, girl! I haven't seen you in ages…years. You haven't changed one single little bit."

Translation, in case you don't speak bitch: "You haven't lost one single little pound."

I give her a tight-lipped smile. "Becca, hi. You haven't changed, either." It's the best I can do. As a Southern girl, I'm well-heeled in phony. I might hate the game, but I sure know how to play it.

I settle onto the surprisingly comfortable waiting room chair beside Mother's, while Becca perches on the edge of one of a row of steel blue recliners across from us, meant to accommodate family members overnight. The dim fluorescent lights flicker and buzz above our heads, and every few minutes a nurse or orderly walks briskly through or an announcement breaks in on the intercom system, all of it background noise.

For what seems like an interminable amount of time, I listen to Becca's inane chatter and the clacking of Mother's needles, adding to the conversation only when politeness forces me to.

"Ladies, I hate to break up your reunion, but you might want to see this." My dad leans across Mother's knitting, angling his phone so we can both see it. On the screen is a picture of a slick-skinned, open-mouthed newborn with his (or her? I can't yet tell) eyes screwed shut, on a clinical-looking platform surrounded by nurses and medical personnel who presumably are weighing, cleaning, and otherwise preparing my new niece or nephew for life on earth.

"Ohmigawd, she's *here*," Becca squawks. Apparently Becca, too, believes she's predetermined the sex of Vivienne's child. She leaps off her chair and starts jumping up and down, or jiggling up and down is more like it since her shoes and dress don't allow much range of motion. I catch my dad staring and give him a dirty look, at which he guffaws loudly.

"George, you sound like a hog," my mother admonishes him.

We glance at each other and smirk, my father looking properly sheepish.

And the next hour passes in slow motion as we wait, and wait, and wait to be allowed to visit Viv and Bradley and (*damn it*) my new niece, Delphine Alexis Cosgrove. And then finally, in the half hour that follows when I get to meet and caress and coo at the tiny, perfect, pearl-pink bundle in my arms, I almost, *almost* manage to forget all about Ian and his heart-wrenching, gut-twisting lie.

And my phone doesn't chime once.

* * *

Late that night I'm back on Jules' sofa, and this time she's the one comforting me. I've come straight from the hospital waiting room, still wearing my rumpled sundress. My stomach is growling audibly, as I refused every snack my dad offered from the hospital vending machines, but I'm too shaky to eat the cheese and crackers Jules has spread onto a wood cutting board and set on the coffee table. I can't even drink the wine she was gracious enough to pour for just me.

"Look. It's obvious that this is eating you up," she says after watching me stare into space for a protracted moment. I've already shown her Ian's text. "You have to break down and talk to him."

"I don't know if I can."

"Why not? What do you have to lose, really? You've already left. You're four thousand miles away from him, for God's sake. He can't hurt you anymore."

I scoff out a hard breath. "Hummphh."

"Unless…" Her voice trails off.

Glancing up at her, I can feel the lines of dread etched on my forehead. "Unless…?"

She's peering intently at my face, and I watch as the dawn of realization breaks through her mask of worry.

"Unless you're in love with him?"

I try to control my reaction, but it doesn't work this time. First my lips press into a thin line, and then I feel my mouth turning down at the corners. Finally I sniffle, trying my hardest to keep the tears from springing to my eyes, but my efforts are fruitless. My face crumples up, and in the next moment Jules has pulled my head onto her shoulder.

"Oh, honey." She embraces me for a long moment, rubbing her palm against my back. "Oh, Quinnie. I had no idea."

And then she pushes away, holding me at arm's length and giving me a stern look. "How could you not tell me something like this? You fell in love with him? You traveled halfway around the world and met a boy and fell in *love* with him? That's a pretty huge thing to keep from your best friend in the world."

Her cheeks grow pink as she realizes what she's just said. "I mean, not that I don't understand needing to keep some things private," she mumbles.

Her allusion to her situation adds perspective and calms my hysteria somewhat. She reaches for a box of tissues on the end table and hands it to me, and we both wait while my tears subside and I attempt to clean myself up.

"Go figure." I shrug. "When I finally fall in love, it's with the wrong person—somebody who lies to me and who I can't trust and who doesn't honestly feel the same way. It's what you've always accused me of. Anybody who might have a chance of being something real, I push him away for some stupid reason, like his nostrils are too hairy or he stared at Savy too long or he wears seersucker shorts." (In Jules' defense, all of these *are* reasons I've broken up with guys in the past.) My lips tremble for one miserable beat as my composure slips. "Ian doesn't love me. He was just using me."

My face crumples, and the tears start to leak again. Jules hands me another tissue.

"You don't *know* that he was using you."

I give her a dubious look. "Yes, I do."

"No, all you have is the word of this Pamela woman. And you said yourself that she's stuck-up as hell and extremely unpleasant. *And* she has a thing for Ian. Why on earth would you trust what she says over what Ian says?"

Because it's easier to believe the bad stuff. Because it fits with my past experience. Because Ian was too good for me to begin with and too good to be true, and it only makes sense that he never wanted me in the first place.

I don't say any of these things, though.

"Because Miranda hasn't denied any of it." My tone of voice has the "duh" implied in it.

"Just because Miranda was lying to you doesn't mean Ian was lying to you," Jules says, echoing what Savy has been telling me for weeks.

"Miranda's known Ian for, like, twenty-five years. She's known me for like two months. They spent their childhoods together. They share a history, and a culture, and a *motive*. They have every reason to trust each other. I have zero reason to trust either of them."

"What if Pamela was telling the truth?" Jules says quietly, ignoring my blustery logic.

I harrumph again. "Yeah, I believe she *was*. That's my *point*."

"What if Miranda really is in love with Ian? And what if she was doing this all on her own and planning to push you two together and therefore become Ian's savior and then, when things ultimately didn't work out…which, let's face it, is pretty likely considering the two of you live thousands of miles away from each other, she'd be the one to enter from backstage and pick up the pieces?"

I'm shaking my head before she's even finished. "That's crazy. She'd have to *be* crazy to try something so delusional. That's, like, she-needs-medication crazy."

"People do crazy things every day. Especially when they're in love with somebody who doesn't love them back."

She swallows hard and blinks rapidly, her hand flitting absentmindedly to rest on her lower abdomen. The double meaning in her words hits me like a tsunami, and my eyes pop wide in their sockets.

"Jules," I whisper, gaping at her.

She shrugs. "I'm not admitting anything," she says after a beat. "I'm just saying, when you've got nothing left to lose, sometimes you do things that might seem crazy. But ultimately everything happens for a reason."

She closes her eyes, and I can tell we've reached the end of this subject. For now.

I stare at her for a long time, but she doesn't open her eyes.

"I don't see where Miranda had nothing left to lose," I finally say. "If she wanted Ian, why wouldn't she have just told him? Why not go after him herself instead of pushing him onto me, a stranger?"

"I can't answer that," she says. "But Miranda can. And maybe Ian could, too. But you have to talk to him to find that out."

"And I can't do that," I say, shaking my head. "I just have to forget about him. That's my only path forward."

"We'll see." Jules is careful not to look at me when she says it, instead watching Keisha, who's pranced over to us in a sleepy zigzag after waking up and audibly shaking herself out of sleep from somewhere in the back of the house. She leaps onto the sofa, and Jules begins stroking behind her ears as Keisha settles onto her lap, tags jangling.

I pick up my glass of wine and sink back into the sofa cushions, trying to digest everything Jules has just told me and knowing it will take time—a lot of time probably—to process all of it.

And that would be fine if I had time. Nothing but time and space to face the memories, the emptiness, the hurt. But sooner rather than later, I have to go back to London. I don't have to see Ian or even tell him I'm coming, and now that I've separated myself and my work from Miranda, she doesn't have to know, either.

But just knowing I'll be back in his city, and soon, is gut-wrenching. It's not just that I can't face him. It's that I can't face my own gullibility, my own *culpability* in so openly, stupidly trusting and befriending and even loving people who found me such an easy target.

Jules is right about one thing. Everything happens for a reason. And I consider this a lesson learned.

I won't make the mistake of trusting so easily ever again.

CHAPTER FIFTEEN

———

One of *Those* Women

The week leading up to my return to England is another nail-chewing, stress-inducing, late-working, client-appeasing seven days of crisscrossing the city, trying to fill every request and troubleshoot every problem and satisfy every client before once again abandoning them to our design assistants. I'll be lucky, when this is over, if I have a client roster left.

I've been in regular contact with Jane, and with only a few minor hitches that I've managed to address via middle-of-the-night calls to my contracting team—middle of the night for me, morning for them—the work on Jane and Adam's house has progressed smoothly. The painting is done, and the old upstairs wallpaper is stripped, the walls either repaired and repainted or rehung with newer, more stylish patterns. The new windows and light fixtures and hardware are installed, and the stairs are newly refinished and carpeted with a chic gray runner with patinated brass accents that complement the antique-meets-modern design scheme.

The kitchen cabinets, shelves, countertops, and plumbing fixtures are installed, though we're still waiting on a couple of appliances that will hopefully arrive soon after I do. Every remaining furniture piece has been received at my hastily arranged new warehouse, just waiting for me to come and oversee its move and installation. I've been in a flurry of ordering accessories and planning final touches, even quick-sketching renderings of a couple of rooms to plot out the hanging of artwork.

The puzzle pieces are laid out. All I have to do now is arrive and put them together, usually my favorite part of a project.

Since I won't be going back again, I've hired a photographer to shoot the finished space for my portfolio, something Jen reminded me to do.

Since I won't be going back.

The words fill me simultaneously with relief and with a melancholy so deep it mirrors the width and breadth and depth of the Atlantic itself. It feels endless. I don't plan to see Ian again— not on this trip, never, not ever again—and already the lack of closure is a gaping wound I'm not sure how I'll ever close. But I know I can't handle seeing his face. I still can't handle returning a text, not even a text that tells him never to text me again.

The days pass. Monday. Tuesday. WednesdayThursdayFriday. Saturday comes and goes a bit slower. I've done all I can do work-wise to get ready for my trip, and so Saturday afternoon I stop by Vivienne and Bradley's house to visit my new niece one more time before my Sunday morning flight.

As soon as I get there I realize Viv is in no mood for company. I ring the doorbell bearing a pair of princess-pink balloons tied to the tag of the plushest, squishiest stuffed animal I could find. Along with Delphine's gift I have something for Vivienne—an essential oils "zen" kit I bought at Whole Foods and a paperback copy of the latest novel by her favorite author.

She mumbles her thanks along with something along the lines of, "Yeah, like I have any time to read." But she does seem grateful that I'm there, especially when I start folding the pile of teeny-tiny onesies and newborn gowns and burp cloths dumped in a heap on one end of the living room sofa, and when I offer to feed Delphine her bottle. Apparently Viv is having trouble nursing, and that's why she's in such a foul mood.

"This is the third kid," she says in a grouchy voice. "I thought this was supposed to get easier."

I give my brother-in-law a look that says, *"Don't ask me. I'm the childless aunt."* He shrugs back with a befuddled, helpless look in his bloodshot eyes.

"So, I heard George say you're going back to London next week?" Bradley asks once I'm settled into one of Vivienne's stiff wing-back side chairs with Delphine nestled into the crook of my arm, the nipple of the bottle clutched in her rosebud lips and her eyes squeezed shut.

"Yes, tomorrow," I say, not looking up from my niece's face. Her rhythmic sucks are mesmerizing, and her sweet baby smells stir up a wistfulness somewhere inside me that I didn't know existed. I try with all my might to keep my attention focused on the baby, not on my impending trip and especially not on London and the paralyzing memories it brings to mind. Desperately I scan my brain for a new subject.

"Speaking of traveling, Mother said that Caroline is coming back into town next week?" I direct this at Vivienne, but it's Bradley who answers.

"Yes, Friday," he says. "She's bringing Catherine with her, so Vivienne is excited. Right, sweetie?"

Instead of responding, Viv swivels her head toward the playroom down the hall and yells out, "Turn down that blasted TV, Elijah. Aisling, make your brother turn down the TV." She looks back at Bradley with a pout. "Can you control those two? I have a headache."

"I'll get you some Advil." He jumps up, seeming happy to have a task that doesn't involve intervening in the playroom. On his way out of the room, he glances at me, continuing to talk as he rounds the island into their open-plan kitchen. "How long will you be overseas this time?" He pulls a glass from a cabinet and fills it from the spout in the refrigerator door.

"I'm not sure," I answer him. "As long as it takes to get everything installed and to wrap up all the finishing touches. And stage the house for photos."

"So a while, then?" He's walking back into the room now, holding a bottle of generic ibuprofen in one hand and Viv's glass of water in the other. "I'm asking because I'm going there myself in a little over a week. If you're still there, maybe I could meet you for dinner, introduce you to a friend." He waggles his eyebrows a bit.

"Nice of you to rub your escape route in my face," Vivienne says, tipping back the pills and then hunching forward to rub her temples with both hands. "Sure, I'll be fine here, all by myself with *three* children, recovering from the trauma of delivering your spawn safely onto the earth." She looks up at me. "I asked him if he could take a leave of absence, but his company doesn't offer *paternity* leave."

"Viv, I've told you over and over again, you should hire a nanny."

"Yeah, like I'm going to pass off the raising of my children to some stranger just so I can leave to go shopping and play tennis at the club. I'm not one of *those* women."

I have the urge to say, "You could go back to work," but something tells me I'd be better served by staying out of this debate. Besides, though I have the benefit of distance to look at Vivienne and see that she's miserable—that as much as she wants it to be, stay-at-home motherhood is not her calling—from her position right smack in the middle of it, Vivienne doesn't have the perspective to see that herself. It's a lesson she's going to have to learn in her own time.

Bradley glances at me with a strained smile. "Sorry," he says. "As I was saying, I could introduce you to a colleague I think you might like to meet. I'd been meaning to text you to find out when our trips might overlap."

"Much as I love that you're attempting to set me up"—I shake my head as vehemently as I dare with Delphine on my lap, to emphasize my sarcasm—"I'm going to decline your thoughtful invitation. I'd be happy to meet up with *you*, but I'm not interested in meeting any men. Especially British men."

Vivienne lifts her head from her hands—sensing some new weakness to torture me with, probably. "Why? What's happened?"

I huff out a laugh. "Oh, nothing." I look up to see them glance at each other and then gaze at me with interest, Bradley with his eyebrows raised. "Nothing," I repeat more firmly. And then, since I can tell I'm not going to get away without an explanation, I add, "I went on a few dates with this one guy. It didn't end well."

It suddenly hits me that Bradley works in finance. I'm sure it's a long shot, but I can't help but ask, "Hey, your client in

London doesn't happen to be Myers Chapman Worthings LLP, does it?" I'm pretty sure that's the name of Ian's firm.

"No," Bradley says. "My own firm has a London branch. It's the Raymond James office in Shoreditch." He pauses, clearly trying to work out the puzzle of my train of thought. "Why, does your guy work for Myers Chapman? I don't know anybody there, but I did hear a story not too long ago about a scandal that went down there recently, some dude embezzling loads of cash." He chuckles. "You weren't going out with *that* guy, were you?"

"No, I wasn't going out with that guy," I say quietly. "I did hear about that, though."

He shakes his head. "Wow, small world."

That's exactly what I was afraid of when I brought it up, but I don't tell him that. "No kidding."

"I also heard they just made a bunch of cuts. Redundancies, they call it there. I hope your guy still has a job—er…or not, I guess, if you hate him."

My heart sinks a little deeper in my chest, torn between hurting for Ian, for the thing he feared finally coming to fruition, and hurting for myself—that I clearly still care enough to fish for information about him in the first place.

"I don't hate him. I hope he still has a job, too." I sigh, and Viv and Bradley exchange another uneasy glance.

"Yeah, well, anyway, I'll try to text you," Bradley says, though we both know he won't. That's fine by me—I'll be busy and anxious to finish my work and get out of town.

"Yeah. That sounds good."

Delphine pushes the bottle out of her tiny mouth. She looks to be fast asleep, though her lips are still moving in a methodical sucking motion. I hold up the bottle to gauge how much of the thick, murky white liquid is left. Viv reaches over and takes it from me, handing me a burp cloth. Heeding Viv's warnings to "support her head," I lift Delphine carefully and rest her soft, sweet-smelling cheek against the crook of my shoulder, rubbing her back in firm circles the way Vivienne and Mother taught me when Elijah was born.

Once she's settled, I glance at Viv and see her watching me closely. "You'll be good at this someday." Her voice is gentle, kind…which sort of freezes me with surprise. "Better at it than me, I'm sure."

I don't know if she's feeling sorry for me because my love life is a disaster or if her hormones are just out of whack, but I feel touched nonetheless.

"Thanks," I say, kissing Delphine on the top of her downy head after coaxing out a burp that sounds more like a high-pitched hiccup. "I'm not sure we'll get the chance to see how I do with it, based on how things are going so far." I smile to show her I'm kidding…or at least that I've made my peace with spinsterhood.

"There's no hurry," Vivienne says. "Trust me. Especially with your career going as well as it is. You have plenty of time for all this." She spreads her arms in a sweeping gesture that takes in the entire living area, a beautiful room whose expensive antiques, custom rug, and tasteful upholstery are right now littered with the detritus of newborns and toddlers.

"Oh, by the way," she adds, reaching out her arms to take Delphine from me. I carefully hand her over. "Speaking of your work, Mother told me a few days ago that she wants to hire you to redesign the dining room and foyer and maybe the kitchen. I've been meaning to tell you so you don't get blindsided and have time to come up with a good excuse. I can't *imagine* what she'd be like as a client." She shudders.

I'm so stunned by what Viv's just said that I can't answer her at all. I'm sure she takes my silence for agreement, but inside, my brain's in a whirl. My mother wants *me* to work with her on the house? My childhood home, the house that made me fall in love with houses?

The world feels like it's just tilted slightly off its axis. For this to be true, there's no question that the earth must be wobbling toward a fiery cosmic demise.

"Wow, thanks for telling me," I finally mumble, noncommittal.

And then Aisling runs into the room, stopping short when she sees me sitting in the side chair. "Aunt Quinn! I didn't know you got here." She dashes over and launches herself onto my lap amidst shushing from both Viv and Bradley. Viv's just laid Delphine in a cradle attached to the top of a Pack 'n Play set up by the fireplace.

As Aisling pulls me by the hand toward the back of the house, I glance back at my sister and see her and Bradley exchange a smile as they tiptoe away from a sleeping Delphine. Even if she tends to emphasize the hardships, it's clear that she also finds joy in this life she's constructed.

Holding my niece's plump, sweaty hand in mine as she babbles on about unicorns or sparkles or ponies or…something—honestly, it's hard to keep up—I can see what all the fuss is about.

For just a fleeting moment, I have the thought that it's too bad Vivienne and I can't switch places—bodies, lives, choices, uncertainties, all of it—for just, like, a few days or a month or maybe even six weeks. Long enough to get a taste of the type of life neither of us is ever likely to get a chance to live.

My thoughts flit to Ian and his text, and the despair fills me up again. I push him out of my head and zero in on Aisling's happy chatter, wishing I could remember that time in my life when hope and happiness depended on nothing more than a zealous belief in unicorns.

CHAPTER SIXTEEN

———

London Calling

As soon as I step through the front door of Jane and Adam's townhouse, I know something is wrong. Not with the project—the house looks fantastic. The century-old structure has that new-house smell, thanks to fresh paint and new cabinetry and refinished woodwork and revamped flooring. Everything is crisp and bright and fresh and Euro-modern, and where before the house felt musty and dated and like it was wheezing out the dying breath of a departed century, now it feels young and bursting with light and life and energy. And this is even without all the furniture and the art and the finishing touches.

My heart swells just looking at it.

But I watch Jane's face as she welcomes me through the door and ushers me into the entry hall, and it doesn't reflect these same emotions. She looks distracted. Distraught. Maybe even a little annoyed or angry—something I've never felt coming off of her before.

She gives me a brief hug, one of those barely touching kind. "Quinn, it's so good to see you."

"Same here." My voice is much more enthusiastic, though inside, I'm worried. *Has something gone wrong? Are they unhappy with the work?*

It wouldn't be shocking to me if some big problem has come up. Something goes wrong during pretty much every major project, and this one has been quite smooth—which, now that I think about it, is worrisome. I swallow the lump in my throat, and it slides down to become a rock weighting the bottom of my stomach, but I keep the bright smile plastered on my face.

They're so quiet and reserved. Did I read them wrong? Do they hate some choice we made? Is there a problem with the kitchen? Is it still under construction? I can't stop the nervous monologue sliding like a news ticker in my brain. But when we pass the pantry and step into the kitchen, my breath comes out in a whoosh of relief. It looks like my renderings come to life.

The cabinets are in place, the stainless steel shelving is hung against a backdrop of white subway tile that runs all the way to the crown molding, the quartz countertops are installed, and the newly enlarged island is finished with a pristine, crisp navy paint job. Above the island hang three aqua-lidded, industrial-inspired pendant lights. New, larger windows above the apron sink overlook the sun-bright conservatory, with a view through to Jane and Adam's lovely enclosed backyard. Everything is beautifully in place, a 3-D, living depiction of the vision that's for months lived inside my head.

I whirl to face Jane, not sure what mix of emotions I'm wearing.

"What do you think?" I hold my breath.

Her eyes flicker to me for a brief moment during which she seems confused, and then she follows my gaze to the kitchen.

"Oh," she says. "Oh, it's wonderful. Yes, we love it." She pauses while I exhale in an audible whoosh. And then she brushes past me into the room, her heels clicking on the new porcelain tile. "It's a little bare," she says with an apologetic smile over her shoulder. "We've been waiting for you to tell us where to put things. We don't want to muck it up with our inept decorating skills. But the kettle's good to go, of course."

She lifts the stainless steel pot off its electric pad and begins filling it with water from the tall Rohl faucet. I relax when I see that *she's* relaxed a bit.

"Would you rather have coffee?" She pauses before setting the kettle on its mat. "Tea's become an automatic reflex for me, but I forget that you're American, too. I can dig out the Keurig…it's in a box somewhere in the extra guest room. That's where we relegated all the 'stuff' from the cabinets." She makes air quotes with her fingers. "We want to parse through it and get rid of things before we put it all back, maybe find a charity shop to donate to, but we haven't taken the time yet. We've only got the bare bones essentials in here right now." She pauses and smiles at me again. "You know us. Any excuse not to cook."

I smile back at her. "Tea is fine with me. All caffeine is good caffeine."

Since there are no barstools at the new island seating area—they're hopefully in my rented warehouse along with the other new pieces we ordered—I lean my hip against the edge of the counter and watch as Jane bustles around and retrieves two light blue mugs from a lower cabinet across the room and sets them on the island countertop. I can see, as she opens and closes the doors, that she's correct and the cabinets are almost empty. She then walks around the island and pulls out a sugar dish from the cabinets beneath it, on the sink side.

My designer hat is on, studying her habits to get a read on how I'll need to organize the finished space—the teacups, plates, and glasses on the stainless steel shelves above the sink…all within easy reach. The sugar dish and teabags arranged in neat containers on the pretty tray I've already ordered for the countertop, making these frequently used items as accessible as possible. Storage of pantry staples—larger quantities of sugar, tea, coffee pods, etc.—in canisters that live on the pullout racks beneath the island, exactly where she went for them.

Design isn't just about making things pretty. It's about making life easier and happier, a lesson I didn't learn in school but from making my own home. It's about taking control of the little things that make us either content or frustrated—also something I didn't learn in school but from life.

Within minutes Jane places a teacup and saucer into my hands, and we carry our cups into the conservatory, where we perch on the lonely wicker settee—the rest of the room's new furniture is at the warehouse. It doesn't take long for me to finally find out what's troubling Jane. And it knocks me backward.

"So, how much do you know about that friend of yours who came here with you a couple of times? That other designer…Miranda, is that her name?"

Just hearing Miranda's name is enough to make me choke on my tea. I'd hoped I wouldn't have to be confronted by her at all on this trip, that she wouldn't even know I was here.

Jane watches as I literally choke, sputtering with my eyes watering as my drink goes down the wrong pipe.

"Oh, my gosh. I'm so sorry. Here let me get you…um, water? A tissue?" She jumps up, setting her cup on the one table remaining in the room, a small round accent table they've pulled to the front of the settee to use as a coffee table.

I wave a hand to stop her. "No, no, I'm fine," I manage to choke out. I take a slow sip of my tea, and the creamy milk Jane added soothes my throat on the way down. After setting my cup down beside hers, I reach up and press the sides of my nose with my fingers to stop the burning, tingling sensation. Then I dab my paper napkin at the wetness in the corners of my eyes.

Jane watches me with concern, her mouth slightly agape. I chuckle because I can't help it and say, "Does that answer your question?"

She giggles nervously. "Kind of," she says. "So, she's not someone you trust, then?" Her forehead is taut with worry lines.

I shake my head, feeling my lips turn down outside of my own will. "I thought she was," I say. "But I've since learned otherwise." The lead weight has returned to my stomach, accompanied by a sick feeling of growing nausea. "Why? What's happened?"

I almost add *"I'm sorry for bringing her into your lives"* but force myself to hold my tongue. After all, I don't yet know that anything *has* happened.

Jane seems hesitant to continue. After a torturous moment she says, "Well, something strange, and we don't know for sure that it's her who was involved in it, but we feel very certain it wasn't you, and, well…here, let me just show you."

She jumps up from the settee so quickly that she bangs her knee on the table, and a drop of tea sloshes over the side of her cup and plunks onto the floor. Jane doesn't even notice. She dashes from the room, and I reach down with my napkin and wipe it up, my heart beating in my throat the whole time she's gone.

About thirty seconds later, she reenters the room with a tablet encased in tan leather. She's tapping at the screen before she sits back down beside me, closer this time so I can lean in and read over her shoulder.

"It may take me a minute to find it," she mumbles, pulling up a web browser and tapping at the keyboard. My horror grows as I realize what she's typing—R-Y-L-A… She stops there as frequently searched terms begin to pull up that include Ryland Pemberton's name.

She clicks one that reads *Ryland Pemberton son*, and my stomach dips in panic.

A website opens, some British news mag or tabloid site that I'm unfamiliar with, and Jane scrolls past the masthead too quickly for me to even see what the publication is called. The article headline reads, "Pemberton Not Who We Thought?" and below it, a subhead reads, "Labour Party upper chamber spokesman harbours secret heir."

My face frozen in what must be a horrified expression, I skim the first few lines before Jane scrolls past them to a large image depicting both Elliott and Braxton. Braxton is looking down, his facial features in shadow and hard to distinguish, but Elliott is staring straight ahead, his chin jutted forward in an expression that reads as defiant, a bit arrogant, certainly haughty…the spitting image of Ryland himself, twentyish years younger.

I register with further horror that the photo was taken just out front, on the sidewalk in front of Jane and Adam's townhouse. I recognize the black iron grate around the thin-trunked tree just off the walkway, the neighboring stoop, even the white Vauxhall Corsa that's almost always parked just off the curb.

I squint at the tiny print beneath the photo to read the caption, but all it says is "credited to our news services."

I look at Jane, and Jane looks at me, and together we look back down at the iPad screen.

"Holy crap" are the only words I can squeak out.

"Yes. Right," Jane says. "So you have no idea either, then, how this might have gotten out." It's clearly rhetorical, since she doesn't ask it as a question. "I was hoping that was the case." She quickly amends, "I told him that it *would be* the case."

"So Ryland blames me for this?" My voice raises a decibel or two by the end of the sentence, my jaw going slack.

She seems to struggle with her answer for a few seconds, finally saying, "Well, he thought you might have had something to do with it. I told him I didn't think that sounded like you at all."

"Trust me when I tell you I had *nothing* to do with this." A realization hits me with the force of a gale wind, and I add, "So, is it true, then? Is Elliott Ryland's son?"

I mean, I suspected as much since the resemblance is so striking, but I hadn't asked Jane about it since she and Ryland were clearly being secretive about Elliott, and it was none of my business, regardless. I also never talked to Miranda about it outside of the couple of minutes when she witnessed Elliott and Ryland here herself, the afternoon when I brought her by to see the progress on the house.

I don't hear Jane's response to my question because it's just occurring to me that while I didn't talk to *Miranda* about Ryland, I did mention him to *Ian*. Casually, while we were lazing in bed one evening in the week before I left. I try to remember exactly what it was I said. I'm sure I didn't mention any suspicions I might have had about Elliott. In fact, I'm not positive I even brought up Elliott at all. Did I tell him what Ryland had said about me resembling Elliott's mother? I can't remember.

"Quinn?"

Jane jerks me back to the present moment. "What? I'm sorry. What did you say?"

"I said no," she says. "That's the funny part. Elliott is his cousin, like I told you. His mother was American. I never met her. And his father, Mr. Pemberton's first cousin, died when Elliott was very young. The poor boy, he has such a tragic history. I feel really bad for him. That's partly why we've encouraged Braxton to spend time with him while he's here, before he starts boarding school in winter term. He needs friends, stability, a home." She bites her lip and glances back down at the screen, which has gone dark. "This isn't helping, I'm sure. He can't even be seen outside right now because of the photographers. And of course, he does look so much like Mr. Pember…I mean, Ryland. The family resemblance is very strong."

Even in the midst of this seriousness, it strikes me as funny that Jane *still* calls him Mr. Pemberton, though they've obviously become closely acquainted. It's as if she has to force herself to call him Ryland. I wonder if it's the House of Lords thing, a show of respect. But I grew up around senators and congressmen, and trust me when I tell you, most politicians don't *need* to be referred to by their formal titles all the time, lest their big heads and egos become even more bloated than they already are. We all put our pants on one leg at a time. That's my take on it, anyway.

I shake these thoughts off. Something else is bothering me, and Jane's answer to my question isn't satisfying it. "Are you *sure* Ryland isn't Elliott's father?" My eyes narrow as I study her. "I'm asking because, well, I'm just going to come right out and tell you this. Ryland approached me once while you weren't here and told me Elliott's mom, mum, looked exactly like me. And, well, the way he looked at me…" I pause, trying to put it in the right words. "Well, it looked like he was staring at the ghost of his own past."

Jane bites her lip, gazing back at me. "I'm fairly certain," she says. "It's just a family resemblance. Ryland also very much resembled his cousin, from what he's told us. But…" Her voice trails off, and she chews her lip again. "I don't know that I should tell you this, but I guess there's no harm done. No further harm, at least." I sit a little straighter, feeling accused, and she raises one hand. "No, no. I'm not blaming you. I believe that you didn't have anything to do with this story." She nods toward the tablet.

"But after it came out, and Mr. Pemb…" She smiles. "Ryland came here to ask Adam and me about it—not the most comfortable moment of our lives, I can tell you—he did tell us something about his past that he said is *imperative* that we keep to ourselves. His word, not mine." She eyes me gravely.

I nod, my brows furrowed. "Of course, I won't tell a soul."

"You're part of the 'ourselves' in my opinion. Otherwise I probably wouldn't tell you. But you're a part of all of this since you've been here through it. And I trust you."

"Thanks." I nod again, my eyes wide and steady on hers.

"After his cousin died, while Elliott was still a young child, Ryland had a relationship with Elliott's mother. I believe it was serious, and to tell you the whole truth, I believe he really loved her. But when they went public with their relationship, or public to their families, at least, Ryland's grandmother threw a fit. Not because Cassie—that was Elliott's mum's name—was his cousin's wife, but because she didn't have the right type of pedigree. So it wasn't just that she was American but that she was a *common* American, not from money or prestige or prominence. That still matters here in some circles, or at least it still did to Ryland's grandparents' generation. And by adopting Elliott and potentially having more children with her, especially as the oldest male in the lineage and heir to his family's estate, he was muddying up their bloodlines or something like that. Ridiculous, I know," she adds when she sees my expression. "But his cousin had practically been disinherited for marrying Cassie in the first place."

"And so when Cassie died…" I start.

"She had Ryland listed as sole guardian in her will. I don't think either of them had ever gotten over the other."

Well, that would explain Ryland's weird intensity around me, the strange, probing, and sometimes longing looks, the difficulty he had in looking at me or talking to me. It also explains his attachment to Elliott. But it doesn't explain…

"How does Miranda fit into any of this?" I burst out suddenly.

Jane is nodding before I even finish. "That's the other reason I wanted to tell you this," she says. "I want to get to the bottom of this story getting out and why." She pauses. "Ryland trusted us not only with keeping Elliott, but with keeping his secrets…and with keeping Elliott out of the public eye. We've let him down, and I just don't understand how it's happened."

The sinking feeling returns to the pit of my stomach.

"I have my suspicions," I mutter. I close my eyes and purse my lips, cursing Miranda internally and bracing myself.

"Did you say anything to her about Mr. Pembert…Ryland, or Elliott, after that day she saw him here? I'm sure she must have recognized him, right?"

"I didn't tell her anything apart from the fact that he has a house next door—to explain what he was doing here. And I'm positive I told her the truth, that Elliott is Ryland's cousin and his mother had recently passed away and that he's friends with your son. And that was that, from what I can remember. Though yes, Miranda was curious, and yes, she definitely recognized him."

Jane sighs. "I suppose in retrospect I should have told you more and limited who was coming in and out of the house. But that would have been very difficult with all the workers and deliverymen and that sort of thing, and besides, Mr. Pemberton told us not to go out of our way to change our lifestyles. He's very private, but he's also considerate. He didn't want to inconvenience us or impose, but he also really wanted Elliott to be comfortable and make friends and not be miserable while he was making arrangements for his future. We all thought this would be a brief, inconsequential situation. And of course we didn't mind a bit, looking after him and taking him under our wing."

I'm listening and nodding along, but something in Jane's speech triggers a question. As soon as she pauses I interject, "Like you said, workers have been coming in and out of the house for weeks. How do you know one of *them* didn't go to the press with the story about Ryland and Elliott? What makes you think it was Miranda?"

Jane nods. "We thought about that, and I might not even have remembered your friend if not for the fact that Mrs. Northfield—you know, our sweet neighbor from two doors down…a pensioner? White hair? Gets out a lot? Usually with that pink pillbox hat pinned to her hair?"

We both smile at this, and I nod. I've exchanged pleasantries with the woman several times during my comings and goings. She's precious and very talkative. She reminds me a little of that "Hyacinth" character from the British show *Keeping Up Appearances*, which Jules used to watch religiously on BBC America.

"Well, there's very little that escapes Mrs. Northfield's notice. And she told me in passing, a little over a week ago, that she saw a woman lurking out front with a camera. She described her as having dark hair with colored streaks running through it and wearing all black apart from a pink jacket and chunky—I think she called them 'unkempt'—black boots. The boots were the kicker. I remembered them from that day you brought her here."

She pauses as I process this. I'm shaking my head with teeth clenched.

"Less than a week later, this photo turns up in *Tattletale*. And from there it went everywhere. It went viral. Being that our child is in it, and he's obviously a minor, Adam has been looking into legal steps we can take, though I doubt we'll do anything about it. The harm's already done, and nobody's bothered Braxton about it, at least so far as he's telling us. And no one has called or bothered us, either. It doesn't seem like anyone has linked us to the story. The press is just bugging Ryland to death. And he's barely let poor Elliott leave the house. He's hired a private tutor. I doubt Elliott will be going back to school here and probably won't be living here much longer."

My emotions are vacillating between pity for Elliott, sympathy for Ryland, and pure, black fury for Miranda. *How could she?* Was she really so desperate for money that she made up a story about Ryland and Elliott to sell to the press? My fingers are itching to grab Jane's tablet and Google the story to see what's being said and what types of publications are reporting it—all gossipy, tabloid-type rags and sites, I'm sure. The legitimate press surely would have vetted its sources a little better and dug up something of what Jane's just told me. And maybe they have.

But I can't think too hard about that right now because, along with being pissed beyond words at Miranda and regretting the day I ever met her, my mind is spinning over Ian's role in this situation. Because surely he had one. If he's been plotting with Miranda, surely he told her about the night I carelessly brought Ryland up to him. The thought roils in my stomach, sending up a bitter, bile-like aftertaste.

He and Miranda are probably right now enjoying their newfound cash, hers to save her shop, I guess, and his to keep him afloat after, I can only assume, losing his job. I wonder how much trouble he's in? I wonder if they fired him under the guise of layoffs or if they actually found something on him—something that linked him to his former roommate's scheme. Because now I have no doubt that Ian was probably involved. If he could lie to me so easily about Miranda, about how he feels about *me*, I'm sure he lied about plenty of other things, too.

They're probably together at this very moment, reveling in how well they snowed everybody over and got exactly what they wanted. *Disgusting.*

"I'm so sorry," I say in a voice barely above a whisper. "I'm sure it was Miranda who took the photo and who sold the story. She's not…she's not who I thought she was, and I only learned that recently. I'm really sorry that I involved her in your project and that I brought her here. I'm usually a much better judge of character than this."

Jane waves a hand in front of us, shaking her head. "No, no, no, don't be sorry," she says. "You have absolutely nothing to apologize for. It wasn't you who did this, and you had no way of knowing something like this might happen. If anything, it's my fault for not bringing you into the loop on the whole thing in the first place and for not exercising more caution. You must have thought the whole situation with Mr. Pembe…Ryland was awfully strange."

Her assurances have relaxed me enough that I can laugh, just a little, the smallest huff.

"Honestly? It just made the project even more interesting," I say. "The whole thing, the secrecy, the way this mysterious neighbor kept appearing through the back gate, the way he was so stiff and formal—nothing like that would ever happen at home. It was so freaking *British*."

Jane chuckles, too. "Yeah, I can see that. I guess we've gotten used to the more reserved culture, living here so long. Honestly it suits us well. I can't imagine ever leaving England and going back to the States." She pauses, glancing at me. "Don't tell Jen that. Adam's entire family is salivating for us to move back. Especially his mother."

I mime zipping my lips. "Mum's the word. Literally."

"I believe you." She grins at me. "Well, you know what? That's that. What's done is done, and there's nothing much we can do about it anyway. So let's look at the house, you think?"

"I think that's a *fantastic* idea." I pick up my cup and follow her through the rooms, dying to get to work.

CHAPTER SEVENTEEN

———

Insults & Injuries

Two days later I'm trekking my usual path from the B&B to the Dawsons' townhouse, pulling a roller bag packed carefully with four small folk-art canvases I bought at a gallery in Memphis to add color to a blank corner of the living room as well as a touch of the family's Southern roots. My plan is to show them to Jane before I take them to a local shop to have them framed.

I'm almost to Jane and Adam's front stoop, obsessing about the chip I discovered yesterday on the leg of an accent table that was delivered to the warehouse and not paying much attention to my surroundings, when I hear someone call out my name.

"Quinn!" The voice is deep, unfamiliar.

I spin on a heel, bewildered.

At first I don't see anyone in the direction of the voice, which seemed to come from the opposite sidewalk. There's a woman walking a poodle on a turquoise leash directly across from me, but she doesn't look up as she passes by. And then a tall man emerges from between two cars, several yards farther up the sidewalk, and glances left before jogging across the street toward me.

My thoughts freeze, and it takes a second longer than it should to register that it's Thomas. As in, Miranda and Ian's friend Thomas. *What the hell is he doing here?* I fight the urge to take off at a sprint, flutters swirling in my stomach.

How does he know I'm here? By "he," I mean Ian, not Thomas…because this can't possibly be a coincidence. I've practically sworn off social media, not wanting to leave any clues about my whereabouts, even though my profiles are set to private and I unfriended Miranda, Ian, and even Eleanor on Facebook before I left the last time.

Thomas has no reason to look for me, unless Ian or Miranda put him up to it. *But which one?*

My stomach roils into a tight, almost painful knot.

"What do you want?" My voice is icy and reaches Thomas before he even steps onto the sidewalk. His face registers surprise at my tone.

"Right," he says, stopping several feet away from me, his hand curled around a black phone that I immediately regard as suspect. Has he already texted Miranda? Ian? He tucks it into his front pocket.

"Right?" I cock my head, glaring at him. "What's right about this? What, are you stalking me for them? What do they want from me? They've already taken it, I assure you."

Now he's looking at me like I'm unhinged.

"They?" he repeats, a smile playing at the corners of his lips. It only makes me angrier. "Who are *'they'*? I only happened to be walking by and thought that it was you I saw. And here it is."

"You *happened* to be walking by? By *my* clients' house?" I let go of the handle of my bag, which rocks backward and lands upright, and clench my fists. "You don't even know me," I growl. "You barely said a word to me all those times I hung out with you guys at the pub. What, are you in on this…this *threesome*, this money-grubbing scheme or whatever it is that Miranda's been pulling? I can't give you any more information for your *sources*. God, you people are sick."

Thomas's eyes grow wide. He winces slightly at the word "threesome" but otherwise looks genuinely confused, not that I buy his act for a second.

"What are you on about?" he says. "Sources? What money-grubb… Scheme? Is that what you called it?" His head gives a rapid shake, as if he's totally taken aback. "I have no idea what you're talking about. Although yes, you're right that I didn't just happen to be walking by."

He shakes his head again. "He said you'd be angry, but…yeesh."

At this veiled reference my body goes taut. "So you're here for Ian." My voice is completely flat. As his name comes out of my mouth, it brings a physical stab of pain.

"Yes, I'm here for Ian. I don't *want* to be here, but to be quite honest with you, he begged me. He said that if you saw him, you'd run the other direction but that you might listen to *me*. And he's been through it, my old friend. I didn't have it in me to say no, no matter how mad he is. How mad you all are." He gestures toward me, infuriating me further.

"Don't lump me in with them," I bellow, affronted. "*I'm* not the one who took advantage of an innocent young boy for *money*."

He stares at me again with that baffled expression. "I don't have the slightest idea what you're talking about. What boy—?"

"What did he tell you to say to me, anyway?" I interrupt, taking a different tack to hopefully throw him off guard. I don't want to talk to him about Elliott. I don't want to give any of them any more ammunition against the poor kid, against Ryland, than they already have. I don't want to be involved in it in any way.

Thomas's face instantly changes, grows sheepish. His ears turn a deep shade of pink.

"He told me to tell you he loves you." He shrugs. "And that he hopes very much that you'll talk to him, give him another chance." Taking a step backward, he holds up both hands. "I'm here. I've done it. I've delivered the bloody message. And now I'll leave you to it." He shoves his hands into his pockets and starts to walk away.

"Wait." My whole body is pulsing at the sound of that word. The *L* word. The most unfair word that's ever been spoken. "How did you know I was here?"

Thomas whirls to face me but doesn't approach me again.

"I didn't," he calls out. He laughs incredulously. "I've been walking an extra two blocks on my way to and from work and at lunchtime every day for more than a week, trying to spot you out for him. Don't ever say I'm not a loyal mate." He laughs again, shaking his head before spinning on a heel and starting away again.

"Lovely to see you again, Quinn," he calls over his shoulder.

He continues to the corner and waits for the pedestrian signal, still shaking his head. I stand frozen in place, watching him for several more seconds, trembling all over.

In the next moment I feel the faint vibration as my phone chimes in my bag with a new text.

* * *

Standing on Jane and Adam's stoop a few minutes later, I'm waging an internal war. So far I've managed to stop myself from taking out my phone, and if I ring the doorbell, I'm essentially committing to not reading Ian's text—because it has to be from Ian; the timing is just too coincidental—until I leave late this afternoon. I don't want to come undone in front of my client, and I have a strong, sinking feeling that Ian might be my undoing.

As I stand there deliberating, my finger stretched toward the doorbell but not pressing it, another text comes in.

It has to be a sign.

Tears already welling, I stand my bag next to the doorway and reach into my purse for my phone. With a shaking hand I pull it out, and then I smooth the hem of my jersey dress under me as I sink to perch on the top step.

I breathe deeply as I wake up the screen. Ian's number blurs before my eyes, though I don't even know yet why I'm crying. I open my text messages and click directly into Ian's thread. The first message, the one sent just after Thomas walked away from me, reads, *I have to see u. Please stop shutting me out. Please talk to me.*

The second message, the one that just came, reads, *This is killing me. I didn't do what Pamela said I did. I didn't do anything to hurt u. I nev want to hurt u. Pls let me see u. At least reply. Please.*

A hot, round tear drips off my cheek and splashes onto the screen of my phone, distorting the words of his text. The words aren't new, apart from the part about seeing him, which is torture—just the thought of him being so close by, knowing I won't give in, that I can't give in, it's torture.

But you did hurt me, I think. *You did do it. And worse, you helped Miranda hurt somebody else.*

Another tear splashes onto the screen. As I watch it slide to the corner, it feels as if I'm outside my own body, as if I'm watching the person sitting here rather than sitting here myself. And then some dam inside me breaks, and before my brain catches up to what my fingers are doing, I'm typing a message back to him.

I can't believe you're stalking me. Leave me alone, Ian. You used me, and I can't forgive you for that. I won't. I don't trust you anymore. Please, please stop texting me.

I click *Send* before I even realize I'm doing it, my instincts sprinting out in front of me. And then less than a second later, I'm horrified. By breaking my silence, by weakening, I'm only opening myself to seeing him again. I'm opening myself to being hurt by him again. I know this. I'm sure he knows this. I stare at the screen, thinking *What have I done?*

His reply comes within seconds.

I can't stop texting u. I love you. Quinn, I LOVE YOU. I'm terrified to lose you.

Tears are pouring down my cheeks again, too many to bother wiping them away. A new text follows right on the heels of the last one.

If u feel anything for me at all, please see me. Just give me a chance to talk to u in person. On your terms, anywhere u want. In a public place, on sidewalk, even. Just pls see me.

I don't know how to reply. I don't move at all; I just keep watching the screen as more words appear. As I knew it would, answering his text opened the floodgate for more texting, more torture.

Tonight? 18.00? Outside your hotel?
Just to talk. We don't have to go anywhere.
Please.
Quinn?

After this text a full three minutes pass in which I can imagine him waiting for my reply, his eagerness and hopefulness that I might respond again fading. And then, finally, another text comes.

I'll be there. 6 oclock, today. If u don't come I'll leave u alone and respect that u don't feel the same. I'll be shattered but won't bother u again. Please.

After I read these words the phone clatters from my hands onto the step, and my head drops into my hands, elbows sinking onto my knees. My tear ducts are caught in a web of confusion—I feel cried out in one respect and like I'll never stop crying in another.

I sit frozen in this position for several minutes before finally taking a long, shaky inhale. I have a job to do. At any moment Jane might glance out the window and see me sitting here on her stoop, an unprofessional nervous wreck.

I wipe my cheeks with the backs of my hands and then dig around in my purse for something to clean myself up with, finding a crumpled-up tissue buried in the bottom. I dab at my face and then pull out a compact and apply powder to try to mask the redness. It's no use—I look terrible.

"Damn you, Ian." My voice is a shaky whisper.

Trying very hard not to start crying all over again, I sit up straighter and then will myself to stand. I mount the steps, grab the handle of my bag, and ring the doorbell before I lose my burst of resolve.

I will not meet Ian tonight. And I will not let him ruin my day.

There. Done. Decision made.

Jane swings open the door.

* * *

"Oh, I love *them*." Jane's voice lilts up at the end of the sentence, the English influence infiltrating her dialect as it does from time to time.

It's twenty minutes later, and I've just finished unwrapping the four paintings from their reams of packing tape and bubble wrap, which now forms a carpet of debris around our feet. I'm sure Jane could tell I'd been crying when she opened the door, but she didn't mention it, for which I'm grateful. In response, I'm overcompensating by being super bubbly, annoying even myself. But I can't help it—it's either fake it or break down.

Together we're gazing down at the four canvases, which I've laid out gallery-style across the new table, delivered only yesterday by the woodworker in North Ruislip who built it by hand.

"I hoped you would. I'm going to have them framed like this." I mime the shape of the mat and frame openings. "And hang them geometrically. With all the neutrals in that space, they'll be like the jewelry in the room."

That's how I thought of them when I found them—they reminded me of the way Jane tends to pair a bright scarf or pair of earrings with her tailored, neutral outfits. They contain the colors that tend to be her go-tos, aquas and corals and kelly greens. The front room, in particular, is inspired by Jane's style, and I'm hoping it also captures her charm and grace.

"That sounds amazing," Jane laughs. "I'll have to remember exactly how you said that so I can impress my friends with it later."

After carefully stacking the artwork and cleaning up the mess from the packing materials, I lead Jane from room to room, discussing plans and gesturing widely to show her what's going where, both to keep my hands and brain occupied and to explain to Jane what she can expect during the final installation. Right now it's planned for early next week, though that could change depending on delivery schedules and subs.

The important thing is that I have plenty to do to keep my mind off of Ian.

Along with juggling communication with clients and coworkers back home, I have to shop for more accessories and for installation materials, orchestrate the schedule, finalize the space plans, and verify all the times with my various subcontractors. And, of course, troubleshoot when things go wrong.

Having never done an install outside the US, I was already a nervous wreck. Now, with what's just happened with Ian, with Thomas showing up here...I'm so shaky and mixed-up I'm actually twitching. If I had the Xanax I keep in my carry-on for flights on me right now, I'd take one. Leaning against the wall in Jane's downstairs powder room, I wish desperately I'd packed it in my purse.

I was already dreading nighttime, even before Ian's text. Unlike my last two trips when my evenings were occupied mostly by hanging out at the Lion's Gate or with Ian, I've spent the past two interminable nights in my room at the inn, unable to concentrate on TV, mostly surfing my phone and consuming the entire internet, line by line. I can name every quiz BuzzFeed has produced in the past two months and tell you my result, and I've watched enough dog, cat, and dancing toddler videos to span five lifetimes.

And now it's late afternoon, and six o'clock is tearing toward me like a ballistic missile already launched. I'm terrified of the minutes passing. Though I've tried to keep Ian's texts off my mind, that's been impossible, and my emotions are crashing in waves, zigzagging dizzily from high to low to high tide as I wrestle with deciding to meet him, then changing my mind, then changing it back again.

There's a part of me that needs to scream at him, to get it all out. All afternoon, imagined scripts of what I'd say to him have sprinted though my head.

How dare he send his friend—like we're twelve years old—to be his spy and messenger? How dare he contact me at all, after what he and Miranda did? How dare he continue to lie about it? To lie about how he feels about me? Because it's all a lie—I know it is. I know he's just continuing to manipulate me, and I know it's because I'm so easy to manipulate. And the cruelty of that is…I can't bear it.

And worse, I'm not the only one he's hurting. My attraction to the wrong kind of men has reached such epic proportions it's now ruining the lives of others. I haven't seen Elliott since I've been back, and that's heartbreaking. He'd actually seemed happy the last time I was here, or at least normal, stable—but Miranda and Ian ruined that, too.

I want to hurl these hurts at Ian, to hurt him back. And I have my chance. He'll be right here. He'll be so close.

And it's that thought that makes me know I can't do it. I can't meet him. I can't talk to him or even scream at him because having him here, having him close, I can't trust myself. If I see him, how can I be sure I'll scream at him when what I really want is tell him how much I miss him, how I've been miserable without him? How can I be sure I'll slap his face when what I really want is to throw my arms around him and never let go?

I *hate* him. I hate him, and I love him, and whoever said the line between the two is thin was so right I want to slap him, too.

I love Ian, and that's why I can't text him or talk to him or see him. Because I'm weak.

The hot tears threaten to spill over again, and I squeeze my eyes shut. *Get it together, Quinn. You're at work.*

I turn on the faucet, splashing water on my face that I pat off with a tissue. And then I force up my façade of fake cheerfulness again before reemerging into the hall.

"Want a cup of tea?" Jane asks as I step into the kitchen.

"No, thank you. Maybe just some water." As shaky as I am, caffeine might not be the best idea for me right now.

"Sure thing."

I've been avoiding my phone, afraid Ian might have texted again or tried to call, and so as Jane moves around the kitchen, I glance out the windows and peer through the conservatory to get a read on the sky, to try to gauge how much time has passed. As late as the sun sets here, it's hard to tell, and the omnipresent clouds are obscuring the sky anyway. My fingers twitch without my phone in them to instantly answer my question. It's amazing how I can't function without my phone in my hand—clock, flashlight, level, window to the world, lifeline.

A part of me wishes it were already past six so this would all go away—not the hurt, which will take a long time to leave, if it ever does. But the situation, the decision, the part of it that's in my hands.

But Braxton is still at school, and Adam at work, and Jane seems in no hurry, and Ian's presence still looms in my future. Even if I'm not there, he will be. And knowing that is torture.

"Is everything OK?" Jane asks as she places a glass of water in front of me, along with the two-thirds empty bottle she poured it from.

"Yes, fine," I answer automatically, my voice dull to my own ears. I drain the glass in seconds, unaware of how thirsty I was. I realize I haven't eaten anything all day.

"You're not worrying about what I told you yesterday, are you? About Elliott? Because I really don't want you to think about that at all. They'll be fine. This will all blow over and be yesterday's news, and Elliott is in good hands. Mr. Pemberton is a good man, as good as they come."

"Thank you," I say. "I've been worried about it, I admit, especially since it was probably my friends who are responsible. But that's nice of you to say."

"We didn't get this far yesterday, but…why do you think she did it? That girl, Miranda? What was in it for her? Besides money, I assume. Someone probably paid her very well for that photo."

"Yes, that. Money," I say with a sigh. "I learned recently that her business isn't doing well. But don't worry," I add quickly. "She has nothing to do with my work on your project. I'm not even renting her warehouse space anymore."

"I'm not worried about that," Jane says. "But I'm glad you learned the truth about her sooner rather than later. At least she can't do you any more harm."

I huff lightly. "Yeah, at least there's that." *Besides break my heart all over again every time I think about Ian, probably for the rest of my life.*

Sighing, I reach for a subject change. "Hey, did I ask you about the chair in the study? I've been meaning to. Are you OK with swapping out that wingback for the armchair and ottoman in the extra room upstairs? It might be more comfortable when you use that room to read, and we can put a floor lamp in beside it."

"Ooh, I like that idea," Jane says. "We never even use that upstairs chair. And we bought it new when we lived in Georgia." She picks up her teacup and rounds the island toward the doorway, and I follow, breathing a sigh of relief.

Time to go back into distraction mode.

* * *

By four thirty I've run out of ways to procrastinate. I've gone over every element of the rooms with Jane and contacted every member of my construction crew. I've pored over my space plans so exhaustively that I probably won't even need to refer to them during the installation. I have to shop for quite a few more items, but it's too late to head out and do that now, and I wouldn't be able to concentrate anyway.

Braxton is now home and he and Jane are in the kitchen, where she's helping him with some element of his homework. At this point I'm starting to feel in the way.

I pick my bag up from the antique walnut hall tree in the entryway, a piece we're keeping as-is, and check my phone. No new texts.

"Well, I'm heading out," I call to Jane, my stomach swimming with a nauseating mix of anger, dread, anticipation, and, for some inexplicable reason, guilt. I can't put off leaving any longer, and if I don't want to be stuck out in the city, afraid to go back to my hotel in case he decides to wait me out, I need to go back now.

"OK," she calls back. She pokes her head through the doorway from the kitchen.

"Remember that I have an appointment tomorrow at ten thirty? You won't need me to be here then, right?"

"No, I have some shopping I need to do tomorrow, accessories for the living room bookshelves and cabinet organizers for the kitchen. I'll be out of your hair all day. But remember that the plaster guy will be here at two to patch that spot in the dining room."

"Got it." She smiles. "I hope you have a nice night."

My gut takes a nose dive as her words tip the roller coaster car of my emotions over the ledge. For a second I can't answer, and when I do I sound like I'm choking. "Thank you. You, too."

"I'll see you soon. Thanks, Quinn."

I give a little wave before I close the front door behind me.

*　*　*

Once I'm out on the sidewalk, my mind spins with conflicting ideas of what I should do next. My hotel doesn't serve meals apart from breakfast, which I skipped, so unless I want to be stuck in my room all night with nothing to eat, I have to stop somewhere. *Do I go to a store? A restaurant?* I can't think clearly enough to figure it out, and despite my low blood sugar and dizzying emptiness, I'm too nauseated to think about eating.

I debate heading straight to the hotel and ordering takeout later, but I might risk Ian seeing me through the window when I come downstairs to collect it. I know he said six, but I have this strong feeling that when I don't show up, he'll wait. Maybe as long as it takes. And I can't risk letting him see me, not at all.

The indecision is so overwhelming that I decide to do none of it and instead call Jules. I've been dying to tell her and Savy about Thomas stalking me and Ian's texts, even though I dread what they're going to say—I know they'll tell me I should meet him.

I sit on another stoop a few doors down from Jane's and dial Jules' number. I hold my breath as it rings, and rings, and rings. When it goes to voice mail, I click *End Call* without leaving a message. I glance at the clock…four forty-five UK time, which means it's almost eleven a.m. at home. Jules is at work and probably not checking her phone. I curse myself internally for not calling earlier.

Next I dial Savy—a little less enthusiastically, only because I have a feeling I already know what she's going to say, and it's not what I want to hear.

She picks up on the fourth or fifth ring, and immediately I can tell that her voice is strange, sort of high and too perky. "Quinn! What's up?" I hear her add a muffled, "Sorry. I'll be back in just a minute."

"Where are you?" I ask, confused by the sound of cars and the low wail of a siren in the background. It sounds like she's outside, not in her office.

"I'm outside Pontotoc Café," she says. "I'm meeting…um, somebody for lunch."

Somebody? "Isn't it a little early?"

"He has a meeting at noon, so we're eating at eleven. They're not open yet, so we're standing outside. What's up?"

"*He?*" I ask, momentarily distracted.

"Yeah," she breathes, her voice quieter. "I met the *most* amazing guy."

"When?" I say, bewildered. "I only left Memphis four days ago. You met him that fast?"

"Last night."

"At Alchemy?" She'd texted me that she was going out with her sister, Lexi, but I haven't heard from her since then.

"No, after, at Celtic."

"And you're already meeting him for lunch?"

"Yes." Her voice drops even softer, and I hear her heels clicking on the pavement. "I have a really good feeling about him."

"Wow, that's awesome. I guess you can't really talk about it right now?" I squeeze my eyes shut. I can't lay my dilemma at Savy's doorstep right now and ruin her date. Even though maybe, just maybe it needs to be ruined—I moved fast with Ian, and look where that got me.

"I'll call you tonight, OK? After work." I hear more clicking, and then there's a muffled sound as she shifts the phone around and says to somebody, "Oh, they've opened the doors? OK, be right there."

She breathes into the phone. "I've got to go."

"OK." My heart is like a lead weight, but I try to keep the disappointment out of my voice.

"But, hey, Quinn?"

"Yeah?"

Her voice drops to just above a whisper again. "I know you said you weren't going to talk to Ian while you're there, but I think you should. I really, really think you need to text him and at least let him know you're there. If not, you'll spend the rest of your life wondering what could have happened and whether you did the right thing."

She pauses for me to respond, but I'm too stunned to speak.

"I really think you need to hear him out," she presses. "If nothing else, you need closure." And then she calls, louder, "I'm coming."

I lick my lips, my mouth suddenly gone completely dry. "Closure is overrated," I finally croak.

I'm not sure she hears because suddenly the outside sounds are replaced by muffled noises of dishes clinking and people talking, so I know she's stepped inside the restaurant.

"Text him," she says. "Do it today." She pauses, and then her voice drops back to a whisper and is sort of muffled, like she's holding the phone right next to her lips. "I have a good feeling about today, a great feeling. Today's a good day for falling in love." She giggles and then adds at normal volume, "I've got to go."

Staggered, I'm not sure whether to laugh or cry. It's as if fate's handed me a fortune cookie, but the message inside is a prank.

"Have fun at lunch," I say. "Love you."

"Love you, too," she trills. She giggles again before she hangs up the phone.

* * *

Glancing at my phone screen, my stomach dips in panic. It's two minutes till five. If I stop for something to eat, even if I take a taxi, which is probably my best option at this point, I'll be pushing it close, time-wise. And my alternatives aren't great. I'm carrying a rolling suitcase, so wandering the streets or hanging out at a bar or restaurant all night will be awkward. I wish the suitcase was packed with the things I'd need to spend the night elsewhere…because I'm almost chicken enough to do that, to book another hotel room on my own dime just to avoid the risk of seeing him.

I'm so torn by indecision that I finally just head in the direction of my hotel, resolving myself to a miserable, anxious, lonely, sleepless, hungry night.

I arrive there at ten minutes after five. Feeling fully deflated, head down, I reach the steps, grab the brass railing, and start to climb the carpeted steps, carrying my empty suitcase by its handle. I'm almost to the top when his voice stops me short.

"Quinn."

It startles me so much I miss the next step and stagger backward. All in the same instant, I drop the suitcase, which clatters down the steps behind me, and clutch at the railing to keep from falling. But my fingers don't quite close around it, and the next thing I know I'm tumbling backward, grasping at air.

An instant later I'm crashing up against something solid and warm, and there's a searing pain in my right ankle. The sweet, elderly porter from the inn has rushed outside, and behind him emerges the front desk worker, a middle-aged woman named Patricia I've talked to several times.

Everyone is talking over everyone else, so all I hear is a jumble of voices and phrases.

"I've got her."

"Is she all right?"

"Oh, my heavens."

"Shall I call an ambulance?"

I can't say anything yet, in part because my brain hasn't caught up to what's happened and in part because all of it—the pain, the noise, the shock—is eclipsed by the feel of Ian's warm, strong arms wrapped around me from behind. He must have raced up several steps to catch me as I fell, and he managed to keep us both upright as he staggered back down. Now we're both standing on the sidewalk just off the bottom step, or at least he's standing and I'm leaning, the full length of my body pressing against his as I try to keep weight off my right foot. I twisted my ankle—or broke it, or something—as I fell.

And then, to my horror and for the second or third time today, hot tears sear my cheeks as the chain of events begins to catch up to me. I start sobbing, uncontrollably, and even though it's creating even more havoc and confusion around me, I can't stop.

"Where does it hurt?" Ian whispers in my ear, his voice laced with panic, his breath hot on my cheek.

Everywhere. My ankle, my pride, my heart especially. I can't answer him, but if I could it would be some combination of the above.

"I think she's twisted her ankle," says Patricia, who's descended the steps and is hovering around me like an anxious mother. "Look." She points toward my feet. "She can't put any weight on it."

"Shall I call an ambulance?" the porter keeps repeating.

"Dear, are you all right? Can you talk to us?"

"I'm…I'm fine," I manage to gasp, my teeth chattering against each other. "I don't…I don't want an ambulance." Tears are still streaming out in hot waves.

"Are you sure? I think we should have that looked at. There's a surgery just up the way." Patricia is wringing her hands and shifting her weight from foot to foot.

"No…real…really," I stutter. I try to put a little weight on my foot and have to bite my lip to keep from crying out. "I'll be O…K-K-K."

"I can take her there," Ian says, his voice strong and assuring, though I can hear the strain and worry coming through. "I'm parked just there." He gestures with his head since his arms are still wrapped firmly around my midsection and then tilts his chin back down to me. "Is it OK if I pick you up?"

His warm breath ruffles the hair at my temple and tickles my cheek. Feeling it, hearing his voice, I'm unable to think straight. But right now, I don't have many good options.

I nod slightly.

Next thing I know, the sidewalk disappears from beneath my feet and I'm cradled against Ian's chest. He's very careful to avoid jarring my injured foot, though it throbs with pain anyway at the change in altitude. The next few minutes are a blur—Patricia following us to the car and opening the rear door after Ian awkwardly digs for his keys and clicks the doors unlocked. She continues hovering as Ian helps me gingerly into the back seat. I slide backward over the bench seat, searing with pain but slightly more in control of my emotions, and Ian yanks off his sports jacket and folds it into a sort of nest onto which he carefully rests my foot. I grit my teeth against the pain.

"Which way?" he asks Patricia, reaching out to take my purse from her. I'd seen her hand my empty suitcase off to the porter before we crossed the street. I feel helpless, like a child. I'm at a disadvantage in so many ways. But instead of making me cry again, this realization helps me regain control. I take a deep breath to steady myself as Ian shuts the door, says a few words to Patricia, and then climbs into the car.

"Are you OK?" he asks, turning back to face me the second he's inside with the door closed. "How badly does it hurt?"

I close my eyes. "Please just take me to the hospital." My ankle feels like someone's shooting nails from a nail gun into it, but that doesn't hurt nearly as much as looking into Ian's concerned face.

"The hotelier said there's a surgery just up the high street with late hours," he says. "Is that all right?"

I haven't heard the term "surgery" used in quite this way before, and it sounds ominous. But from the context I assume it must be some kind of medical clinic. "Fine."

Thankfully Patricia is correct and "just up the way" is an accurate description. I only have to endure a few short minutes of searing pain and crushing, awkward silence before Ian spots the clinic. It takes longer for him to find a parking space than it did to drive here, but thankfully, being that it's rush hour, someone pulls out of a curbside spot before he has to make the block a second time.

And then he's helping me out of the car, and I have no choice but to let him put his arms around me again, to lift me up and cradle me once again into his broad, familiar chest. I fight the urge to nestle my head into the warm pocket of his shoulder, the even deeper urge to press my lips against the white broadcloth of his shirt, the exposed skin of his neck.

My head is swimming with pain, confusion, anger, frustration, hatred, love.

It's hard to deny, with him holding me like this, that I'm in love with Ian. The expression on his face is heartbreaking, a mix of worry, tenderness, and determination. I'm hurt, and he's rescuing me. I don't see how this could be going better for him. My entire body clenches with the indignity of it, sending a new throb of pain through my ankle.

He walks with me carefully over the sidewalk, taking care to angle me to avoid bumping into any of the gawking pedestrians. "This isn't the way I wanted this to happen at all," he murmurs, as if he's overhearing my thoughts.

Despite everything, a hard laugh escapes my throat. "You might like it better than the alternative," I say, careful not to look at him.

"You weren't going to meet me." It isn't a question.

"No."

His lips are set in a grim line as we reach the sliding glass automatic doors of the clinic. Neither of us says anything else as he carries me toward the reception desk. With one look at us, someone behind the desk jumps up and rushes through a door into a rear hallway, and another minute later, a black male nurse comes through another door pushing a wheelchair. Ian gently helps me into it.

He speaks with the clinic staff, and they hand him a clipboard with paperwork to get my information. He brings it over to me, meanwhile handing me my purse so I can dig out identification. Thankfully I'm carrying my passport, and I hand it to him to pass to the receptionist.

He pushes me into the small waiting area, an entirely white space with blue faux-leather armless chairs and a TV mounted in the corner. There's only one other person in the room, an elderly lady with a neat bob of bluish-gray hair, holding a purse primly in her lap. Since she doesn't appear to be sick or injured, I assume she must be waiting for someone.

I spend a couple of minutes filling out the blank fields of the clinic forms, Ian hovering just beside me. Unnerved, I shoot him an irritated glance.

"You can leave now," I say through my teeth. "Thank you for catching me when I fell and for bringing me here, but I don't have anything else to say to you."

His chiseled jaw is set. "I'm staying."

"They won't let you come back with me," I say. "I'll tell them not to."

"Then I'll be here when you're finished." His voice is quiet, and I can't tell if it's just the typical English reserve, trying at all costs not to create a scene, or stubbornness.

"I can get a taxi back," I say. "I don't need you."

"But I need *you*." His face, so composed, so determined a moment earlier, crumples into a mask of anguish. "You don't understand. I can't let you walk away from me again. I need you like I need the air in this room."

I make the mistake of looking into his eyes as he's saying this, and I see my own pain reflected back at me. I see a world of things I'd hoped for, things I'd only ever glimpsed while I was with him, things I'd resolved myself to losing forever. And then I feel my own hard mask slip away, and I'm crying. Again.

"Ian, I can't. Not now. Not here, not… I can't talk to you."

Across the small space, I can feel the eyes of the elderly patron glued to us. Ian reaches up and catches a tear on the tip of his finger, his face so close to mine. He looks to be on the verge of tears himself.

"Quincy Cunningham?"

Both of us jump at the call. I glance over to the desk and see that the receptionist is holding out my passport. Ian jumps up to retrieve it, meanwhile slipping the clipboard off my lap and handing it to her in exchange. "We'll have her back in just a minute," the receptionist says, and he nods.

It's infuriating—him acting like he has a right to be here, like he's my husband or boyfriend or significant other. It's infuriating that I want him to be these things.

"Please just go." This time it's a whisper, and I can feel my own determination fading.

He shakes his head. "I can't."

And then I hear my name again, and someone is standing with a door open to the rear hallway, and Ian rises to push me in my chair toward the doorway, where they switch off, and the same nurse as before takes over and wheels me down the white hall.

"We'll get you fixed right up," he says.

As the door swings to a close, I hear the woman in the waiting room say, "That was more riveting than *Coronation Street*. I hope you…"

And then the door clicks shut, and I miss her parting words of advice. I hope she's telling him that I'm obviously in distress and vulnerable and that no means no, but somehow I fear that's not the case. I want to call back to her, "He's not my tragic, star-crossed lover. He was scheming with my former friend and possibly his current girlfriend to hustle me for money." But I'll let her write her own ending.

In the meantime, now that Ian's not in front of me as a distraction, my ankle is screaming with pain again, and it's hard to concentrate on anything but that.

* * *

The next forty-five minutes does wonders for my ankle, which is sprained, not broken, and now tightly and expertly wrapped. But it does nothing for my mental state, nor does it provide me with a solution for what to do when I find Ian still waiting for me out front, as he'd said he would be.

The nurse holds opens the door again and waits as I hobble past on crutches, issued courtesy of the National Health Service—I have no idea how any of this will be billed, but no one else seems to be concerned about that, so I figure I'll worry about it later. Ian jumps up from his chair and rushes over to me.

I see that the elderly lady is gone, and now a Middle Eastern woman in a burka is seated, filling out forms, with a young boy wiggling in the chair beside her. I grimace up at Ian.

"Fine," I say before he can speak. I'm stubbornly not meeting his eyes. "Yes."

"Yes, what?"

"Yes, you can drive me back."

He almost smiles. "Is it broken?" He glances down at my wrapped ankle, and it occurs to me for the first time that I have no idea what's happened to my shoe. As far as I can remember, it was missing before I even got into Ian's car.

"No, just sprained. I have to keep it elevated for several days and come back in a week to have it looked at. I have no idea how I'm going to get my work done in the meantime."

I glance over at the receptionist, who nods at me. "All ready to go," she says.

I thank her and begin hobbling toward the doors, Ian close by my side.

"So that means you might be here longer?" The hope in his voice is painful.

"Ian…" I start, but I don't finish because we're now out on the sidewalk, and the blur of city life around us is distracting. I can't talk to him like this. But I have sort of come to the realization that I do have to talk to him. If for no other reason than, as Savy said, closure.

When we reach his car, there's an envelope tucked under the windshield wiper. "Oh, no. It looks like you got a parking ticket."

He shrugs. "I forgot to pay the meter. No worries."

I feel guilty for a split second and then remember that if either of the two of us should feel guilty, it's him. My face hardens back into its inscrutable mask.

This time he helps me around the car and into the front seat, disorienting me since I'm still not used to the "wrong" side of the car. He's so gentle, so tender, and every point of contact between our skin singes with electricity, bringing back memories too painful to bear.

And so as soon as he climbs into the driver's seat, I snap, "I guess you have plenty of money to pay for parking tickets now."

His head swivels, and he looks at me with an expression of pure bewilderment. "What is that supposed to mean?"

I watch his face for the smallest reaction as I say, "The photos. You must have made a fortune selling the photos. Or hasn't Miranda shared the money with you yet?"

At Miranda's name his features twist with some strange mixture of pity, pain, and revulsion. "I haven't the faintest idea what you're talking about when you say 'photos,' but I can promise you I haven't accepted any money from Miranda. Nor will I, nor do I want to or need to."

"So you're saying she *has* offered you money."

He closes his eyes, leaning his head back against the headrest. Outside the thick silence of the car, the cacophony of the city envelops us, horns honking, car engines gunning just inches from my door, a siren blaring with a foreign-sounding wail in the distance. "I don't know what in hell's name Miranda is thinking these days," he admits. "She's gone quite mad."

I'm silent, staring at him for a long moment, but he doesn't open his eyes. "You're going to have to explain that to me," I say.

He chokes out a hard laugh, finally lifting his head and opening his eyes. "I wish someone would explain it to *me*." He looks straight into my eyes, his wide and imploring. "All I know is the same thing you know, the things Pamela accused her of the night you left…" He pauses for a beat and adds with a tone of dread, "Along with a little bit of history I suppose I should have made you aware of."

"Does it have to do with Thomas?" I blurt out. Thomas's placement in the jigsaw puzzle of their relationship has had me baffled since the beginning.

He looks taken aback again. "Thomas?" he says. "No." Then he looks off into space for a moment, seeming to consider it. "Well, maybe. Sort of."

I shake my head. "You're right," I say. "You're going to have to give me the history. Start at the beginning, please."

He nods slowly. And then he gestures with his head toward the street. "Can we at least drive someplace more comfortable first? You really need to put that foot up."

I grimace again. The last place I want to be with Ian is my hotel room, but I can't exactly elevate my wrapped ankle in a restaurant or a bar.

He lifts both hands. "I have no ill intentions. The instant you want me to go, I'll go. I promise. Even if you tell me to leave and never talk to you again." His voice breaks on the last couple of words, making my heart trip over itself for a second or two.

I consider the offer as he seems to think it through. "If you don't want me to come to your hotel we can go to my flat. That might be the most comfortable place for you anyway."

I'm shaking my head before he even finishes his sentence. "No way." We have too much history there. I can't even imagine the pain of facing the photograph in Ian's entry hall, the sparse, bachelor charm of the kitchen where we shared takeout meals, the bed where we shared…everything.

My stomach gurgles loudly, and this somehow decides things for us. He calls in an order to a nearby curry house, and, apparently feeling my ankle situation is too urgent to wait for the food, he gives them the hotel name for delivery and then carefully angles the car onto the street.

The next ten to fifteen minutes are occupied with navigating the confused, zigzagged disaster of London rush hour traffic. Ian can't find a parking space near the hotel on the first pass through or the second or the third. He continues circling the maze of roundabouts, dealing with the city's frustrating and complicated network of one-way streets, until finally someone is pulling out of a space within a block of the inn's front steps. This time he remembers to pay the meter.

I'm able to hobble to the bottom of the steps on my crutches, but once we reach them, Ian decides it will be easiest just to carry me again. It's getting less difficult for me to say yes, though I have a feeling that will only make it more difficult for me to say no to him later, which makes me uneasy.

Holding my crutches in his left hand, he sweeps me up easily into his arms again, and by the time we reach the top, the porter has the door wide open. Several more minutes pass while he and Patricia fuss over me, asking Ian and me questions and expressing relief that I'm back in one piece and not sobbing this time.

By the time we get through all of this, the food's already arrived, and Ian pays for it and helps me onto the elevator. It's only when we're standing outside the door to my room and I'm digging in my bag for my room key that it hits me how very, very different this night is turning out than I expected when I approached the hotel steps hours earlier.

And suddenly I'm unsure of myself, of everything.

"Ian." I pause with the key card in my hand. Meanwhile he's holding my purse, the bags of food—and my shoe, which Patricia handed us before we got onto the elevator.

His expression is somber, as if he knows what I'm thinking.

"You weren't going to meet me," he says, as if he still can't believe it.

"I don't think I can do this."

"I'll leave if you want me to." He glances at the items in his hands. "I'll just drop these things off and help you get settled, and I'll go."

His chin is lifted in a stoic expression, but his lower lip trembles, and I can see that he means it. That he'll do this for me.

"No," I say quietly, shaking my head. "No, it's all right." I hold the key card up to the panel on the door until it flashes green, and then I turn the handle. "Come in."

Once we're inside with the door closed, my mind flashes back to the last time we were in a room together in this hotel. It was a different suite, but it looked much the same, and my heart twists with a wistful pang. I force the memory out of my head.

Ian busies himself with setting the bags of food on the desk, hanging my purse from a corner of the desk chair, and taking my crutches when I hand them to him, leaning them against the wall by the door. He puts an arm around me and helps me hobble to the bed, and then he searches the room for extra pillows—which he finds in the top of the wardrobe—and helps me get propped up in bed with piles of pillows behind my back and another pile under my wrapped-up foot and ankle.

"Do you need anything? Water? Pain medicine?"

"Some Advil would be great." I nod toward my purse. "Hand me that bag, please. I'm pretty sure there's some in there." There's an unopened bottle of water on the desk, and he brings it to me, waiting as I take the medicine and get settled. And then there's a long, awkward silence.

"I'm not sure where to begin," he says. He looks around for a place to sit, and finally he drags over the heavy wooden armchair from beside the desk. The bed is a tall, queen-size four-poster, which means that when he sits, he's a good foot or more below me, awkward for conversation.

"Maybe you were right about your apartment being more comfortable," I admit.

With a sigh I gesture for him to get up, and then I point to the end of the bed. Neither of us even looks at the food. I couldn't eat right now if I tried, despite my gnawing hunger.

He climbs onto the bed, careful to avoid disturbing my ankle. Having him up here, close enough to feel his body heat, the bed moving beneath me every time he moves, is unsettling. But at the same time, I don't want him to go. Being here, in another country, halfway immobile and still in some pain, I'm almost able to forget how mad I am at him and remember only how being with him makes even this foreign place feel like home.

A wave of sadness threatens to crush me, sadness over what we might have had before he made it impossible for me to trust him again. We stare at each other for a long moment, until I have to break the gaze and look away.

"First…" he says. He stops until I glance back up at him. The look in his eyes is so raw and tender it almost knocks me breathless. "First," he repeats, his voice quiet and even, "I love you."

I suck in a sharp breath. It was one thing to read the words on my phone's screen. To hear them from a third party. Hearing them in Ian's voice, watching them come through his lips, it's more than I can bear. I look away again, willing myself not to cry.

He continues in a hoarse voice, "If there's one thing I've figured out in these weeks past, that's it. I love you. Quinn, I'm in love with you. And even if you won't believe me, even if you think I'm mad, even if it makes you suspect even more that I'm guilty of the things Pamela accused me of, I have to have you know this. I have to be sure that you hear me, that you believe me. I'd never forgive myself if I let you go without fully explaining how much I need to be with you. How much I need you and miss you."

A single tear streaks my cheek. I can't move a muscle. I can barely even breathe.

And suddenly I'm quaking with emotion. Love and hate again, crossing over each other in an indefinable blur. "But you would say that, wouldn't you? If you wanted my money? If you wanted a…how did Pamela put it, a 'trust fund heiress'? How much of Miranda's little plot were you in on, anyway?"

"None of it," he explodes. "I didn't even know there *was* a plot. If anything, I was happy Miranda wanted to introduce me to someone, because I thought it meant she'd moved on from what had happened before, that it meant things might get back to normal."

I shake my head, completely lost. "*What?*" I stare at him for a couple of seconds, my brow furrowed. "This is where you have to start at the beginning."

Ian sighs and rubs his forehead for a few seconds before he meets my eyes again. "You know we've all known each other since we were kids, right?"

"Yes. You, Miranda, Thomas, and Eleanor, right?"

"That's right. We were all mates. There was no tricky love stuff in the way most of that time. Until after university, in fact."

I raise an eyebrow.

He quickly continues, "And then Thomas got it in his head that he wanted to date Miranda. And they did go out together, for several months. This was about, oh, seven or eight years back."

I nod, one piece of the puzzle clicking into place. I was sure they'd had a history together. "And then what happened?"

"Well, they broke it off. *She* broke it off. And Thomas never got over it. We'd all gone our different ways at that point, and they both had other relationships. I knew Thomas was still sort of hung up on Miranda, but I thought it was all based on the past, a nostalgia sort of thing. But then we all found our way back to one another again, here in London."

"And so Thomas asked out Miranda again?"

"He did." Ian nods, his eyes far away. "And they did go out again, for a brief time."

There's a long silence. "And then what happened?"

He takes a deep breath. "And then, well, I told you what happened with my job, and then with my brother and Joanna."

"Yes," I hedge, not sure how this can all possibly tie in.

"Well…" He pauses again. "I was in a bit of a state. I mean, all right, I was lit-rally a mess. And in the middle of the worst of it, Miranda asks me to go to dinner with her, to cheer me up. We actually went to the same restaurant you and I went to on our second date, on the canal." His eyes grow distant for a moment. "In retrospect, that wasn't the best idea, taking you there. But it's just so lovely. I wanted to experience it with *you*."

"What happened?" I ask, impatient. I don't want to hear him bringing up *our* memories of what was hands-down the best night of my life and tainting them with stories about *her*. "What happened when you went there with Miranda?" My voice twists on her name.

He sounds strained when he answers. "She told me she didn't really want to be with Thomas, that she'd always preferred me," he said. "I was gobsmacked. I'd never suspected, and I'd always thought of Miranda like a little sister. I just don't think of her that way. But she caught me so off guard, and I was in such a bad place, and…"

His voice trails off.

"And?" I prompt. "What happened between the two of you?"

"Nothing," he answers too quickly. And then he sighs, a rasping, dragging sigh. He pinches his nose between his thumb and index finger before continuing. "Well, not nothing, I suppose. She kissed me. I let her kiss me. One kiss, barely a kiss at all. But I felt wretched about it later, on Thomas's account."

"As you should have," I say, my tone making it clear that I have no sympathy for this.

"I told Thomas what happened," he says. "The next day. And he confronted Miranda and forgave her, and me as well, but she broke things off with him."

"Wow."

"Yes, wow." He sighs. "And then we went our separate ways again, or at least *I* went my separate way. I still met up with Thomas from time to time, and he told me eventually that he and Miranda were speaking again. I hadn't heard from her in months when she texted me to tell me about you. When I went to the pub that day, the day that I met you, I thought—stupidly, I realize now—I thought it was all behind us, that she'd moved on. And I thought it looked like things were finally patched up between her and Thomas, that we were at least all friends again."

I gaze at him, processing his story. He seems exhausted from telling it, and I almost feel sorry for him. Almost.

"But what about the money part of it? What did Pamela mean by saying Miranda set me up with you so I could bail you out of debt or whatever? She made it sound like you two had cooked up a plot together to cheat me out of my fortune…which doesn't exist, by the way. I mean, yes, my family is financially stable, but I'm hardly a trust fund heiress. And I don't have any interest in taking my parents' money. I make my own way."

Ian looks as flummoxed as I feel.

"I couldn't figure that part out, either," he says. "I haven't asked her. I haven't talked to her at all since you left."

"She hasn't tried to contact you?"

He shakes his head. "No. You?"

"No. Honestly, I thought it made you seem more suspect. If none of it were true, or even if it was, wouldn't she have tried to deny it?"

"I don't know. I don't know what was going through her mind with any of it. All this has made me frightened for her. I haven't spoken to Eleanor, but I've talked to Thomas, and he hasn't seen nor heard from her, either."

"My friend Savy thinks she's too embarrassed to contact me. I told her I thought that was unlikely, that Miranda is far too self-assured to be embarrassed."

"You might be surprised by that," Ian says. "I've always found her to be quite insecure." He shakes his head. "She didn't have the easiest way growing up. You heard that story about her mum and my dad. Well, it wasn't the first or only time something like that happened. Her mother is, well, let's just say her mother's lifestyle choices affected Miranda heavily, and not in a good way."

He says this with a look of mild revulsion, and that reminds me of what he'd told me about his own mum, about her financial situation. And that reminds me…

"Hey, whatever happened with you at work? My brother-in-law, who works with an investment office out of London, told me your firm just had a big round of layoffs. Did you…?" My voice trails off.

He shakes his head. "I made the cut," he says. "They've kept me around. In fact, I've been promoted."

"Well, that's good to hear." It also explains why he's wearing a suit, or most of it, anyway. His jacket is probably still crumpled up in his back seat, and he lost the tie somewhere in the midst of our medical clinic adventure.

Which leads me to another question.

"How is it that you were already outside my hotel when I got here?" I ask suddenly. "It was barely after five. You asked me to meet you at six."

He half smiles. "I'd been here since three," he says sheepishly. "I had a feeling you wouldn't come, since you hadn't been answering my texts. I wasn't taking any chances. I'm sorry for the stalking, as you put it, by the way." He shakes his head, studying my face. "You really were killing me, Quinn. I couldn't figure out exactly what I'd done or why you were so angry with me. Nothing of what Pamela said made sense, but it seemed to make sense to *you*."

He pauses, and in the silence that ensues, he seems unsure of himself.

"You asked…you asked if Miranda has tried to contact me, and she hasn't. But I have tried to contact her. I've been trying to reach her for weeks, actually, almost as long as I've tried to reach you. *She* hasn't returned my texts or calls, either. I haven't gone so far as to try to track her down at work or through her friends. But I was a step away from that. I was desperate to talk to her because I thought it might help me reach *you*, to find out what it was she did that upset you so much that it ruined my life."

"Ruined your life?" I raise an eyebrow. "Is that maybe overstating things?"

"Are you kidding me?" His voice takes on a new timbre, drops so that it's lower and husky. The same raw tenderness I glimpsed earlier, at the clinic, returns to his eyes.

"Haven't you heard the most important thing I've told you tonight?"

"What is that?" My head feels fuzzy, like I'm floating on a cloud of cotton. I don't think it has anything to do with the pain or the medication. It's only beginning to hit me that I don't feel so angry with him anymore.

That maybe, just maybe, he's been telling me the truth.

Though Ian doesn't move a muscle, his eyes flood with so much warmth it's as if I can feel it touching me, wrapping around my body. He holds his gaze steady with mine, making me wonder how I could ever have doubted his sincerity as he says the words again.

"I love you."

I can't move. I can't even breathe, but my good leg twitches involuntarily toward him. His eyes flicker down to it and then back up to my face. He seems to take it as a cue that maybe it's OK to come closer and scoots forward on the bed, drawing his knees in toward his chest and leaning so that his face is only a foot or so from mine.

"Is there any chance, do you think, that you could ever feel the same way?" He says this in nearly a whisper, his gaze probing mine. "About me?"

I close my eyes. I keep them closed for a long time, how long I'm not sure. When I open them again, his face is even nearer, so near that I gasp. His eyes hold mine for a few seconds, and then he bends his head toward me and lowers his lips to meet mine.

The kiss is gentle, sweet, soft. Like a sigh of relief. When he releases my lips and pulls away, I experience the strangest sensation…almost like panic. Panic that I might lose this again. I never want to lose this feeling, this gnawing need inside me being filled. I reach up to wrap my hands around the back of his neck to hold him here. And then I draw him back toward me until his mouth covers mine.

This kiss moves past sweet and soft to urgent, insistent. His tongue probes my lips and explores past them. Our breathing turns into short, uneven pants. Before I lose myself completely, before I forget, I break my hold on him and press against his shoulders.

He pulls back at once and stares into my eyes, stricken. As if I'm going to push him away, tell him to go. As if that could possibly happen now.

"What is it?" His voice contains a fresh note of panic.

"I just, I…"

He studies my face, searching my eyes. "Wha—" he begins again when the silence stretches on. I stop him with a kiss. And then I pull back to look at him again.

"It happened that first night," I say slowly. "That first night at your apartment."

"What happened?" His forehead is creased with confusion and concern.

Making sure his eyes are on mine, I whisper, "That's when I fell in love with you."

I watch as his expression changes. Gradually the worry lines disappear. Gradually the emotion in his eyes moves past concern to disbelief to understanding…to hope.

"You love me?" He says it softly, his lips so close I feel his breath.

"I am *so* in love with you," I whisper back.

And I can't say anything else because my lips are suddenly very busy.

My head grows fuzzy after this point, but one thought does manage to break through my dreamlike haze and rise to the surface of my mind. It's about Savy, of all things.

Savy was right about something, something very important.

Today is definitely a good day for falling in love.

EPILOGUE

———

We're right smack in the middle of dinner—or *tea*, as Ian's family refers to the evening meal—when Ian's pocket begins blaring Beyoncé's "Crazy in Love," which would strike me as the most hilariously nonsensical ringtone ever to come off a proper English businessman's phone if not for the fact that, A) Ian is not really all that proper, and B) It's me who he's "Crazy in Love" with. He changed it as a joke while we were lazing in bed one night at my condo in Memphis, and it stuck. Now it's as much a part of him as late-night curries and copious misuse of the word "lit-rally."

It's been seven months since my sprained ankle saved my life—or, as Ian would tell it, saved his. Seven months of transatlantic flights bridged by hours-long phone calls, lengthy emails, and steamy Snapchat conversations with imagery graphic enough to make Herbert the Pervert seem chaste as a chapel full of nuns. Seven months of learning favorite colors and places and books and bands and sharing memories as vital as our first broken hearts and as mundane as our first lost teeth. Seven months of navigating cultural chasms and coming to the incredulous conclusion, many times over, that people who live thousands of miles and oceans away from each other are way more alike than we are different.

For the first three to four months, we floated on a cloud of bliss and avoided all talk of the teensy-tiny problem in our relationship—that trivial little matter of the ocean situated inconveniently between us. In the months since, we've managed to plant our feet back on the ground and admit our growing need for a solution…and begin to make plans.

Those plans are the reason we're here, seated across from each other in Ian's mum's dining room, a warm, friendly space with coral walls, a time-worn china cupboard, and dim lighting emanating from a blackened brass chandelier that's older than my grandparents. The oblong table is stretched as far as its leaves will take it and covered by a white cloth with scalloped embroidered edges. It's laden with crockery teeming with fresh, steaming, hearty foods, from the platter of roast beef dripping with au jus to the huge bowl of creamed potatoes to the delicate tureen of green peas—and unlike the experience around my own family's dining table, here everyone is urged to take generous helpings and to have seconds or thirds if they like.

Ian's sister, Charlotte, whom I've become quite good friends with, and her husband, Paul, are seated to my right. Their two kids, Samantha and Charles, are across from them at Ian's left. Ian's mum, Viola, is at the head of the table between Ian and me, and squeezed in at the other end is Ian's brother, Michael, and his new wife, Joanna, who's petite with a sharp, irreverent tongue and a wild mane of fuzzy dark curls—not someone I would have pictured Ian with in a million-jillion years, but she's the perfect counterweight to Michael's quiet, pleasant reserve. I attended the wedding on Ian's arm, and yes, he and Michael are on speaking terms again.

His phone still blaring, Ian reaches under the table and clicks the button to silence Beyoncé's booming voice, but not before everybody gets a good listen.

"That's an…interesting ringtone you've chosen there, brother," says Michael, as Joanna snorts.

Ian gives an easy laugh and glances at me. "Usually I keep my mobile set on silent," he admits. "At work, particularly."

"I think it's very sweet," Charlotte says, nudging my arm with her elbow and giving Ian a satisfied smile.

I've just dipped my head to pop a bite of Yorkshire pudding into my mouth—homemade by Ian's mum and so delicious, puffed and crispy and drizzled in brown gravy made from the juices of the roast—when Ian's voice mail chime goes off. Seconds later Beyoncé's voice rings out yet again.

Ian and I exchange a quizzical look, and Charlotte says, "Someone really wants to ring you up. It must be important."

"Right, sorry," Ian says, digging into his pocket for his phone and rolling his eyes at Michael, who's sniggering loudly. When he glances at the screen his eyebrows shoot up, and my brow furrows in response. After silencing the ring again, with the phone still buzzing, he holds the screen up to show me. The display reads, *"Miranda mobile."*

"Oh, my God," I say.

"Shall I answer it?"

I stare at him for a beat. "No, we should probably wait until after dinner. Particularly since…" We continue staring at one another, eyes wide, as everyone else glances around, mystified by our exchange.

"Yes, particularly since…" Ian's voice trails off just as mine did.

"Shall we just tell them, then?" he asks, his eyes intense.

"Definitely. Let's just tell them."

After several seconds of silence, during which Ian's voice mail chime rings out a second time, Joanna finally cries out, "Oh, for flip's sake, are you going to tell us or not?"

"Tell us what?" Ian's mum looks alarmed, and beside me, Charlotte looks well chuffed, to put it the English way. She's the only one besides Ian and me who already knows.

"You're engaged," Michael pronounces.

"Quinn is pregnant," Joanna says at the same time.

Ian and I both burst out laughing. He points first at Michael and says, "Not yet, mate," still chuckling. And then he points at Joanna and adds, "Not to my knowledge, no."

"Well, out with it, then," Viola trills impatiently, her eyes already glistening. "I've been waiting for this, whatever it is." I barely hear her because my brain is still whirling over Ian's *"Not yet."* We haven't actually discussed marriage, but that doesn't mean I haven't been thinking about it. And now I know that Ian's been thinking about it, too…

Ian reaches across the table and grabs my hand, wrapping my fingers in his and gently caressing my wrist with his thumb. "I'm moving," he says in a low voice, gazing at me as he says it and then shifting his eyes slowly from me to his mother. He's been afraid of how she would take the news since they've always been close. "I've been offered a job by an investment banking firm in Memphis. I interviewed for the position in March, and I've started the paperwork process for my visa."

"We have a long-term plan," I add, glancing apologetically at Viola. "For now we'll both live in the States, and then when situations allow, we'll both look for jobs in England and move back here one day." I shift my gaze back to Ian, directly into his eyes. "Together," I add softly. He squeezes my fingers.

Over the last three months we've discussed this at length, and Ian's insisted each time that he's the one who should move. He says that before we met he was already looking for some new adventure, some big way to change his life, and he just hadn't realized the opportunity he'd been waiting for was…me.

I love the idea of living in England, and I would move for him, too, but if I'm completely honest I can't bear the thought of leaving Jules right now, with baby Dimitry due to arrive any day. And Savy is freaking out at the thought that everything is changing, that Jules and I are moving on and she's losing both of us at once. She hasn't said as much, but I can tell.

And no, in case you're wondering, Savy's lunch date didn't turn out to be the love of her life. In fact, she dumped him after only three dates, after she spied him shooting up in her bathroom and then swiped his phone and figured out from his text threads that Prince Charming's ex-wife had an order of protection against him and he was getting daily threats from his dealers over nonpayment.

Poor Savy's prince might never come. She's OK with that idea but not OK with losing me. Or Jules. Maybe one day I'll convince her to give up on the Memphis dating pool and move across the pond.

Viola jolts me out of these thoughts by clapping her hands together rapidly and letting out an excited giggle. Ian and I glance at her, and then back at each other, and then back at her. This wasn't the reaction he'd expected, not by a long shot.

"Ooh, I knew it," she squeals. "I just knew it. And I've been waiting for it." She gives us what almost seems like a chastising look. "It's taken the two of you long enough to figure it out." She claps her hands again. "Oh, and you'll have to let me visit, of course."

"And me," Charlotte chimes in.

"And me," adds Samantha, Ian's niece, in her eight-year-old's trill. We all laugh.

"Of course," I say, a warm rush of pleasure flooding my cheeks. "Anytime." Glancing at Samantha and Charles, I add, "While you're all there we should plan a trip to Disneyworld." It takes a minute before anyone can hear me over the kids' excitement, and then I add, "And Ian and I will visit here, too, as much as we possibly can."

Ian's new firm happens to be the same one my brother-in-law Bradley works for, which means it happens to also have an office in London. And since completing the work on Jane and Adam's townhouse I've gained two additional English clients, so a portion of my traveling in recent months has been for work. I haven't run into "Mr. Pemberton" again, but I have visited Jane and Adam, and Jane's assured me that Elliott is comfortably settled into his new school in Switzerland, and the press hubbub around Ryland's "scandal" fizzled out pretty quickly.

The pieces of the puzzle have all fallen together rather nicely, I'd say. There's only one exception, one missing piece in the otherwise finished picture…and she's just left two voice mails on Ian's phone.

Until now, Miranda hasn't spoken a word to Ian or me since Pamela's meltdown in the pub, though we've both tried reaching out to her multiple times. We do know where she is and what she's been doing, however, because Ian stays in regular contact with Thomas.

She lost her shop. It turns out she had been operating so deeply in the red that it was a wonder the business was still open the day I first ventured into it. Not long after my trip when Ian had confronted me and I'd sprained my ankle, Miranda's landlord evicted her and her inventory was repossessed; the money she might or might not have made from selling the photos of Elliott clearly hadn't been enough to bail her out of her financial mess. And, within weeks of her shop closing, she'd entered a rehab program to deal with the alcohol and drug addiction none of her friends—apart from Thomas—knew she had. I learned from Ian that Miranda's mother had spent time in the same treatment center in years past.

It explained a lot.

And speaking of Thomas, he's really stepped up for Miranda and walked beside her through all of it. She's in recovery, from what he's told us, but she's remained too mortified to contact either Ian or me. This call from her, it's a huge step. I'm dying to hear her message and for Ian to call her back and have her actually answer this time, to work on putting the past behind us.

Maybe one day we can all be friends. Maybe. It's not so hard to imagine, after witnessing firsthand the depth of Thomas's love for her. Surely not even Miranda, bold and unpredictable Miranda, can repel an emotional connection with that much force. And I should know.

I glance away from Viola to catch Ian's eye and find him gazing at me. It's that look he sometimes gives me, the one that melts my insides and nearly knocks the breath out of me—the look that makes sense of my past and promises my future. Seeing that look, the depth of love in his eyes, my breathing hitches and I struggle for air as my stomach performs a series of fluttery somersaults.

Around us, Ian's family is buzzing with chatter about the trips they're going to plan and the places they want to see in America and the way they all knew this was coming—"No, really, *I* did," pipes in Charlotte—and the way that, no matter who knew what and when, none of them are surprised at all. They could see from the beginning that this was the real thing, that Ian and I would find a way to be together.

I hear it all, but really I'm barely hearing it.

Across from me, Ian is smiling our private smile, and his words to Michael are still pulsing in my ears—"*Not yet.*"

Ian Murphy wants to marry me, and I want to marry him.

It's only a matter of when.

Acknowledgments

This book is close to my heart because of its setting, and it couldn't have come alive without the help of my aunts and uncles and grandparents and cousins, who've welcomed my husband, my son, and me into their homes through the years and given us awe-struck Anglophiles a taste of life in the land of thatch-roofed cottages, striped-awning markets, villages with streets named "The Street," cathedrals with white spires reaching into a daytime sky that's not *always* cloudy, and postcard-perfect meadows with undulating grasses cradling thousand-year-old stone churches that are as alive today as they were when my parents and grandparents and grandparents' grandparents stood smiling on their foot-worn steps. I'll never get enough.

More specifically, I could not have finished this book without the help of two early readers, my cousins Joanne Hamling and Michaela White, who, respectively, assured me that Ian's pronunciation of "lit-rally" is true to his regional dialect and informed me in clear terms that Marmite is an English invention that inspired the Australian copycat version, not the other way around. Thank you so much, Joanne and Michaela! I'm thrilled that for all its faults, Facebook is around to keep us in each other's daily lives in spite of the miles between us.

Thank you, too, to Jamie Hopkins and Gretchen Ledgard, and to my sisters, Maria Porter and Cindy Trail, for reading the book's early draft and for always, always being such amazing cheerleaders and supporters of my writing. It means more to me than I can express. Thanks also to my writing buddies and confidantes Traci Andrighetti, Tracie Banister, and Meredith Schorr. Your witty words, both on paper and in real life, inspire me and keep me super-excited about doing what we do. The same goes for all of my online and real-life friends in Chick Lit Chat HQ—thank you for the daily laughs, insight, encouragement, and motivation.

Of course, a gigantic thank you goes out to my editor, Wendi Baker, and my publisher, Gemma Halliday, for your amazing work and incredible support. You're a joy and a pleasure to work with, and I'm lucky and honored to be doing this alongside Gemma Halliday Publishing's talented, supportive, and FUN team of authors and editors.

Finally, one more enormous thank you to Lance and Colby for giving me the love, time, support, and encouragement I needed to finish this fifth novel...with hopefully many more to come. I love you, and I love our adventures.

ABOUT THE AUTHOR

USA Today bestselling author Stacey Wiedower had barely blown out the candles on her 21st birthday cake when she took her first job as a reporter at a daily newspaper. She later followed her passion to interior design school and spent three years working at a firm with bizarre similarities to the set of Designing Women. Today she funnels that experience into her work as a full-time freelance writer, penning everything from magazine articles to website copy to a bi-weekly column called Inside Design. She also writes romantic comedy, and the zany characters she's met poke their heads into her stories from time to time. Stacey lives in Memphis, Tenn., with her husband, also a writer, and a son who's inherited their overactive imaginations.

To learn more about Stacey Wiedower, visit her online at:
www.staceywiedower.com

Enjoyed this book? Check out these other romantic reads available in print now from Gemma Halliday Publishing:

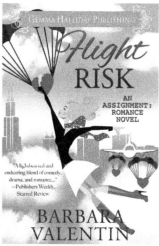

www.GemmaHallidayPublishing.com